TO LOOK UPON THE SUN

SHANNON ST. HILAIRE

WILD SAGE

ISBN (eBook): 979-8-9899658-3-0
ISBN (Paperback): 979-8-9899658-2-3
Library of Congress Control Number: 2024903182

Published By Wild Sage

Book Cover by Jessica Bell.

Title Production by The BookWhisperer

First edition 2024

"*As for herself, she said, it was not proper for the victim of a deed of such wanton insolence to look upon the sun, and plunging a dagger into her breast she slew herself.*"

— Diodorus Siculus, The Rape of
Lucretia, *Library of History*

PART ONE
SEED

This generation of youth is learning nothing other than to think German and act German. And if this ten-year-old boy and girl enter our organizations . . . they'll go from the Jungvolk to the Hitler Youth four years later, and we keep them there for an additional four years . . . And they won't free themselves for the rest of their lives.

— ADOLF HITLER, REICHENBERG SPEECH

CHAPTER ONE

I lse tried to listen to the reading on a woman's duty to bear at least six children, but all she could think of were blades of grass tickling her ears, warm air, warmer skin on hers. Felix's hands, long fingered and smooth from a life of leisure, tracing her edges. One of their stolen moments had changed everything. But which one?

The other girls in the circle listened, rapt, as Ilse usually did —memorizing the words, letting them infuse her mind until she couldn't tell her own thoughts apart from the lessons. Pale-eyed and serene, Fräulein Glücks read aloud, "The goal of female training is, without deviation, to be the coming mother."

The words pressed in on Ilse, making it hard to breathe. She looked at the damp earth beneath her feet. Tried yet again to remember the last time she'd bled.

Weeks ago, months. How many had it been?

She couldn't remember.

Unable to sit still, she shifted on the low stump and her

Hitler Youth badge dug into her chest. Fräulein Glücks looked up from the pages, her mouth still moving, and met Ilse's gaze expectantly.

Silence. Ringing filled Ilse's ears.

Fräulein Glücks must have asked her a question. She hadn't heard a word. It was the first time in four years in the Bund Deutscher Mädel that she had no answer. She looked down, away from the BDM leader's gaze, unsure what to do or say. Fräulein Glücks's voice, far away, asked, "Anyone else?" and another girl piped in. Now Ilse had failed in front of the BDM, her one sanctuary.

Fräulein Glücks tucked her tattered copy of *Mein Kampf* away and gave instructions for which fruits and herbs they should gather to take home and preserve. Today it was nettles. The other girls were dusting off their skirts, picking up their wicker baskets, and dispersing into the woods of Bürgerpark. Ilse watched them as if they were actors in a film, separate from her. Some of the girls had been her friends once, Rosalie and Gerda and Friederike. But their constant laughter baffled her. Plus they'd gone on to Gymnasium after eighth grade. Ilse would have liked to continue her education, but it simply wasn't possible; she'd gone straight to work for Herr Anschütz, cleaning and cooking in his manor.

The BDM leader's gaze was on her again. Ilse snapped to attention, shoved on her own gloves, and began her search for the jagged leaves and stinging hairs.

Foraging was Ilse's favorite BDM activity, one of her favorite activities generally. When she moved deep into the trees and far away from everyone else, the roar of life became a whisper and the crisp freshness of the air made her more awake than she felt anywhere, anytime else. All that mattered was finding small green shoots, bright dots of flowers, splashes of berries. When she kneeled and touched the plant she was looking for and took it for her basket, it felt like she was one of them, a tender, soft, green thing in the shade and dappled sun and fresh air. What more could any living thing need?

But today she couldn't concentrate on foraging.

It had taken her too long to notice that her breasts ached and her bone-deep fatigue was not normal, that the scent of fish was not, in fact, more pungent than usual, but that her sense of smell was stronger—strong enough to make her gag. She hadn't had time to think about these things, could not afford for them to be real, so she'd ignored them for far longer than she should have. It wasn't until her stomach had begun to round, despite her sparse diet, that she'd known.

Ilse knelt before a nettle plant and checked the underside for white spittle, then began cutting the leaves.

If she told her father, he'd cast her out on the street before the words left her mouth. He must never know.

She could marry Felix. Someday, when his career as a mathematics professor advanced or perhaps when he inherited his family's wealth, they would have their own house with a garden. She thought of the cocky, boyish grin that she wanted to kiss, then smack right off his face, and then kiss again. His long, lean frame that slouched when he was standing. His odd and wonderful mind she'd spent hours exploring. If they made a life together, it would be better than any she could have imagined in her small existence.

She would be safe. The burden on her shoulders could lift.

If he would have her.

When the sun shining through the leaves of the trees turned gold, Ilse returned to the circle of tree stumps, her basket half-full. The other girls trickled in, some with full baskets, others with nearly empty ones. Fräulein Glücks's long, narrow face peered into the girls' baskets and murmured words of praise for the ones who did well and encouragement for those who did not. When she arrived at Ilse's basket, she merely glanced up at her, then walked on. Ilse stared at the ground. In all her time as a member of the group, she'd never disappointed her BDM leader. Today, she'd done it twice. She had always fancied Fräulein Glücks to be something of a big sister: She'd taught Ilse and the other girls to cook and camp and knit scarves for charity. She'd taught her about the national community and how important it was to care for others. And now Ilse had disappointed her. Her shoulders, normally rolled back straight and strong, hunched. She couldn't find the energy to stand straight.

As the girls got ready to leave, Fräulein Glücks announced, "Be sure to clean the combed-out hair from your family's hairbrushes and bring it to your hairdressers. They will pass it on to produce felt for the military—a service to your country."

The girls left in ones and twos. While Ilse was reattaching her basket to her bike, the tall, athletic shape of Fräulein Glücks appeared before her. Ilse braced herself for punishment, a lecture perhaps, but when she looked up, the BDM leader cocked her head, eyes soft.

"You gathered enough today, but I've never seen you return with a basket that wasn't overflowing." It was a question.

Ilse blinked and averted her gaze. Fräulein Glücks was only a few years older than Ilse—in her early twenties while Ilse was not yet eighteen—but she seemed much wiser and more worldly. The BDM leader was easy to talk to; Ilse felt that if she turned to her, she would listen, and care, and help.

But what if, instead, Fräulein Glücks told her how stupid she was? Ilse would have to risk it; she had no one else to turn to.

She couldn't find the words, so she placed a fingertip on her belly. Fräulein Glücks's eyes flicked down for just a moment. They sparked with understanding—and excitement?

"Does the father know?"

"Not yet." Ilse swallowed, confused. The scolding would surely happen now.

"Tell him soon. It's better that way. He is of good blood?" Her tone was matter-of-fact, not angry, and certainly not disappointed.

"Of course."

"Then probably you two can get married." Fräulein Glücks smiled encouragement. "All will be well."

Ilse nodded, but fear welled within her. This meant she, the daughter of a carpenter, would have to crawl to Felix, the son of a lawyer, and share the news that would compel him to marry her. Maybe he would think she'd done it on purpose, to entrap him. They hadn't been officially courting. There'd been no talk of marriage. Perhaps he would turn her away in disgust.

Fräulein Glücks studied Ilse's face. From her satchel she pulled a pamphlet and handed it to Ilse. On the front was a red, three-pronged symbol, and in blocky letters: *Lebensborn*. Fount of Life.

"I'm sure everything will work out with the father, but just in case, you have options. I know girls who've gone here before, at my recommendation."

Ilse was taken aback. This was what Fräulein Glücks thought of her?

"Isn't Lebensborn an SS brothel? A stud farm?" That was what Ilse had heard in the few times the name had come up. Why was there such secrecy around it, people wondered. They must do depraved things behind those walls, breeding Aryans like farm stock. Even dedicated Nazis like her father paused at the mention of Lebensborn.

"It's nothing like that." The BDM leader looked perturbed. "The Lebensborn Society is a maternity home, with the best medical care, high-quality food, luxurious accommodations. It's perfect for girls of pure blood who can't marry the father of their child and need discretion. Your reputation would remain intact for those with old-fashioned ideals who still don't understand that what's important is propagation of the Aryan race, regardless of marriage. A child of good blood is always a wonderful thing. At Lebensborn, they would celebrate you."

Ilse opened the brochure. Dozens of pictures depicted homes—mansions really—nestled among rolling hills; large, well-appointed rooms with chandeliers and velvet-upholstered chairs; grounds dotted with plump babies and rosy-cheeked staff in crisp uniforms. It looked perfect. Too perfect. At least for someone like Ilse.

"Thank you." She handed the pamphlet back. Better not to bring it home, where her father could find it. "But the father is a good man. I think he will marry me."

Beneath flat, gray skies, Ilse pedaled toward Felix's home in the Schwachhausen neighborhood. She'd told one person; now she could tell another. Soon she would begin to show, and she needed to be married before that happened.

She often wondered what Felix saw in her. Was it her looks? She knew people found her golden, waist-length hair, sky-blue eyes, and athletic build attractive. The small scar on her left temple seemed only to make her more intriguing to others. Certain things seemed to come to her: a discount at the market, a free drink, a place ahead in line, along with winks, comments, and unwelcome propositions. But it took more than looks for someone like Felix, intelligent and interesting, to spend time with her.

She passed a man playing his drehorgel. As he cranked, the small organ churned out a nursery song.

Maybug, fly,
Your father is at war,
Your mother is in Pomerania,
Pomerania is burnt down!
Maybug, fly.

She'd say it as soon as she was alone with Felix, and with it would come relief. The problem would be shared then, and perhaps even solved. She pedaled faster.

Felix's house came into view. Large and white, it looked gray and flat in this light. No light streamed through the gaps in the drawn curtains. She propped her bike against the fence and walked to the door. With a forced exhale, she rapped her knuckles against the door and waited.

She knocked again, harder.

"Moin, Fräulein," a voice drawled. Her eyes snapped toward the sound and locked on Gregor, Felix's neighbor. He was one of the few people who knew about Ilse and Felix, out of pure nosiness. He'd found them out a few months ago, when it was too cold to spend time outside and Ilse had come to Felix's instead of meeting in the park. She used the back door, but one day Gregor had been taking a leak on his parents' rhododendrons and caught her. Ever since, he'd enjoyed commenting on her comings and goings.

"You won't find him here," Gregor said.

Ilse narrowed her eyes at him. "Why do you say that?"

Sprawled on his bench, Gregor watched the bottle in his hand as he swiveled it on its bottom edge. He was making her wait.

"The Weidemanns are gone. Their visas were approved yesterday, and they absconded in the night." He made a little gesture with his fingers, tiny legs running away.

Her body went cold. Time slowed to an excruciating pace.

A pair of birds passing overhead seemed to fly too slowly to stay airborne.

"What? Why?"

"Didn't you know? They're Jews."

"But there are hardly any Jews in Bremen," Ilse said. It seemed far more likely that Gregor, the trickster, was toying with her. But though he wore a self-satisfied smile, his usual devilish gleam was gone.

"There were at least five, until today."

"I would have known. You're making this up."

"They didn't exactly go around announcing it. Would you?"

The birds in the sky vanished, blotted out by the sunlight piercing through the clouds.

"Felix wouldn't leave without saying anything."

"Oh, but he did."

Ilse peeked through the window. Beyond the lacy curtains, she saw the sitting room, empty of people but full of furniture. Some of the bookshelves looked less crowded, and things were scattered on the coffee table, as if gone through hastily. She stepped back, feeling as if she were floating away.

"Don't be sad," Gregor drawled. "When people get their visas, they tend to leave right away. While they still can."

It was hard to breathe. She felt strangely hot. She pulled at her collar, shifted from one foot to the other. If Felix was truly gone, she was lost. Completely alone.

He couldn't have left, couldn't be Jewish.

She wouldn't cry here, in front of Gregor. Not before she had the truth. She gripped the handle of her bike and hopped on.

"How about you join me?" He raised his bottle at her.

"Not even if you paid me," she called over her shoulder as she rode away.

Out of his sight, the impact of what he'd said hit her. If it was true, she had committed Rassenschande, the intermingling of Aryan and non-Aryan blood. A crime.

The penalty for having an intimate relationship with a Jew was fifteen years' imprisonment with hard labor. She would most likely be sent to a camp—a KZ, short for Konzentrationslager. Ka zet, sounds that cut.

She arrived at the abandoned, crumbling wall and pried at the loose brick. This was their secret spot, Ilse's and Felix's, exactly halfway between their homes. The brick came free, and her heart skipped: there was a note, folded and folded again to become a tiny white square.

Her hands shook, only a little, as she opened the note. It was scribbled in a hurried hand and riddled with his usual dashes, a manifestation of thoughts too fast and too bright for the usual punctuation.

Ilse—

I wish I could say goodbye in person—My family is leaving Germany tonight. We had to go someplace safe while we still could. I'm sorry I wasn't honest with you about who I am—I only wanted to spend time with you, and I didn't know how you would react.

I hope we will meet again, in a better time—
Bis dann, Lehitra'ot—

Felix

Her eyes skittered over the page. It took her several tries to read the words, but she understood long before she finished.

Felix was gone. He had left her without a goodbye.

Her heart was pounding. She examined his handwriting,

looking for anything left unsaid. Her eyes blurred. She could find nothing, no subtext that would explain everything. Was she not looking hard enough?

He'd left her for some unknown location, far away. He would be safe there.

Ilse, however, was not safe.

Leaning against the wall, she pressed a hand to her chest, trying to breathe. The cold metal edges of her Hitler Youth badge pressed against her palm. She had unknowingly committed one of the worst crimes, the one she had constantly been warned in school, in the BDM, on the radio, never to commit. There was nothing worse than to corrupt bloodlines, to allow her body to be defiled by a Jew.

She had memorized these ideas, but never analyzed them—her father's belt had taught her not to. But she didn't feel defiled. If she was, she should feel it, and yet she didn't. There was no room for anything but fear. For Felix and for herself. For their child.

What would her father do if he found out? What would the Reich do?

She was not only pregnant out of wedlock, she was a criminal—with a secret that would be impossible to keep.

CHAPTER TWO

A big bone with scraps of meat clinging to it. Suppengrün: a bundle of carrots, leeks, celeriac, and a sprig of parsley. The items scattered on the kitchen counter looked unreal. All she wanted to do was lie down, but her father would be home soon, expecting dinner. With shaky hands, she lit the stove and set water to boil, then added the bone, which sank to the bottom of the pot.

Mischling of the first degree—that's what her baby would be. It was the term given to those with one Aryan parent and one Jewish parent. The word itself was almost too filthy to say out loud, a schoolyard insult.

She wondered what it meant that the one man she'd ever been close to was a Jew. Was there something wrong with her that she'd been attracted to him? Was she blind to his viciousness, his inferiority? What, then, would his child be like? The back of her throat burned. With nausea or tears or both, she wasn't sure.

On her way home, she'd stopped to stare at a flyer with a caricature of a Jewish man, hooked nose overwhelming his face, raping a German woman. Looking at it, she'd felt sick.

Felix must be different from the rest of the Jews. The exception.

That made her feel better.

But he was a Jew, different or not, and he'd hidden the truth from her. What else had he done? And how could she have been so swept up that she missed it?

She'd met Felix several months ago, as summer began to fade. She'd gone with her employers, the Anschütz family, on a boat trip to one of the nearby islands. After laying out platters of cured meats and potato salad and glasses of shandy for them to graze on, she'd been free for the afternoon. She'd left the crowded island and swam across the river to another, unpopulated island, the water salty in her mouth this close to the sea.

When she heard splashing behind her, she swam faster.

The shore, when she reached it, was similar to the one she'd left—sandy, grassy, with a few beech trees—except more rewarding since she had put in effort to reach it.

Behind her, more splashing. She looked: there was a young man coming to shore—mid-twenties, with a narrow build and broad shoulders, his damp brown hair already threatening to spring back into lively curls. A big smile slashing his face.

She sat down on the sand, toes grazing the water. He flopped down next to her.

"What did you think of the swim?" he asked.

She spared him a brief look, a smirk, but didn't answer. He wasn't deterred. He looked at her, longer and more intently than anyone had before. It should have made her self-conscious, that much staring. But his gaze emboldened her, made her feel that anything she did or said would be fascinating.

"It was fine," she said. "Except someone was chasing me."

"*Racing*, you mean. He's a good sport, too. He's taking his loss in stride."

"Why is that?"

"There are many ways of winning. For example, if one finds good company, I consider that a success." He flashed a grin.

She'd never done anything like it before, but within fifteen minutes she was lying on her back, looking up at the sky, and listening to him talk about his passion for mathematics.

"I believe there's an equation for everything," he'd said. "We should find the mathematical equation for trees." He gestured to the nearby beech trees, eyes lighting up.

"Why?"

"Because we can. We should know everything about the world, for the sake of knowledge."

He was unlike anyone she'd met before. With him, she felt a bubble inside her like laughter. It told her that she was young and healthy, that she could do anything. That she *should* do anything while she still could.

After that day, she'd started meeting him a couple of Sundays a month at Bürgerpark or isolated spots on the river or even his home when no one was there. They never met in public, and she assumed it was because he was ashamed of their difference in station—he lived in the elegant Schwachhausen neighborhood, while she was born and raised in Gröpelingen, dirty and reeking of fish. Their relationship could never be serious because she couldn't be a proper gentleman's wife, someone who hosted parties and discussed philosophy and literature. She too had kept Felix a secret; she'd always told her father she was attending a BDM outing or that she had errands to run.

One day, early in their relationship, Felix was leaning back on his forearms, well-developed for a scholar, when she'd felt a nearly uncontrollable urge to melt into him. Perhaps it was the early autumn air, or the wine he'd brought, or the blanketed feeling of peace the trees gave her, or the way his curly hair sprang up with a life of its own. She'd leaned forward and pressed her lips against his. That day, and many Sundays after, she'd yielded to desire. She allowed herself this one indulgence. Through the winter and into spring, she had indulged again and again.

These meetings had seemed separate from her daily life. She'd felt no shame, only a spark of aliveness, a moment of escape. It hadn't occurred to her that her stolen moments with Felix could cross the barrier she'd created and change the very fabric of her life. The mistakes were obvious now: trusting Felix to prevent this disaster, trusting him at all, indulging in a futile affair.

Felix hadn't trusted her with his secret, in all the time they spent together. He must have thought she'd turn him away in disgust if she knew the truth. Would she have?

She washed and chopped the few nettles she'd gathered and added them to the pot. A scrawny rat skittered across the kitchen floor. With all the factories nearby, she'd given up the battle against the vermin long ago.

Barely identifiable scraps of pork detached from the bone and floated in the broth. Tonight, she was making an Eintopf, a one-pot meal. One-pot dinners were cheaper and quicker than a golden roast with buttered vegetables and thick slices of bread, but the right touches could transform even a simple Eintopf into a delicious meal. Ilse normally liked applying those touches, learned from the BDM and the cook at the Anschütz house— but not today. She kept forgetting which ingredients she'd already added. Stirring the soup with the ladle—metal, not wooden, lest the wood soak up any fat—she stuck her nose in the pot to sniff for bay leaf or rosemary.

She was supposed to hate Felix now. All this time she'd thought he was superior—with his fine clothes, his large home, his university education—when in fact she was the one who belonged to the master race. This thought buoyed her. He couldn't hurt her. He wasn't worthy of her. But the idea felt off, discordant, and it melted away.

At 7 p.m. exactly, the same time as every other night, Ilse's father came to the table and sat, like a well-trained dog. He began whittling away at the table—he'd built it himself, years ago, and every night he took out his smallest knife and worked more on the pattern. Long ropes of intertwining ivy, animals in motion, flowers in bloom. He was never done.

When she was younger, he'd taught her to whittle, too, and she made cruder versions of his own carvings, the two of them working in silence that was almost companionable.

When she pulled the cone-top off a can of beer, she cut her trembling finger on the jagged metal edge. She sucked the finger, the taste of iron coating her tongue.

Her father didn't take his eyes off his Eintopf as she placed the beer in front of him and sat down. His bald pate stared at her. Between them, on the wall, a red wax portrait of Hitler, mottled by the years, surveyed them.

The small whittling knife lay next to her plate, waiting for her. Her hands shook too much to render any carving today.

Her heart pounded. When she looked down, she could see the fabric covering her chest pulsating. She took a deep breath. Her panic mustn't show.

She didn't know what to do. Each of her frantic ideas was more impossible than the last.

Termination was illegal. She could find a back-alley doctor, but the danger to her health was high, and both she and the doctor would risk imprisonment, and she didn't have the money anyway. Two hundred marks, she'd heard.

Lebensborn only received German babies. One-hundred-percent Aryan. She'd seen in the pamphlet that they would check the genealogical records of both mother and father, and the records would not lie.

Whatever she did, she would have to do it soon, before tightening her girdle and wearing her loosest dress stopped working, and her father noticed.

The scraping of their spoons punctuated the radio in the background, which delivered some news report that her father had trained her not to listen to, so she wouldn't develop opinions. Her education was limited to her duties as a woman of the Reich, which included deferring to the head of the house when it came to politics.

Still, she heard mention of the Autobahn and how many jobs the Führer had created, bringing to an end the inflation that had had ten-year-old Ilse filling their wheelbarrow full of Reichsmarks to buy one loaf of bread. Her father grunted in approval at the radio. He hadn't liked being hungry and out of work any more than the rest of Germany had. When the Führer came to power, he'd raised the country out of the gutter, dusted the German people off, and told them they were the best in the world. They had work now, and food. But more than that, they had pride.

The flavors of the soup somehow didn't complement one another, too bitter one bite, too sour the next. The large, uneven chunks of carrot were sweet and mushy. Ilse could barely choke them down. Her father didn't seem to notice, slurping bites while whittling and grunting in agreement with the radio.

"When do you leave for land service?" he asked.

She cleared her throat. "In a month."

By then, she would either be starting to show and she'd have to go somewhere, anywhere, before he noticed, or there would be no baby and she could actually proceed with her year of land service, which she'd so looked forward to—good, hard work with people whose values aligned with hers.

"Where?" He dug his knife into the leaves of an oak tree he was carving.

She rested her spoon against the bowl so he wouldn't see it tremble in her hand.

He looked up. Her pause was too long. Was he studying her more closely than usual? His eyes narrowed.

It had to be a plausible lie, a patriotic lie.

The words came out of her, rough as her father's.

"There's a farmer in Silesia whose wife is about to have their sixth child and they need someone as soon as possible. Since I live in a household with no children, I'm assigned to look after them."

Her father looked down again, and Ilse regretted saying that last part. At times, particularly at meals, she imagined her mother sitting in the spot she was in now, closest to the stove. She and the sister who'd never been born would have sat across from each other, perhaps kicked each other under the table. But Ilse had wanted to be a good big sister, looking out for her, taking care of her. Seen to it she ate her vegetables, but also slipped her bits of Bremer Kluten.

Just like that, Ilse had found her way into a place she couldn't control, an overwhelming desire for a mother who would make sense out of all this. Emptiness and uncertainty—a spinning top that would soon skid to its own demise.

The smell of the soup sickened her now that it was cold. Bits of fat had already congealed at the top. She swallowed hard, willing herself to keep down the rancid bile rising to her throat. This would be the third time she'd thrown up a meal in front of her father in the last few months. She could not do it again. She emptied her bowl back into the pot, to be eaten another day.

As she began washing the dishes, she remembered what she'd forgotten. Salt.

.   .   .

When her father finally disappeared into his bedroom and she could hear his steady snoring, Ilse sat her exhausted, aching self on the side of the bed and retrieved Felix's note from her pocket.

She felt a twinge of shame as she tried to find meaning in a few thoughtlessly scribbled words. The sparse letter was a blow to the gut each time she read it.

She'd never really known Felix. He wasn't a gentleman of leisure as she'd believed. He'd dropped out of university, and she'd assumed it was because he was no longer interested, but he would have been forced to leave for having Jewish blood. For that same reason, he hadn't been able to take her out for dinner or dancing. They wouldn't have been allowed in the same establishments. To be seen together could have led to severe punishment.

Though he'd never shown it, he must have been afraid all the time. No wonder he'd found escape in her as she had in him. Perhaps he'd found a place where he could devote himself to the mathematics of every elm and pine he encountered.

He'd been her lover and the closest thing she'd had to a friend, and he'd left in the night, and she would never see him again.

Her hand lay on her belly, as if her touch could tell the child who its father was. It was the strangest feeling, for her body to be someone else's home. How could it make another tiny body, while she had nothing to say in the matter?

She would erase Felix now, from her life and her child's life. To the world, he wouldn't be the father anymore. It would be better if she forgot, too.

Silence filled the night air as she held the paper over the stub of candle next to her bed and touched the top corner to the flame, watching it turn to ash.

"What is that?"

Her father stood not three feet away from her. One hand

was on her belly, visibly rounding in her threadbare nightgown, the other on the burning note.

Fear crashed through her in one blinding haze; she cringed, retreating to the farthest corner of the bed. Hide the belly, hide the note. But there was too much to hide, to reverse, so she did nothing. Paralyzed.

He snatched the note out of her clumsy hand. It was at least half-burnt. She hoped at least Felix's sign-off had burned away. Why had he left the mark of his incriminating language?

Her father's ribs stood out against the colorless fabric of his nightshirt as he read the note. His chest heaved. Sinews threatened to pop out from his neck. He looked at her, eyes shadowed and seething.

Instinctively she clutched her hands over her belly. She shouldn't draw attention to it, but she couldn't fight the urge to protect it.

He lowered the note. Looked at her. Looked at her protective hand over her stomach. She saw it in his eyes: he knew.

He crumbled the remnants of the paper, which fell to the ground in ashes.

"Was I not clear, all these years, that you are not to shame this family?" His voice trembled with rage. "You will leave this house."

He stepped toward her. She shrank back, but her head thudded against the wall behind her. There was nowhere to go.

He did not use his belt this time. He used his fists.

Chapter Three

Ilse shuffled down the streets of Gröpelingen, weak and shaking.

For the first time, she had not submitted. She'd taken her beatings quietly before, but she'd been younger then—she was fourteen when the last one had happened. This time, she'd had nothing to lose by defying him. The worst had already happened.

She hadn't hit him back, only raised her arms, a chair, a book —whatever she could find—to protect herself. When he'd realized she wouldn't surrender, something had changed in him. His hands had dropped to his sides, his back bowed. His face looked old and haggard. She'd wondered if he was going to cry, and her own eyes burned.

She'd taken advantage of his stillness to find a canvas knapsack and shove a few things inside: a dress, her BDM uniform, a comb, a book on plants that had belonged to her mother. On the way out, she'd stopped to look at him, still frozen in the dim room. It was her fault; she'd destroyed their small family. For thirteen years, the two of them had only had each other. He would be alone now, with no one to take care of him. She'd pushed the door open and left her home for the last time.

She had no money, nowhere to go.

Though it was nearing midnight, the streets bustled with people coming home from swing shift or on their way to work the graveyard shift, or who had no jobs at all. She rarely ventured out at this late hour, and for good reason. Drunks leered at her from stoops. The eyes of criminals bored into her, sizing her up, seeing what worth she might have that they could take. She fixed her eyes on the ground and walked purposefully.

After she'd walked for several minutes, she found a sheltered doorway on a quiet street near a few other bedraggled figures and settled in. Her extra dress served as a blanket and the knapsack a pillow. She leaned against it and imagined it was her mother, warm and soft. Ilse doubted that any of this would have happened if she were still alive. With a mother's guidance, she probably wouldn't have gotten herself in trouble in the first place.

Huddled in the doorway, she noticed the throbbing in her arms and hands where her father's blows had landed. She pushed up her sleeves and inspected the red, angry splotches that stood out against her pale skin. Tomorrow they would bloom into bruises.

Perhaps she would miscarry. She could never return to her father's home, but she wouldn't be shunned by the world, wouldn't have another mouth she couldn't feed.

Inside, she felt shattered. She could put herself back together somehow, but she would never be whole again. The night's chill began to sink into her skin. A tear trickled from her eye and she wiped it away.

The other people on the streets stirred at the first sign of dawn. In the gray light, they looked worn and filthy. They arranged their belongings, worthless to anyone else, with such care. Children, wide-eyed and too thin, hung on to their mothers' skirts. The sight filled her with dread.

Her head felt too heavy to lift; she hadn't dared to fall asleep last night. The bruises from her father's blows had become hideous purple splotches on her arms. Her body ached so much from the beating, and from shivering through the cold night, that it felt impossible to move, but even more impossible to remain on the hard ground. Her hair was frizzy to the touch, and her body felt grimy with dirt and sweat. She stifled a groan as she forced herself to stand and put her dress on over her nightgown.

Where to go? She'd spent the night racking her brain. There was one answer, one house she knew that stood empty. She set off on foot toward Schwachhausen.

Felix's home was not empty.

Ilse slowed as she passed the front gate and watched from the corner of her eyes as Reich officials swarmed the house. Brownshirts carried furniture into awaiting trucks, like ants bringing food to their hive.

Her heart raced. How narrowly she'd escaped being caught inside the house. If they'd come just a few minutes later, they would have found her making herself at home. Would they have thought she was an opportunistic squatter—or a friend of the family? Neither was good, but one was far worse.

She'd thought she would be safe in Felix's home for at least a week or two. She stifled the shudder that threatened to run up her spine.

Her usual twenty-minute bike ride had taken two hours on

foot, and she'd come all this way for nothing. Rain fell, more mist than drops. The swastika-adorned flags attached to every house flapped halfheartedly in the weak breeze. She'd once seen the flags as a comfort; the solidity and power in them made her feel safe. Now she felt the need to hide from the swastikas as if they had eyes.

Bürgerpark was close. She headed for the protection of the canopy of trees.

For the first time in her life, she had nothing to do. No apartment to keep, no father to take care of. No meals to cook, nowhere to cook them. No work until tomorrow. She was at sea. What was the point of her?

The green park was sprinkled with people taking walks and having picnics, like she and Felix used to do. Like people with no worries.

Now, her burdens were insurmountable. The world was a horror with no escape.

She made her way deeper into the park, where there were fewer people and wild brambles and vines and thick mosses like carpet. She knew a few of them: chamomile, ivy, celandine. Hemlock, too poisonous even to touch.

She stopped. The answer popped into her head, quiet and clear. She kneeled before the hemlock, almost grateful. An answer to her problems.

The rounded tufts of white flowers looked harmless. She traced the smooth stems down to the earth and uprooted them. How many would it take? Based on the warnings, she thought it only took a little, but she didn't want to do the job halfway. In a trance, she pulled a few more, then gathered them up and put them in her knapsack. This could all be over with just a cup of tea. It was comforting to have the option.

She knew where she could go now. She retraced her steps out of the park and entered the Anschütz manor through the employee entrance at the back. It was Sunday; the servants had the day off and the master and mistress of the house were at church.

In the kitchen, she put together a plate of bread, cheese, and a few pickled vegetables. The sight of ham made her mouth water, so she dared to cut a slice, so thin it was translucent. Even after she'd devoured the food and cleaned up all traces of her presence, her stomach begged for more, but she didn't dare make another plate. Instead, she grabbed a roll—a delicacy made with white flour—for later.

After freshening up in the bathroom upstairs, she passed the closed door of Herr Anschütz's study and pressed her hand against its polished, warm wood, safely lodged in a beautiful home.

Before, Ilse had had a plan. Every day, after she'd finished the cooking and cleaning at the manor, she'd stolen a few minutes in the study to teach herself typing and shorthand. Someday, Herr Anschütz would find himself in desperate need of a secretary, and then she'd step in. She'd help once at first, and then he would need her assistance again, and again, until he officially appointed her as his secretary.

It wasn't that she was passionate about secretarial work. She'd felt the same tug of longing when she saw captains sailing boats, or marine engineers building them, as when she saw a smartly dressed woman downtown, clacking into an office building. Ilse had been determined to move up in the world, school or no school.

But now there was a child. Once her condition became obvious, the Anschützes would have to let her go. There was no respectable career in her future. There would be no warm hearth to come home to, no meat on the table. Her small world would never expand. Instead, she would be a vagrant with a child.

With a sigh, she pushed herself away from the door and continued down the stairs toward the part of the house only servants entered. Family portraits in thick frames adorned the wall along the stairs. Several generations of Anschützes looked down at her over large mustaches and tiny spectacles. Further down the stairs hung a picture of her employers, Herr and Frau Anschütz, with their son Rudolf between them. Rudolf, a tall, strapping, blond fellow, had joined the Luftwaffe not long ago. During a training flight in Austria, he'd crashed his plane into the side of a mountain. He was only twenty-two years old. Looking at his wide grin, the tragedy of it threatened to overwhelm Ilse.

The hemlock called to her.

The clatter of shoes and the rumble of voices announced the return of the Anschützes. She was halfway down the long flight of stairs that opened into the foyer, with nowhere to hide, so she tried to make herself look at ease.

Frau Anschütz, elegant as always in a gray silk dress that highlighted her dancer's body, looked like a bird perched on the arm of her stout husband. Herr Anschütz's face was a pleasant blend of amiable and intelligent. He wore a monocle that he sometimes dropped in feigned surprise, which always made Ilse giggle like the young girl she'd never felt she was.

Herr Anschütz was muttering to his wife. "He's the best tailor in northern Germany. I don't care if every Brownshirt in the country stands guard in front of his shop. I won't be intimidated."

Frau Anschütz said something too quiet for Ilse to hear, but she was clearly ridden with anxiety. Ilse knew from the cook's gossiping that Herr Anschütz stubbornly patronized Jewish businesses. There were very few Jews in Bremen, but Brownshirts stood outside the doors of their shops, daring people to enter. Most didn't.

Frau Anschütz caught sight of Ilse. Her mouth opened in surprise. "Ilse? What are you doing here?"

"I forgot something—my jacket—so I came back to get it." Ilse raised her forearms to show the brown BDM jacket she wore. "Since I was already here, I thought I'd inspect the house to make sure all was well."

"That's very sweet of you." The tension left Frau Anschütz's body, though she seemed perplexed. For good reason —Ilse had never roamed the house on her day off before. Probably none of the staff did.

"Indeed. Good girl." Herr Anschütz absently patted her on the shoulder as he wandered toward his study.

"Is there anything you need while I'm here?" She forced herself to look benignly at Frau Anschütz, who was watching the closed door of the study with a quizzical look, which Ilse figured was how the woman showed concern. Even after working for her for almost four years, the lady remained as elusive as a ribbon dancing in the wind—something to admire from a distance.

"No. Thank you, dear."

"I'll be off then."

Frau Anschütz bobbed her head and floated down the hallway to take her afternoon nap. She always held herself as if poised to begin a dance, but on the rare occasions Ilse had seen her without makeup, she saw shadows under the woman's eyes and sallowness in her skin—a look of long suffering. Ilse knew from the cook that there had been attempts to have another child in years past, involving at least one operation. The attempts had gone poorly and left Frau Anschütz with pain, constant and unrelenting.

Ilse plodded to the back door, opening and closing it loudly. Then she headed toward a little-used linen closet just large enough to lie down in. She closed herself in with the thick scent of lavender and fresh linen. It was a risk—if caught here, they would likely fire her—but it was quiet and felt safe enough to breathe. And she'd be fired soon anyway.

She'd finished making a bed for herself out of a couple of spare eiderdowns when, deep inside her, there was a faint fluttering sensation. She flinched. Something was wrong.

No—the baby was kicking.

The strange sensation thrilled her. She touched her hands to her stomach. A part of her that had been dormant seemed to wake up, yawning and stretching its legs.

An idea glimmered in her mind. A crack of light shining behind a door.

The Anschützes' son, Rudolf, had been a perfect Aryan. He met—even exceeded—all the standards, as far as Ilse could tell. He would be a perfect Lebensborn father. And he was dead. If she named him as the father of her child, he couldn't refute her claim.

Nor could he confirm it—would they need to confirm?

Ilse thought of whispers she'd heard about the program, that it was a brothel for SS whores. How many people would that deter? If few women joined the program and she had the desired qualities, they might accept her without looking too closely at the details.

The problem was that he'd been stationed in Austria for the last several months, which meant he'd been away when the baby was conceived. But there was no reason to think they would notice that detail. She could say that he'd come back for a visit, or even that she'd traveled to Austria to see him.

Her heart leapt with an unfamiliar sensation: hope.

But what about Herr and Frau Anschütz?

They'd been good to her all these years, even given her Rudolf's bike when he'd left for university around the time Ilse began working for them. It had been a luxury she'd never expected, and one they'd given freely. She used to imagine they were her parents: a kind, talkative father, an existent mother, a feeling of warmth. That dream had faded as she'd grown up, but their kindness had remained.

Would she repay them by tarnishing their son's reputation? It was no small claim to say he'd gotten her pregnant and left her to fend for herself. It was a betrayal. They would certainly fire her. Her stomach twisted at the thought. She would have to carry that guilt with her, of hurting others to help herself.

But she had to do something.

There was the hemlock in her knapsack. Surely the Anschützes wouldn't want that fate for her. And it wasn't as if she could ruin Rudolf's life. In fact, it wouldn't even tarnish his memory—it was unremarkable for a gentleman's son to get a serving girl pregnant. There was no reason to think Lebensborn would tell the family. He was dead, and he alone could refute her claim.

It would work—wouldn't it?

She would at least try.

She curled up on the soft eiderdown, took her mother's book out of her knapsack, and thumbed through the pictures of the plants, too tired to read. The book was *Physica*, written by Hildegard von Bingen, a twelfth-century Christian mystic. Her mother had added pages to the back of the handbound, felt-covered book, filling them with new plants and pressed clippings or sketches to identify them, along with their medicinal uses and any lore that went with them. The images, and her mother's looping handwriting, were a comfort.

Inside her, the baby moved again.

CHAPTER FOUR

Two days later, Ilse sat on a stiff table facing a dowdy, middle-aged doctor.

"Il-sah Rad-ah-mann," he said, slowly enunciating the five syllables of her name as if it were a verdict.

He scanned the contents of the envelope she'd handed him. Yesterday, when she'd gone to the Race and Resettlement Office —RuSHA—she'd filled out forms about her entire genealogy, family health, race, and religion, along with a complete work history. She'd completed an excruciatingly detailed questionnaire on the father as best she could with what she knew about Rudolf and his family, then an affidavit swearing he was the only person she'd had intercourse with during the window of conception. Her palms had become so sweaty that the pen kept slipping from her hand.

As she'd left the office, she'd been given a sealed envelope with instructions to deliver it to the doctor for her physical exam, which would check that her health and race were up to Lebensborn's standards.

The doctor cleared what sounded like a large blockage of phlegm in his throat and picked up a caliper, which she recognized from her examination to enter the BDM. It looked like an instrument designed for torture, and Ilse forced herself not to flinch as it yawned over her face. The doctor measured the height and width of her skull, muttering as he wrote the measurements down, along with his racial assessment: "Skull: long and narrow." Then her nose—"small, upturned"—and jaw —"square, strong." He held up to her eyes a color palette, each color eerily shaped like an iris, complete with pupil: "ice blue." And her hair: "beeline honey blond." Next: "Height: 1.72 meters. Weight: 58.9 kilograms." Then, lower: "38.1 centimeters, good, strong hips for a woman." Her shoulders, square like her jaw, 45 centimeters.

He tapped the dash of scar on her temple. "What is this from?"

"I fell as a child and hit the corner of a table." He jotted that down.

Ilse felt like livestock. It was dull, but still, her heart pounded.

When he finished with what felt like a hundred measurements, he said, "Now undress." He examined the file, which he rested on his belly. Ilse made no effort to remove her clothing. She felt frozen.

"It's alright." The doctor waved the form at her. "This is standard. All aspiring Lebensborn mothers receive the same examination."

He waited, staring at her blandly.

Only one man had ever seen her naked, and that had been under very different circumstances. There had been the shelter of trees, a soft blanket beneath her, and desire. The doctor seemed to have no intention of leaving the room, so Ilse used a trick she'd learned back in the days of the leather belt: she detached herself and became a formless entity conveniently occupying a body, which unbuttoned its blouse and unzipped its skirt, letting it all fall to the floor.

"Slip, too. All undergarments," the doctor said, clearly finding her hesitation tedious.

The body let the straps of her slip slide off her shoulders, the wrinkled imitation silk gliding against her skin as it fell to the ground, then the brassiere and the underwear and the white socks.

The doctor approached and measured the rest of her. He examined every inch of her skin, looking for blemishes and birthmarks. She was glad she'd thought to steal some of Frau Anschütz's powder to cover up the yellowing bruises her father had given her. Then the doctor told her to lie on the table for the pelvic examination. The instruments were cold, and the whiteness of the room made everything feel colder. She ignored the invasion.

"Four and a half to five months along. Due late October." The doctor didn't ask how the pregnancy made her body feel. She didn't ask why she always seemed to have a runny nose now, a symptom she'd never heard of. He didn't offer any other insights into the child. She had so many questions she didn't dare ask: Was the baby healthy? Was it strong? Questions he couldn't answer: What color would its eyes be? Would he be able to tell the baby was Jewish? Would there be something wrong with it?

The doctor instructed her to sit up and she did, clutching at the thin paper on the table to cover bits of herself.

"You have a large, strong frame. Very good measurements. You're a category-one Aryan."

When Ilse arrived at the RuSHA office, a woman with cat-eye glasses sat at the front desk, her hair in perfect finger curls. She'd been there a few days earlier when Ilse first visited. She looked up from her task of rearranging papers and putting them inside other papers. It looked so easy compared to hauling mop buckets and beating carpets. And Ilse had lost all hope of having a life like hers.

She eyed Ilse with the appraising look of a woman deciding if another was prettier than her. It was clear she didn't remember Ilse.

"What can I do for you?" The woman was sickly sweet in her professionalism.

"I applied for Lebensborn last week." She tried to swallow the faint tremor creeping into her voice. "Has there been a reply?"

"Your name?"

She gave it, and the woman shuffled through a file on her desk.

"Oh yes! You are to speak with one of our officers. Please have a seat and I will let him know you're here."

She rose and sashayed down the hall, a walk she must have practiced.

This was it. They were going to tell her they had discovered her lie. One simply did not deceive the Reich. What punishment would they devise for her? Her heartbeat pounded in her ears.

At last an officer appeared, cold and clear and hard, like glass in the sun. He was young, which only made him seem more severe.

He led her to his office and invited her to sit. Across from her, he placed his elbows on the desk and interlaced his fingers.

"Frau Ilse." She'd never been called "Frau" before, but, as the pamphlet had informed her, Lebensborn bestowed upon every pregnant woman the respect, and the honorific, of a married woman. Using only first names protected the mothers' anonymity.

"Most of our girls work in offices," he said, "but we're pleased that you work in a home, perfecting your cooking and cleaning skills, exactly as the Führer wishes. Also, you are a category-one Aryan. Highly valuable to the Reich."

He flashed perfect white teeth at her. It took everything she had not to bounce her leg. The waiting was unbearable. The officer began flipping through papers on his desk—Ilse's application, she now saw. Her questionnaire on the father.

"We have investigated the originator of the child." He looked at her now with concern. "I'm sorry to inform you that the young man in question has passed away."

"Yes, it's terrible." Ilse fluttered her eyelashes, trying to look devastated. She let her own grief, over her father, over Felix, shine through, if only for a moment. Tears would fill her eyes if she let them—but with the SS, she sensed it would be too much.

"Well. This means he's not able to pay the required subscription for you and the child to stay in a Lebensborn home."

Of course. A detail she'd missed, and now it was too late to do anything else about it, and she and her baby would be ruined. Devastation swept over her. The hemlock.

The officer's eyes flicked to her chest.

"But he died in service of the Reich. We would like to help you and the child. To subsidize the cost of your stay, we'd like to offer you the opportunity to help around the home. All mothers-to-be must do housework; you would simply be asked to do a bit more, your condition permitting, of course."

Ilse wanted to melt into the chair with relief. The Anschützes hadn't denied her claim. Perhaps they hadn't even been told. Lebensborn hadn't noticed that she and Rudolf could not have been in the same place at the time of conception or that he couldn't confirm her story. Her suspicion had been correct: they needed her as much as she needed them.

A few chores would be nothing. She thanked him profusely.

The next day, four months before her due date in October, a car would take her to the home. For four months, she couldn't make a wrong move—never say a wrong word, never let anybody know that her baby was Mischling. They wouldn't tell Ilse the location of the home, only that she would be in the heart of the Reich.

Part Two
Germination

An unmarried mother who rears a healthy and worthy child is immeasurably more valuable to the nation than a childless married woman.

— Walther Gmelin, "Women's Studies and Family Policy"

CHAPTER FIVE

July 1938
Wernigerode, Germany

The half-timbered manor was three stories high, perched atop a hill, looking down on the village below. This was the Lebensborn home in the Harz Mountains, and the grandest house Ilse had ever entered.

The SS chauffeur insisted on carrying Ilse's grubby knapsack into the foyer—an oddly kind gesture for the SS, who in general were aloof and arrogant and feared. The girls in Bremen declined their advances, and everyone went quiet when a black uniform or Mercedes appeared.

But now Ilse was part of the SS.

The foyer alone was larger than her whole apartment back in Bremen. An electric chandelier hung from the ceiling. Velvet-upholstered couches clustered around a fireplace. Ilse wondered if she could sit on them. Of course she could—she lived here now. She wandered over and stroked the plush arm, but couldn't bring herself to sit. It was at least as nice as the Anschütz family's furniture, which she'd cleaned many times but never, she realized, sat on herself. She couldn't imagine being comfortable in a place this fine.

A matronly woman entered with a smile. Her blank, wide-set eyes and broad mouth gave her a toad-like appearance, and her shapeless brown dress swayed as she moved. Ilse reminded herself to speak the High German she'd learned in school, rather than the Low German of Bremen.

The woman spoke with a simpering voice that sounded polite but wasn't.

"Welcome to Heim Harz. I'm Frau Administrator Ingrid. You must be Frau Ilse."

Ilse said yes, though it felt like a lie. She still did not feel like a Frau, a married woman.

The administrator led Ilse to the front desk where more paperwork awaited. One question asked: "Will you raise the child or leave him under the care of Lebensborn?" Her pen hovered over the empty box next to the little square for adoption as she thought about the bones and flesh and life knitting together as she sat there.

Together, she and the baby were doomed. Apart, they both stood a chance. But the pen in her hand quivered. The baby was still a part of her. They couldn't ask her to give up her lungs or her heart; it felt wrong of them to ask her to give up something that felt just as essential, something she needed to protect.

She checked the box. Giving up the child was a matter of will. She would have to do it and accept the suffering that would come with it. Her insides felt like ice.

Frau Ingrid led her up two flights of stairs and down a corridor, past a sour-looking maid mopping the floor. At the administrator's knock on one of the doors, a young woman swung it open. Rosy-cheeked and round-eyed, she looked like a perfect doll. If she was pregnant, she did not yet look it.

The girl's wide eyes took in the sight of Ilse in her rumpled dress, the one she'd been living in for over a week. Ilse felt dirtier than she'd ever been in her life. She itched to rip off her clothes, burn her dress, and take a long bath before any more of these perfect people could see her. She hadn't considered what it meant that Lebensborn mothers worked in offices, if they had to work at all. Yet another way she wouldn't fit in.

"I'll leave you to it," said Frau Ingrid. "Dinner's in an hour."

"I'm Karola," Ilse's new roommate said, pulling her into the room. Blond curls floated about her face, punctuating her words.

The room was the loveliest Ilse had ever called her own. Delicate floral wallpaper, polished wood floors, two large wardrobes, and two bedside tables—everything simple, but high quality. It was a place designed for respite, which she could not allow herself.

"Your bed is on the far side, by the window. And that wardrobe in the corner is yours. Is your father SS?"

Ilse ached at the memory of how she'd left him, looking years older in a matter of moments, a broken man, while her arms stung from his blows. "Hardly. He's a carpenter in a factory."

"Ah. And the originator?" She pointed at Ilse's belly.

"Luftwaffe." Ilse swallowed, her throat dry, hoping Karola wouldn't ask more questions she couldn't answer truthfully.

"That's something. My father and the originator are both SS. The originator is actually a friend of my father's. It's all worked out really well."

Ilse's face was turned away, which was fortunate. The thought of sleeping with a man her father's age, much less his friend, filled her with a revulsion she was too surprised to hide.

"The originator is the one who made arrangements for me to stay at Lebensborn," Karola continued. "He wanted to make sure I had the best accommodations during my confinement."

"And then you will give the baby up for adoption?"

"Absolutely not! This baby keeps me in the originator's life forever. He'll take care of both the child and me." She patted her belly with a smug smile.

"How nice," Ilse said, hoping her voice sounded cheerful and not at all disgusted.

"You're giving up yours?"

Ilse nodded, unable to say the words aloud.

"That makes sense. Then you can return to your life without having to worry about the child."

What life? Ilse couldn't summon a response.

Karola rolled onto her back and cupped her barely rounded belly. "I've gotten so fat," she moaned. "And I'm not even five months along. I shouldn't be so big already."

Ilse arched an eyebrow at Karola, who could easily have been a model even considering her condition. She knew she was meant to tell Karola how thin she still looked, but she couldn't bring herself to make a statement that was so obviously true.

On the bedside table, she placed her mother's book of plants. It was a stroke of luck that Lebensborn had brought her to the Harz. Her mother came from these mountains, and now Ilse would become a mother here.

A second door led to the bathroom, which adjoined another bedroom. Only four girls would use it. At home, there had been a toilet down the hall shared by all the tenants on the floor, and a bathhouse a block away. Ilse slipped inside and took in the milky white porcelain and green-tiled walls, listening to the silence. She showered but didn't wash her hair; she couldn't go to dinner looking like a drowned rat.

As soon as she'd left the RuSHA office yesterday, she'd returned to the Anschütz home only to tell the cook she was leaving and gather her things. She couldn't bring herself to look Herr and Frau Anschütz in the eye. She didn't know if Lebensborn had contacted them, or if they would have fired her before she could quit, but she didn't want to risk hearing from their lips that she was a lying whore. For that last night in Bremen, she'd slept in the park.

This morning, with an empty stomach and dirty clothes, she'd gotten into the sleek black Mercedes, the first car she'd ever been in, and left everything she knew behind.

In the bathroom mirror, she tried to smooth her frizzy hair and drape it over the faint scar marring her temple, but she was doomed to look like the working girl she was—perhaps endowed with wide, ice-blue eyes, full lips, and perfect bone structure, but lacking the style and grace of girls like Karola.

When she emerged, Karola linked their arms and led Ilse downstairs to dinner. Karola reminded her of a hummingbird, flitting from one colorful flower to the next, and she swept Ilse along with her. It felt nice, being swept—and why shouldn't she be friendly with Karola? The girl seemed nice, and she ached from keeping to herself for so long.

But she couldn't let go. As much as she wanted a friend, she couldn't relax and be a regular girl. Not anymore. Not even for a moment.

In the dining room were four cloth-covered tables that seated six or so people each—room for twenty-four expectant mothers. Most of the chairs were occupied, but Karola led her confidently to one of them and sat her down. Karola introduced her to the girls at the table: Brunhilde, Gisela, Hetty, Sabine. Their names immediately blurred together in Ilse's mind. A beautiful, heavily pregnant woman looked Ilse up and down with a cruel glint in her eye, then smirked. Gisela, Ilse thought her name was. The rest of the girls, perfectly groomed and elegant, seemed uninterested in Ilse after cursory glances and wrinkled noses. She smoothed her hair over her scar and wished she could have at least ironed her dress before dinner.

Most of the other girls looked fifteen or sixteen. She felt old in comparison. At the same time, she saw in them, with a small amount of horror, her future: Girls so large they looked as if their stomachs were about to burst open at the seams, expelling gore and infant across the polished floors. Girls off balance, tottering on each other's arms. She saw the labor they would soon be in, which Ilse, too, had no choice but to face. How many of them would give up their babies, she wondered.

"Lebensborn requires all of us to eat two-thirds of our vegetables raw," Karola advised, pointing at the colorful salad at every place setting. "Herr Himmler believes they're healthier than cooked vegetables."

At the center of each table were enormous serving plates piled high with roasted pork, sauerkraut with lard and broad beans, roasted potatoes with linseed oil, and crisp Zwieback. Ilse's mouth watered. She hadn't known there was this much food in Germany, much less at a single table. Karola nudged her.

"Eat up. If you don't, the baby won't be big and strong."

"And then the Führer won't want it," said Gisela, who was probably having twins. She looked older than the others, more woman than girl.

Ilse couldn't remember the last time she'd been truly full. She hadn't eaten since lunch the day before, and now, even though her midsection was full of baby and getting fuller every day, her insides felt like a yawning abyss that would suck her into it if she didn't eat soon.

She heaped her plate full and ate so quickly she had to remind herself to slow down, to taste the food and not let these girls think any less of her than they already did. The roast was hot and rich. She'd forgotten the rich taste of butter, almost sweetening the wholemeal bread. There was no better flavor, she decided.

As dinner died down, an employee with glamorous curls and bold, laughing eyes entered the room and bellowed over the din of talking women, "Motherhood class is about to begin in the second parlor." Ilse thought she saw the woman give her a shadow of a wink.

Fighting back the pain from her overfull stomach, Ilse followed the women and their protruding bellies out of the dining room and into a parlor-turned-classroom. There, Frau Ingrid delivered a long lecture with a reading from *The German Mother and Her First Child*, the Reich's definitive text on mothering.

"'Whatever you do, do not pick the child up from his bed, carry him around, cradle him, stroke him, hold him on your lap, or even nurse him. The child will quickly understand that all he needs to do is cry in order to attract a sympathetic soul and become the object of caring. Within a short time, he will demand this service as a right, leave you no peace until he is carried again, cradled or stroked—and with that, a tiny but implacable house tyrant is formed.'" Frau Ingrid closed the book and looked up. "Besides, the screaming is good for the child's lungs."

Ilse felt a flicker of wrongness. Though she had no younger siblings, it seemed to her that children cried because they needed something. It would be cruel to listen to their suffering and do nothing. Doubt mixed with the lessons of the Reich and curdled in her veins; she pushed the thoughts away, shaking and suddenly too hot. Doubt was never allowed.

The room had gone silent. It was thick with the breaths of so many girls and a strange tension. She looked up; Frau Ingrid watched her, eyes narrowed and glinting.

"Are you well, Frau Ilse?"

She sat up straight and said yes, she was, but her voice sounded small. She felt dirty and wrong. Wrong for questioning the doctrine, wrong for tainting herself with Jewish blood.

The Reich had to be correct. Look at this place, this refuge, which had taken her in when her father had cast her aside. She need only believe.

❦

Ilse woke early after nightmares of a tall, hard man and a flaxen-haired woman who held her baby tenderly, then wrung its neck. Her heart raced. She stared at the ceiling for a few minutes before she gave up on sleep and got dressed.

For her morning housework assignment, she ironed and sorted old clothes that previous mothers had left behind, which current tenants were invited to claim for themselves. Ilse took two simple but well-made dresses and a nightgown, addressing the least of her problems. With food, shelter, and clothing taken care of, her mind was free to worry about the baby: The dark hair it could be born with, the wrong measurements the caliper could reveal, any number of defects that would prove she'd bred with a monster—and created one. She felt as though the fear could snap her in two at any moment. She tried to swallow it. Panic could give her away as surely as the caliper.

When she'd finished her chores and changed into one of the new dresses, she followed the sound of voices toward the dayroom. Books lined the far wall, a gramophone stood silent in the corner, and clusters of couches and chairs were scattered throughout. All the pregnant girls, about twenty of them with their enormous bellies, seemed to take up the whole room. Karola spotted her at once. She waved Ilse over to the empty armchair next to her by the window. It was a gesture both welcoming and casual, an assumption of friendship. Ilse joined her, warmth blooming in her chest.

"Everyone keeps to their group around here," Karola said, putting her feet up on the ottoman and gesturing to the gaggle of mothers in the center of the room. "The married ladies stick

46

together. I'd say half of the pregnant women here are wives of SS officers."

"Wouldn't they be more comfortable at home?" Ilse was surprised; she thought the biggest benefit of Lebensborn was the discretion, the protection of her reputation. Why would an SS wife, elite of the elite, need that?

"I think their husbands know that the program is Herr Himmler's pet project and want to get in the good graces of the leader of the SS—who wouldn't? The program doesn't get the respect it deserves because of the rumors, so having married women makes it more reputable. It's meant to be a holiday, a time away from their responsibilities. Then there's the fact that Lebensborn offers the absolute best care. All the right food, prepared the best way for the babies. Unfortunately that includes cod liver oil." She grimaced, turning her pretty bow lips grotesque. "But they like to complain about having to share rooms and do chores. If they don't like it here, they should have stayed home. That's what I think. Don't let them get to you." She sniffed.

"Alright."

Karola was a picture of relaxation, reclining in her chair with an unopened copy of a magazine, *Das Deutsche Mädel*. She stared out the window and tugged on a curl that had fallen onto her shoulder. Turned the curl into a braid, undid it, and braided it again. Ilse fidgeted. Sitting still felt odd—wrong, even.

Someone turned the radio on and the Hitler Youth song, "The Rotten Bones Are Trembling," jangled through the speakers. A few girls began singing and dancing to the bois-terous tune. The result was cacophony. Ilse knew she should be more vivacious like the others—in addition to being tall, blond, and tan, German women were expected to be lively—but she simply didn't have it in her.

"What do we do now?" Ilse asked Karola.

"Anything. Nothing."

"We're supposed to do nothing but sit here for several months?"

"We work in the mornings, and then there are three meals and two snacks per day. Twice a week we have classes on motherhood and National Socialism. Sometimes we get to watch a new film that hasn't even been released in theaters yet. We're doing our part just by being here and making these babies."

Eating five times a day sounded like heaven to Ilse, but she didn't know what to do with no tasks—besides worry.

Through the window, she could see red-roofed houses cascading downward into the town, nestled in a valley. She'd only been farther than Hamburg once, an hour's bus ride away from Bremen—the time she went to the Nuremberg rally with the BDM. On the ride to Heim Harz, she'd marveled to see the flat landscape she knew so well yield to hills that loomed larger and larger. She'd passed haunted-looking moors, then cliffs of granite reaching for the sky, then hills of green and gold. The varied landscapes had seemed surreal, a trick of the light, a hallucination.

The baby fluttered in her stomach, saying hello. She smiled.

Then an unfamiliar sensation: a pulsing. It happened again. Then again, moments later. She sat up straight, all her attention pulled inward, listening. Fear rippled through her.

"What is it?" Karola asked.

"The baby is doing something. It's jerking. Regularly."

"I wonder if it's hiccups."

"They get hiccups?"

"Sure. The others talk about it. It's actually a bad sign. Could mean something's wrong."

Ilse thought of Felix's Jewish blood snaking through the child's veins, turning it, possibly, into something terrible. Scales for skin, a snout for a nose, extra fingers and toes. Perhaps it could leach the life out of her, a true parasite. At her alarmed expression, Karola sat up. She placed a hand on Ilse's.

"I didn't mean that. It was thoughtless of me. If it keeps up, you can ask the doctor next time he examines you."

Karola leaned back in her chair and studied Ilse's face.

"Maybe it's easier if it doesn't survive, given your situation. You wouldn't have to wonder about it."

How could she say that? She, who also carried a baby? Was it because Karola could keep her baby and thought those who weren't able to wouldn't care?

They were such a human thing, hiccups. The baby was very much alive inside her.

Ilse placed a hand across her belly. She opened and closed her mouth, unsure of what to say. Her alarm felt primal—all her senses alert, the world slowing.

"It's not like that." Ilse's voice sounded hoarse. She excused herself to take a walk.

As the baby hiccupped again on her way out, she decided not to ask the doctor about it, in case it made him look too closely.

CHAPTER SIX

During her first weeks in the home, as her body swelled, her skin thickened, her hips widened, and a long, vertical line appeared on her belly, Ilse perused the small selection of books provided, most with titles like *Raising the Ideal German Child: A Guide for Modern Mothers*. Her chafed washerwoman hands began to heal and soften, and she slept until the sun in her eyes woke her. She often placed her hands on her belly, closed her eyes, and sank inward. She felt the baby there, in conversation with her own body. It didn't feel like a monster. It felt like magic. This was the least alone she'd ever be. And she had to give the baby away.

She took advantage of the endless supplies of yarn to knit a sweater so the baby would have something to remember its mother by, then several hats and pairs of socks. She imagined, and tried not to imagine, the little head and feet that would occupy them in less than three months. It terrified her that she was making an entire person. It seemed far too complex to do properly, even in the best of circumstances.

In the afternoons, her restless hands found brooms and dusters, which were pried away from her by Schwestern—the employees in the home, most of whom were former Lebensborn mothers themselves. "Rest, for the child," they told her. But she couldn't rest, even for a moment. So she explored the home. She needed to know every inch of the place as a cat did. To find a way out, if she needed it.

Heim Harz comprised three buildings: the largest one, which Ilse lived in, contained all the pregnant women and the hospital ward. The smaller building next door housed the Lebensborn employees, administrative offices, and the kitchen. A third building housed the administrator's quarters, new mothers, and the crèche for infants and children.

The pregnant women weren't allowed near there for reasons no one would share with Ilse.

She walked around and around the grounds, despite the near-constant drizzle of the Harz. She didn't mind the rain, even though it caused her spun rayon jacket to stretch permanently into an odd shape that no longer fit her. The grounds consisted of a swath of hill surrounded by a wooded area, dotted with a gazebo and a picnic table. It seemed untouched, with no garden or landscaping.

There were no cars or trams whizzing by, no workers commuting, no hustle or bustle of any sort. Apart from the church bells clanging proudly across the town every hour, the insistent chirping of birds was the only sound.

Compared to her last days in Bremen, this home was a peaceful paradise. But unease followed her. Whenever the evils of Jewish blood were mentioned, whenever the other expectant mothers boasted of their SS originators, whenever Frau Ingrid eyed Ilse a little too long, she was reminded that she didn't belong here, and that at any moment the Anschützes could reveal her lie. The lie itself was a crime, but revealing the true father to Lebensborn would be disastrous. Felix's neighbor, Gregor, knew, and any number of people could have seen them in Bürgerpark. She'd been so careless. And, of course, the baby might fail the racial examination. What would happen then? If only she could keep the child inside her forever, where it would be safe, or, at least, safer.

She remained friendly with Karola, but what she'd said reminded Ilse not to become too close to anyone. She'd keep her guard up, with Karola and everyone else, every moment until she left Lebensborn, no matter how friendly they became. If she became too comfortable with someone, she could slip. Everyone here was, or seemed to be, a devout Nazi who would denounce her if she made the slightest misstep—if she revealed her secret, but also if she neglected to salute, if she asked too many questions in class, if she expressed anything but perfect patriotism.

At night, she lay on her side facing away from Karola. With a hand on her belly, she read her only book, her mother's book. She hadn't had the time or energy to read in years, and she marveled at the rustle of turning pages and the smell of old paper and ink. Her mother had pressed clippings of various plants from the Harz's unique ecosystem between the pages and annotated them in her elegant scrawl. Ilse ran her fingers over the letters, taking what comfort she could from them. Poppy, hops, red foxglove, black bill weed. Sometimes her mother noted medicinal uses, other times the origins—Nordic or oceanic, remnants of the last ice age. Ilse tried to remember her mother's voice, imagine her saying the words, but she couldn't. She could only hear light laughter echoing in her mind. For all she knew it wasn't her mother's laugh at all.

What she did remember was the scent of lemon that clung to her mother after she cleaned, and how she wore her hair down in voluptuous curls, though the mode for married women was a knot at the base of the head. She remembered that her mother threw her head back to laugh whenever Ilse surprised her, and she knew her mother had named her after a fairy tale, Princess Ilse of the Harz.

Her mother's frequent flights of fancy had made Ilse's father both fall in love with and disrespect his wife for her impracticality. Ilse had witnessed his feeble attempts to rein her mother in, but she'd grown up running wild in the mountains, barefoot in summer, sun-bleached hair streaming behind her. Ilse wasn't raised with that spirit, but an inner part of her yearned to stretch, to be free. It was buried too deep for her to notice most of the time.

When Ilse was five years old, her mother had disappeared into the bedroom, a hand on her back, face contorted in pain, her belly full of a sibling for Ilse. And she never saw her mother again. She never saw the baby at all—a sister, stillborn.

Ilse had liked to put her hands to her mother's belly and feel the child within. How magical the life inside her had felt, only to turn out not to be a life at all. Perhaps the same thing would happen to Ilse. She would simply disappear, fade from life, the child along with her.

A deep need for her mother rose from Ilse's gut, as if from the baby itself. She wondered what her mother would say about her predicament. Would she shame her for getting pregnant out of wedlock? For having a child with a Jew? Or for entering Lebensborn? The questions cycled endlessly, but no answers came.

❦

Ilse waddled down to breakfast, feeling as if she'd been constipated for seven months and having her monthly just as long. According to last week's checkup with Dr. Bartz—a short man, bald and pink-nosed, who disconcertingly always seemed to have the sniffles—she'd gained seven kilos, but it felt like twenty.

She sat down at her usual table, along with Karola and two new girls. They introduced themselves as Lucie and Metta.

Porridge again, porridge every day. Ilse had never thought of complaining about too much food until now. But the congealed porridge, smelling both pungent and bland, was enough to make any pregnant woman run for the toilet. Himmler, head of the SS and mastermind of Lebensborn, required every woman to eat it daily. We must be like the British, he said. Do not worry about your figures—the British eat porridge every day and look how thin they remain, how annoyingly superior in every way.

Weren't Germans supposed to be the superior race?

Lucie and Metta both had perfectly coiffed hair and glowing skin and airy demeanors, and looked so similar Ilse couldn't tell them apart. They eyed the porridge with suspicion. One of them—Lucie?—pushed the bowl away, and a brown-uniformed Schwester descended upon her. She pushed the bowl back in front of the girl.

"You must eat the porridge. Don't think you're better than anyone else here."

Nose wrinkled in disdain, the girl reached for the sugar bowl and piled heaping spoonfuls into the porridge. The Schwester hovered until she took a bite, chewed, and dramatically swallowed.

Ilse locked eyes with Karola, asking each other the same silent question: What was that about? But neither had the answer, and soon the chatter rose once again.

The reluctant porridge-eater had thick, dark eyebrows that made Ilse suspect she wasn't a natural blond, but was otherwise a picture of the Aryan race. She ignored Ilse and Karola, choosing to speak only to the other new girl. Both women had flat stomachs; they couldn't be far along.

Normally if someone didn't talk to Ilse, she left well enough alone, but nothing ever happened at the home and she needed a distraction from the plague of worry. So Ilse spoke.

"Where are you from?" she asked them.

"Frankfurt," the one with dark eyebrows said. Probably Lucie.

"Cologne," said the other. Metta. She had a mole below her left eye—moley Metta, that was how she would remember. "By way of Tegernsee."

The two women exchanged a knowing look.

"How so?" Karola asked.

"Well," said Lucie, lowering her voice, "there's a castle outside the town, where, incidentally, Herr Himmler's family lives. It puts this quaint little house to shame. I believe it was confiscated from Jews. Anyway, the castle is only for the most ideal of the Nordic race. I myself am half a head taller than just about any girl in Frankfurt, and, well, you can see the rest. I can prove my German lineage back to the sixteenth century, even further back than is required to enter the SS itself." She looked around for impressed faces. "Once my picture appeared on the front page of *Das Deutsche Mädel*."

Did this girl really want to talk about her looks this much, or was she dragging out the suspense?

"Through the BDM, I was selected for a program, the most secret part of Lebensborn."

"We shouldn't say," said Metta, though she clearly brimmed with the desire to tell.

"You might not even call it Lebensborn at all," said Lucie. "It's sort of a top-secret SS operation."

Then why announce it, Ilse wondered. Just to brag?

"We were there for a few weeks and we got to meet the most handsome men I've ever seen—"

"Lucie, don't," Metta said.

"—and all of them SS." Lucie carried on, undeterred by Metta's pleas or the secrecy she claimed she'd sworn to. "Tall, blond-haired, blue-eyed, strong—I've never seen such a selection. I made my pick, got pregnant right away, and now I'm here."

"They were *so* handsome," Metta sighed.

"We'll have to go back." They both looked delighted at the prospect.

"You mustn't tell anyone," Metta said, looking Ilse and Karola in the eye. "Please. We'd be in so much trouble."

"Of course, we won't," Karola said, her voice soothing— though it was clear she was dying to share her latest shiny bit of gossip, which she gathered like a magpie.

They were lying about this castle, lying for attention, feeding on the rumors about Lebensborn that could ruin all their reputations. The idea of breeding for the SS in such an organized manner was ridiculous. Ilse hoped she wouldn't have to interact with these girls much. In less than three months the baby would come, and then she'd be in the mothers' ward. She touched a finger over the spot where the baby pummeled her ribs.

Metta looked at Ilse. She nodded and promised, too, though she wasn't sure she had room for another secret. She decided to forget about it instead.

The conversation moved on to objects found around the home. There were myriad hiding places where treats, photos, champagne, and other contraband could be found.

"I found a collection of love letters underneath the floorboard near my wardrobe," said Gisela, who'd just taken a seat at the table, her chair groaning under her. "Very romantic. *Very* explicit."

"I didn't know any girl here loved their infant's originators," Lucie said.

"One did, anyway," Gisela said, eyes glinting. She never seemed to say anything about herself or her life before Heim Harz.

Ilse's thoughts turned to Felix, handsome in a particular way, but with such interesting thoughts, a way of squinting into the middle distance and finding so much more there than anyone else she had known. Once, he'd told her that all the matter in the universe already existed, and could only be transformed. She'd wondered, in that case, how a plant could make leaves and blossoms out of nothing but sunlight.

But she couldn't have loved him because she'd never truly known him. Perhaps she would have, in another world. The thought sent a pang through her chest. Instead, she was like the other girls at the table, pregnant, unwed, at risk of ruin without Lebensborn. It was no prison—she could probably leave if she wanted to—but she was trapped all the same.

After her morning chores, Ilse fetched *Physica* and headed to the dayroom to read. Coming down the stairs, she nearly ran into two important-looking men in black SS uniforms. Ilse jumped aside. Her heart pounded. Had they come for her?

"What lovely thing do we have here?" said the shorter one, whose pallid skin and colorless hair reminded Ilse of a corpse. His smile looked more like a leer. She recognized him from a photo in the foyer: Sturmbannführer Pflaum, head of Lebensborn.

"I'm Ilse, sir."

"And what are you reading?" asked the other man. He was tall, with wavy blond hair, a long straight nose, and sincere, deep-set eyes. The insignia of three oak leaves on his collar told her that this was an important man.

She lifted the book to reveal the cover.

"*Physica*." She willed the tremor to leave her voice.

"An herbalist! How wonderful." His smile was warm. "We should all return our attention to the soil."

The pallid man cleared his throat. "We should be going."

"May we meet again, Ilse," the taller man said.

She reached the dayroom but sat with the book unopened in her lap. She felt unsettled, somehow. Her heart continued to flutter frantically in her chest. The attention of SS officials couldn't lead anywhere good. But, she reminded herself, nothing at all had happened. She would probably never see them again.

CHAPTER SEVEN

The moon shone so brightly through the sheer curtains that Ilse didn't understand how she'd ever slept through it. But she didn't roll away; instead, she gazed at the white light streaming through the window.

Lately she'd been imagining a scenario in which she kept her baby: the two of them living in a boarding house in a sleepy town somewhere far away, sharing a narrow bed, the child warm and soft and curving into her body. But even if she somehow managed to find the money for travel and the first month's rent, Ilse wouldn't want to live in any place that would accept a young, single mother. It certainly wouldn't be fit for a child.

She listened to the thumping of her heart, willing it to calm down. She needed to sleep.

No one had warned her of the constant sickness that came with pregnancy. She had a constant cold, with a stuffy nose and body aches. Fatigue pervaded her body, yet she couldn't sleep. The weariness in her body had no effect on her state of mind, alert and alarmed. For all she knew, she'd say something incriminating in her sleep and Karola would hear. A part of her listened constantly for the stomping of SS boots coming for her at last. She'd been lucky so far, but how long could it last?

Before, she'd been spared the energy for insomnia, the comfort required for contemplation. Now, the many contradictions in her life became impossible to ignore: how she was praised for creating a German child despite it being a shameful secret outside of Lebensborn, how that child was actually a Mischling, how she had more than enough to eat while the people outside barely scraped meals together. The leaders of the Reich surely knew what they were doing, but she found herself running in mental circles trying to find the logic in it.

She left the warmth of her eiderdown for the chill and damp of the air. She walked to the window, peered out at the garden, the brick wall, the hills beyond, then turned and walked back to her bed, then back to the window. Fortunately, Karola slept deeply and was undisturbed by Ilse's roaming.

The Freimarkt would be starting in Bremen soon. She couldn't imagine an October without the bustle of the folk festival, the crowds and music and dancing, the beer and the bratwurst. Girls in the BDM discussing which boys would give them gingerbread hearts with inscriptions like "Ischa Freimaak" —It is Freimarkt and everything is allowed. But she'd left that life behind forever.

Ilse wanted to keep the baby.

She couldn't keep the baby.

Words like "could" seemed to matter less and less.

She could become a Schwester after the birth—work at the home, stay close to the baby, keep them both fed and clothed and sheltered. It was a position of honor, one that could lead to opportunities for a better life. One that allowed her to keep the baby.

But the danger was too great. Every day, under the nose of the Reich, they'd risk discovery. What if the baby was born without hair, but then it grew in dark and curly? What if its nose grew into the wrong shape? What if his nature turned evil as she'd been taught? What if Ilse became too comfortable, made a friend, and slipped?

As she paced back to the window, a floorboard creaked beneath her foot. Remembering the breakfast table conversation, she crouched down and wedged her fingernails in the groove between the boards. It remained stubbornly in place. She fetched a shoehorn she'd found in her wardrobe and worked at the seam. After a minute or two of prying, the loose board gave way with a scratch and a groan.

Ilse checked that Karola was still asleep. She lay sprawled on her back, one foot dangling off the bed. Ilse put the floorboard aside and peeked into the space it had covered.

Inside was one object: a book. She pulled it out. It was compact and dense, a comfortable heft in her hand. The brown leather cover was stamped with bold letters: *Jane Eyre* by Charlotte Brontë. Ilse had never heard of the title or the author.

She returned it and slid the floorboard back in place. Given its illicit location, this book must be forbidden, which meant she could get in trouble.

She slipped back into bed, and the full moon continued to stare at her on one side, and Karola's belly, itself a half-moon under the white sheet, stared at her from the other. Ilse was still exhausted, but more awake than ever.

Jane Eyre by Charlotte Brontë.

Jane Eyre.

Charlotte Brontë.

The words rolled around in her head. The book, heavy and beautiful, begged to be opened, to reveal its world to her.

Ilse had loved school during the years she'd gone. She still remembered everything from all her classes—mathematics, history, literature, science—perhaps because she'd studied so hard, cared so much. Because she knew that once she turned fourteen and graduated, she'd never have the time to learn again; her life would be consumed with the tedium of taking apart garments to save every bit of thread, button, and elastic, of cutting newspaper into squares for toilet paper. There would be no time for study.

So she'd borrowed books from the school library to read late into the night instead of sleeping. She hadn't needed much sleep back then. But when she was not quite thirteen, literature had disappeared in flames and most of the reading material left was about National Socialism, or at the very least written by National Socialists. A year later, she'd left school and there'd been no energy or time for reading. But she had time now.

Somewhere in the building, a scream echoed. Her stomach clenched. A girl was having her baby tonight. With each birth, Ilse felt herself moving up in line. Soon, the screams would be hers.

She looked out the corner of her eye; Karola slept open-mouthed, her breaths slow and easy. Ilse slinked to the forbidden floorboard, retrieved the book, and fled back to bed like a spy to a safe house. She flicked on the lamp beside her bed and held the book open inside the small halo of light, ready to hide it should Karola wake up, and began to read.

※

None of Ilse's clothes fit her anymore, not even her shoes. She couldn't believe she'd ever fit into the little black saddle shoes she'd worn to the home—they looked like child's shoes compared to her feet, which had inflated like two oddly shaped balloons. Some girls had stopped treating her with indifference—they'd moved on to snickering and whispering behind their hands at her. She knew she looked ridiculous squeezed into her only pair of shoes, yet another marker of her inferior status.

In the dim light of the closet off the laundry room, she went through the clothes left behind by previous mothers. The walls were lined with shelves of neatly folded dresses, blouses, skirts, and shoes. She was running her fingers across the shiny leather, weather-beaten patent leather, and scuffed rubber, when someone barged in. It was the laughing-eyed Schwester—Ilse had learned her name was Hannelore. Tall and slim and buxom, her coppery hair carefully styled so it hid one eye, she seemed far too glamorous for Lebensborn. She vibrated with life.

"I had a feeling someone was in here," she said.

Ilse recalled a rumor that Hannelore stole from the home; perhaps that was her true reason for being here. As a secretary, she had no reason to be in the laundry room. Hannelore glanced at the shelves Ilse was perusing, then down at her feet, and her face transformed into a confidential smirk. "Need some help?"

Ilse wished she could hide her feet. Or find some way to preserve her dignity. "No, I'm alright."

"Well, you've turned into a rod of steel, haven't you!" Hannelore said. "You'll want to get better at hiding your emotions if you're going to survive here." She slipped delicate fingers through Ilse's arm and jiggled it. "There, now, loosen up. Be a willow, swaying in the wind. And take help when it's offered."

Hannelore nudged Ilse to stand against the wall, then pulled over a stool from next to the laundry machines. She stepped on it to reach the highest shelf, which Ilse had thought was empty, and started rummaging around.

"You're the quiet one," Hannelore said. Ilse didn't know what to say to that. "Don't worry; it's good. Better than chattering without saying anything."

Ilse watched her rummage around the shelf, which seemed

to be quite full—but she rearranged them with practiced confidence. At last, she brought down a pair of enormous wooden shoes.

"They're not much, but better than going barefoot, which is how you'll end up with those sausages. They look like they're about to burst out of their casing."

Ilse didn't love this commentary on her body, but found herself trying not to laugh anyway. She slipped out of her own shoes with relief and put on the wooden ones.

She felt an unexpected rush of warmth toward Hannelore. Such a simple kindness. "Thanks."

"Up there in Bremen, you're practically Dutch. These suit you."

Schwestern and mothers weren't supposed to socialize, but Hannelore seemed like the first genuine person she'd met in a while, and Ilse was tired of having no one to talk to except the pregnant wives and mistresses of SS officers.

"Would you like to take a walk with me sometime?" Ilse asked. She would be careful to keep Hannelore at arm's length—an acquaintance, not a confidant. Still, her palms dampened with sweat.

"I have a better idea." Hannelore's eyes sparkled. "Meet me at the picnic table tonight."

It turned out Hannelore's concept of a better idea was to sneak Ilse into the Schwestern's building, along with a bottle of vodka. She got the impression that Hannelore did this kind of thing often. When Hannelore took her hand and pulled her toward the small, half-timbered building next door, Ilse balked. Pregnant women weren't permitted to enter the Schwestern's building.

"What are you doing?"

"Don't you ever tire of the girls?" Hannelore leaned in close to Ilse and wiggled her eyebrows. She raised her voice an octave, simpering and breathy: "Oh, isn't my baby's originator the handsomest man you've ever seen? Isn't the Führer so brave and smart, Herr Goebbels so charming?"

Ilse stifled a chortle. It was identical to any mealtime conversation, and she was indeed sick of hearing it.

"Come take a break with me," Hannelore said. "I know how to make sure you won't get caught."

Hannelore's bold confidence made Ilse believe her. The Schwester didn't seem dishonest, but she was intelligent—wily, even. She was in good standing with Lebensborn, so being friendly with her wouldn't hurt Ilse's reputation.

She nodded, and Hannelore grinned, tugging her along. Ilse's heart skipped—in anticipation of fun, she realized. She hadn't felt that way since she'd last had a good friend, more than four years ago.

Hannelore made quick work of sneaking her in, up the stairs and past the silent hall lined with fleur-de-lis. Although simpler than the rooms of the mothers-to-be, the Schwester's room was still better than any room Ilse had slept in before Lebensborn. Two beds framed a table with a pitcher of water and a small window overlooking the grounds.

"I have this room to myself until another Schwester is hired," Hannelore said. "Make yourself comfortable."

Hannelore draped herself casually but elegantly across the pillows, looking like a work of art. She looked in her early twenties, yet she seemed at once both older and younger than Ilse.

She sat against the footboard, the baby wedged between her legs and torso. They passed the bottle back and forth. Ilse took the smallest possible sips; she needed to keep her wits about her.

Prints of unusual art, some of it pastoral, some Gothic, some abstract, adorned Hannelore's half of the room. On the wall above the headboard, there was only one picture: a woman pilot.

"Who is that?" Ilse asked.

Hannelore tilted her head up. "Hanna Reitsch. She was the first woman to cross the Alps in a glider *and* the first woman to fly a helicopter. She was the first. I will be the second."

"You want to fly planes, too?" Ilse had never heard of women doing such a thing.

Hannelore's eyes lit up, the fervor in them almost manic. "I do fly. Or rather, I have flown. Glider planes. From the sky, everything is beautiful, even the things that are ugly. And all of it is unimportant. Someday, when I fly again, I'll take you."

"Is that why you work here? To pay for flying lessons?"

"I haven't flown since my parents were alive. My mother died of influenza. Then, during the inflation, my father lost his job and his copious savings, and took his life."

Ilse flinched, but Hannelore stated it matter-of-factly, almost breezily, as if she took even this in stride.

"Flying is the best thing in the world. It changes you."

"Into what?"

"I don't know." Hannelore flapped her hand. "Yourself, I suppose."

"Am I not myself already?"

Hannelore's eyes narrowed, appraising her. "Not yet."

Ilse chuckled. If she wasn't herself, who could she be?

Hannelore was unlike anyone she'd met before. She made Ilse feel at ease and alive. Hannelore seemed to cast a spell on everything around her, turning it to magic, including Ilse herself. She began to feel that she really could fly, that anything she did in Hannelore's company would be . . . *fun.*

"Did you know I'm one of the only Schwestern here who wasn't originally a Lebensborn mother?" Hannelore said. "I came here just for the job."

"Are you from the area?" Ilse asked.

"No, why?" Hannelore clearly spied the hope in her eyes.

"My mother came from here—a town called Thale. My father met her when he was a journeyman carpenter and brought her back to Bremen with him."

"What is she like?"

How to describe her mother, a myth who existed only in her mind? "She was . . . a free spirit. She had a yellow canary, a Harz Roller, that she brought with her to Bremen in a little gilt cage. My father wanted to get rid of the canary—another mouth to feed, no matter how small, was one mouth too many—but my mother refused and fed the little bird seeds and insects she gathered and sang along with him. When she died, the canary followed her not long after. But I kept the cage."

Hannelore sighed and took Ilse's hand and closed her eyes. They sat like that for a moment.

"I'm so glad I found you," Hannelore said. "You're nothing like the others, with their empty heads. If I hear the 'Horst-Wessel-Lied' one more time I'll scream. So many daffodils in this house."

Ilse went still. She studied Hannelore's dancing eyes for a sign.

Daffodil was a term for a female Nazi. Only those who were against the Nazis used it.

People were careful not to reveal such negative sentiments to those who didn't share them—which meant that Hannelore thought Ilse shared them. It made Ilse feel uncertain, as she had when she'd found out the truth about Felix. She passed the bottle without drinking from it, her stomach in a knot. She hated when people knew things about her that she herself was unaware of.

"Do you know who stayed in my room before me?" Ilse asked. Whoever stayed there before her could have been the original owner of *Jane Eyre*. Hannelore might be the only person who would give her a straight answer.

She furrowed her brows. "Agathe, I think her name was."

"What was she like?"

"Feisty. Always talking back to Frau Ingrid. She up and left one day—before her baby's birth. There were rumors that she was removed from the home."

Ilse absorbed the information, filling in the picture of the girl whose place she'd taken, whose book she now read. Spirited. A rebel. Her heart leapt a little, and if she didn't know better, she'd think she was excited. But she pulled herself back. She must conform.

Hannelore launched into stories of the Schwestern. How sometimes they neglected to take out the chamber pots in the crèche for weeks at a time, causing a stench that leaked into the hallway. How an epidemic broke out in another home after the Schwestern failed to notice a case of diphtheria. "They quarantined for weeks, all together. Can you imagine the torture?"

"I don't understand how that could happen. This is the best facility in the country, with the best care. How could they be so irresponsible?" Ilse's voice came out aggressive, ready to attack—not Hannelore, but those who'd lied to her, those who might bring harm to her baby.

Hannelore swept her hair back, revealing her left eye for the first time. "That's what the pamphlet says, sure. At first they brought on people with actual experience, but no one else wanted to work here—with the reputation as an SS whorehouse and all—so they started keeping on any mother who meets the 'racially valuable' criteria and gives birth to a healthy child. Those are the only two requirements now."

Ilse wondered how Hannelore felt so free to say what she thought, danger and all, when Ilse didn't even know her thoughts well enough to speak them.

"Sometimes my baby has hiccups," Ilse said. "I worry that something's wrong, that the child won't come out right."

"Why would something be wrong?"

Ilse's tongue thickened in her mouth, grasping for words that wouldn't come.

"Darling, hiccups are normal. I'm sure your baby is fine."

The air was heavy with the warm, sweet scent of pumpernickel bread pudding as Ilse tidied up the kitchen after her extra chores. While she was scouring the already-spotless countertop, Frau Ingrid entered the room, her clipboard propped against her stomach. Ilse ceased wiping the rag over the counter and stood at attention. Whenever any mother-to-be completed a task, the administrator inspected the work. Many Lebensborn mothers were unenthusiastic workers, and the administrator could often be heard scolding pouty-faced girls all over the home. Frau Ingrid examined the spiral coils of the stove, the porcelain sink, the checker-board floors, and the wooden cabinets, then scribbled her notes.

"How did you make that dish?" Frau Ingrid asked. Pumpernickel bread pudding was rarely made, since the bread itself had to be steamed for a full day before being turned into pudding. Ilse had only made it once before, while assisting the cook at the Anschütz manor.

"I hope it was alright?"

"Yes, yes, it was good. Very good." Reluctance was thick in her voice.

"Orange and lemon zest is the trick. The citrus balances out the other flavors."

Frau Ingrid made a noncommittal sound that Ilse chose to

interpret as approval. It gave her the courage to do what she'd been thinking about since talking to Hannelore.

"I was wondering"—Ilse nearly lost her nerve at the sight of the administrator's unfriendly eyes, but pressed on—"could I become a Schwester after the birth?"

She would do any job to stay with the baby, and perhaps as a Schwester she could move up in the world, become a secretary or even a nurse.

"You want to stay?" Frau Ingrid's eyes slid down to Ilse's belly, then back up to her face. "We'll see."

Once Frau Ingrid left, Ilse took off her apron and lumbered outside. Lately she'd taken to moving slower, partly because her new body, large and achy, was difficult to maneuver, and partly to fill up the time so she wouldn't be alone with her thoughts. When she pushed open the door, a gust of brisk wind whipped her hair and dress against her body. She braced against it and gulped in the fresh air, then made for the unoccupied picnic table.

Since their conversation two days ago, the fact that Hannelore had chosen Ilse to confide in continued to rattle her. Hannelore had used the word "daffodil." She'd criticized the program. She wouldn't say those things to just anyone. True, of late, things Ilse had taken for granted no longer made sense to her. Felix wasn't the monster, the pig, the poison mushroom she'd been taught Jews were. Unwed mothers who didn't meet the racial criteria were denied the sanctuary Lebensborn offered. Babies meant to be safe in the home were beaten. And then there was *Jane Eyre*. The novel revealed a different world, a new perspective that had nothing to do with the Reich, and one that did not fit with the reality Ilse knew.

Jane Eyre had been written a hundred years ago yet was ahead of Ilse's own time. That must be why the book was forbidden; it was about a woman who lived for herself, and to make matters worse, she was English.

Jane was the same age as Ilse, so similar to her and also so different. They were both motherless and penniless. But Jane was certain of herself and possessed a thorough thoughtfulness that was foreign to Ilse. She had an "inward treasure born with me, which can keep me alive if all extraneous delights should be withheld, or offered only at a price I cannot afford to give." She followed her sense of right and wrong with no doubts. Her own self was all she needed to live. Ilse supposed Jane had it easier, living in a different time and place, perhaps a simpler one—and her inward treasure was not outside of her, as Ilse's would be. A child changed everything.

She was becoming increasingly uneasy with her situation. She was a racially valuable mother in a land that wouldn't allow her to be anything else, a land that was sending away everyone who didn't fit its narrow requirements for existence.

If only she could ask Hannelore questions, so many questions, ones she couldn't even articulate to herself. But even thinking them frightened her.

What did it mean when her experience of the world contradicted everything she'd been taught? How could she know what was right? How had she ever thought she'd known?

A hazy memory rose in her mind of her friend Mitzi from school, the only Jewish friend she'd ever had besides Felix. Mitzi had faded from Ilse's life years ago. She'd nearly forgotten about her.

Slumped against the picnic table, Ilse strained to remember, listening to the urgent chirping of the birds as if they held an answer for her.

. . .

Ilse, just turned fourteen, was stealing a few moments after her errands to soak her aching feet in the river Weser, the refreshing cold spreading up her legs as gooseflesh, which settled as they warmed again from the sun. A voice called her name. She hadn't seen Mitzi in several months, since Mitzi had left school. Ilse jumped up, splashing them both with water, and embraced her friend—she hoped they were still friends.

Mitzi's face was soft and round, but she sometimes tilted her head in a defiant way that made it clear there was no weakness in her. They sat down, facing each other.

"Where have you been?" Ilse asked. "I've missed you."

Mitzi ducked her chin.

"My parents took me out of school."

"Why?"

"I go to school through our synagogue now. The other children . . . well, they can be mean."

"I'm not."

"No." She smiled, turning away to look at the water. "You're not."

Ilse remembered seeing Mitzi walk home from school, surrounded by boys who pulled her hair and tugged on her bag as she hunched over the books she carried. From far away, Ilse had thought they were teasing her the way boys who liked girls sometimes did. But there had been something off about it that she hadn't been able to name.

Since the Nazis had come to power the year before, all Jews had been removed from political positions, including Mitzi's father, who'd been a senator. No one would hire a Jew now. And to leave Germany to find work elsewhere, they would have to give up all their possessions and all their money, moving to a new country with nothing.

Whenever Ilse had to salute the block warden who informed on the neighborhood to the Nazis, or learned in school that girls grew up to be mothers and boys grew up to be soldiers and that Jews had no business being in Germany at all, there was a twisting pain above her navel and below her ribs. It was the kind that came when she'd done something wrong—but she hadn't done anything at all, so she could neither take it back nor fix it nor even apologize.

Ilse's stomach began to twist now. Though it made her want to hunch over, she swallowed the feeling. Mitzi held her back straight.

Mitzi's black shoes sat side by side with Ilse's in the sand, Ilse's patent leather ones coming apart at the soles and Mitzi's leather ones looking as if they would disintegrate into the earth at any moment. For some reason, seeing Mitzi like this was harder to look at than Ilse's own shabby clothes and worn shoes. Perhaps it was because Mitzi wasn't used to being poor, and Ilse was.

Ilse's father was glad when the one Jewish girl at school had left. He'd said it was disgraceful for Aryans and Jews to interact. In the past, Ilse had tried to explain to her father that Mitzi was different. When she did, he took off his leather belt and showed her that she was wrong. But her father couldn't see what she did at school, so Ilse continued being friends with Mitzi until she left.

Mitzi's stomach gurgled. She tilted her head back and pretended the sound hadn't come from her. Ilse realized she was hungry, too.

"Should we have some lunch?" Ilse asked.

"I'm not hungry."

Ilse said the same thing sometimes when there was no food at home and she smelled everyone's lunches at school and watched their potato salads disappear into their mouths, her mouth thick with saliva. Ilse couldn't bear that Mitzi must be feeling the same way.

"Come to mine. By the time you get there, maybe you'll want to eat something with me." Mitzi agreed. The twisting came, the twisting went.

In Ilse's apartment, they made her favorite: Labskaus. Mashed potatoes, pureed beets, a fried egg, even a bit of corned beef. A feast. And Mitzi ate.

That evening, long after Mitzi had gone home, Ilse's father arrived and sat in his chair by the fireplace. He called her and she came in from the kitchen.

"Labskaus tonight," he grunted.

Time slowed. So did her mind.

"I can't make it."

"Why not?"

He looked at her for the first time that day. His eyes were an otherworldly pale blue, the same as hers.

"I had it for lunch."

"Then make the rest for me. You couldn't have eaten it all yourself."

Ilse opened her mouth and closed it. Her mind went blank. No lie came to her, no version of the truth that would save her. It had been so exciting to see Mitzi, she hadn't thought of her father and how he would surely notice missing food.

"Who was here?" he asked, steel entering his voice.

"A friend."

"Who?"

A pause.

"Mitzi."

He stood. Though he was not a large man, the lines of his body held a threat. She knew the strength hiding in that wiry frame.

"You know you're not allowed to speak to her."

Twisting, twisting.

Something snapped in Ilse.

"I want to know why I can't spend time with my friend. I want to understand."

"She is not your friend. You have risked our reputation by bringing her kind here."

Ilse tossed her head, annoyed by the familiar words that never gave her the answers she sought. More than anything, she wanted the twisting to stop.

"I like Mitzi better than all the other girls in my class. Why should her father not be able to work? How is she inferior?"

Her father unbuckled his belt and slid it through his pant loops. The sight was enough to make her back tense up, as if the belt had already slashed across it.

Softly, not looking at her, he said, "I've told you, many times, that these questions are not appropriate for girls to ask. You are not to think of politics. You will do as I say. In this family, we are National Socialists, and that is all you need to know."

Ilse swallowed. Her whole body went cold. She turned around and bared her back to her father. She buried her fist in her mouth and refused to cry out with each lash. Soon drops of blood speckled her knuckles from where her teeth had cut them.

It was the worst of the many whippings she'd received. He'd used the buckle end of the belt. She missed two days of school and lay in bed on her stomach, only getting up to prepare food for them both.

"I do this for your own good, you know," he said once, standing over her. He sounded almost remorseful. "It's no life for someone who doesn't believe."

For two weeks, Ilse slept on her stomach to let the welts heal. The pain pulsed across her back to the rhythm of her heartbeat, especially in the places where multiple strikes had landed.

She disobeyed, she was wrong, she was bad—each throb told her this. So she would be good from now on, and do exactly what her father said, and think what he wanted her to think. It was easy enough to do: When she dreamed of a different life, she reminded herself that she was born to be a Hausfrau. When she thought of helping someone who was not a member of the German people, the Volk, she told herself that they were not for her to help. By the time her back had healed, she barely remembered why she'd made herself think those things.

And the twisting ache in her stomach went away completely.

Chapter Eight

Too claustrophobic, these grounds. Ilse felt a compulsion to leave the home, even if just for a walk, so she put on her coat and went to the wooden gate. A bored-looking SS guard stared into the distance, not noticing her. She cleared her throat and he looked at her. His dull eyes seemed to snag on her face, unable to look away. She gave him her best smile. Dazzling even, she hoped.

"May I go for a walk, Officer?"

"Certainly, Gnädige Frau." He opened the gate and stood aside for her to pass through.

She thanked him and took her first sip of non-Lebensborn air in months. It was as if she could suddenly take fuller breaths than before.

It only took a few minutes to walk through town, but she kept going. As cobblestones turned to dirt paths and the shelter of buildings yielded to spruce and pine trees, she looked for the plants her mother had drawn in her book. The BDM had instilled in Ilse the ability to identify flora, but she knew only the dozen or so from northern Germany that the BDM had deemed useful. Now, she wanted to learn about plants simply to satisfy her curiosity.

It was too late in the season to identify the alpine anemone —her mother had proudly noted that the Harz was the only place in Germany where it grew. Instead, she looked for ferns and mosses. She found the fir clubmoss, sticking out of the ground like miniature Douglas firs, and aromatic spignel, useful in teas and tinctures for stomach and joint ailments. She broke off a soft sprig and bit into it; it tasted like fennel, just as her mother's notes described. She imagined her mother tasting this same taste, touching this same plant. Ilse rolled the sprig between her fingers and dropped the tiny ball to the ground.

She felt heavy and sluggish, so she tottered downhill toward town, with the distinct impression that if she moved too quickly, she'd tip over. She held her belly as she walked to relieve the pressure from her back, her bladder, her everything.

Her body was going through all this, being changed, in some ways forever. Even though she was giving the baby up, it would be impossible to forget. The baby was rewiring her, changing her in every way. She was filled to the brim with fear and lies and an impending loss she would always carry with her.

In town, the rows of houses, a thousand years old and all connected to one another, transported her back in time. Parts of Bremen were like this. The town square especially, with its gothic spire, reminded Ilse of home. Perhaps she could find work here in town once the baby came.

It was market day, the square bustling. Strange to think she had bought nothing in three months. She didn't have a single pfennig to her name. Here were fresh cheeses, marmalades, Pottsuse, the local spiced pork spread—the kind of foods that rarely reached larger towns like Bremen anymore. Drawn by the warm, yeasty smell, she found her way to the baker's stall, tended by a long-faced man whose legs seemed to go all the way up to his armpits. She smiled politely at him.

"Whore." He hissed the word into the loaves, but she heard it.

She looked up. His mouth was a straight line as he met her gaze.

"Hitler's whore. You're not welcome here. This is a respectable town."

Ilse took a step back. Other shoppers and vendors looked on. No one said anything. Her heart thudded in her chest.

The way they all looked at her—they were unwelcoming, even threatening. What would they do to her?

A short, squat peasant woman holding a bucket said, "You sit in luxury, up on your hill, eating chocolates, while we work and have nothing to show for it."

Ilse, confused, opened her mouth to say something, anything, to defend herself. Before she could, the woman heaved the bucket and sloshed its contents at Ilse.

She squeezed her eyes shut, bracing herself, for burning heat or jolting cold or stinking filth. Instead, she was pelted with what felt like dozens of birds—hard bodies, soft wings, pointed beaks. Silence fell and blood pounded in her ears. She opened her eyes and found herself covered in food scraps—peels of onions and potatoes, nubs of carrots and celery, grounds of ersatz coffee, cooking oil dark from use and reuse. One hand had protected her face, while the other covered her enormous belly. She lowered them both now and met the squat woman's gaze. Her beady eyes glinted back at Ilse.

The crowd of villagers closed in.

Ilse took another step back, then turned. As soon as she did, something hard hit her in the back. Blow after blow landed, the villagers using whatever was on hand to hit her, hurt her, yelling things Ilse couldn't hear. She tried to run but slipped on the slick cobblestones. Then she was on the ground, her hands and knees screaming in pain. She swung a fist but only caught air.

Something hit her head. Her teeth crashed and her brain knocked against her skull. There was darkness, then she saw stars. Was this it? Death at the hands of these strangers?

"Stop!" An authoritative voice rang out over the jeers of the villagers. The voice was familiar. She tried to get up, but couldn't manage her shaking, ungainly body. She fell again.

Pain shot through her right hip. Too close to the baby.

The crowd parted and Hannelore muscled her way through, strong and blazing. Her dress whipped around her like a small gale-force wind. Ilse had never been happier to see anyone.

"Go away. She's done nothing to you." She shooed the villagers, and even though most of them were older and bigger than her, they obeyed, dispersing and grumbling. They'd had their fun, shaming the unwed Lebensborn mother.

Hannelore crouched down beside Ilse. Calm eyes, steady voice. "Can you get up?"

Ilse tried again to stand, but she felt dizzy and off-balance. She desperately wanted to leave the square. Escape from the village. Return to Heim Harz.

"Hold on to me." Hannelore reached out her hands and pulled her up.

Freshly washed and her wounds tended, Ilse lay in bed in the hospital ward. Dr. Bartz had assured her the baby was alright, but she'd been frantic, pestering him with questions and concerns. Then he'd given her something for the pain and the world swam pleasantly. She couldn't remember what she'd been worried about; everything would be fine and the baby would be perfect. Hannelore sat beside her, looking radiant. Like an angel.

"You saved me." Ilse smiled. She'd never felt more magnanimous. She wanted to give Hannelore a hug and all her worldly possessions. Then she remembered she didn't have any possessions and laughed.

"I'm glad you're feeling better," Hannelore said. The walk uphill to the home had been arduous, Hannelore half-supporting her while Ilse gritted her teeth and tried not to cry from the pain and the fear. "Those barbarians acted like you were personally responsible for Lebensborn, probably the whole Reich, too."

"I've *never* felt better." Ilse sighed contentedly. Her words slurred. "It's so nice to have a friend. My last friend was Felix, and he left me. Didn't even say goodbye. He left me in a terrible position. Didn't mean to but he did."

"What position?" Hannelore pointed at Ilse's round belly, rising and falling under the white sheet. "That one?"

"That's right. But he had to go. He wasn't safe here. I want him to be safe. But now I'm not safe."

Hannelore said something, but she sounded too far away. Ilse couldn't hear. Then Hannelore grasped her hand so hard it should have hurt. "Stop talking. Go to sleep. I'll stay here until the drugs wear off."

⁂

The following afternoon, body still aching and bruised, Ilse was released from the hospital. She'd woken that morning with the memory of her loosened lips. Cold fear had frozen her chest. When she'd tried to get up and find Hannelore, the Oberschwester in charge of the hospital ward had pushed her back into bed, saying, "We're not taking any chances where a child of pure blood is concerned. Rest."

Now, she must beg Hannelore not to share what she'd revealed in her drug-induced stupor. Ilse couldn't remember exactly what she'd said, how much danger she'd put herself in— and Hannelore, by extension—but she knew it was enough. Now Ilse would find out if she could trust her.

But she couldn't find Hannelore anywhere. She scoured the laundry room, the kitchen, the grounds, anywhere Hannelore might go that Ilse could access.

It was as if she'd evaporated into thin air.

When Ilse returned, defeated, to her own room, all three of the mothers-to-be who shared the bathroom were crammed into it. Lucie—the one with dark eyebrows—was the most recent addition, assigned to share Gisela's room. They welcomed Ilse back raucously, fussing over her wounds, then just as quickly forgot about her as they returned to primping themselves. As Ilse jockeyed into a position in front of the sink, her belly bumped Karola's. Karola burst into giggles over it, and Ilse couldn't help the corners of her mouth rising, too.

"I'd die for rouge," Lucie said, peering over Ilse for a view of the mirror and pinching her cheeks.

"Your glow is all you need," Gisela said.

Lucie whacked her on the arm with the back of her hand— "Stop, you liar"—but beamed all the same. The two appeared to have become fast friends.

"Me, I miss kohl the most," Gisela said.

"What about you, Ilse?" Lucie asked.

Ilse started and met Lucie's round eyes in the mirror.

"Pencil for darkening my eyebrows." She looked down so she couldn't see if they were examining her thin, blond brows with disgust, but the chatter soon moved on.

Ilse was about to go downstairs to search again for

Hannelore when something Lucie said made her stop. She was telling a story she'd overheard from the Schwestern; somehow she always seemed to know more than the rest of the house combined.

"This SS couple had been unable to have children for many years. It was hopeless. But then the wife, age forty, has a baby. And another. It was a miracle, or so everyone was led to believe. Turns out, they'd *adopted* these children and lied about it to Herr Himmler himself. The husband and wife were shipped off to labor camps, put to work for a few months, and then hanged."

"Just for adopting kids?" Karola's mouth was hanging open a little.

"For lying about it, of course." Lucie placed the final pin in her flawless Olympia roll.

For a moment Gisela looked pale, almost as if she were choking. It must have been a bout of nausea, because she said, "We must be honest, above all."

Ilse's mouth went dry. When the girls headed for the door, Karola looked at Ilse, who remained frozen, hands clutching the cool porcelain sink.

"I think I'll stay here and rest," Ilse said.

Karola nodded, saying something about rest being important and that she would bring food back for her, then left. As soon as Ilse was alone, she took a large, shuddering breath, doubling over.

She'd known she'd be in trouble if she were caught lying to the Reich. She figured she'd go to prison, as the Nuremberg Laws dictated. It hadn't occurred to her that she could hang. But if members of the SS were punished for lying about adoption, surely her punishment for lying about her Jewish Lebensborn baby would be at least as severe.

She'd committed a terrible crime, allowed her blood to mix. Now that she knew her likely punishment, she could practically feel the scratch of the rope around her neck. She tugged at the collar of her shirt, gasping for breath.

But she would only hang if she was caught. After Hannelore, she must return to not being friendly with anyone. And then there was the matter of the baby, who would be born soon, which could mean discovery for them both.

She needed a plan for escape. At the first sign of suspicion, she'd leave, under the cover of night. The gate would be locked, but the wall was scalable, perhaps even with a newborn swaddled tight against her.

She should escape now.

But to leave meant a lifetime of hiding—her against the Reich—and she would lose. She could only leave if she was certain she'd already lost.

She had to relieve herself—she always had to relieve herself these days. But once she'd sat on the toilet and emptied her bladder, she felt she couldn't get up, paralyzed by fear. So she kept sitting there, her head in her hands.

She couldn't believe she'd wanted to stay at the home and work. Now it seemed anywhere at all was better. In the cheapest room in the cheapest boardinghouse in the worst part of any town, she and her baby would be vulnerable, yes, but still safer than they would be at Heim Harz. As soon as she could leave, she would.

<hr />

Ilse wasn't going to sleep tonight.

Over the course of the day, the ache in her pelvis had turned into cramps, dull and far apart enough for her to ignore them. They'd increased in intensity and frequency, now racking her body every few minutes. It was too soon. The due date wasn't for three weeks.

She wouldn't go to the hospital ward. Not yet. She could enter it and never come out. Her body could be torn apart from the inside.

There, she would find out what the baby looked like.

The months of waiting no longer seemed like the torture she'd thought. This was torture, no longer being able to put it off. Just one more day, she begged, but her body had decided.

In a few hours, she could be dead. Her baby could be dead or taken away. Her neck could be in a noose. Too many horrible possibilities.

For a while she could manage the pain, biting the eiderdown to keep quiet and not disturb Karola. With one rush of pain, she sat up in bed, sweating, twisting the blankets as she pushed them off her. With the next, an involuntary guttural sound escaped from her mouth. She rolled to her other side, facing the window, as if Karola wouldn't be able to hear if she pointed her screams in the other direction. Soon the other girl's wide eyes peered over her, the rag curlers in her hair making her look frightening in the dark.

"It's time," Karola squeaked, and disappeared out the door, pale nightgown fluttering in her wake. An eternity passed. Through a haze of pain, Ilse felt rough, inexperienced hands grab her arms. Once they'd guided her down to the second floor, they manhandled her onto a gurney and wheeled her to a procedure room. The Schwestern scurried around the room, ominous-looking metal tools and bowls clattering in their shaking hands.

"Is anyone else coming?" Ilse panted. Her nightgown was soaked in sweat and clung to her body. She wanted to take it off and lie there, naked and unashamed.

"The doctor will be here any moment." The Schwester's voice trembled.

Ilse had heard that the doctor at another home was only a

dentist; no other doctor in the area would associate with Lebensborn. She wondered if Dr. Bartz was a dentist, too, and knew nothing about childbirth. He'd be unable to see her through.

No wonder pregnant women weren't allowed to mix with women who'd already delivered. They knew Lebensborn was all a fraud.

Only their racial examinations were thorough. Dr. Bartz could be the one to find her out.

No dark hair, she bargained. No curls. Anything but that. Anything else could be explained away.

Another contraction seized her. She ground her head into the pillow and all thoughts left her.

Outside, it was a damp, cold night. The moon was nowhere to be seen. No stars peeked through the clouds. Ilse was yet another woman in the house on the hill, screaming, with no anesthetic, only a photo of the dear leader to gaze upon as a pain reliever. She, however, squeezed her eyes shut.

CHAPTER NINE

Ilse knew she would follow her mother into the dark. A part of her had always believed that would happen.

When she was five and her mother disappeared into her bedroom, clutching her swollen belly and almost too pained to walk, Ilse hid under the kitchen table, gripping a chair leg. The screams went on and on, they would never end. Sometimes they mingled with the midwife's quieter commands. Some ladies, her mother's friends, came. Her father paced outside the door. The look on his face terrified her most of all.

Then it got quieter.

Two men came and her father pressed his callused hands against her eyes while they carried something out. It sounded large; the men's voices strained as they maneuvered out the door and onto the landing. Her father left with the men. The ladies moved around, slowly and quietly now. One of them ducked her head under the table to see Ilse. The woman told her to remain calm. Ilse was calm; mostly she was confused.

After some time, when no one was looking at her, she slipped out. She wanted to see her mother. But when she peered inside her parents' bedroom, her mother was gone.

Instead, she found an empty room so clean it shined, a bed made with clean sheets, and a fresh quilt tucked in on the sides, different from the way her mother made it. The air smelled of the tang of earth and metal, so sharp she could taste it. The whole room felt wrong.

In its cage by the window, her mother's little yellow bird fluttered its wings, trying to escape. Its frantic chirps broke the pressing silence. Ilse did not understand then, did not understand for a while, that her mother wasn't coming back.

Ilse labored through the day, and the following night. There could not be this much pain without death. But her body resisted this certainty; it knew other things. It contracted, it pushed, it screamed, too, like her mother's had. The same metallic, earthen smell filled the air. Something was wrong.

The wheezy monotone of Dr. Bartz's voice would have driven Ilse insane if she weren't already. Eventually he told her there was a shoulder dystocia. The baby was stuck.

The doctor cut her.

He had her pull her legs toward her stomach, and he pressed on her pelvis, reached inside, and rotated the baby's shoulder.

He told her to roll onto her hands and knees. He reached inside again and pulled an arm.

The baby slid from her body in a river of fluids. She rolled over and collapsed onto the bed, drenched in matter that had come out of her own body. But no cry pierced the air. Just silence, as there had been when her mother died.

The baby still wasn't crying. Why wasn't it crying?

Ilse cried instead.

Then he did cry. A baby boy, they said.

She leaned forward on the bed, rose to her knees. The pain

of her body and the fear of her mind converged in an overwhelming desire to see him. Her body felt like it had been split
in two. Blood poured down her legs.

What did he look like? What color was his hair? Not dark,
not curly. Please.

Over the shoulders and heads of the staff, she saw that he
was covered in viscera, hairless, and bright pink, a button for a
nose. Nothing to indicate his Jewish blood.

She collapsed onto the bed, not caring that she landed in a
pool of her sticky, cooling blood. The last energy she had left
her. The baby wailed, a sound as primal as the pain that she
was, for the moment, no longer aware of. She asked for him, but
the doctor ignored her.

His bulky, white-clad form hid his examination from view.
Was he measuring the baby now? No hair wasn't enough. The
caliper could still betray her. She couldn't breathe. Surely a
body couldn't take this much fear.

She caught a glimpse of Dr. Bartz's face. He looked bored,
murmuring casually to a Schwester. Nothing out of the ordinary
in the examination, then. He handed the baby to the Schwester.
Ilse's body shuddered in relief.

"Can I hold him?" she asked again.

The Schwester walked out of the room without a response.
Dr. Bartz told her that she'd labored for nearly thirty-six hours.
She sank into the pillows. She didn't need him to tell her how
long the labor had been. He continued, telling her the baby was
big and strong, despite coming early. That meant she'd done
well in creating a perfect Lebensborn child. Now she must rest,
and she will see the baby tomorrow to begin nursing.

"But I want to see him now." The reedy insistence of her
voice was foreign to her ears.

Tomorrow, the doctor insisted, and left. The remaining
Oberschwester, a trained nurse, stitched Ilse up, cleaned her,

changed her bedding, told her to sleep. "You've earned it," she said.

It didn't matter that she begged; no one would let her see her baby.

Ilse did not see him again for twenty-four hours. All of her ached but especially her arms, empty of her baby. She stared at the ceiling and decided to call him Otto. Ottjen, his name would be in Low German. Like *Ottjen Alldag*, the Bremen children's book, one of the only books written in Low German. Everyone in Bremen knew the book. Everyone smiled when they thought of it.

She began to doubt the features she'd seen. Perhaps she'd seen what she wanted to see: a perfect Aryan babe. He must have had Jewish features after all. They'd taken him far away, done something terrible with him.

Her hands developed a tremor. She couldn't stop herself from asking the Schwestern who came in and out how Otto was doing. Their aloof replies did nothing to calm the fear roiling in her mind. Though she was more exhausted than she'd ever been in her life, all she wanted was to throw the covers back, run to the crèche to find Otto, and take him away.

But that would seal their fates. Their only chance was for her to behave as if nothing was wrong.

"Are you ready to see him?" asked Oberschwester Trina, who was in her thirties with strawberry blond hair.

Ilse sat up—or tried to—and croaked, "Yes." She wanted to see him so badly it hurt.

When she finally held the baby in her arms, a small bundle swaddled in white, he was hers. She couldn't remember why she'd thought she couldn't keep him. One day without him had been too much. A lifetime was impossible. She must stay close to him and protect him.

"You have twenty minutes," Trina told her.

There were no Jewish features after all. At least, not yet. His looks still had the vagueness of a newborn; his face had not yet become what it would be. She longed to see it.

Would he look like Felix or like her? Or like her father, or relatives of Felix whom she'd never met?

How could she love something that was wrong, should never have existed?

How could it be wrong to love him?

Otto's pink, wrinkled eyelids squeezed shut against the world and she held him tighter, his shield. He yawned. A large tear splashed onto the baby's blanket. She'd never cried so much.

For most of the twenty minutes, she learned how to nurse with Oberschwester Trina. He latched easily—of course he did, because he was perfect. He kneaded her breast. To her alarm, she caught a glimpse of thick fluid coming out of her, golden like an egg yolk, but Trina told her this was normal for the first few days, and what the baby needed. Ilse felt immensely grateful to Trina, with her knowledge and her calm voice. The Oberschwester rarely smiled, but there was a warmth to her.

Ilse kissed the baby's downy head and told him she loved him a thousand times. Trina tried to stop her. "It's not good for the baby."

Ilse didn't care. She didn't believe her. Perhaps Trina didn't know everything after all.

When the twenty minutes were nearly over, Frau Ingrid came and Trina left the room, as if by unspoken agreement. The administrator approached the foot of the bed and observed the mother and child with disinterest.

"Are you ready to settle the paperwork?"

"What paperwork?"

"To register the birth and confirm the adoption."

She couldn't force the words out of her throat, raw and scratching. She took a breath.

"I've changed my mind about giving him up. I'm going to keep him."

Frau Ingrid blinked. Ilse half-expected her tongue to flick out of her mouth and catch a fly.

"For any mother to take her child home, she must secure permission in advance from the Reich Central Office. This is typically done in advance." She paused, her wide lips working.

"I suppose we could begin the process now. Do keep in mind that to be allowed to keep the child, you must prove your financial ability to provide proper care and education."

Ilse clutched Otto. Such a thing was as good as impossible.

"If, however, you leave him with us, we can ensure he will be raised in a good home, and grow up to be an elite member of the SS."

She wanted to take Otto far away. But even if someone in a distant town consented to hire a mother with no husband, she would have to leave Otto to find that work, and the pittance she could earn wouldn't be enough to satisfy Lebensborn.

To stay with Otto, she would have to remain under the watchful Aryan eyes of Heim Harz.

Jane Eyre, when stuck in a dull and narrow life, had desired liberty, but settled for a new form of servitude. So, too, would Ilse.

She swallowed and opened her dry lips. Her eyes met Frau Ingrid's wide-set, blank ones. One more shuddering breath, and then she said, "May I stay here and work while I'm waiting for permission? I can do any job you want. Cook, clean, care for the children . . ." She wished the last one hadn't sounded so hopeful.

Frau Ingrid paused. Ilse knew there was an open position for a Schwester; she'd seen the empty bed next to Hannelore's. Ilse had the feeling that Frau Ingrid enjoyed her power, such as it was. This home was her tiny kingdom.

She sucked on her teeth, making a show of considering. "Fine. I will allow you to stay on as a Schwester. We already have a cook so you can't have that position, as much as I liked your bread pudding. You'll be a nurse's aide, providing whatever assistance is needed. It's not glamorous work, but you and the infant will continue to receive the excellent care of Lebensborn.

"A monthly fee of forty-five Reichsmarks is charged for every month your child stays at the home. Are you prepared for this fee to come out of your pay? Keep in mind, a Schwester's salary is sixty per month."

Fifteen marks per month, to save up for a life.

"And if the child stays past the sixth month," Frau Ingrid continued, "the fee is raised to sixty marks per month."

Ilse gaped. The administrator's eyes narrowed.

"Don't be ungrateful. If you do well, you will be trained as a nurse and your time at Lebensborn will count as an internship that will qualify you to work in hospitals in the future. Not everyone who passes through here is made this offer. You've done the good work of an Aryan mother; this is your reward."

"Of course. Thank you."

Frau Ingrid wrote on her clipboard. Ilse wasn't sure if she should celebrate or be frightened. She'd gotten what she'd asked for, she could stay with Otto. But what might it cost?

"And Ilse," the administrator said, "there have been rumors about you, and your . . . dedication to our cause. Don't let me find out the rumors about you are true. I'd hate to regret my decision."

Ilse swallowed. "You won't."

Had Hannelore talked? Ilse's throat knotted; if her one

friendly acquaintance had betrayed her, then she was lost. But Hannelore wouldn't have.

On her way out, Frau Ingrid summoned Trina to return the baby to the crèche. When Trina wrenched the baby from her embrace, a dry, unearthly sob escaped from Ilse's mouth. She wanted to scream at Trina. She fantasized about beating the Oberschwester with her fists and taking Otto back.

But she let Trina take him away. The ache in her arms began anew.

Ilse woke to the squeeze of a hand. She pried her eyes open; her eyelids felt as if they were melded together.

Shiny, cascading waves of hair. A grin and laughing eyes. Hannelore. Ilse wanted to weep.

"I have been looking for you." Ilse's voice was hoarse. She cleared her throat.

"And I've been looking for you. I didn't know where you were until the birth certificate came across my desk. Good work. I went to the crèche to see Otto. He's a precious little lump."

"I know."

Hannelore chortled. "How are you feeling?"

"I just want to see him. All the time."

With sympathetic eyes and a squeeze of the hand, Hannelore commiserated. It wouldn't do to be heard complaining about Lebensborn's treatment of its mothers. Ilse realized that Hannelore was everything she wanted to be: smart enough to work the system in her favor, to get what she needed without losing too much in the process.

"Look, about what I said after the attack—"

"Don't worry. I heard nothing. I know nothing. And I made sure no one else does either."

Ilse heaved a shuddering sigh.

"You didn't think I would tell anyone, did you?" Hannelore sounded commanding, and possibly also hurt.

"No. But it's better to trust no one."

"I can't deny you there."

Hannelore completed a full inspection of Ilse's physical and mental states, nosing in her chart and interrogating her. Then, she said, "There's something I have to tell you."

Ilse's stomach knotted. What bad news now?

"I've met someone. A man," she clarified at Ilse's confused look.

"Here? In a maternity home? Or in the village?"

"Haven't you heard? The Schwestern and SS men have mixers sometimes. That's where I found him." She looked pleased with herself. "He has this presence. I've never seen someone so intimidating. And he's a pilot—we have that in common. He's flown combat missions for the Luftwaffe, and has his own plane, which he flies across the country on business."

"He's in the SS?"

Hannelore's chin tilted, acknowledging but not apologizing.

"Either we work for them or we sleep with them. It's all the same to me. Anyway, he took me on a trip this weekend and showed me an apartment. It's beautiful, converted from an eighteenth-century palace. There's an Italian Baroque-style hall decorated with gilded stucco figures. He wants me for himself and says he'll take care of everything. I'll have an allowance. And, when the moment is right, I will convince him to arrange flying lessons for me." She sighed, ecstatic. "Maybe there will be clouds so solid-looking I'll want to fly around them. Or maybe birds will include me in their formations."

She looked at Ilse. "Do you understand? The desire to fly is a constant hum inside me, and now that it's so close, it's grown into a roar. If people were elements, I'd be wind and air. I can only breathe in the sky."

Ilse nodded. She didn't understand, really, but she could see the truth of it etched in Hannelore's face.

"You never seemed like a Schwester anyway. I'm surprised you were here at all."

"It was my older siblings' idea." Hannelore smirked. Ilse got the impression she never did anything that was someone else's idea.

"I'm happy for you," Ilse said. "Will you be close by?"

Hannelore shook her head. "I'll miss you. It wasn't supposed to be hard to leave. I didn't think I'd find a friend here."

"Me neither." Ilse's eyes burned. "Could you do me a favor? If you can before you leave, visit Otto. Let him know he's loved."

"Of course."

Exhaustion and sadness made her feel heavy and slow. Sleep threatened to drag her down.

"One more thing," she said with effort. "I knitted a scarf for you, yellow with a fisherman's rib stitch. It's in my wardrobe. I thought you might wear it while flying."

Hannelore leaned over and kissed Ilse's forehead.

Ilse spent the next week in recovery. She slept for much of it; the doctor told her it was because of the blood she'd lost. Several times a day they brought Otto to her. As soon as he finished nursing, he was taken away. It nearly broke her every time.

When Ilse had been in the maternity ward for three days, Karola arrived with a slightly deflated stomach and wan, pasty cheeks. She was wheeled in next to Ilse.

"You made it," Ilse said. "How did it go?"

"Why don't they allow us Dammerschlaf?" she asked, her voice hoarse.

Though drug-induced twilight sleep had been the norm for childbirth for the last few decades, Lebensborn mothers weren't allowed it. They were supposed to experience childbirth in its purest form, as a nearly religious experience.

"Because they don't know how awful it is," Ilse said.

Karola had already fallen asleep. Ilse closed her eyes and imagined it was Hannelore next to her. Hannelore, whom she would never see again. Another friend lost.

Ilse and Karola remained side by side for two days. All mothers were encouraged to nurse—what was natural was best for the baby—but Karola, like many others, refused because she wanted to keep her figure. Ilse tried to explain that nursing would help her body recover faster, but Karola wouldn't hear it. Ilse was asked to feed Karola's baby, too, a strapping boy with a shock of yellow hair, and she did. It felt strange, almost wrongly intimate at first, for another baby to suckle at her breast, but soon the wrongness faded. When Karola had recovered from her uncomplicated delivery and left with her baby in her arms, Ilse imagined her returning to the warm home of her wealthy SS family and being praised for her service. Karola's life could not be more different than hers.

Alone in bed, Ilse often stared at a crack on the ceiling above her and imagined it lengthening across the whole room until the ceiling crashed down on all of them. She saw the house in ruins, overgrown with ivy, little dolls and chamber pots amid the rubble.

CHAPTER TEN

W hen she had sufficiently recovered, Ilse and her few possessions, including the forbidden book tucked in among her clothing, moved to the staff building. Two brown dresses, two white aprons, and two beige hair kerchiefs became her drab uniform.

Her new room, functional and comfortable as her previous one, offered a view of the snow-frosted castle and the medieval town.

She shared the room with Traude, who worked in the office. She was tidy, with a torso shaped like a box and no eyebrows to speak of—in fact, she rarely spoke at all.

Ilse hoped to win her over so she would help Ilse train to be a secretary. That was a career; she could make a good living for herself and Otto. She'd spent so many stolen hours at the typewriter in Herr Anschütz's office, she was halfway trained already. Besides, she wanted to be privy to the inner workings of the office, to make sure she and Otto were still safe. She tried to be friendly when Traude was getting ready for bed her first night.

"How long have you worked here?" Ilse asked from her bed,

where she was already tucked in.

"A long time."

"Oh?"

"Long enough to know you're a Lebensborn mother, and your child a bastard."

"Well, yes," said Ilse, carefully. "That is true of most of us."

"Not me. I'll marry before I have a child. As it should be." Traude pulled off her brown dress and turned away from Ilse, revealing an unsightly mole with two dark hairs growing on the fleshy expanse of her back. Ilse looked away.

"It must be difficult working here if you feel so strongly about us."

"It doesn't matter what I want. I'm a servant of the Reich."

"Perhaps you'd prefer to work for the Reich elsewhere. You work hard; you deserve to be somewhere you're happy." If Traude left, there would be an opening in the office.

Traude scoffed and turned off her lamp. Into the dark, she said, "I can bear anything in life as long as it is for the greater good of Germany. Good night."

Before breakfast the following morning, Ilse trudged across the sodden grounds to the crèche to feed Otto. She wandered through the empty halls, blue in the predawn twilight, following the sound of crying babies. But at the door, a Schwester—Ursula, Ilse thought her name was—barred her entry.

"Visiting hours aren't for another twenty minutes," Ursula said, blinking slowly. The ruddiness of her cheeks and her thick shoulders gave her away as a farmer's daughter.

"He's my child. I'll see him now."

Ursula shook her head. "Those are the rules."

"Please? Let me in, just this once."

"It's not possible."

The finality in her voice told Ilse it was useless to argue and dangerous to press.

"I'll wait then."

Ursula's mouth gaped a little, then she closed the door, and the fussing of the babies grew quieter. From the room at the far end of the hallway, toddlers' shrieks of delight and despair echoed.

Ilse tucked herself into an alcove near the crèche and tried to quiet her racing heart, partly from anger at being denied access to her own child, and partly from excitement about seeing him for the first time without the Oberschwester's supervision. And she was desperate to nurse; at the sound of crying, her breasts had begun to leak. Two wet spots were soaking through her brown dress.

As the church bells chimed eight, Ursula opened the door and stood aside so Ilse could enter. She didn't bother to thank the Schwester before rushing to the cribs, peering into each one. There were three rows of them, many empty, but four or five contained squirming infants. She hoped she would recognize her baby—what did it mean if she didn't? But there he was, the pinkest and most wrinkled of them all, her Otto. She scooped him up with care—every part of him was so breakable. His little mouth puckered, and the pressure built in her breasts.

By the window, Ilse spotted an enormous rocking chair cushioned with green velvet and she sat in it. She put Otto to her breast and he began to nurse, bringing her instant, tingling relief. His head resting against her arm felt small and hard and soft and hollow and, more than any of those things, comforting. He was here, he was safe.

The window held a view of the castle, just like the one in her own room. She imagined Otto looking out the window while she looked out hers, and they would look at the castle together, even when they were apart.

She traced his apple-round cheek and something fierce and wild rose up in her, a force bigger than herself. She would tear the world apart for him. She would work hard, get promoted, save money. Stay out of trouble.

What she needed was to find a life for him in the real world, to bring him up safe and healthy. To teach him everything he needed to know about life and how to live in it, though she wasn't sure she knew herself. She had no idea how to get him out of Lebensborn, but she would channel her feral energy into finding a way.

Ilse began her work as a Schwester, which entailed, as far as she could tell, being given the work the Oberschwestern didn't want to do. She ran around the home all day, an activity made difficult with her ongoing pulsing, aching soreness, though it was just as well; she would rather not sit on that soreness. Her breasts leaked into the gauze now lining her brassiere while the extra flesh she hadn't yet lost jiggled and chafed inside her uniform.

Her training took no time at all; the job required no mastery. She fetched things alternately for the Oberschwestern and for the new mothers. There were rooms to be tidied, instruments to clean, beds to make, and medicines to organize. She was familiar with this kind of work, but now she had something very important she'd rather be doing: spending time with Otto, keeping him safe. She was missing every new hair on his head, every yawn, and somehow worst of all, every tear. Instead, Schwestern like Ursula who seemed only slightly interested in their work were caring for him.

Ilse was only allowed to see Otto for a few short increments every day. The rest of the time he was fed from a bottle, lest she spend too much time coddling him. The windows of the crèche were often thrown open despite the cold, to let in the brisk mountain air, which Lebensborn had determined was essential for the health and strength of the children.

When she nursed Otto, she studied his face, as all mothers study their children, but also to discern whether his hair was growing in curly, his eyes turning dark, or his nose changing shape. She whispered, into the tiny ear that she inexplicably wanted to bite, to chew, to devour, that she would get him out of there and then she would hold him all day.

Ilse now became privy to the half of Lebensborn that had been hidden from her when she was pregnant. Most mothers left within a month of giving birth, about half of them taking their babies with them. Married women often left right away, as soon as the day after the birth, disgruntled by what they considered to be poor treatment. Others seemed to be removed sooner than they wanted—a reminder to the others to be on their best behavior. Then there were mothers who stayed on for months, because they worked as Schwestern, or simply because they were favored by the unseen powers of Lebensborn.

As for the children, those who remained for adoption became residents of the home. Some of them had been there for two years. If there was such a demand for children of pure blood, Ilse was surprised they weren't being snatched up. She never saw a prospective family visit, though sometimes children were transferred to other homes, and she supposed that's where adoptions occurred. She was gladder than ever that she'd decided to keep Otto.

At mealtimes, Ilse had first tried sitting with Traude, but the secretary had made a point of scarfing down her stew and leaving only a minute after Ilse sat down. She was still chewing her last bit of bread as she walked away.

Eventually Ilse found a table, close to the kitchen and the

clattering of pots and pans, with another Schwester who didn't seem to quite fit in. Ursula, who worked in the crèche, had a slowness about her, her movements and words, that gave her a cowlike appearance. But her sweet smile rarely left her face. Her stomach protruded against the folds of her brown dress; in a few months she would be relieved of her duties and move in with the mothers-to-be in the main building.

"Aren't you looking forward to the mixers?" Ursula asked Ilse one day, cheeks rosy.

"Mixers?"

"Yes. Sometimes SS men staying in a hotel in the village come to the home. We dance, we drink, we flirt . . ." Her flush brightened her whole face now.

When Hannelore had told her she was leaving, she'd mentioned mixers—the opportunity for Schwestern to prove their devotion to the Reich by making babies with SS men. That must be where the bulge in Ursula's uniform had come from.

"I don't think I'll go," Ilse said. "I'm so tired by the end of the day, I couldn't possibly have any energy left for dancing."

"But you must." Ursula looked up, nonplussed, from the meat she'd been sawing at.

"I'm still recovering from my baby's birth." Ilse didn't want anyone going near that area, still red, swollen, and aching, for a long time. But mostly she was disturbed by the idea of a casual encounter with a strange man, and having another baby to either raise on her own or give up.

"As soon as you can, you should go," Ursula said. "You'll have the best time, living here and enjoying the company. Maybe even the time of your life."

A sudden anger flared in Ilse. Anger that women were nothing but breeders. That the girls here seemed so pleased with themselves for getting pregnant when really it was all they could do. She put down her spoon and stared, unseeing, at her plate.

❧

Solitude was a rare commodity at Heim Harz. Between her work and worrying about Otto, she lacked the time and will to take dreary, wintery walks. But if she couldn't be with her baby, she must at least find quiet.

Her shift had ended and visiting hours at the crèche were over, so her feet led her away from the noise of the main building, across the grounds, and into a back room behind the kitchen. Large bags of pearl barley, rye, and split peas slumbered against the walls, and the air was stale with disuse. She sank onto a sack of barley.

Yesterday, a girl had a stillbirth, and as a result, she'd been required to leave Lebensborn in the morning. Ilse had helped the girl dress. She could barely walk. Ilse was furious that she'd been forced to leave while still recovering, still grieving. The knowledge that it could have been Ilse in her place made shivers run up her spine.

The room was silent. But instead of finding peace in it, all she could hear were the echoes of the girl's plaintive voice, asking to stay just one more day. Ilse had tried to reassure her, telling her again and again that it would be better if the girl went home to recover there.

Her eyes closed. She'd stayed up so late reading *Jane Eyre* the night before that her eyes felt like sandpaper and her brain throbbed against her skull. The novel pricked at her mind, opening the door to thoughts she didn't know she could have. As she made new connections, she saw everything as interrelated, and it was more wonderful than any national community because it was made up of more than Germans; it included everything. In her sluggish yet awakening imagination, everything, living or not, had more nuance and complexity than she'd ever known. It was dizzying, the contrast between this new world and the straightforward one her father and the Reich had carefully crafted for her.

These thoughts frightened her. She shrank from them as if from a leather belt. If the foundation of her existence was swept out from under her, she might fall into some unknown, dark place. But the thoughts always found her again, and as time went on, the belt, and her father, were drifting to the background of her mind.

When she finally opened her eyes, her gaze fell on something she'd overlooked before. It looked like a cupboard door, painted the same eggshell color as the walls, and its handle had been removed, making it nearly flush with the wall. She went to it and wedged her fingernails into the crack between the door and the wall and swung it open. Inside, it looked like any other large cupboard, but with a pulley system inside it. A dumbwaiter—there had been one in the Anschütz manor, though this one was much bigger. Big enough to fit a person.

She closed the door, making sure the seams blended back in with the wall. Directly above the kitchen were the administrative offices. It could be useful someday.

On her way out of the kitchen, she heard Frau Ingrid's voice, devoid of the simpering, overly polite tone she reserved for new arrivals and those she wished to impress.

Ilse's heart stopped. She stepped back and hid behind the door, not daring to breathe. Though she hadn't done anything wrong, technically, she felt guilty, and it could show.

"The files are backing up. There are so many letters coming in from homes all over the country, and from the Central Office. It's impossible to read and respond to and file them all, even with Traude's help."

Ilse's breath caught. This was her chance to make a better life for Otto. She waited for Frau Ingrid and the person she was ranting at to pass, then left her hiding spot. Safely in the hallway, she could have come from anywhere. She waited until Frau Ingrid parted ways with Trina, then caught up with the administrator.

"Excuse me," Ilse said. Frau Ingrid's back stiffened, or maybe Ilse imagined it. The administrator turned, somehow looking down at Ilse despite their being the same height. "I couldn't help but overhear a moment ago that you might need clerical help. I'd like to offer myself for the job. You'll never find a harder worker."

Frau Ingrid glanced around. "Where did you pop out from?"

"I was just walking back to my quarters after my shift." She hid her hands behind her back to hide the faint tremor.

Frau Ingrid looked Ilse up and down. She felt very aware of the remaining flab in her belly, how slovenly she must look in her brown dress. "Do you have administrative experience? Can you type?"

"My previous employer taught me." That was close enough to the truth. "He would have made me his secretary if the baby hadn't come along."

Frau Ingrid raised her eyebrows. "You didn't go to school for it?"

"I'm more than up for the challenge. What I don't know I can learn quickly." The administrator continued looking skeptical. Ilse drew in a breath. "And if my work isn't satisfactory, I can go back to being a nurse's aid. Nothing will be lost."

"I'll think about it," said Frau Ingrid. "Though it's not clear to me if you have the devotion to the cause that is required for a more advanced role."

The "thank you" died on Ilse's lips. Her heart pounded.

"I'm devoted. I'll prove it to you." Though she couldn't think how, and her interest in being a good daughter of the Reich was dwindling.

"Will you?" Frau Ingrid's frog eyes widened at Ilse. "Have you attended a mixer?"

Her heart dropped to her stomach. She'd barely begun to bleed again. If she hadn't witnessed it so many times in Gröpelingen, she'd have thought it wasn't possible for a woman to get pregnant again this soon.

"I will." Her voice felt raw as she scraped the words out. "As soon as I can. It was a difficult birth."

"Well, perhaps once you've recovered, you'll be able to demonstrate your devotion. Then we will see."

The door closed. Ilse stared at the grain of wood, wondering if a raise was worth giving her body to strange, frightening men. Her stomach tossed and burned. The answer to that question was easy: No.

But was it worth it to remove herself from suspicion and protect Otto?

⚜

The parlor of the Schwestern building, safely segregated from the gestating mothers, was aglow with dimly lit chandeliers. A string quartet played in the corner. The air was heavy with forced romance, and something else, too—a giddiness, or nervousness, in the twinkly high-pitched laughter of the Schwestern. The men postured like peacocks in their black uniforms, medals gleaming. They were hard at work, wooing girls just like Ilse, in looks at least. She got herself a beer and downed it far too quickly.

If proving her loyalty to the Reich was necessary, then she would make an appearance, though she had no intention of breeding with anyone if she could help it. The thought made her want to crawl deeper inside her shell—in fear or disgust, she didn't know. Perhaps both.

A tall, cocky-looking young man with beady eyes approached her. He offered her another drink, although she was still standing there, in front of the free bar. She said no, thank you, shooing him away. Polite but unfriendly. All she had to do was be seen there. Perhaps she could appear to go back to her bedroom with someone. Another beer in hand, she walked in laps around the room, milling. She tried to look like she was going somewhere, doing something, and did not need to be kept company. She sat at the chair by the window and stared into the black.

Then, out of the darkness, a face appeared. It hovered bodiless in the air. She started and whipped around—she'd seen the reflection of an SS man, whose body, clothed in black, did not catch the light. He had a lean, strong build and was supporting himself on the back of a chair next to hers, too drunk to stand. She'd seen him earlier, at the bar. It appeared he'd made quite a dent in the supplies.

"Now, we kiss?" He leaned toward her, his eyelids drooping, his lips puckered. Ilse cringed into her chair. That was his line? His introduction? Did he actually think it would work, or was he simply too drunk to use language properly?

"I don't think so."

With great effort, he opened his eyes, confused.

"Yes." He nodded. "You and I."

In the corner of her eye, she saw Frau Ingrid surveying the room. Sensing Ilse's gaze, she turned and their eyes met. Ilse looked back at the man.

"What's your name?"

"Max." His freshly shaven upper lip gleamed with sweat.

She set her jaw. This was for Otto. For their future.

"Fine. Let's go."

She stood up and led the way out of the room, making sure Frau Ingrid saw her. Max caught up to her and linked their arms together. He smelled of kaloderma soap and stale beer. She resisted the urge to pull away.

Then Frau Ingrid stood in front of them.

"This way." She summoned them with a gesture and marched out the door. Ilse and Max followed as she led them upstairs. Max was so drunk he could barely manage them; she dragged him as best she could given his bulk. She hoped the administrator wouldn't notice his condition and figure out what Ilse was up to. Frau Ingrid stopped at a door that Ilse had thought led to a closet and opened it for them. As they entered, the administrator gave her a nod, then closed the door.

Inside, a dim light flickered overhead. There was a narrow bed and nothing else—not much else would have fit in the tiny space. At least Traude wouldn't walk in on them here. She hadn't been sure what to do about that. Now, however, she was alone in a bedroom with an SS man, trained for brutality. She gave him a light shove in the direction of the bed and he flopped across, arms and legs spread wide.

She stood over him for a full minute until she confirmed her hope: He was far, far too drunk to do anything but sleep. A sigh of relief escaped her, shoulders sagging. She pulled the throw blanket from the foot of the bed out from under him.

"You're so beautiful," he mumbled. "Thank you."

"Sure," she said, not caring what he was thanking her for. She curled up on the ground with her back pressed to the wall, as far away from the bed as she could get. The floor was hard, and the boisterous music from the parlor below made it vibrate. Cool air leaked in from the window above her. She would wait an hour or so—long enough to satisfy Frau Ingrid—then escape to her room. She didn't want to be there when Max sobered up.

He was so much larger and stronger than her; he would be terrifying sober, and she would have to do whatever he wanted.

"Turn off the light," Max grumbled into the bed.

"I'd like it on." She felt safer that way, even though she knew it would make no difference.

He groaned. All she could see was the side of the bed and the top of his slick blond head, but she heard the shuffle of fabric and a snap, then a cock.

Something was about to happen. She didn't know what. She stilled and tensed, every sense alert. A black barrel appeared.

A bang—loud, violent, terrible.

A gunshot.

Ilse had covered her head with her hands before she understood what had happened. Something was raining down. She opened an eye and saw broken glass, porcelain, and plaster scattered across the floor. In the ceiling was a crumbling hole where the light fixture had been.

In the darkness, covered in powdery residue, Max began to snore.

CHAPTER ELEVEN

I n the recovery room of the hospital ward, Ilse stood at an empty bed, folding a freshly washed mountain of towels. It had been two days since the night with Max. She hoped she'd bought herself time—a month at least—before she'd have to face the mixers again.

She'd never been that close to a fired gun, never known the ringing it would cause in her ears, or the terror that would live in her body, every muscle tense. Sometimes she jumped at a slammed door.

She'd spent the last few restless nights reading, a welcome escape. She hadn't dared to bring out *Jane Eyre* since moving in with Traude, who would love a reason to have her removed from Lebensborn. But Traude was visiting her family in the Rhineland, and last night, Ilse had finally finished the book. She'd reread the last pages over and over. It had been hard to breathe, as if the words were oxygen.

Her mind still inhabited the estate on the lonely moors of the English countryside. Jane said she was no bird and no net ensnared her—what would Jane do if she were ensnared? Ilse rolled this idea around in her mind, because if she could figure out the answer, she was sure it would be the key to understanding her own place in the world.

She continued to come up empty. National Socialism only made sense when you didn't think.

She had been almost thirteen when Hitler took power. She'd never seen such commotion. Bremen's inhabitants scrambled as if they were passengers on a train that had arrived at their stop without warning. They couldn't hang up their homemade swastika flags fast enough. On some, the swastika had been sewn on backwards.

Ilse had already been in Jungmädelbund, the BDM for girls aged ten to fourteen, and the group grew large, splintering into two, three new groups. Ilse excelled in all the physical activities: swimming, gymnastics, hours and hours of marching. Because she did so well, she and a few other girls, and some boys from Hitler Youth, got to go to Nuremberg in 1935 to see the Führer. Planes thundered overhead, tanks roared, and tens of thousands of people cheered. Hitler traveled right past Ilse's group in his Mercedes limousine, the biggest, longest car she'd ever seen.

Hitler spoke, working himself and the crowd into a frenzy. The more agitated he became, the less Ilse understood him. But the jostling crowd created a pulse that made her feel like part of one enormous organism, and there had never been such a display of hope, of enthusiasm, of pride in the subjugated Germany Ilse knew, and she was swept up, jumping and cheering with everyone around her.

The Führer announced that Europe and America had humiliated Germans by calling in debts the Fatherland could never repay. And humiliated they were: Inflation was so crippling that sometimes a thief coming upon a wheelbarrow filled with trillions of marks would overturn it, emptying out the cash, and run off with the wheelbarrow, which had actual worth. Children starved and their fathers took their own lives. But now things had changed. This was what it felt like to be a victor after being downtrodden. This was the national community. Ilse did not feel alone. She felt—though she hardly dared think it—joy.

After the speech, Hitler came to meet high-achieving Hitler Youth from across the country. Some got to shake hands with him and had their pictures taken by Hitler's photographer. Those who got to speak to the Führer, to touch him, were ecstatic. Some of them wept. The rest of them, including Ilse, were jealous.

She stored the memory of that day in her mind. She'd cherished it as the highlight of her short life.

Until recently.

Max's violence, his casual abuse of his power, had woken her up harshly to the realities of her world. *Jane Eyre*, too, was waking her up, but gently. Jane tapped her on the shoulder, asking her to think, to notice what she felt. She'd spent so long ignoring herself.

The faint sound of babies wailing trickled in from the examination room and echoed against the polished surfaces of the hospital ward. Gisela had gone into labor the night before and delivered her twins. Deposited in a bed close to Ilse, she stared, blank and drawn. Her usual glint had faded. Ilse knew she was giving up her babies, and felt a twinge of pity. Was giving up two children twice as hard? The place where she'd been cut during the birth pulsed faintly. She moved closer, bringing her towels with her.

"How are you feeling?" Ilse asked.

"They're girls." Her voice was flat.

"I heard."

"As soon as they were out, the doctor told me not to worry—I'll have more children, and at least some of them will be boys." It was clear that this had not made her feel better.

"I'm sorry."

"Don't be. I knew this was coming. And now I'll go back to my life as if nothing happened at all." She lowered her voice: "You know, I hated it here, every moment."

Ilse gaped at her. Gisela reigned at Heim Harz—how could she not have enjoyed herself?

"It's true," Gisela continued, so quiet that Ilse had to concentrate on the girl's lips to understand her words. "I never wanted to come here, but what else was I supposed to do?"

"Why didn't you want to come here?" Ilse whispered.

Gisela looked at her meaningfully, but Ilse shook her head, not understanding.

Across the room, the radio cut out Wagner's triumphant music and began broadcasting the familiar, cool voice of propaganda minister Goebbels. Mechanically, Ilse turned her attention to it. Goebbels didn't come on the radio unless something significant had happened.

Goebbels announced that the parents of a seventeen-year-old Polish Jew had been expelled from Germany, back to Poland, along with many other Polish nationals. When the young man received this news, he shot and killed a German diplomat in Paris. Goebbels suggested that this assassination had been the collective plot of all the Jews in the world.

Last night in response to the diplomat's death, the people of Germany had burned down one thousand synagogues. They had shattered the glass windows of seven thousand Jewish businesses and destroyed everything inside. Ninety-one Jews were killed, and 30,000 Jewish men were deported to KZs.

And it was all the Jews' fault for provoking the Volk. They were parasites, poison mushrooms, aliens.

Ilse's hands went still. All those innocent people dead, wounded, punished, for one assassinated German. And Otto could be one of them someday.

There had been laws segregating Jews, excluding them from public and economic life. There had been occasional violence by drunken Brownshirts. But nothing like this. Until now, Ilse had thought that most Germans wanted Jews out of the country, somewhere far away—but not dead or imprisoned. Had one boy's actions changed that overnight? Had all of Germany become like Max?

Goebbels completed his speech: "We shed not a tear for them. The synagogues stood in the way long enough."

The voice faded to static. Then a click, and a new voice came on, the announcer's.

"New laws have been put into place to account for the actions Jews have driven us to take. Jewish children may not attend German schools. Jews may not drive cars or be admitted to theaters, cinemas, or concert halls. Jews shall be held liable for the damages caused during this night, to the amount of one billion marks. More announcements to come."

"How hideous of them," Gisela said. Ilse whipped her head toward her. Hideous of whom? In the woman's wide, sad eyes, flecked with green among the blue, she saw the truth.

Gisela, who all this time had pretended to be the perfect Nazi, did not believe in the Reich. In the glow of her eyes, Ilse saw her hatred of Germany, of Lebensborn, of having to give her babies to the SS—but at the same time, she had no other options. What situation must she have faced at home that this was what she had to do? Poverty? Religious parents? No parents at all? Had an SS officer forced himself on her? They stared at each other. Ilse's mouth grew dry. What could be said in response to this wordless confession? Then Gisela shrugged and looked away.

That was the most honest conversation they would ever be able to have.

Ilse wanted to go to Gisela and put a hand on her shoulder,

but she knew Gisela would shrug her off. Instead, she wrapped her arms around her gut, the hollow that was there.

She longed for truth. To turn the radio dial to the real news, to the BBC or Swiss Radio International, and find out what was actually happening. But it was impossible. The People's Radio didn't have those stations.

She looked out the window. Wernigerode was as sleepy as ever, a medieval village existing outside of time, its orange-tiled roofs tucked into hills of green trees. If not for the radio, she would have had no idea that any of it, what they were calling Kristallnacht, The Night of Broken Glass, had happened. The horrors were invisible, almost as if they didn't touch her.

But they did. They were part of her, always.

Otto would grow up in this world, and she must protect him from it. An objectless fear filled her body, tingling and vibrating to her fingertips, her feet, her head, until it overflowed. She fled the hospital ward, not stopping until she reached the nursery and had buried her nose in Otto's squirming neck.

⁕

Ilse couldn't breathe.

She woke clawing at her throat, clutching at the neck of her nightgown. Her breath came—for it did come—in wheezing sounds she'd never heard herself make before.

In the bed next to her, Traude, returned from the Rhineland, snored peacefully. Ilse pressed her hand against her chest to feel it rising and falling, but found instead that she wanted to tear at herself, her clothes and skin, until she lay in pieces on the floor. This was disgust—for the life she lived, for who she was.

For who she had been, because she no longer believed.

She'd brought Otto into the world with doubt in her heart, inexcusable doubt. He was perfect, just like his father.

Follow the rules. That was the single lesson her father had taught her about life. Maybe he was wrong.

So quietly and easily she'd gone along. Everyone else had; it seemed natural. National Socialism was about freeing Germans from the debt and humiliation they had endured for so long. They were a strong people and deserved prosperity.

But at what cost?

The Reich had shown its true self to her, and she could no longer ignore it.

A sickening feeling rose from her gut, pulsing nausea through her.

She climbed out of bed and went to her wardrobe. Inside, her BDM uniform hung neatly. Why had she brought it with her when she'd fled home? She hadn't been able to imagine not having it; it was her key to the national community, where she belonged, where she was useful. She took the uniform out, thinking of burying it in the ground or burning it in a fire.

But she couldn't. She needed the uniform to pretend.

Many Germans pretended. They put out their red and black flags when ordered, they saluted Nazi officials, they donated to the Winter Relief Fund, because what other option was there?

Out in the world, among people who only went along because they had to, she could sometimes get away with saying "good morning" instead of "Heil Hitler." But inside Lebensborn, surrounded by the most enthusiastic, fanatical supporters of Hitler, revealing even the slightest doubt would have consequences.

Her situation had not changed. She had to continue working and living in the home, attending indoctrination classes, listening to the People's Radio. And spending more nights with men like Max.

Here, no one would suspect that she, or her son, wasn't a one-hundred-percent Nazi.

The thick material of the uniform scratched her fingers. She buried it underneath her knapsack at the bottom of the wardrobe.

⁂

A Schwester, still glowing from her recent birth, let out a pure, carefree laugh, bracing herself against the breakfast table. Ilse couldn't imagine feeling light enough to let a laugh ring out. That was the luxury of the unburdened.

The eerie similarity of all the girls struck her: they were tall and blond with blue eyes and straight or snubbed noses. Yet they seemed different to her as she spooned porridge into her mouth. There was almost an innocence to them. They walked with straight backs and easy gaits. Their eyes were clear of doubt and secrets. Ilse, meanwhile, was adrift.

National Socialism, she tried to tell herself, wasn't all bad. So many social services were offered. There was appreciation and respect for the German people, trodden upon for so long by the rest of the world, stripped of their resources and humiliated ever since the Treaty of Versailles. Shouldn't Germany raise itself back up?

Just like that, it was so easy to slip. She put down her spoon and stared into the half-empty bowl.

She had to remember what her body had woken her up to tell her the night before. For a moment, she dwelled on the suffocating sensation she'd felt. The weight of the Reich. The guilt of being a part of it. The danger to her son. There could be others in this room who were here out of necessity, who also didn't believe in the Reich, but had nowhere else to go. It would be nearly impossible to find them. Gisela's moment of honesty had been a risk to them both, and such a thing was unlikely to happen again—unless Ilse sought it out. And she couldn't take that risk.

Her porridge had gone cold and lumpy. A thick, bland smell rose from it. She could add more sugar and attempt to choke it down, but it seemed a waste. No longer pregnant, she wouldn't be forced to finish it.

The hair on the back of her neck tingled. She turned and saw Frau Ingrid's eyes on her. Her blank expression held an undercurrent of something foreboding, something that made Ilse's skin crawl. As if the administrator could read her mind.

Slowly, Ilse picked up her spoon and took a bite of porridge, fighting the urge to gag. When she looked up again, Frau Ingrid was still watching her.

CHAPTER TWELVE

Winter passed slow and mountain-cold. Snow blanketed the ground, the mountains, the whole village for months. Ilse rarely went outside anymore except to crisscross the grounds between the crèche, the main building, and the Schwestern's quarters, but from the windows she saw that snow had turned everything, even the trees, a blinding white. She didn't understand how the snow tucked itself under and in between branches; there was no green or brown in sight.

All was a blur to her except for Otto. He made sounds, nondescript coos. His eyes began to focus on toys, her hands, her face. She wondered if he would be smart like his father. Perhaps he would grow up to study mathematics as well and discover the equations for birds and stars and mountains.

She came to know every corner of him, soft, plump, with no features that would endanger him. The infants in the crèche and the toddlers playing on the grounds did not look like the elite Aryan race Lebensborn had promised; only some of the children were blond, and even fewer had blue eyes. They didn't seem healthy; many had persistent coughs and they all cried often and smiled rarely. Hannelore had been right about the Schwestern: their inexperience and lack of care was made clear in the growth the children. Ilse hated to think of what happened when she wasn't with Otto.

She'd discovered that by bribing Ursula, she could see Otto outside of visiting hours. If she paid enough, the Schwester even let her bathe him sometimes. Spending the money was painful, but she couldn't stop herself. It felt important to care for him, not just visit and play with him. She'd learned all about child-care in the BDM, but with him it was all new, and devastatingly important.

Occasionally other mothers visited, but most only stayed long enough to nurse, barely looking at their babies before hurrying off. Ilse couldn't understand it—how did they not feel the same uncontrollable pull toward their children that she felt toward hers? Had they some mastery over their emotions that she lacked? Had they swallowed what they'd been taught, that the babies they birthed were nothing more than future soldiers for the SS, and affection would do them no good? Or did they simply pretend not to care because it was what they were supposed to do?

As Ilse saved what was left of her meager salary, she imagined a little home in a faraway town. It would have a garden and she could grow her own vegetables and Otto would play among the plants and earth and sun. But that was very far off, judging by the ledger she kept in her mind.

One day the falling snow made Ilse think of ice-skating. Ursula had left when Ilse arrived, as if she were there to relieve her from her work, so there was nothing keeping her from sweeping Otto up and around the room in a dance that made his eyes widen and his arms flail gleefully. She even sang a jolly little tune, something she never thought she'd do.

All over Bremen, there were shallow lakes that froze quickly in winter. As soon as they did, everyone, children and adults alike, headed for one of these lakes with their wooden Dutch ice skates, curved up at the toe. Even Ilse had owned a pair.

When Mitzi was still her friend, they'd gone to the lakes together and skated in unison, with arms intertwined or in a gliding waltz. She and Mitzi had twirled around and around, Mitzi's round cheeks growing increasingly rosy. Her nose, too. And Ilse had laughed and laughed. So much laughter had been pulled out of her that she couldn't breathe, a victim to joy.

Now, at the memory of Mitzi, the twisting feeling in her stomach returned. She hoped Mitzi had left Germany long ago. It was the only way she could still be alright—Kristallnacht had made that clear.

Ilse knew Mitzi had gone to synagogue but was aware of little else about her religious practice, or Judaism at all. As far as she knew, Felix and his family weren't religious, but she hadn't really known him. Ilse regretted that Otto would never know his heritage, and she'd once gone along with the powers that made it so. She swallowed against the rock in her throat.

Ursula came back from her smoke break and Ilse returned to the rocking chair. She stroked Otto's wispy hair and watched his face take on a perplexed expression that made him look like an old man. His back arched against her arms, much stiffer than any baby's should be. She bounced him a few times to loosen him up. His back remained stiff but he broke out into a bright, gummy laugh.

⁂

March brought Otto's name-giving ceremony. Frau Ingrid had advised her of the date and what to wear, but apart from that, Ilse knew nothing of what to expect.

On the scheduled day, she followed a group of mothers and

Schwestern into the dayroom with Otto in her arms. He absorbed his new surroundings, eyes wide with curiosity. Ilse felt uncomfortable in the formal setting, wearing a starched, hand-me-down dress and Tyrolean hat, not to mention the men clad in black uniforms with skull insignias glimmering on their caps. Everyone adopted an air of solemnity upon entering the room, as one would a church, because, it became clear, this was a National Socialist baptism.

There was an altar draped with a swastika flag and a banner inscribed with the words "Germany Awake." The room was decorated with winter jasmine and crocuses. Along with the SS men, there were about ten infants held by their mothers or by Schwestern: these were the children who'd been born in the months since the last name-giving ceremony. Because Harz was one of the smaller homes, the ceremonies were infrequent.

The mothers and the Schwestern holding the babies took their seats in the row of chairs across from the altar. The SS men gathered around the altar like priests.

Danger, the room said to her. Every cell in her body yearned to run away. The ceremony, her and Otto's mere presence in a room with these men, felt wrong and dangerous.

The ceremony began. A middle-aged SS officer dressed like a priest took his place behind the altar. He informed the gathering that "National Socialism is an ideology that demands the whole person." Two other SS men read from *Mein Kampf*. The air in the room grew stuffy. Ilse wondered if it would be against the spirit of solemnity to crack a window. The "priest" gave a blessing in a voice that was either reverent or monotone:

> *We believe in the God of all things,*
> *And in the mission of our German blood,*
> *Which grows ever young from German soil.*
> *We believe in the race, carrier of the blood,*

And in the Führer chosen for us by God.

Blood and soil, the RuSHA motto. Then a pretense at religion, with Hitler as their God.

These men were terrifying. She couldn't imagine letting them into her bed. She certainly couldn't imagine having their babies. She'd stayed far away from the mixers since Max, but she would need to go again soon for a hope at getting a promotion—and out of this place. She held Otto closer and he squirmed.

One by one, each mother—or if she had already left, the Schwester assigned to the infant—were summoned to bring their children to the altar, where they were ushered into the SS. When Ilse was called upon, her heart beat in her throat. Revulsion and fear oscillated through her so quickly she trembled. Surely now these racial experts would identify what she had spent countless hours searching for and could not find: the Jewish blood that ran through Otto's veins. She rose and brought the baby to the altar.

As instructed, she passed him to the officer assigned to be Otto's "godfather." She recognized him as the tall man with deep-set eyes who'd commented on *Physica* all those months ago.

She had seen what was to come, and she dreaded it. The priest unswaddled the baby, revealing his soft pink skin. Otto arched his back as he often did but did not seem distressed. The priest attempted to uncross Otto's legs, which in the last couple of weeks had begun to cross. Ilse herself couldn't straighten them out without fearing she would hurt him. Though she hadn't found anything about it in the books, she was sure it was his tendons and ligaments growing slower than his bones. Perfectly natural. She started forward to stop the priest from tugging at his legs but was held back by an officer. The priest gave up and produced a dagger.

The godfather, introduced as Gruppenführer von Thiel, took the dagger and held the blade over Otto's belly. She noticed that the man hovered it, almost imperceptibly, over the baby so the blade didn't quite touch, whereas the other godfathers plopped it right on the babies' flesh, so soft, and the blade sharp enough to draw blood—perhaps that was what they wanted, these men devoted to blood and soil. Ilse felt grateful to this Gruppenführer.

The priest addressed the baby: "We take you into our community as a limb of our body; you shall grow up in our protection and bring honor to your name, pride to your brotherhood and inextinguishable glory to your race."

With that, Otto was officially ushered into the SS, elite of the master race.

What have I done? What have I done? The words raced through Ilse's mind as she tried to silence them. Otto was returned to her arms, a warm, sleepy bundle, heavier by the day. Another child began to cry and, undaunted by glares from the SS, did not quiet until the ceremony was over.

Afterward, coffee and cake were served and music played on the gramophone. The mothers and SS men were meant to mingle. Ilse found the milling about uncomfortable, but she was glad to have the extra time with Otto. She retreated with him and a slice of spice cake to the bay window, recessed enough to fit a couch and a table. Though she was tempted to pull closed the curtain that would separate this nook from the rest of the room, she settled for cracking the window and gulping in the fresh air.

Someone appeared in Ilse's line of vision. It was the man, Otto's new godfather. His face rested in a pensive expression; his serious eyebrows prepared to rise and knit together.

She jumped up to greet him. It was best to make a good impression on an SS officer who held one of the highest ranks.

"Hello, Frau Ilse," the man said. What was his name? "I'm afraid we weren't properly introduced when we met before— I'm Erich von Thiel. It is an honor to play a small role in young Otto's life."

Ilse wasn't sure what to say. "Thank you."

She didn't know what it meant for Otto to have a godfather —would this man be a part of their lives? She'd assumed not, that he was designated godfather only for the purpose of the ceremony, but here he was, holding something out to her—a savings bank book and a silver candlestick.

"Gifts for your son," he said. "Soon every Lebensborn child will receive a candlestick upon his birth, and one every year after that. I happen to have access to the factory where the candlesticks are made, so you're among the first to receive one."

"Such a kind gesture, Gruppenführer." She took the items, the candlestick cold and heavy in her hand, and placed them on the table.

He smiled. "Call me Erich."

Ilse summoned a smile in return, but she would never call a high-ranking SS officer by his given name.

The Gruppenführer leaned in and tickled the baby's cheeks, then his belly. Otto was delighted. Then the officer produced something else, a small wooden train painted bright red.

He held it out to Otto, who grasped the toy for a moment before it fell out of his hands. The officer seemed surprised as he stooped to sweep the toy off the floor.

"He's what, four, five months old?"

"Yes, five."

"A bit behind, is he?" The officer cleared his throat. "Well, then. I'm sure he'll catch up soon."

Ilse took the toy and held it for Otto to look at.

"You must have a full crèche at home yourself," she said.

"I have two boys and a girl, though they're all out of nappies and in school now. I'm afraid my duties take me away from them more often than not."

"I hope you will be able to see them again soon. I can't imagine being away from Otto any more than I already am."

"Yes, I can see that. Although I think it is different for a mother. The father's job is to discipline. It is a duty I do not relish."

Ilse could almost smell a whiff of leather tinged with sweat. She swallowed and looked down.

"I recall you were reading Hildegard von Bingen when we first met. Have you kept up with your studies of herbalism?" he asked.

"Not as much, anymore. I haven't had the time."

Otto's legs spasmed and he began fussing. She bounced him a little, pressing him close to her breast to hide the spontaneous lactation that had begun at the sound of his cry. Her brassiere was soaking, and now her slip and soon the gray wool of her dress would be drenched and it would never stop.

Von Thiel seemed to sense Ilse's discomfort, or at the very least Otto's.

"I must excuse myself. The drive back to Munich is a long one. I will check in on the two of you from time to time, to see if I can be of service."

She thanked him and scurried back to the crèche to feed Otto.

CHAPTER THIRTEEN

One soggy day at the end of May, Ilse entered the crèche and scooped Otto up, cooing and making faces at him. She sat him down in the play area, casting a guilty glance at the other babies fussing in their cribs who received no visits at all.

Several brown curls, just like Felix's, had sprouted from Otto's head. Neither she nor Rudolf Anschütz had hair like this. Straight and pale like straw, both of them. Someone someday might think to question it. Otto lay on his stomach and she handed him various toys, which he examined and touched and tried to grab, but everything fell out of his hands. The books said he should be able to hold on to small objects by now, but as the Gruppenführer had said, Otto was sure to catch up.

Schwester Ursula was hovering near her. Ilse looked up, impatient to return her attention to Otto. Ursula's brown-clad belly now protruded prominently.

"Is there something you need?" Ilse asked her. More money probably.

"Not exactly." Ursula's usual vacant smile was gone from her face.

"Alright," said Ilse, turning back to her baby and wishing the Schwester would go away.

"It's just . . ." She twisted her apron in her hands and looked down at Otto, a shadow darkening her eyes.

Ilse looked back at her sharply. "What is it?"

"I've just heard from the doctor that Otto has some . . . delays. He isn't developing as an infant should."

Ilse felt very still, chill and rage freezing her. And something else—a fear creeping in the back of her mind that she hadn't allowed to surface.

"Have you noticed that when you pick him up, his head falls back if you don't support it?" Ursula said. "At six months, he should be holding it up. His back arches, and his legs are stiff and crossed; sometimes they spasm. These are all issues I haven't encountered before."

Ilse hadn't either. She had no explanation for the quirks she'd noticed. But they had to be no more than that. He was healthy, strong, a bright, glittering star.

"Dr. Bartz has examined him and found these behaviors concerning," Ursula continued. "He's consulting with Lebensborn headquarters, and no one knows what will happen next. I shouldn't be telling you this, but I thought you might want to know."

"You thought? Of course I want to know. Dösig." She slipped into Low German to call Ursula stupid, knowing the farm girl from Thuringia wouldn't understand. "It's good the doctor is consulting. That's why we're here, isn't it? The best medical care Germany has to offer."

A tremor had crept into her voice and her heart pounded with fear. Nazis believed that a physical condition meant impurity, meant not Aryan. If they pursued the issue, they could find out the truth about Otto's father, or simply assume that his genes were wrong because he was a bit behind the other babies.

Ursula nodded, looking cheered, and went back to folding clean diapers. Ilse thought she must be rather simple after all. Otto was healthy, he was perfect. There was a misunderstanding somehow. She picked Otto up, took him to the window.

"Look at the castle," she said, pointing at the view. He reached for her finger. She kissed the top of Otto's head and all over his face and there was nothing delayed about his laugh.

Ilse went straight to Frau Ingrid. She suspected from her chilly relationship with the administrator that she wouldn't help, but that didn't stop her from trying.

Frau Ingrid was in the kitchen, conferring with the cook. Ilse lurked in the doorway, struggling to be patient, until at last they had finished discussing pork shortages. Frau Ingrid nearly stumbled over Ilse on her way out.

"Frau Ilse. What is it now?" She sounded exasperated already.

"I was hoping to have a word with you in private."

"Now? I'm quite busy."

Ilse should stop, wait for a better moment. But she felt a pressing urgency that forced her to continue.

"It'll be quick."

Frau Ingrid sighed and led Ilse to her office. The room's four brown walls were lined with file cabinets, one small window the only relief. Ilse stood in front of the desk as the administrator sat behind it, busying herself with little tasks, not looking Ilse in the eye.

"I've heard about Otto," Ilse said.

"Have you?"

"Yes. And I wish to be kept informed, and involved in any decisions made."

"I'm afraid that's not how it works. You know by now that the Lebensborn Society takes responsibility for the health of its charges."

"Even so. What has Dr. Bartz said?"

"He said that Otto has some delays. You must have noticed this yourself; I hear how often you visit." She frowned.

"I hadn't noticed, actually, and I don't believe it's true. I'd like a second opinion."

Frau Ingrid puffed up like a toad about to croak. Her eyes bored into Ilse's.

"I assure you, we always provide Lebensborn babies with the best treatment. This is not your concern."

"What will happen to Otto?"

"As I said, that remains to be seen."

"But what are the options?"

"Ilse. That's enough." Frau Ingrid rose and held open the door, waiting for Ilse to leave.

⁂

Word about Ilse's situation had gotten out by morning; the Schwestern avoided her in the halls and at meals—Ursula had stopped sitting at her usual table, instead crowding in at the one next to it, where there was no room for Ilse to join. When she walked across the grounds, the mothers-to-be clustered at the gazebo and muttered quietly, casting occasional glances at her.

There was a mixer that night. She wasn't sure she'd be wanted now, if her viability as a German mother was in question. But no one had told her not to go, and she thought it best to continue doing all the things a daffodil eager to fulfill her purpose in life would do.

Back in her room, she felt too agitated to do anything but pace or, better yet, burn down the building and escape into the night with Otto. She forced herself to put on a cornflower-blue dress with a royal-blue velvet ribbon around the waist. Her hands shook too much to do anything with her hair, so she simply smoothed it down.

In the parlor bustling with couples, she stood in a daze. Colors swirled before her, the dresses and hair and suits and sparkling glasses blending together.

"Frau Ilse," a low voice said from behind her left shoulder. Ilse whirled around and saw before her Otto's godfather.

"Gruppenführer von Thiel." She pulled the corners of her mouth upwards.

Beneath his thick brows, his eyes met hers, intently, sincerely. She was unused to people looking at her that way; she averted her gaze to hide the mysterious pricking sensation in her eyes.

"I am pleased to see you this evening." He offered his arm. She didn't understand what he could want with her, but at least with him, other men wouldn't approach her for the time being. She took his arm, and they continued on the path she'd set out for herself.

"How have you been, Gruppenführer?"

"Erich," he corrected cheerfully. "I've just met with Herr Himmler to tour Wewelsburg Castle, not far from here. I'm quite excited by the prospect. Herr Himmler is fascinated by the mystical, as am I, and he plans to transform the SS into an elite society. As you can see, we are well on our way." He gestured around the room. "It is at Wewelsburg that we will rebuild a new chivalric order based on the Knights Templar. SS officers will meet for important rituals aimed at mental concentration and accessing the fullness of our mystic potential."

His eyes lit up, but his words ceased to make sense to Ilse's ears. Her mind scattered in twenty directions at once. What would happen to her and Otto? Would they be run out of this place? Imprisoned? Killed?

He paused, waiting for her response. She blinked and looked at him. She must look like a cow in the field with her blank gaze.

Swallow the fear. Do what needs to be done. For Otto.

"That sounds fascinating," she said, lowering her voice to sound husky, sensual. She kept her response as generic as she could in the hopes that it was appropriate. For good measure, she added a side smile she knew Felix had liked. "And where did your interest in this area begin?"

That got him talking again, and she leaned in, brushing her breast against his arm, lightly enough to be an accident. Almost. She felt like a wild animal, careening toward the nearest viable mate, indiscriminate in her frenzy.

But it wasn't indiscriminate: Here was a powerful man who happened to be her baby's godfather. Who might have an interest in helping his godchild. Would he be involved in the decision about Otto? This was her only hope against the forces of Lebensborn. With the right maneuvers, she could seduce him into helping her.

His low, quiet voice continued as she led them to the double doors that opened to the grounds.

"Are you sure?" He paused at the door. Through the panes, the grounds were pitch black and uninviting. She opened the door a crack. Crisp mountain air rushed in.

"Yes," she said. "The room is stuffy, isn't it? I need a bit of fresh air." And to get him alone.

Ever the gentleman, he opened the door the rest of the way and held it for her. Nearby couples glared as gusts of cold enveloped them. Ilse stepped into the night. He followed and closed the door behind her.

As if observing from far away, she could tell it wasn't cold; it was freezing. Her body immediately began to shiver. If she could have felt anything besides fear for Otto, she would have returned to the warmth of the parlor immediately.

Instead, she turned to von Thiel and stepped close to him.

"Have you ever danced outside on a spring night in the mountains?" She held out her arms. She'd hardly ever danced, but she'd seen it enough. Besides, the woman's role was to follow. She at least could do that.

His shoulders were hunched against the cold, but his eyes lit up and he stepped close to her. She was instantly warmed by his heat.

"I'd offer you my jacket, but it's my uniform, you see. It isn't permitted."

"Of course. I'm fine." She'd rather freeze than wear the SS insignia anyway.

He slid an arm around her waist and took her right hand in his left. They swayed slowly to the music that emanated from the parlor.

Now was the moment. She should let him know that he could kiss her, or even kiss him herself. Take it just far enough that he would do anything for her.

Instead, to her horror, she was overcome. Wrapped in warm, strong arms—even though she feared the man they belonged to —something cracked inside her. She lowered her head. A tear dripped into the blackness where the night and his uniform met. She swallowed.

"What is the matter?" When he spoke, his chin touched the top of her head.

She looked up, arranged her face in her best all-clear expression—*with the Führer all will be well*—and said, "Nothing." But then she looked down again, staring at his chest. She hadn't wanted it to happen like this, to lose control instead of whipping him into a frenzy of lust. It had been ridiculous to think she could do that.

"Ilse, tell me." His voice rumbled against her. On his sleeve, the white background of his swastika armband reflected light from the parlor.

With a finger, Von Thiel gently tilted her chin up so she had no choice but to meet his eyes. She hadn't received this much attention from anyone since her Sundays with Felix and she felt flustered under his gaze, unable to do anything but tell the truth. Even though he was SS, and dangerous, for reasons she didn't understand, her fear of him was slipping away.

She told him about Otto's delay, her request for a second opinion, how she wasn't permitted to be involved. How she didn't know what would happen to him. As she spoke, his eyebrows knitted together, rising to the middle of his forehead.

"This is unfortunate news. You have my sincerest condolences." His voice was low and soothing.

She mumbled a thank you and willed herself not to let another tear fall. Not when he could see.

"It is clear that you would prefer not to socialize. Shall I see you back to your quarters?"

She was surprised that that was all he had to say, but she'd lost all hope of seducing aid out of him after crying onto his tunic. At least by going back to her quarters with von Thiel, everyone would assume they were off to make another Lebensborn baby.

"Yes, please."

With her fingers tucked into the crook of his arm, they entered the parlor and walked through the room to the entrance to the Schwestern's quarters. Fortunately, Frau Ingrid did not materialize this time. He kissed her fingertips, gave them a squeeze, and said, "My thoughts are with little Otto."

He bid her farewell, and she felt a hint of relief—as if some of her worry had transferred to him and there was less for her to carry. She fled up the stairs to her room before Frau Ingrid could catch up with her.

⁂

The dumbwaiter door creaked loudly as she opened it. Ilse cringed and waited, but silence surrounded her; no one was in the kitchen. She climbed in and closed the door. She fit comfortably enough if she put her knees up to her chest. The boards were thin but held her weight. The air smelled of stale wood, perfect for kindling a fire. She gave the pulley a good tug and, though the dumbwaiter moved, its joints creaked from lack of use. Ilse hopped out and raided the kitchen for linseed oil and cloth, which she used to dab at the stiff hinges. She climbed back in and pulled, gliding upward. When the dumbwaiter docked, she held still, listened.

Before this, she'd checked the second floor, directly above the kitchen. She'd found the other door to the dumbwaiter, painted over and just about invisible. On either side of it were the offices of the administrator and the doctor.

After a few moments of silence, she heard footsteps approaching: women's voices. She could hear every word of their rather dull conversation about nail varnish. Good—the dumbwaiter wasn't soundproof. Breathing shallowly in the stuffy space, she pressed her ear against one side of the wall, which must be shared with another room. There was nothing. It was late, after all. On the other side, which she tried next, there were muffled sounds. She could hear Frau Ingrid, barely, on a phone call, discussing two mothers-to-be, one a mistress to an SS officer and the other an SS wife, who had discovered their babies had the same father. Now the mistress was being transferred to a home called Steinhöring.

136

There was the muffled shuffling of papers and occasional footsteps, Frau Ingrid speaking with Traude, asking her to type up letters for her.

If Frau Ingrid was going to discuss Otto and his health—or his origins for that matter—Ilse wanted to hear it. The situation she'd carefully crafted for herself and Otto to survive here was crumbling. Her whole file would be under scrutiny, and it would not hold up.

Frau Ingrid received a call and spoke for some time with a person who was clearly important. She was deferential for the first time in Ilse's hearing. The conversation was peppered with "Jawohl" and "Right away." As the conversation progressed, she began to sound flustered.

"We have been writing to SS families to tell them the truth, that the Lebensborn Society is a reputable institution. We send them photos of our most racially pure children; they would melt a heart of stone. I don't know what more we could do . . . Yes, Sturmbannführer. I will think of something."

Ilse thought of the cacophony of sound that came from the room where the toddlers were kept. Frau Ingrid must be facing pressure to find homes for them all.

The administrator's footsteps sounded on the floor, louder and quieter as she paced back and forth, punctuating her steps with heavy sighs. At last she put on a record and all Ilse could hear was the blare of Wagner. She cringed at the sound, the preferred music of the Reich. Desperate to get away, she began her descent.

Ilse had hope today. A doctor, who had nothing whatsoever to do with Lebensborn, was coming from nearby Halberstadt to examine Otto. She'd tried to be present for the examination, but arguing with Frau Ingrid was like trying to persuade a statue. So Ilse waited. She was certain it would be good news; he would direct them to a specialist and a cure. There was never nothing to be done. She nearly skipped as she brought new mothers their meals and cleaned out chamber pots.

When she was halfway through sterilizing instruments, there was movement at the door. She looked up. Frau Ingrid and Dr. Bartz loomed in the doorway, straight-faced. Ilse set the instruments and the cloth down, aware of her hands brushing her thighs, her lungs pumping, her heart beating. She swayed slightly.

"What did the doctor say?"

Dr. Bartz took out a handkerchief, unfolded it, blew his nose, and refolded it while Ilse waited. "*I* am the doctor. He was the consultant. He agreed with my assessment that the child has birth palsy. He has been sent to a hospital in Brandenburg for special treatment."

All the blood left Ilse's body, she was sucked dry as a rock. She grasped the table to support herself.

"You took my baby away? I didn't say you could do that. You *can't*."

"It was our decision," said Frau Ingrid firmly, as if enforcing a bedtime for an unruly toddler. "I must say, you are far too involved in this child's life. It's unhealthy."

"What is the special treatment?"

"It means that he's getting the care he needs."

Rage tore through her. She wanted to throw the instruments at them, overturn the tables and bury them underneath. Instead, her breath came in short gulps. She couldn't suck in enough air. Her lips were numb.

"Which hospital?" Her voice shook. "You must tell me. I have to be with him."

The worst had happened. As long as they were together, she

could have protected Otto. That was her one desire. She'd failed. Otto had disappeared into the Lebensborn system, which was designed to cover its tracks. How could she find him now?

"It is not your place to tell us what we must do," Frau Ingrid said. "You're becoming hysterical. Sit down and the doctor will give you a sedative."

Chapter Fourteen

The next day, though still groggy from the drugs Dr. Bartz had stabbed into her arm, Ilse worked with an industrious speed that exceeded her previous efficiency. She channeled her worry and anger into the physical exertion of her tasks, fetching cool glasses of water and hot towels, sanitizing equipment, and changing bedpans. Before everything happened with Otto, she'd been about to learn to give injections, and then perhaps she would have gotten a raise. There was no talk of injections or raises now, and she didn't care. The part of her that was a mother was so big and so close that, even though the other parts of her were still there, she could not see or feel or care about them. Her breasts leaked, the only relief from the pain and pressure that built from not nursing. Her arms were empty and aching.

When she'd finished her work, she sneaked into the dumbwaiter and listened for Frau Ingrid to mention Otto or Brandenburg or special treatment, whatever that was.

Curled up in the tiny wooden box, cloaked in the familiar scent of old wood, free of light, often free of sound, Ilse closed her eyes and thought of nothing. She cried silently, knees hugged to her chest. The voices of Frau Ingrid and various employees of the RuSHA department were audible through the walls, but she only half-listened to the humdrum tones of applications, adoptions, and subscriptions, as well as the mediation of petty dramas among the mothers. Her ears perked up at a discussion of high infant mortality rates in the homes, mutterings of better care needed, and Ilse wondered for a moment if Otto had received substandard care, if that was why he was crippled. But they were questions for which she couldn't expect an answer, so she pinched her finger-nails into her wrists and thighs until they left marks and counted every mistake she'd made that had gotten Otto into this situation.

Before Frau Ingrid left her office for the day, Ilse heard her speaking in soft tones to a "Kurtchen," probably her son. Ilse didn't want to think of her as a mother, as a human.

Perhaps, after the treatment had been done, they would finally realize nothing was wrong with Otto at all. They would see what she saw—a perfect child.

Or maybe in the course of their tests they would realize that he was Jewish, and it would be over for both of them.

Or this treatment was what Otto needed. It had been thoughtless of them not to let her say goodbye, but she wanted him to get the proper care; that's what she'd been advocating for since all this started.

She refused to consider what else special treatment might mean.

⁂

He had been gone for two days when Frau Ingrid came into the hospital ward. Ilse was scrubbing the tiled floors, yet again stained with blood and gore and smelling of birth—heavy, sickly sweet and metallic, the smell of her mother's death, of Otto's birth.

The mop stilled in Ilse's hands. The administrator approached, pulling out her clipboard, but not to inspect Ilse's work.

"Tell me the addresses of your family members, please." Frau Ingrid's mouth was a straight, firm line.

"Excuse me?"

"Where does your family live?"

"Why do you ask?"

"Your relatives must undergo an inspection."

This was it: they knew Otto had Jewish blood and they were finding out if it came from Ilse's lineage. They could find anything wrong with her or her family, should they want to.

Frau Ingrid was becoming impatient now. "We can find this information ourselves, of course, but it is important that you comply. Otherwise, we may begin to doubt your loyalty to the Reich."

Ilse knew a veiled threat when she heard one. She gave her father's address in Bremen.

"Any other family?"

"I have some relatives in the Harz and outside Leipzig, but I haven't seen any of them in years. I don't even know their names."

Frau Ingrid scribbled on the form. "Your information along with an inspection of the originator and his line should be sufficient. Thank you for your cooperation."

In her bedroom, the door locked, her chest heaving, Ilse wrenched open the wardrobe and threw the worn knapsack onto the bed. In it went her clothing—only hers, not the borrowed clothing from mothers and Schwestern past—and her mother's book.

How long would it take to uncover her lie? Her only hope was for the infinite bureaucracy of the Reich to give her a head start.

With her knapsack tossed over her shoulder, she strode to the window.

She paused, staring at the castle on the hill. Her plan had been to climb out through the window—fortunately there was a bay window below and she could land on the ledge and jump from there to the ground—then scale the garden wall. From there, run somewhere. Seek refuge in a farmhouse, perhaps. She would find her way.

But if she left now, she would lose any chance of finding Otto again.

The knapsack fell to the ground. Residual adrenaline pumped through her chest, her arms and legs.

She sank into the chair and watched the castle, her mind blank, her emotions gone. She could think of nothing at all to do, nothing that would save her and Otto.

CHAPTER FIFTEEN

Half a kilometer from the home, Ilse studied the tree, its thick trunk striped with layers of bark, twisted branches forming knots around it.

Machandelboom.

The thought had come to her as she woke—which meant she must have fallen asleep at some point. She remembered something her mother had written in her book, that an offering to a juniper tree, made by a mother, was thought to heal a child. Ilse didn't go in for such fanciful ideas normally, but she didn't even pause to be embarrassed for considering it now.

She retrieved the scrap of gray wool she'd cut off her borrowed Ulster coat and the bit of wholemeal bread she'd stolen from the kitchen.

With a look around to make sure no one was nearby, she took a breath and spoke the words, willing her voice not to crack: "Dear Hollen and Hollinen, I bring you something to spin and something to eat, so that you might forget my small child and leave him in peace."

Her voice was low and gravelly. She stood at the tree for a moment, unsure what to do. Then she pressed her hand against the trunk, feeling the scrape of the bark against her skin. The tree felt alive, palpably so, as if it had a heartbeat. She pulled her hand away and returned to the home.

***

Four days after Otto was taken, Traude intercepted Ilse on her way to the dining room.

"You're needed in Frau Ingrid's office," she said, clearly pleased with herself for having orders to give.

Ilse was just going to dinner to eat sauerkraut and cod liver oil and far more vegetables than she wanted. She didn't want to go to Frau Ingrid's office, but Traude was waiting for her, and Ilse had no choice but to go with her. Each time her foot fell against the ground it felt like someone else's.

Frau Ingrid's door was open. Before Ilse went in, she smoothed back her flyaway hair and wiped her palms against the side of her dress. Traude lingered at the door, so Ilse closed it as she entered.

The administrator looked up. Her eyes revealed nothing. She invited Ilse to take a seat.

There was no preamble. She simply said the words. Like an anchor dropped at sea, like a gunshot in the night. Words that changed everything.

"The child is dead."

The administrator's voice sounded like nothing, like ringing, like the roar of an ocean.

Ilse shook her head.

"Who? Who died?"

"Otto."

Frau Ingrid handed her a postcard. It was stiff in Ilse's hands. Typewritten words in black ink. A stamp bearing Hitler's face in the corner. Postmarked from Brandenburg.

Ilse's eyes leapt to his name: Otto Rademann, from Heim Harz, Wernigerode.

It read like a certificate.

Date of death: May 29th, 1939.

At the bottom, a notice: The body will not be returned because it has been disinfected.

Disinfected.

Ilse pushed words out of her mouth, rough like sandpaper.

"What was the cause?"

"He was a weak child. He could not be saved and would have been a burden on society. He was Lebensunwertes Leben." Life unworthy of life.

Ilse stood. She watched her hands push open a door, then another door. She couldn't breathe.

She was outside. For once there was sun. She hated its glare and heat.

It was nausea, bile, the crawling out of one's own skin. On the other side of the lawn, the children had been brought out for their daily two hours of fresh air, their cornsilk heads gleaming in the sun. Painfully alive.

There was a bench. She sat on it. She would stay there, until the shreds of her body became one with it.

There was no body.

Was he really dead?

If he were dead, she would feel it.

It was unreal, would be unreal until she saw it for herself, and she never would.

She imagined his body, his ashes, and vomited.

. . .

Ilse lay on the floor next to her bed the rest of the day and the night that followed. Clutched in her hand, the postcard—Otto's death notice—became crumpled, then soft. She reread it whenever she began to believe that it had all been a nightmare.

Otto couldn't really be dead. They wouldn't kill a baby. No one could do that.

But what could they be doing to him instead? Why would they keep him from her if they hadn't killed him? She forced herself to think of every gruesome experiment, every possible torture, and still knew her imagination fell short. Then she thought of how to find him.

Take a train. Find the building, hop the fence, sneak into the room, find the little bundle that was Otto, snatch him up, run.

Hitchhike. Pretend to be a nurse, find Otto, snatch him up, run.

Walk to Brandenburg. Seduce the guard and steal his keys. Find Otto, snatch him up, run.

Write a letter. Get a lawyer. Request his release.

The release of a child declared dead?

It would never work. Run.

When she had exhausted her futile plans, she stared out the window at the castle. The ache of the knowledge that Otto was not there to see—it consumed her until it turned into revulsion.

Was she so sure that they wouldn't kill a baby?

She knew the Nazis. Knew what they did, and how, and why. She'd been one of them. After everything she'd been taught and everything she'd seen, she couldn't think of a reason why they'd lie about this one murder when they'd been so proud of their other acts of violence.

She returned again to her plans, cycling through each thought, again and again, knowing it was pointless.

While Traude slept, she rested her cheekbones on her knees and cried silently. Her eyes were so swollen she could barely see out of them. Her mouth was dry. A voice in the back of her head told her she needed to drink water, but she lacked the will to pour a glass.

Now was her time to escape, before the false originator was discovered, or some flaw in her body or her heritage was invented, but what for? She was overcome by a lethargy that went to the core of her being. The noose was not her concern when she felt she was going to die any minute.

Her bones dug into the hard wood but she remained; the discomfort only made her wish for more physical pain, something to equal and exceed the loss of Otto and make it so she couldn't think.

She did not move from the floor until the next morning when a guard came to the door and asked her to come with him. It was not a choice.

CHAPTER SIXTEEN

"Haven't I already done this?" Her voice felt brittle, about to crack. "Perhaps you can refer to my records."

Dr. Bartz inspected her, measuring and probing with calipers and gloved fingers. During her first examination, her stomach had been round with pregnancy. Now it was flat. The rest of her body had reshaped itself, too. Her hips were wider, as were her fingers. Not in a way that others would notice, but in a way that she alone could feel. A portrait of Hitler stared at her, the same one mothers were supposed to gaze upon during labor.

"We're looking for any imperfection that may have been missed before," the doctor said.

She gritted her teeth, crossed her arms over her chest. What moles or bumps or red patches or dry patches could reveal about her hereditary health, she didn't know. When Dr. Bartz pushed her arms aside and prodded at her breasts, swollen and engorged from not being able to nurse, milk leaked out of them. She should have been embarrassed, but instead she found herself hoping it was he who was ashamed. He was the one milking her like a cow.

They could find any defect in her, real or imagined. Perhaps they would discover she'd lied to the Reich. She felt the noose tightening around her neck.

When Dr. Bartz was finished with her, she fastened her clothes with shaking hands. She emerged from the room to find an SS guard waiting for her, the doctor's report in hand. He led her down the staircase. The home was devoid of the usual clusters of girls, as if they feared her predicament was contagious.

Blood pounded through every vein in her body with such intensity it almost hurt. She must run. But she'd wasted her opportunity to escape. Now her fate would be decided for her.

Adrenaline was jolting her awake. It was the threat to her physical self, she knew. The body is determined to survive, to avoid pain. She should be running across the mountains to freedom. She'd had the opportunity, but she'd used the time for torment and tears and it was too late for that now. Perhaps she would die for that mistake. She wasn't sure she cared. The pulse pounding through her body sounded like Otto's name.

The SS guard opened the great oak door and ushered Ilse in. Behind a long table against the picture window, the local administrators, race experts, and black-clad officers sat in a row. The guard placed the medical report on the table and left the room. The door groaned closed.

She smoothed the wrinkled pleats of yesterday's dress. As she walked on wobbly legs, her head light, she realized she'd had nothing to eat or drink in almost a day. The room must have been cold, because every hair on her body stood on end.

At the end of the table was von Thiel, his eyes even more serious than usual under his heavy brow—perhaps it was pity his gaze held. Ilse avoided looking at him. It was humiliating for someone who had seemed to view her as a person to now see her like this. She was at her basest form, stripped to the bone, just as naked as she'd been in the exam room.

She moved to take a seat across from them at the table, but Sturmbannführer Pflaum, head of Lebensborn, raised his hand. She'd met him once before, on the stairs while she was still pregnant. Gray eyes, colorless hair, he was disconcertingly generic. Such a bland man to wield such power over her life, her child's life.

"Please remain standing," Pflaum said, his voice scratching like dry leaves. Of course—this committee was assembled to assess her body, its worth. Ilse loosened her grip on the chair and resisted the urge to cross her arms and hide herself.

"We have some questions for you, starting with your heritage."

They questioned her about her family history, whether there were any illnesses, disorders, abnormalities that she'd neglected to mention before. Alcoholism, abuse in the home? What consisted of abuse, Ilse wondered. What father did not reprimand his daughter if she misbehaved? She didn't know of such a family. So that wasn't abuse, but then what was? She answered no to all the questions.

"Perhaps you have forgotten to mention something?" Pflaum spoke as if it were an innocent mistake she could have made, one that could be painlessly rectified. All her problems would go away if only she said yes. She said no again.

The bright morning light shone in from the windows behind them. Looking at the people cast in its shadow made her eyes water. She mustn't let them think she was crying. She blinked and tried to appear to be looking at them without really looking.

Pflaum moved on to her political opinions. When had she joined Jungmädelbund? Age ten? Wonderful. And then BDM from age fourteen on? Yes, all very good. They went down the line of adjudicators, each one asking a question: Recite a quote from *Mein Kampf* concerning the Jewish question. What rank did the Führer achieve in the Great War? What was the destiny of the Aryan race and where had it gone wrong in the past?

Ilse answered the questions as best she could. The words were sand in her throat.

The questions went on and the faces before her turned increasingly to unsympathetic stone. They stopped taking notes and only stared at her, looking bored, as if she were an uninteresting creature in a zoo.

To answer the questions was not enough. She must demonstrate her enthusiasm. Her eyes must go glassy with admiration at the mention of the Führer, her voice must be filled with awe at the power and superiority of the Aryan people, even though the Reich had killed her baby, and she was disgusted by National Socialism, and disgusted with herself for having had anything to do with it.

But this was a test she must pass. She must pretend to be infected once again.

She sank into her past self, that unthinking girl who believed what she was told. More than that, she willed herself to become a Karola, a Traude, a one-hundred-percent Nazi. A woman who aspired to be a mother, perhaps also a BDM leader. A woman who, beyond that, had not a thought in her head at all. A vacant smile lifted her mouth, eyes looked beyond the room, enraptured by the sight of something heavenly.

"What was the Führer's mother's name?"

"Klara." The word came out soft and reverent.

"What is a woman's role in society?"

"Children, kitchen, church." Her eyes brightened with fervor.

She even found herself singing the "Horst-Wessel-Lied" in a hearty voice that was nearly a yell.

The row of stern faces softened, and there was even a nod

here or there. But Ilse couldn't tell if it was working, or if it would be enough.

After what felt like a thousand questions but was probably less, she was told the committee would deliberate and come to a decision tomorrow. Ilse clicked her heels together, puffed up her chest, summoned the *Heil Hitler* from deep in her gut, and pushed it up and out of her body. As she left the room, she thought she saw the Gruppenführer standing up as if to address the committee, but the thick door closed behind her, sealing out all sound. There was no one in the hallway.

She'd been given no instructions, so she went to the dumbwaiter. She curled up inside the dark box and pulleyed herself up, feeling weak and shaky. Her eyes, wide open, took in the darkness. There was silence, except her pulse saying *Ot-to. Ot-to.*

She replayed the meeting in her head again and again, wondering if she'd said the right thing, discovering too late the perfect words to say instead. She pictured the faces of the committee members—had they nodded or had she imagined it? Perhaps they were only being polite to her face to keep her calm.

Finally she exhausted herself. Her head rested against the thin wooden siding and slipped into the liminal space between sleep and waking, her first reprieve from consciousness in over thirty hours. On the other side of the wall, Frau Ingrid entered her office with someone else and they struck up a conversation. Ilse might have missed it all, but then they uttered her name. Her eyes snapped open. Instantly awake, she strained every part of her body to hear.

"Anschütz is dead, so we cannot inspect him, obviously." That was Frau Ingrid's voice. "None of the originator's family members revealed hereditary conditions, but we cannot be certain."

Ilse's exhausted heart picked up speed again, thumping painfully in her chest. Had the Anschützes revealed Rudolf's whereabouts? Had they alerted Lebensborn to her lie?

It was Pflaum's voice that she heard next. All he said was "very well." It seemed that no one had doubted that part of her story enough to look closely, so concerned were they about her physical imperfections and his.

Quiet reigned as he shuffled papers. How could something so important be so dull and tedious? Soon she would die from it.

"The mother seems devoted to the Reich," Pflaum said. "That counts for something with Herr Himmler. Perhaps she deserves a second chance."

"I'm not sure she is as devoted as she appeared," Frau Ingrid said. "I've never seen her so enthusiastic before. There's a look she gets sometimes, as if she's thinking about things she shouldn't. Perhaps," her voice lowered, "doubting the Reich. She does not participate in the national community. And she barely pays attention when I teach *Mein Kampf*." She sniffed.

"Ah. Well then. The child has already been liquidated?"

"Yes."

Otto. Liquidated. She doubled over, her body breaking in two, torn apart by anguish. All sense of what was going on around her disappeared. The blind pain was like nothing she'd felt before, a hundred times worse than childbirth, a thousand times worse than the loss of her mother.

He was really gone. His baby laugh, the first bits of a voice that would never form words. His tiny fingers that would never grow long and callused. The world would never know his eyes, his hair, his personality.

Gradually, a part of her became aware again. On the other side of the wall there was more silence, then the sound of papers being tapped against the desk. Pflaum spoke again with a tone of finality: "In the absence of sufficient information to determine whose fault the defect was—mother or father—we recommend sterilizing the mother as a precaution against any impurities in her blood."

"Yes, Sturmbannführer."

"The sterilization procedure has not yet been perfected, so there are likely to be complications. Please be prepared for all contingencies and document them. It will be helpful to our doctors as they further their research."

The door opened and closed, swishing against the carpet, and confident steps retreated down the hallway.

They were going to sterilize Ilse. It was simply another administrative decision, a letter to be written, arrangements to be made.

With shaking hands, she pulled herself down and fled to her room.

Not only had Otto been taken from her, wrenched from the world, but now she was losing the possibility of having another child. If she couldn't bear children, then she would lose her value to the Reich. And if she wasn't useful, then why would they keep her alive?

In school she'd learned about the new law that allowed for compulsory sterilizations. She'd thought it was one of those things that could be done but never was. Apparently she was wrong. She shuddered to think of how many had suffered this fate before her, probably not even told what was happening to them. Their choices ripped away from them in a moment by the cruel hands in power. Soon she would be one of them.

Pflaum had said there would probably be complications. What did he mean by all contingencies? Death was certainly one possibility. Or worse. She thought of a similar operation Frau Anschütz had received years ago—how she'd never been the same after, in constant pain, sickly. Ilse could not imagine being unable to work. She would have no way to survive. It would be a slow death from hunger and exposure on the streets.

There was a numb voice in her head, telling her to get out. Nothing else inside her was functioning, so she followed the voice.

She haphazardly threw some things into her knapsack. Her brain didn't work, her hands didn't work. She would sneak out during dinner, when everyone else was in the main building. In the back of her mind, an alarm sounded that she still hadn't eaten, but she didn't feel hungry. She put on her coat and made her way out of the empty Schwestern quarters onto the grounds. Now she needed to slip past the main building where everyone was gathered, in daylight, without being seen. She took a breath and skirted along the edge of the grounds next to the bushes. Almost to the main building. This was the last time she would see the half-timbered walls of the home.

Frau Ingrid rounded the brick corner of the building. Her eyes were on a paper she held in her hands. There was time—barely—for Ilse to hide in the bushes.

She held her breath as the administrator strode past. If she was going to fetch Ilse, then she didn't have much of a head start. As soon as Frau Ingrid disappeared into the building, Ilse darted out from her hiding place. A guard and his dog were at the gate, so she found the lowest part of the garden wall. The ancient stones were covered in ivy and slick with rain, with hardly any place to gain purchase. But she had to climb it; there was no other way. With part momentum and part sheer force of will, she mounted the wall and hopped down on the other side. Her ankle twinged. She must have landed wrong. But it wasn't broken or sprained, and she set off at a run, down the hill into town. She was halfway to the train station—the fastest way to distance herself from the home—when she realized that was the first place they would search for her.

She took a hard right, crossed a tiny bridge, and headed for the hills. With her mother's book, she could live in the woods for a while. Or she could sneak into the castle and hide there for a few days; they would never think to look for her there. But where would she go after? Where would she be safe in the long run? She couldn't think about that now.

Soon her ribs seared in pain and every step had her gasping for air. Her head spun. Hunger, lack of sleep, and fear were catching up with her. Just one more step, she told herself. One more step. Don't think of anything else. Especially not Otto. And then she was thinking of him again, but she could walk at a brisk pace while crying, tears dampening the front of her jacket. She moved blindly, not knowing or caring where she went, as long as it was far away.

Her breathing became difficult and each step strained her legs—because, she realized, she was going up, toward the castle.

A stone wall blocked the most direct route to the castle. It surrounded what appeared to be a bed and breakfast, with rows of uniform windows staring blankly. There was no time to find a way around—the SS would be after her any minute. They probably already were.

She found the gate open and crossed the lawn. Walk confidently and no one will take note of you, she told herself. There was the back wall; it came up to her chest and was about a foot wide. She hoisted herself over it and picked up a narrow trail that did not appear to be maintained. Just as well; she was unlikely to run into anyone this way.

Sweat trickled down Ilse's back and each breath came out as a wheeze. All this time, she'd thought hiding in plain sight would keep her safe. Instead, she'd made it worse by lying to the SS. They would make an example of her if they caught her.

The trail took a sharp turn and the castle appeared, large and looming. From the stone terrace, she could see not only the town below but rolling green hill after rolling green hill, bright from the spring rain. She tugged and pushed on the immense door. It wouldn't budge—locked. Not that that would stop her. There was sure to be a window she could climb through. She tossed her knapsack to the ground and began pacing the wall like a wild animal. All the windows were sealed shut. The walls were high and smooth, no ivy or deep grooves between stones for climbing. How could she enter a castle built to be impenetrable? It would be better to put as much distance between herself and Wernigerode as possible. She headed back to collect her knapsack.

"Frau Ilse."

She froze. Her entire body went cold. It was over. This was the sound of her own death. The rustling of the trees in the wind. The endless twittering of birds. The thud of hobnailed boots as SS men surrounded her. The panting and pawing of their hounds.

She turned and looked at Frau Ingrid.

The administrator, out of breath and very, very angry, looked her up and down. Her eyes nearly bulged out of her face. Then she smiled. It was worse, much worse.

"Where are you going?"

"For a walk."

"You've missed dinner."

"I wasn't hungry. I wanted some fresh air."

"I'm sure." Frau Ingrid's eyes told her that she knew exactly what Ilse was doing. She was silently grateful that she'd tossed her knapsack away moments before. "We were worried that you'd gotten lost. Let's get you back to your room."

There was no escaping these SS guards—there were two of them, she now saw—each with a lethal-looking dog. She walked beside Frau Ingrid, back down the hill and into a black

Mercedes that returned her to the building she'd hoped never to see again.

As the administrator walked her to her room, she was aware of every panel of every grain of wood on the floor, the clacking of their shoes sounding *Ot-to, Ot-to*. Every fleur-de-lis on the wallpaper, repeating over and over, insufferably persistent. Nothing would save her. Nothing would bring Otto back. At least she would join him soon.

She was locked in her room with a guard stationed outside the door. Alone in the silence, she bristled with the energy meant for her escape and paced back and forth in her room. The guard's footsteps thudded as he also paced. A Schwester brought her food. It was not a Lebensborn meal, with fresh vegetables and meat. It was a sandwich on hard bread with a glass of water. She wasn't hungry at all.

It grew dark. Traude returned to the room and gave her a self-satisfied look. Ilse didn't know if Traude knew what had happened, but it was clear she thought Ilse deserved whatever punishment she got. Ilse turned her back to Traude and looked out the window. She had no desire to see the broad expanse of the woman's naked back one last time. The mole, in particular, she wouldn't miss.

Long after Traude was snoring into the night air, Ilse finally calmed down enough to feel hunger. The sandwich tasted like sandpaper but she ate it anyway, in the dark, seated at the edge of her bed. Ilse had no idea what the next day held, but it was best to face it with as much food in her as possible.

The guard knocked on her door before breakfast. Ilse had barely slept. Everything felt unreal.

"Come with me," he said.

The guard was young and freckled and his eyes, which were

no doubt blue, were in shadow. She looked at him, tried to see if he might help her, or if he cared at all. Under her gaze he blinked and looked away; he must be newly minted SS.

"Now," he said, resolute.

She followed the guard across the damp grass and inhaled the fresh spring air. It was her favorite season, which seemed cruel. Even this was taken away from her. It might be the last spring morning she ever saw. She breathed in again.

As she passed girls at their morning chores, some looked at her with curiosity, and Ilse knew she would be the subject of conversation at breakfast, and mid-morning snack, and lunch. Others looked at her with the same disdain as Traude. And others saw her and scattered with fear in their eyes, as if her crimes were catching.

Up the stairs. To the hospital ward. At the door of the examination room, the guard stood aside for Ilse to enter. One slow step after another, she entered; he closed the door and took up his station outside of it. Oberschwester Trina arrived and, without a word or even a look, gave Ilse a paper gown to change into, then methodically examined her body and marked it with a pen. For incision lines. They were going to cut her open and—do what? Ilse had no idea how it would work, and she doubted anyone would tell her. She didn't even know the hospital ward, or Dr. Bartz, were equipped for operations. Though they probably weren't too concerned with creating ideal conditions in this circumstance anyway. She'd heard it in the dumbwaiter: she was an experiment.

Ilse swallowed pointlessly, her mouth dry, and asked, "When will it happen?"

"This afternoon," Trina said. Like the guard, she didn't care —even though she'd seen Ilse through the birth and then supervised her at her work. They were all automatons now. Something was breaking inside her. Everyone around her was

160

uncaring, unfeeling. There was no one good, no one to help her. She longed for Hannelore. If she were here, she would at least visit Ilse and lessen the agony of waiting alone.

The Oberschwester left and Ilse slumped on the narrow bed. She'd cleaned this room a hundred times. She never thought she'd be a prisoner in it.

CHAPTER SEVENTEEN

Ilse passed the better part of the day in the hospital room with nothing to do. At first she tidied up just to have an outlet for her nervous energy, but she stopped herself. She passed the time fidgeting with the edge of the bedsheet and considering a way out. Maybe she could hit the guard on the back of the head with the chamber pot and run for her life. But there were guards at the gates, too, and a dozen people to pass before she even reached them. It would never work.

She tried to imagine her life after the operation. Where would she go? Would she be able to work? She imagined a life with no one to turn to and no one to burden. She would be worthless to the Reich. She knew what happened to those who held no value.

Life unworthy of life.

Would she be sent to a labor and reeducation camp to be worked until she reformed or died? That seemed likely. The cold hospital air cut through her thin gown and she shivered.

A Schwester entered the room, carrying the clothes Ilse had been wearing that morning in a neatly folded stack.

"You're to go to the meeting room," she said. She placed the stack at the foot of the bed and left before Ilse had time to ask questions.

She didn't dare to speculate about what this meant. Perhaps they were going to skip the sterilization and ship her straight to a KZ. She put her clothes on. When she opened the door, the guard was gone. Hope sparked in her veins, unstoppable.

When she made it to the meeting room, only Sturmbann-führer Pflaum was there. He stood, smiled, and gestured to the chair across the table from him, the one she hadn't been allowed to sit in the day before.

"Please sit, Frau Ilse." His voice had a strange warmth in it, forcibly kind.

They both sat. His large forehead loomed as he bestowed a smile upon her.

"You must be wondering what all this is about. New infor-mation has been brought forth related to your case. It has been determined that the child's defects were due to conditions at the birth and not, in fact, genetics. Because of this, along with the originator's heroic sacrifice and your dedication to the Father-land, I am pleased to inform you that we are bestowing an honor upon you: you will join the order of the family of blood, the SS. You will be appointed to an esteemed role in another Lebens-born location. You will have a couple of duties, which you will learn about there. And if you don't fulfill them properly—though I'm sure you will—then we will revisit your verdict. Think of it as a second chance. To prove yourself."

Ilse reeled with relief. Her head buzzed. She would not be cut into; a vital part of her would not be taken away. She would not be imprisoned in a camp.

Then confusion crashed over her. Anything was better than what had been about to happen to her—but what exactly was happening now, and why?

"Thank you," she said. "May I ask what new information

was brought forth?" She had to find out what had saved her, if she could.

"Let's just say you have good friends who took the time to do their research."

Ilse had no idea what that meant, but now Pflaum was beaming at her, looking like a teacher proud of his pupil as he stood to open the door for her. She tried to force a smile in return, but her lips didn't move at all.

Early the next morning, Ilse returned to the castle to retrieve her knapsack. It was a marvel to be allowed to leave now with only a nod from the guards. Her sentence had been dropped, though replaced by a newer and more confusing one.

Before she got into the car that was waiting for her in front of the home, she took one last look at the castle, still and gray and constant, offering neither comfort nor pain. She was leaving all traces of Otto behind her, except the ache. She would keep that; she wanted to.

The opaque partition was up, obscuring her view of the driver and the front window. The curtains on the side and rear windows of the car were shut, and when she tried to push one aside, she found they were fixed in place. No one could see her, and she couldn't tell where she was going—yet another Lebensborn secret. A dark, claustrophobic, almost womb-like environment. Ilse swallowed the urge to panic; that wouldn't do her any good.

Trapped with nothing but her thoughts, she was forced to contemplate her fate. Such a narrow escape, only to find she'd been shackled into the most feared, elite sector of the Nazi Party, the SS. She didn't understand what had changed. How could she have evaded a wretched punishment only to end up with an equally wretched reward?

In the dark warmth of the car, she hugged herself and listened to her own breathing: proof she was alive.

PART THREE
DORMANCY
CHIEF OF THE SS RACE AND SETTLEMENT MAIN OFFICE

Just as we breed Hanoverian horses using a few pure stallions and mares, so we will once again breed pure Nordic Germans by selective cross-breeding. . . From the human reservoir of the SS we shall breed a new nobility. We shall do it in a planned fashion and according to biological laws.

— RICHARD WALTHER DARRÉ, CHIEF OF THE
SS RACE AND SETTLEMENT MAIN OFFICE

Chapter Eighteen

The kitchen was pristine, industrial-sized with milk-white tile counters and state-of-the-art Cromargan appliances—everything a cook could wish for. This was where Ilse would spend her time now.

She knew she was in a villa, and that villa was an administrative center for Lebensborn, located somewhere in the vicinity of Munich. Some Lebensborn bureaucrats lived and worked on the third floor. The rest of the villa was occupied by several young women who did the clerical work, the laundry, the cleaning.

And Ilse was to cook for all fourteen residents, six days per week.

There was a time when she would have been pleased with moving up from maid to cook. It was no secretarial position, but at least she wouldn't spend her days on her knees, combing out rug fringes and cleaning the crusted rims of toilets. Cooking was a craft, something to hone and be proud of.

She did not feel proud now. She felt nothing, a fog blanketing every emotion. Behind that dense gray wall, there was deep mourning, and disgust at having to serve the SS, and fear, because they did not tolerate mistakes. Her work had to be flawless.

Ilse had learned how to cook essential German dishes from the BDM. Then at the Anschütz manor, she'd often assisted the cook. But she'd never run a kitchen that served a whole villa's worth of SS officials before.

Though her body felt slow and heavy, her heart pounded. The conflicting sensations befuddled her. She forced herself to grab an apron hanging from a hook by the door and tie it on. With less than two hours before lunch needed to be on the table, she forced herself to focus. She gathered up beef, apples, and armfuls of produce, deposited them on the kitchen island, and got to work.

Yesterday, upon her arrival, she'd been inducted into an extended version of the SS, what was unofficially called the Little Blond Sisters. It had reminded her of joining a religious order, swearing loyalty to the Führer as the savior and forsaking all others, but instead of a church, she was in a small office, and instead of a priest and a congregation, there was only an SS man and the new administrator, Frau Herta, a rail-thin woman with an affectless face whose perfume smelled like rotting roses and talcum powder. And there had been considerably more paperwork.

They'd made it clear to her that once someone entered the SS it was a lifetime commitment, disguised as an honor Ilse was not given the option to decline.

After the ceremony, Frau Herta had advised, "Be sure not to have sexual relations with any men unknown to the Lebensborn office." Ilse had no plans to engage in any sexual activity at all, but she'd nodded dully. Then the administrator had shown her the villa, which Ilse found unfamiliarly modern and geometric in style—Art Deco, Frau Herta had called it—though not without a bust of Hitler on every floor.

As she pounded tenderloin with a mallet, Ilse contemplated her son's death: Had he been alone? Outside in the wilderness in the Spartan way? Or had he been surrounded by cold, unkind faces? Was it quick and violent, or slow and full of suffering? Had he been afraid, felt pain, missed his mother? Yes yes yes.

She contemplated how many other babies had been killed for failing to meet the criteria of the Reich. Surely Otto wasn't the only one, and he wouldn't be the last. She didn't understand how anyone could look at a human and see *life unworthy of life.*

By the time she finished with the mallet, the meat was so thin there were holes in it.

A flicker of movement caught her eye. She looked out the window and saw several young women in colorful day dresses with Waffen-SS soldiers, gathered at the far corner of the large grounds. They were drinking fussy little cups of something and playing lawn games and performing traditional German dances. Then, a dimpled Little Blond Sister passing by on the arm of a broad-shouldered SS man caught a glimpse of Ilse through the window and winked at her. The girl vibrated with a nervous giddiness that was all too familiar to Ilse. This must be another mating ritual like the ones at Heim Harz.

She moved on to chopping apples, arm aching from her work with the mallet, and added them to a sizzling pan of butter until they were softened but still crisp. Then she removed them and browned the pork in the same pan. Broth and wine to loosen the brown bits of meat sticking to the pan; cornstarch and apple juice for thickening. Boil, slurry, simmer. If nothing else, she had the smell of roasting meat and caramelizing fruit, the texture of the dough she kneaded, the sound of knife against cutting board she chopped.

When she checked the clock on the wall, she saw that lunch was to be served in only fifteen minutes. She'd been working steadily, but she must have been so sluggish that she'd fallen behind. Already she could hear people arriving in the dining room, the voices of middle-aged men, punctuated with the piping of girls, rumbling through the swinging doors. She spooned mustard into the pan on the stove, then remembered she'd already added some—or had she? Nothing to be done about it now. She plated fourteen salads. Little green leaves scattered across the counter. Sweat beaded on her forehead and dampened her underarms.

From the dining room entrance, the administrator appeared. Her narrow body was rigid and clad in a gray dress with a fussy quantity of buttons. Her mouth was like her body: a thin, straight line. Frau Ingrid had been a toad, but Frau Herta was sharp and pointed like a bird.

"Almost finished?" The administrator shaped her mouth into something resembling a smile.

"Almost."

"I hope you will be up to the task."

What if she wasn't? The question wasn't worth asking. An icy rock settled in her throat.

"I just need a few more minutes."

As Frau Herta left, the voices coming from the dining room multiplied, the girls mingling with the officials.

By the time Ilse put lunch on the table, her dress was soaked in sweat and her hair had frizzed around her head. The diners gave her disdainful looks as she brought out the dishes. She would have to focus and work faster if she was going to make it here. And keep better track of her ingredients.

When Ilse had finally finished lunch and dinner and cleaned up the kitchen, she tossed her apron down the laundry chute and trudged up the dark, ornately carved stairs toward her room. The broad-shouldered SS man she'd seen earlier was on his way down the stairs, looking flushed and rumpled. As he passed her, she felt a pinch through her brown dress, right at the spot where hip merged with bottom. She flinched and whirled around. The SS man grinned at her and lifted an eyebrow. Abhorrence curdled in her chest. He'd barely finished with one girl and already he was grabbing at the next? She ducked her head and ran up the stairs, not stopping until she'd reached her bedroom and locked the door.

The room was well-appointed: Royal-blue velvet covered the chaise lounge and chair at the vanity, upholstering the bed and the surrounding curtains. Accents of silver—framed paintings, trim on the furniture—made the room glitter.

She sank onto the eiderdown and allowed the exhaustion she'd kept at bay to wash over her. Her fingers ran along the embroidered pattern of swirling flowers. That contact was all she wanted.

What mysterious forces had brought her to this villa? How had she narrowly avoided a horrific punishment? Her sluggish brain came up with no answers. It must be another nuance of a bureaucracy she'd never understand.

After a while, when the sky outside matched the dark blue of her room, she fetched her copy of *Jane Eyre* from a floorboard that, until Ilse and her shoehorn arrived yesterday, had not been loose.

She should have left the book at Heim Harz, but when she'd packed, numb with grief, all she'd wanted was something that made sense. The risk of bringing it seemed worth it. After turning on the lamp by her bed, she splayed the book wide open with one hand and angled it to catch the light.

She read from the middle of the book, when Jane leaves Mr. Rochester upon finding out his dark secret.

"If I could go out of life now, without too sharp a pang, it would be well for me," I thought; "then I should not have to make the effort of cracking my heart-strings in rending them from among Mr. Rochester's. . . ."

Don't leave him, she thought. Why cause yourself suffering if there's a way to avoid it? Ilse wouldn't have done it. She wished she'd had such a choice to make.

Pain radiated throughout her entire body, a burning ache. It was the physical sensation of missing Otto, the chasm widening, yawning, stretching. With her eyes squeezed shut, she conjured his smile, his warm head. His tiny laugh sounded in the room as if he were there. She rolled onto her side and squeezed her knees up to her chest. Then rolled to her other side. Gasping for air, she hauled herself up and flung open the window. With her head leaning into the night air, she focused on the breeze dancing across her face. The freshness of the air slowed her lungs. She imagined bits of herself floating away on the wind, into the clouds, until there was nothing left.

She was surprised to find she kept living from one moment to the next, but she did.

When the night air had made her cheeks tight with cold, she went back to bed.

❦

Ilse ate lunch at a little wooden table in the corner of the kitchen by the window. Painted white with green trim, almost like a child's table, it was tucked away in an alcove that hid it from both the main and dining room doors. In the two weeks since she'd arrived, she'd been too busy trying to keep up with the demands of the job to eat alongside the others in the dining room. It was just as well; she preferred the quiet and the view of the great linden tree rustling in the breeze.

Today she'd prepared Labskaus using her mother's recipe. It made her think of Mitzi taking dainty bites back in Bremen, but with it came the memory of what happened after. How she'd let her friendship with Mitzi slip away, swallowed the doctrine she'd been taught.

She spooned mashed potatoes into her mouth. They were good because she didn't have to chew them. Food was flavorless to her now, and anything that took too long to chew was harder to get down. Warm and smooth, the potatoes slid down her gullet. She wondered if others found her food to be off, since her tongue and nose—the most essential of a cook's tools—could no longer be trusted. To make up for the lack, she tried to pay extra attention to her recipes and not lose her place, but it was hard to tell if she was successful.

The air filled with the scent of roses and talcum powder, and Ilse stood to greet the administrator.

"Frau Ilse," she said, "do you have a moment?"

She must have forgotten something, the beets or the eggs or the flavor. "Of course."

"I wanted to see how you're settling in."

Ilse swayed. Was she actually expected to be "settling in"? What did that entail? "I'm doing fine."

"And have you found anyone to your liking?"

"What do you mean?"

"You mustn't forget every woman's duty to the Führer." She gave Ilse a meaningful look.

Ilse's only thought, a small one, was *oh*. They couldn't expect her to be willing to have a baby again, not a month since they'd killed her firstborn. She couldn't just have another child for the Führer to do with as he pleased.

But in the few weeks Ilse had been at the villa, she'd noticed that this place was different from Heim Harz. There, the same few women had remained for months on end, with some change as women had their babies and left, and new ones arrived. Occasionally there were mixers and sometimes Schwestern got pregnant. Here, there were no expectant mothers, no babies, only girls who had been at the villa for a few days or weeks and were actively trying to get pregnant. They devoted much of their free time to having picnics and walking around the garden with the steady supply of Waffen-SS soldiers, who it turned out came from the convalescent home adjoining the villa. Often, girls left in black Mercedes, smug and glowing.

This was no maternity home. It was a conception facility. The goal of every girl here was to conceive, then be shipped off to a home, as Lucie and Metta had been. And Ilse was one of them. Would she be put on an endless loop—breeding facility to maternity home and then breeding facility again? She tried to swallow the rock in her throat.

"I won't forget, Frau Herta. I only need some time."

"Time. Interesting. The Führer wishes for every woman of German blood to have six to eight children, at least. There is no time to spare. This is the rebuilding of our country at stake. When we take back our land, we must repopulate it with pure-blooded men and women."

Ilse had no response, so she nodded.

"Do your best to keep the same partner through the completion of a cycle. We need to keep track of the originators." The line of the administrator's mouth turned to an upward curve, while her eyes, the color of a river on a cloudy day, remained unchanged.

Seated on a burlap sack of lentils in the corner of the storeroom off the kitchen, where she was unlikely to be found, Ilse poured a finger or two of whiskey she'd stolen from the cellar. She preferred beer, but whiskey was easier to smuggle. Her heart fluttered in her chest like a trapped bird and she needed it to stop. She slumped against the wall and poured herself another finger. She'd never had whiskey before and didn't care much for the first round. During the second, however, she began to notice the complexity of earthy, sharp, and sweet flavors that changed on her palate the more she paid attention and let it linger on her tongue. Her heart ceased to feel as if it would fly out of her chest. Instead, her insides began to warm and tingle.

She wouldn't be as lucky as she'd been with drunken Max and chivalrous von Thiel. In a place this small, with its true purpose so thinly veiled and frequently acted upon, she wouldn't be able to manufacture the appearance of fulfilling her duties. Frau Ingrid had been an aggressive monitor of the girls' behaviors, but Frau Herta, with her calculating, hawklike vigilance, was a class above. She would miss nothing.

Ilse had thought, after Otto died, that she would never attend a mixer again. There could be no reason to subject herself to them. But here she was, trapped in a breeding facility.

She had a modern sensibility about intercourse. In school, in the BDM, throughout this new society, the message had spread: sex leads to procreation; therefore, sex ought to be encouraged.

Giving herself to Felix had been something she wanted to do and so she'd done it. She'd enjoyed it, but she never spoke of it to anyone. Whether that was from shame or lack of a confidant, she didn't know.

But she'd chosen to do it. Well, now she'd choose to do it again. There was always a choice, if you looked hard enough.

SS men were constantly milling around the villa. They stayed at the convalescent home anywhere from one week to a couple of months, and seemed to have nothing to do during their time there besides flirt with the girls. A handful wore a cast on a wrist or had a few scratches, but overall they were very much on the mend. The soldiers' arrogance repulsed Ilse, and their uniforms reminded her of Otto's death.

She chose a day when she felt the rumbling discomfort, the off-ness of her body and soreness of her breasts that heralded menstruation, the time when a woman was unlikely to get pregnant. She had to be seen making an effort, but that didn't mean she would be successful.

The grounds of the villa were quiet and humid. Thirty-foot-tall spruce trees crowded each other at the perimeter, making it impossible for anyone outside to see what happened within. It also made any view to the outside world impossible—except for one corner. This part of the grounds was raised several feet higher than the rest. There, the trees faded, and only ferns and bushes lined the fence. The corner overlooked a quiet, uneven cobblestone street fifteen feet below. It was in this area that the girls and SS men gathered. From across the grounds, their combined voices mimicked the sound of a rushing river, interrupted by occasional high-pitched, unnatural laughter.

She'd come straight from the kitchen, on her way out making sure to pass Frau Herta, who was chatting with the medical superintendent in the plush chairs by the fireplace in the main room. Ilse was still wearing her brown uniform. Given the utility of the arrangement, looks hadn't seemed important. As she arrived at the grassy knoll, she realized her mistake; all the other girls wore their best dresses, bright blues and yellows, polka dots and florals, with strategic darts nipping at their figures, and carefully curled hair.

Ilse would have to make do, frumpy as she was. Standing for

a moment by herself, she noticed the way the girls cocked their heads just so and smiled with knowing looks. Had she looked like that with Felix? No, it had been much more natural.

The men were really more like boys. Their youth was in their skin, smooth as milk, and their bodies, brimming with energy. They looked ready to pounce, to fight or to take. She resisted the urge to retreat.

One of the boys approached Ilse, slipping a glass of punch into her hands. His hot fingers grazed hers.

"And who are you?" he asked smoothly. He was a head taller than her with a slender frame, Himmler-esque glasses, and spotty skin. He wasn't exactly the ideal SS specimen, but he had the air of someone who knew his way around his weaknesses.

"Ilse. You?"

"Emil. Isn't this a situation?"

"I suppose you could say that." Ilse didn't know what he meant.

"It would almost be a joke. If it weren't a serious duty, I mean. We're like birds in springtime, each one of us trying to sing the loudest and build the prettiest nests."

"It's more of a business arrangement." She eyed him. At least he wasn't a frightening thug.

They discussed, with continued awkwardness, their situation, pretending they were above it by addressing it directly. Finally, after what felt like hours, he invited himself up to her room. She realized she could have done that much sooner and gotten it over with. What had she been waiting for?

From a second-floor window, Frau Herta watched Ilse and Emil walk toward the villa. The administrator jotted something in the notebook she held. One suitor per cycle, she'd told her. Frau Herta was sure to keep careful track.

On the way up to her room, Ilse reminded herself of what her father had taught her: a task was a task. Unpleasantness was a matter of perception; it didn't matter how she felt about doing something when it had to be done. She'd cleaned toilets with this same mentality. She unlocked her bedroom door and led Emil inside.

Her only hope was that it wouldn't hurt. She hadn't been touched since the birth, since she'd been cut and stitched and slowly healed. For all she knew, she would tear all over again.

Emil's lovemaking could be best described as fumbling. He seemed unsure of how to get from the door of Ilse's room to the bed, then struggled with the order of taking off the necessary items of clothing and climbing on top of her and administering close-mouthed kisses. At one point, he reached for her breast, but she saw in his eyes that he decided against it. He placed his paw on the mattress next to her instead. Perhaps he thought it would be unprofessional.

In a few minutes he was done. He stood up, embarrassed by his semi-nakedness as he hurriedly dressed. He thanked her and escorted himself out.

The very best she could think of him was that he hadn't been rough and she was not hurt. That was a success.

She cleaned herself up and stripped the bed of its sheets to be washed, willing her womb to remain empty.

If only she had a way to make sure Emil's huffing, sweaty efforts were unsuccessful. In the thousands and thousands of years that women had been having children—and often not wanting to have them—they must have found a way to avoid it.

Of course they had.

Ilse dropped the soiled sheets. Heart pounding, she fetched out *Physica* from the bottom of her wardrobe. She opened it and skimmed through each plant, eyes hunting for the right words, though she wasn't sure what those words would be. Pregnancy, contraception, prophylactic, fetus? She wished she'd paid closer attention during her casual perusals.

Marshmallow for fever, savin for worms, dauwurtz to purge the stomach . . .

Nothing she was looking for. Though she could not blame Hildegard von Bingen or her mother; these were the sorts of things ladies did not write down. Her body surged with pointless adrenaline that made its home in her thighs, pounding heavily there.

She snapped the book shut and tossed it back in the wardrobe with a thud, then gathered up the laundry to take down to the cellar.

With fresh sheets on her bed, she perched on the wide windowsill, looking out on the darkened shapes of the spruce trees and drinking pilfered whiskey from her water cup.

She finished her second glass and poured another. She'd never been properly drunk before. When would she have had the time or the money to drink enough alcohol to reach—whatever that state was. Oblivion? Bliss? In the storeroom a few days before, she'd stopped herself before she lost lucidity. Now she wanted to find out what it was like to be fully and properly drunk—in private.

After several sips, she decided it was quite pleasant. Floaty. She felt far away from herself and any problems she thought she had. As long as she had this moment, everything was just fine. She leaned her head against the wall and reveled in the sensations, in themselves a form of entertainment.

When she hopped down to visit the toilet, she caught sight of her reflection in the vanity mirror. She couldn't remember the last time she had really looked at herself, taken the time to perceive her face in its entirety, as another might see her. She sat down at the vanity.

She inspected the sharp line of her jaw and the point of her chin. Her large eyes, cast in shadow now, looked droopy and pleased, though they did not always look that way. And her hair, look how it cascaded past her shoulders in golden waves after spending the day in a braided knot. The scar on her temple was dainty, a beauty mark almost, letting the world know she had a story to tell. Yes, she saw how she could be thought beautiful.

Then as she continued staring—this face her only company —it seemed to transform before her eyes. It turned splotchy. Uneven. Hideous. There were shadows under her eyes that made her look sickly. The scar marred her skin, revealing that she was damaged. Her hair was limp around her head. She looked shriveled and shrunken, far older than she was. This was the face of the person she could never escape, and the life that came with it.

She turned away from the mirror and poured herself another glass.

CHAPTER NINETEEN

Ilse stared out the window, unable to look away from the people who'd appeared on the grounds. She did not understand what she saw. The ladle in her hand dripped chunks of quark into the glass bowl below.

They wore faded blue-striped uniforms, filthy, patched, and far too large or too small. They looked ready to fall over from weakness and hunger, yet they worked with superhuman speed. A man in a black uniform stepped into view, a rifle slung over his shoulder.

Then she knew.

She'd heard speculation of the KZs but had never known anyone who'd witnessed what happened there. There was no other explanation for who these men could be. They were supposed to be work and reeducation camps—not pleasant places, to be sure—but these inmates were being overworked and beaten.

Another prisoner appeared in Ilse's line of sight: a man pushing a wooden cart laden with produce across the grounds. He was heading for the kitchen door. She flew to the door, nearly upending the bowl of quark. As her hand touched the cool brass of the doorknob, a memory from her first day at the villa floated back to her. The administrator's grim face looming. *Should you encounter any prisoners, do not interact with them in any way.*

Ilse hadn't paid much attention to it at the time; she'd felt as if she were becoming a prisoner that day and hadn't really known what the administrator meant by it, so the information had been tucked away in the recesses of her mind. She looked at her hand on the knob. All she had to do was turn and open it, then she would be face to face with this man. She opened the door.

The man was already there, emptying the contents of the cart to leave in front of the door, and he looked up with a start. Beneath eyes hollow and dark, a comet of freckles streaked across his face. His head was mostly bald with only patches of hair. She could not begin to guess his age. A yellow triangle overlain with an upside-down pink triangle was sewn onto his sleeve. A piece of string served as a belt, holding his much-too-large pants around his hips.

Ilse opened her mouth, but a hello felt insufficient. She closed her mouth and felt her teeth click together. Then, somehow worst of all, the man went back to work, transferring bundles of plants wrapped in newspaper from the cart to wooden crates on the ground.

"Let me help you," she said at last, and grasped the nearest bundle, which was full of bay leaves. His eyes lowered; he looked anywhere but at her.

"That's not necessary," he murmured. His voice was hoarse and quiet.

She said nothing, only continued.

Peppergrass, blackcurrant, sage, thyme—their mingling scents, sharp and earthy, filled the air. They made short work of it.

"Will you be coming back here?" she asked as they unloaded the last bundles.

He ducked his head in a nod. "We're going to come once a week."

"Where are you coming from?"

"Dachau. We work at the experimental herb garden there, the Plantation. This is the first harvest."

There was a sharpness to the way he pronounced his s's, a hint, perhaps, of Low German.

"Snackst du Platt?" she asked.

"Jau, ick bün en Hamburger Jung."

Ilse sighed in relief. She hadn't heard her mother dialect since leaving home.

"Bremen," she said, gesturing to herself.

There was movement at the corners of his mouth. A faint smile. He began to turn the wheelbarrow around.

"Wait," she said, still in Low German. She cast about for something to give him. She crossed the kitchen to the bread box and brought out two Bierocks, turnovers filled with beef and onion. Ilse wrapped them in a napkin and brought them back to the man.

He snatched the food out of her hands. His movements were so quick Ilse could barely track them: One turnover went straight into his mouth in two bites; meanwhile, he took out a neatly folded, filthy handkerchief that contained a crust of bread. He placed the other turnover next to it, folded up the handkerchief, and stowed it away. It looked as if he'd put the handkerchief and its contents in his pants, but there must have been a pocket on the inside. Over the right knee of his pants, a patch had been sewn and the stripes didn't line up.

"Thank you." He looked her in the eye for the first time. They were large and dark brown and dull. They'd been beautiful once, Ilse was sure. "I have to get back."

"I'll have more food for you next time."

He pushed his cart away, the wheels rattling and wobbling.

Long after he left, Ilse stared out the window at them as they plowed and weeded the garden.

Then she brought the porridge and the fruit and the cheese out to the dining room table, where the girls waited for the meal which, they reminded Ilse, was meant to be served at eight o'clock sharp.

⁂

Over the next few weeks, when the man came to the door, they unloaded the cart together, Ilse trying to work as fast as she could to unload the majority of the bundles so he didn't have to —but he moved with an unnatural speed. She slipped him black bread to remind him of home, or apple cake, or roasted meat. She fashioned him a sturdier belt out of the strings from her spare apron. He told her his name was Thomas. He began to look her in the eye.

They exchanged scraps of information in Low German. He gave her small flashes of his life before. He told her about his life in Berlin, where he'd lived for ten years. He'd been a gardener for wealthy families there, specializing in roses.

Then he would leave and Ilse would watch out the window as he and the other inmates continued to work. Hands braced against the ledge of the sink, nausea rising to her throat, she would contemplate the magnitude of the evils being committed, and how small and powerless she was in the face of them. How Thomas's life could be stamped out by the SS at any moment, and the world would continue without him. How there was so much suffering it was impossible to bear, but so invisible to others it may as well not even exist. And then, how there would be less suffering in the world if the prisoners were dead, if she were dead, if so many suffering people were dead. Perhaps the best act to minimize the suffering of the world was to die.

But she stopped those thoughts. To think that way was to give in. Death was one thing. Surrender was another. She had no right to throw away her life when so many outside her window were fighting with everything they had to keep theirs.

And then she would push herself off the countertop and return to work in a flurry of activity. To lose herself in work, in usefulness, was the best antidote to the morbid hopelessness that bordered on evil itself and threatened to consume her. She asked Thomas, many times, what he needed, what she could get him.

He always shook his head. "If we have anything extra, even a pair of socks, we'll be beaten. It has to be food only, things I can dispose of quickly."

Ilse made do with pushing food and small items like aspirin and soap into his gray hands. She fantasized about ways to get him out of there, but she couldn't even free herself.

One day, he finally said, "There is something. There's a canteen at the camp. People from the outside can send money for prisoners to spend there. With three pfennige, I could buy a coffee . . . "

Ilse sent him all the money she had. She no longer had a use for it. No Otto to protect.

Once, she asked one of the many questions that had been on her mind since they met.

"What does the pink triangle mean?" She gestured to her arm, the same location of the patch on his own body. The yellow triangle must represent the Star of David, but she didn't understand the faded pink one overlaying it.

"It means I'm a homosexual." When she blinked in confusion, he clarified, "I prefer the company of men. That's the charge for which they arrested me."

Surprise registered first. Her mouth gaped open. An uncomfortable mix of confusion, revulsion, and pity roiled inside her. She could barely comprehend such a thing, and to imagine Thomas doing it—whatever it was, because she couldn't imagine how it worked—made her take a step back from him.

But she stopped herself mid-step. She rocked forward again, no doubt looking like she was performing some odd dance. She reminded herself: that was her conditioning, and regardless of what she thought, it should not be a punishable offense. At last words came out: "And for that they think you deserve to be a forced laborer?"

Thomas hadn't missed Ilse's reaction. He looked away, his face more drawn than ever.

"I don't contribute to the propagation of Germany, they say. Not that they'd want me to, with the Jewish blood in my veins. I'm a Mischling."

So, he was doubly cursed in the eyes of the regime. The rock lodged in her throat, yet again. Its presence was becoming habitual. All she could think of to say was, "There has never been anyone less deserving of this than you."

His eyes flickered. "No one deserves this."

He grasped the handles of the cart and pushed it away.

Something in her was waking up. Triggered by rage, it was as if her very self was erupting from the grief and weariness inside her, crumbling the facade she'd built. The facade of a daffodil. The girl who had done as she was told—and nothing more—was dissolving, and as she shook off the debris of that identity, she looked out at the world clear-eyed, untethered and bolder.

One day in early August, Ilse fed Thomas roasted pork and potato salad that were part of an elaborate birthday meal for Frau Herta. She hadn't had time to fix something different for him. He stood by the door and told her, between enormous bites, of childhood summers spent on his grandparents' farm in the Elbe marshlands, downstream from Hamburg.

"I ran barefoot and played in the orchard all day with my brothers," he said. "When the plums were ripe, I'd find a nice plump one and stick it into my mouth—you know how the skin pops and juice bursts out? Well, once that had happened and the flavor turned tart, I would spit what was left out on the ground. Later, I'd step on the pulpy, pitty mess with my bare feet. They felt like slugs and stained the soles of my feet purple. Now I wish I'd eaten every bit of every plum."

"You'll go back there someday. And eat more plums than your stomach can hold."

"It wouldn't take very many these days."

He peered out the door—and he was gone. He'd darted out the door while Ilse was still following his gaze, which landed on a black uniform, too close. They'd gotten too comfortable. Thomas had been in the kitchen for several minutes.

She watched out the window as he ran to the rest of the group and reached for pruning shears. The SS guard walked up behind Thomas, almost lazily. The rifle twirled in his hand, the butt aimed at Thomas's back.

It was her fault. She'd given him food that took too long to eat. It had required a plate and fork and knife.

Ilse didn't think. There was no time. She ran out of the kitchen and across the grounds. As she drew closer to the guard, she called out to him.

The man stopped, curious, like a dog sniffing the wind. She slowed to a walk, and he eyed her, clearly assessing her, deciding if she was attractive. He didn't make any attempt to close the distance between them as she tried to catch her breath and reach him at the same time.

When at last Ilse stood before him, she spoke without

knowing what she was going to say, hoping she could string something together as the words fell out of her mouth. "Officer, I've been meaning to speak with you. I apologize for not doing so before. I kept this prisoner for a bit longer today because I needed his help in the kitchen."

"You did?" The man had high cheekbones, pale skin, and a sneer on his thin lips. He reeked of rotting meat.

"The sink was clogged and this man helped me."

"He's not a man."

Ilse thought about doing violent things to him.

"In any case, I'd like his help around the kitchen for the more difficult and . . . unpleasant tasks, which I'm not suited for." She made her voice sweet and breathy with just a hint of helpless pleading. "I hope you can spare him for a few minutes when you come in the future?"

He stared at her for a moment longer.

"I'm Ilse, by the way." She forced herself to smile sweetly and tilt her head as if she were shy but hopeful.

"Alright then. Ten minutes, starting next week. And I'm Streckenbach. Walter."

She thanked him profusely, beamed, and shook his hand, then returned to the kitchen as quickly as possible. She didn't dare to look at Thomas until she was back inside. He'd worked his way into the middle of the group so that when the SS man casually swung his baton in the direction of the working bodies, none of the blows landed on him.

CHAPTER TWENTY

Though Ilse did her best to avoid the girls passing through, eating her meals separately and spending her spare time in her room or in a corner of the grounds, sometimes they said things that caught her attention. Sometimes they said, "France and Britain have declared war on Germany."

When Ilse learned about the war, the dreaded, inevitable war that everyone had hoped would never come, she was on her lunch break, lying on the grass and pretending she was dissolving into a million pieces that would drift away on the breeze.

The words floated to her through a dense thicket. She propped herself up on her elbows. A chorus of other voices chimed in. Girls reported talk of rations and draft letters and glory. This was their chance to show the rest of the world how supreme Germany really was.

Ilse knew what the Great War had been like—she'd heard so many tales from older generations that it felt as if she'd been there herself. Her neighbor back in Bremen often told her the story of eating nothing but rotten potatoes the whole winter of '17 to '18. Everyone had a story like that. None, soldier or civilian, wanted to live through another war again, another guaranteed, humiliating defeat. They were a country of people who'd learned from their mistakes—yet there they were, following a madman. Yes, she went so far as to believe that now. A regime that believed Felix and Otto and Thomas and so many others were not worthy of life was one that had gone insane. Revulsion boiled in her when she thought of Hitler and those who followed him, and of her past self, who had followed, too. And now, so many people would die for it.

As the days passed, she heard more about the war. Once, she turned the radio in the kitchen on, but couldn't stand the sound of Goebbels's voice. Poland fought back, but the radio assured the German people that Poland would fall. She learned that the ration cards only allotted fifteen hundred calories a day, hardly enough for most. Meanwhile, Lebensborn had everything—coffee, sugar, meat, chocolate—and they had it in abundance.

She knew she should feel more at the news that Germany was now at war with most of Europe, whether it be elation at the prospect of the Fatherland having living space, as all of the Lebensborn staff and Little Blond Sisters seemed to believe, or fear of a doomed conflict, as she gathered most of Bremen believed from their subtle hints over the years—but she couldn't take in the idea of any more suffering.

⁂

Ilse greeted Thomas with a plate of beef rolls with cream sauce and a steaming mug of coffee. Real coffee.

She remembered her first cup of coffee back at Heim Harz. After years of drinking burdock and chicory grounds, the coffee had pummeled her tongue with bitterness and richness. She'd had to take small sips, and couldn't finish a whole cup because it made her shaky. Soon she'd begun to crave it, especially the smell—there was no substitute for that. A small luxury.

He now had time to sit in the little alcove, once Ilse made sure all the doors were tightly closed and Thomas couldn't be seen. She retrieved a wrench from under the sink for Thomas to pretend to use if someone came in. He ate and drank until his belly was distended.

Watching him eat, she wondered if the war brought him hope. If Germany lost, there would be no more camps, and he would be free. He'd told her that conditions had worsened in the camp overnight once the war started. Most of the prisoners had been shipped to other KZs while Dachau was converted into a training camp for soldiers. Thomas and a few others remained to keep up the Plantation, all of them living in a greenhouse.

"You know, at the camp, they give us hardly any food," he said, his nose pointed at the mug. "Too little to live, too much to die. Ersatz coffee and watered-down turnip soup to fill our bellies. And it's all drugged." He gulped down the coffee, gripping the mug with both hands.

"Drugged?"

"That's what I've heard. To lower"—he cleared his throat—"testosterone levels, decrease aggression and desire, make us docile."

Ilse tried not to look away. Now was not a time for embarrassment.

"That's horrible."

Thomas shrugged.

She looked out the window and saw Walter Streckenbach, the sneering SS man, beating the prisoner closest to him, for no reason she could determine.

A version of her ran out again, this time throwing her body between the prisoner and the guard. Perhaps she would put a stop to the beating. Perhaps a few unimportant blows would land on her. Perhaps she would die trying to save him.

But she knew by now it would make no difference except that she'd be giving her life over to the SS, a noble sacrifice and nothing more. Instead, she watched as the guard tired of beating the man and returned to pacing down the row of prisoners, swinging the baton against the ground.

She couldn't bear that she had flirted with him. This man was supposed to be the elite? It was his seed she was supposed to allow inside her, his offspring she was supposed to bear?

She blinked.

An idea so obvious, so good, she was filled with a strange feeling. Hope.

"Do you know what the drug is called?" she asked. "The one that kills desire?"

Thomas shook his head.

"I don't. It's probably a rumor. We've lost our aggression and potency because of the conditions we're living in. Why do you ask?"

They barely had time to get to know each other. They had a few minutes, once a week. There was no time for secrets.

"You know what goes on here? Not officially, but unofficially? Young *Aryans* come here to propagate their genes. These young girls' heads are filled with thoughts that aren't their own, and they don't understand what it means to allow their bodies to be used for such a purpose. They hand their babies over to be raised by the SS, to become the SS. The children will grow up to be indoctrinated, to become terrifying soldiers, just like the guards outside. The mothers will never see their children again. And if those children aren't perfect, well, you know what happens." Her eyes sparked. "I've been doing nothing to stop it. I've been a part of it. I want to prevent myself from having a child. If I were to drug the men who . . . come to my room, make it so they were unable to perform, it would still appear that I was fulfilling the requirements of my position, but without the risk of another—a child."

Ilse paused, catching her breath. Thomas stared at her, not unsympathetic, not surprised. There must be nothing left that was unimaginable to him.

"I'm sorry," she said. "This is nothing compared to what happens at the camps. My problems are nothing."

"It's the other side of the coin." His voice sounded hollow.

They looked at each other with empty eyes.

He squeezed her hand between his bony fingers and left, his cart in tow.

In her room that night, Ilse thumbed through the pages of *Physica* again, this time looking for *impotence, desire, lust* . . . She didn't really know what to look for. It struck her that she knew little about the male body. She couldn't find the words to describe what it might—or might not—do.

She scanned page after page, still in her uniform and smelling of onion, as the summer sky grew dark. Upon turning a page, the word *lust* jumped out at her. "A man who has an over-abundance of lust in his loins should cook wild lettuce in water and pour that over himself in a sauna bath. He should also place the warm, cooked lettuce around his loins."

Myrrh could also extinguish lust, but only when held against the skin. Sparrowhawk fat was effective when applied to the loins.

She couldn't exactly do any of those things to SS men without them noticing. She closed the book and sprawled across the bed, staring at the ceiling and willing the need to act to subside. Instead, it bristled inside her.

CHAPTER TWENTY-ONE

Mandatory mixers were held every Saturday night. They were much like the sporadic events at Heim Harz, but even less subtle in their purpose. Though Ilse's task of keeping the buffet table full of food kept her in the kitchen and in an apron, when she emerged to deliver new trays she was the subject of the insistent attentions of the Waffen-SS. It was nearly impossible to reach the end of the night uncoupled, especially with Frau Herta checking in every few minutes, her expectations clear. Under her glares, Ilse had had to sleep with Emil one more time, no less fumbling or uncomfortable the second time, but he was gone now, and she did her best to avoid further dalliances. She told Frau Herta she was waiting for her next cycle, to be sure she wasn't with child. This was an acceptable excuse: the last thing Lebensborn wanted was to be unable to clearly trace lineage.

On a Saturday at the end of September, Ilse prepared cream slices, plum tartlets, and cheese spread with fresh herbed bread. She'd never cooked for more than a handful of people before this position; she found herself flustered with the tripling and quadrupling of recipes and hadn't yet perfected the timing. She was behind, becoming sticky with sweat, and her hair was frizzing into a halo around her head.

The room, elegant with its lavish furnishings and oversized paintings of Norse goddesses, was lined with men and women lounging. A gramophone played jolly tunes, and in the center of the room, people danced, holding each other close. It was all drenched in artifice.

Ilse set down the tartlets, which were immediately descended upon by several lean and eager young soldiers. She looked past them, agog at the sight of the officer who had just entered the room.

It was Gruppenführer von Thiel, his serious eyes shadowed by his brow. She hadn't expected to see him again; without Otto, she had no ties to his godfather. He must have been checking on his department's most secretive project and decided to personally respond to the call to propagate his genes.

Ilse ducked away; she didn't want to be seen like this, frizzled and aproned, by someone on whom she'd cried, who'd seen the humiliation of her trial. Someone who'd met Otto.

When she had no choice but to emerge a few minutes later with more cakes, she noticed that von Thiel hadn't taken up a conversation with some BDM waif. Hands in his pockets, he was studying the painting of the Norse goddess Frigg lying prone on a bed of royal-blue cloth. As if he felt her eyes on him, he turned and met her gaze. Ilse set down the plates. She wanted to flee back into the kitchen, but it would be unacceptably rude after the eye contact they'd made and the way he was walking toward her.

He greeted her warmly. When he leaned in to kiss her on the cheek, she panicked, wondering if she smelled—of herself, of garlic, of meat. He didn't seem to notice, a good sign, and she

could not help but notice his warmth, the actual physical closeness of another body. She hadn't felt more than the graze of a
hand in months, apart from Emil's ministrations, which she
didn't count.

"I did not expect you to be cooking," he said. "You should
not be put to work like this."

"Everyone here works, Gruppenführer. And this position
was likely the only one I'd know how to do." She thought of her
futile efforts to learn to type. That dream was far behind her; it
seemed to belong to a different person.

"Still, it's hard work. It'll wear you out." He seemed ruffled,
pulling on his tunic.

"I'm more than used to it. Besides, there's nothing else I'm
interested in doing here."

He raised his eyebrows. "Nothing at all?"

Ilse kept her back straight but lowered her eyes, away from
his knowing look. He smiled. "Come, sit with me."

"I have more food to serve."

He waved his hand. "Someone else will do it."

"I'm the only one who works in the kitchen."

He sighed. "Very well, then. Perhaps if you finish soon,
there will be time left for us to catch up over a bottle of wine."

Impatience flicked its tongue inside her. What did he want
with her? After how difficult she'd been, getting upset when she
was supposed to be seducing, he certainly wouldn't pursue her
now. He was doing nothing more than taking up time she'd
rather spend alone in her room, but she couldn't think of a
way out.

"I'd like that," she said, and withdrew into the kitchen.

Half an hour later, her duties were complete. She pinched her
cheeks and took her apron off before returning to the merri-

ment. Von Thiel was waiting with two glasses of blood-red liquid, and she made her way toward him, past the leering men and canoodling couples. This late in the evening their foreplay had lost its zest and become habitual, unenthusiastic—but no less patriotic.

As she sank into the chair across from von Thiel, he gave her one of the glasses and offered his in cheers. She took a sip. The dryness popped on her tongue and instantly she felt the beginnings of relief.

What were they going to talk about? They had only one thing, one person, in common . . .

Von Thiel did not seem to share her concerns. He cheerfully populated their conversation with questions about life in the villa, comments about the weather, observations of the well-appointed room. Ilse felt herself loosening. The conversation was painless, if uninspired, and he seemed to have no agenda—an unfamiliar experience for her these days.

So she held up her end of the conversation and asked, "Where do you live? You seem to be everywhere."

"North of Munich, a forty-five-minute drive from here. I come to the villa occasionally on business, so we may see each other a bit more often. I hope that's alright."

"I'd be delighted." She pushed through her weariness to force a smile.

He refreshed their glasses with the vintage bottle. She was glad she'd practiced being drunk in case it happened again.

"You know, I think you and I are friends now, yes?" He was being playful. Ilse wasn't sure his statement was true, but thought it best to go along. What was friendship, really? She couldn't say for sure that this wasn't it.

She nodded. "I am if you are."

He leaned forward, his eyes intent and earnest, made dark by the dim lighting of the sconces along the wall.

"I wish to know you better. I sense something in you, hidden depths that perhaps not even you have plumbed."

So, he was interested in her, romantically, though she couldn't understand why. Confusion and nervousness crowded her mind.

She knew from his aristocratic name and his uniform alone that his station in life was far above hers. He must live in the kind of houses she cleaned. She tried to imagine it—a manor, a villa, perhaps a small castle. Meanwhile, she felt less beautiful every day, regardless of the racial assessments she'd passed with flying colors. Her hands were callused. Her hair flew away from her head in times of stress, much like it was doing now. Grief and hopelessness had turned her skin gray and her eyes dull. And most of all, she lacked the finesse and charm of a lady. Yet here he was, gazing into her eyes. She knew enough to understand his expression. For reasons she didn't understand, he was attracted to her; now it was for her to decide what to do about it.

Von Thiel was a powerful man, but he seemed safer, gentler, than other SS men. If he claimed her for himself, the administrator would stop pestering Ilse to sleep with every Stormtrooper and Rifleman passing through. There was no telling what a man in von Thiel's position could do for Ilse. He might even help her leave the SS someday.

Her gaze lowered to the elbows resting on his knees and trailed on to his clasped hands. On one hand, he wore a ring with a skull etched upon it; on the other, a simple gold wedding band. Ilse imagined a Hausfrau tucked safely away in the Black Forest, looking after the children. Perhaps their marriage was a loveless one, though it was just as likely that von Thiel loved her well enough but believed in the importance of propagating the Aryan race, and bigamy—perhaps even polygamy—was a part of that.

But it didn't matter what she thought; it was not for her to make that moral decision for him. Her only responsibility was to find a way through the mess that had become her life.

"Alright, I'll tell you about myself," she said. She smiled, the kind of smile she hadn't used in over a year, since Felix. It was a natural smile. True flirtation meant not holding back, rather than the forced performances of the other people in this room. It was easier with the hum in her head, for which she silently thanked the wine. "It's not something I've given much thought. There has always seemed to be something else to do. I suppose I'm a girl, trying to make her way through this world." She trailed off, unsure what to say next.

He leaned back, pleased with her, pleased with himself.

"I was right; you don't know yourself yet. But you will. You're a flower bud waiting to bloom, a caterpillar in its cocoon."

Ilse didn't like this image of herself, a small being with no awareness or power, which could be crushed under the sole of a shoe. She rolled her shoulders back and pressed on.

"I like cooking. It's satisfying to make food people enjoy, and probably even more satisfying to work with the food, all its textures, smells, colors. Spring is my favorite season, when I can go outside and lie in the grass and feel the world coming to life around me. I wanted to go to university, but I also don't know what I would have studied so it's just as well I didn't go. Your turn. Tell me who you are."

He chuckled at her boldness. He surely didn't receive commands often, and not from a woman, a cook.

"Well, I spent the first twelve years of my life in Austria, where my German parents waxed poetic about the Fatherland. When we finally returned to our ancestral home in Pomerania, I was dismayed by the castrated ruins I found. Where was this bold country of composers, philosophers, and poets I'd heard so much about? And soon we were at war—I was too young to fight in the Great War, barely. Instead, I studied the origins of our race and discovered them in myth and legend. There is much about Germany that cannot be understood, either because it has been lost to history or because it is simply beyond our comprehension. I choose to dwell in that place, where mysticism meets reality."

"How do you do that?"

"I am at work on many projects for the Reichsführer. I can't discuss most of them. You see, I've been leading the SS's efforts to uncover our mystic roots. For example, I've studied the mythical land of Thule, that northerly island written about by the Greeks, the lost land of ice and summer, of farmers and fair-haired maidens, believed to be the birthplace of the Aryan race. We will re-create this utopia, right here on German soil. Humans will regain their large statures, their superior intellect, and their psychic abilities."

Aryan, SS, superior—she blocked those words from her mind when he spoke them. She could not afford to let her revulsion show, so she listened around those words, smiling as enthusiastically as she could. He edged forward on his seat in his excitement.

"One of my particular areas of interest is Wewelsburg Castle. You likely won't remember that I mentioned it before. It's the spiritual home of our sacred SS brotherhood. All important SS gatherings will take place there once we have remodeled it according to our designs. SS officers will even be buried there."

He lit up, enchanted by the mysteries of which he spoke. Ilse wished she could appreciate anything that much. She nodded along, though most of what he said made little sense to her. Von Thiel stopped talking; as he looked at her, his expression changed.

"I would like to take you to the castle. A pure German woman like you belongs in a place like that."

"It sounds like a place for men. Rather gloomy, I imagine."

"Hardly. It's been decorated in the Nordic fashion. I'd like to know what you think of the place."

"I'm certain that someday you will." Ilse smiled with her eyes.

Von Thiel had been leaning closer and closer to her. Only a few inches closer and their noses would touch, then their lips. She looked at the clock on the wall. *Jane Eyre* had taught her that if she bestowed all her affections at once, he'd lose interest in her. She needed him to come back, and keep coming back for a long time. No more brief, awkward encounters—she would be a mistress. Like Hannelore.

"Oh my." She hoped her surprise sounded genuine. "It's so late. Look, nearly everyone has gone. I must be getting to bed."

"There is a dinner for SS officers this Saturday," he said, rising with her. "I would like you to be my guest."

"Me?" Ilse stiffened. A formal event, SS men—she would be out of place. More than that, she'd be disgusted.

"Yes. I enjoy your company, and the night will be much more pleasant with you by my side. It's a favor you could do for me. Additional perks include wearing a new dress and eating elegant food which you have not made yourself."

Ilse remembered herself and forced a playful smile. "Well, don't get your hopes up. It's difficult to make me presentable."

"You're level-headed, you have the skills any good German woman ought to have, and you're as perfect-looking as it gets— made to be shown off."

Ilse squirmed, wishing he would stop looking at her like she was a goddess or a sculpture. He hadn't called her beautiful, attractive, or lovely—he'd said she was perfect-looking. As if there was one ideal and she met it.

"I'm not sure that I'm allowed outside the grounds," she said.

He flapped a hand. "I'll take care of that."

She felt strangely cold. She could still back out, find some excuse. If she didn't, she would move irrevocably forward on this path.

"I would be honored."

Chapter Twenty-Two

True to his word, von Thiel sent a gown for Ilse to wear. It arrived in a flat white box lined with delicate tissue paper the morning before the dinner. She was relieved that he hadn't sent her a dirndl to emphasize her Germanness. Instead, it was a slinky black silk dress with a deep V in the back that made her feel naked, and black pumps, black gloves, and a black stole to accompany it. Perhaps he wanted her to match his black uniform.

After work, she bathed, scrubbing her skin red. She feared no amount of soap would remove the taint of the kitchen from her flesh. Her hair she pinned back in an attempt at an Olympia roll the way she'd seen Lucie do; though she didn't quite manage the elaborateness of the hairstyle, her hair was smooth and held firm in its position. As she slipped into the gown, which felt like a second skin, she wondered why he would go to the trouble of giving her something so fine.

Von Thiel picked her up in his Mercedes, even getting out and opening the door for her. She took her place on the soft black leather of the seat. This was her first time in the front seat of a car.

"I would have thought you'd have a chauffeur," she said once von Thiel returned to the driver's seat.

"Normally, I would," said von Thiel, inserting the key into the ignition and starting the engine, "but I got my start as a chauffeur, back when I was very young. I've never wanted to give up the independence, and the feeling of controlling a powerful machine."

She watched as he put the car into gear, master of the mysterious levers and pedals that somehow made the car move.

"I like that," she said. "Maybe you will teach me sometime."

"You want to learn to drive?"

"Yes, why not?"

"I suppose there's no good reason why you shouldn't learn, is there?" Von Thiel gave her a hint of a wink as he twisted to look out the rear window. "Alright, I'll teach you someday."

He anticipated a someday for them. There was hope, then, that her plan would work.

As they drove to the dinner party in the heart of Munich, nerves jangled inside her. Not only was she unpracticed in the ways of fine dining, but she was worried that she would be unable to hide her revulsion for her dining companions. At the villa, she simply avoided interacting with the other residents for extended periods of time. If she was stuck with someone one-on-one, she could usually find something human about them, but all together in a group, they blurred into one entity defined by their worst qualities. She would have to be careful—limit her drinks, watch her words, say as little as possible. That was safer than trying to lie, although she was getting better at that.

They arrived outside an enormous neoclassical villa, half-covered in ivy. And she'd thought the Lebensborn villa was impressive. A valet opened Ilse's door.

Stepping into the night air, Ilse braced against the nip of early fall. Von Thiel appeared by her side and held his arm for her to take. Together, they entered the warmth and light of the home. The valet relieved her of her stole, then led them toward the rumbling of voices in the drawing room.

In a blur, she was introduced to dozens of black-uniformed men and their wives, dressed in the height of French fashion. The air was so thick with perfume and cologne that she felt like she was choking on it. A tray of champagne flutes passed under her nose and instinctively she grabbed one. Von Thiel was no longer at her side, swept away by the men. Ilse felt unmoored without him. She made do with nodding, smiling, and providing short responses as the women around her chattered.

The women all wore makeup and couture—finery that defied the values of the Reich. Being in the inner circle of the SS made them above the rules. The women either complimented her or insulted her in such a way that it appeared to be a compliment.

"It's wonderful to see a fresh face," said a woman, petite and blond and delicate. Her voice dripped with condescension.

"And a *natural beauty* at that," said a brassy, bright-eyed woman. She looked like fool's gold. Her eyes snagged on the scar on Ilse's temple. The woman opened her mouth—perhaps to ask about it—but Ilse cut her off.

"How wonderful that you can enhance your looks with French influence. I remain German in all ways." That quieted the women.

It gradually became clear to her that it was not wives in attendance, but mistresses. No wonder von Thiel felt he could bring Ilse. The bright-eyed woman was Fräulein Behrens, a beautiful former actress who was there as the guest of Hitler's secretary, Martin Bormann. Apparently, Goebbels and Bormann had fought for her affections, but she was repelled by Goebbels.

"He threatened to end my career in film. I told him I'd

rather clean stages than be his mistress," Fräulein Behrens declared with a puffed chest, looking as if she expected applause.

The delicate blond sniffed and tilted her chin in defiance, which Fräulein Behrens noticed.

"I'm terribly sorry. What a fool I am. Of course I didn't mean that." Fräulein Behrens placed a hand on the woman's arm and squeezed. The gesture was overly familiar and Fräulein Löhr looked taken aback. Ilse didn't blame her. Who was this flamboyant woman?

"It's nothing. You're right in fact," said Fräulein Löhr. "My relationship with Joseph—Herr Goebbels—didn't end well. I do not recommend crossing his wife."

The ladies gathered in, almost imperceptibly, but the faintest rustling of taffeta and a collective inhale tightened the air in anticipation of gossip. Fräulein Löhr saw that she had her audience. She straightened her shoulders and raised her gaze to meet the women's eyes.

"After we'd been seeing each other for a few months, Joseph gave me a key to a secret passageway in his home. I used it to enter and visit him in secret. We had the run of the house, with his wife sound asleep in her bed. It was a wonderful time. But Magda, the shrew, found out about all of it and had the lock to the secret passageway changed." A few of the women suppressed chuckles. Fräulein Löhr shot them glares and they straightened their faces. "Very petty, if you ask me."

Ilse watched the interaction, nonplussed. How could these women take themselves so seriously? A woman appeared in the circle across from Ilse. The woman's heavily painted lips smirked—laughing at, not laughing with. Her copper hair fell in carefully styled waves, nearly covering one knowing, kohl-darkened eye.

She looked so different with dyed hair and makeup that Ilse didn't recognize her at first.

Hannelore.

Her heart convulsed and squeezed. It was about to burst. Hannelore caught Ilse's eye, winked at her, and melted out of the circle. A moment later, an arm entwined with hers. Ilse squeezed it. A laugh bubbled out of her. She wanted to cry. Her friend, the one she was never going to see again, was here.

Hannelore whispered, "We mistresses can get rather caught up in ourselves sometimes, can't we?"

Ilse arched an eyebrow. She wasn't a mistress—yet. "I'm not sure if I'd choose Bormann over Goebbels myself, but I rather prefer neither."

Hannelore threw back her head and laughed.

"You're with Gruppenführer von Thiel, right? He's a handsome one, in that serious, sensitive kind of way. I prefer them young, athletic, and ambitious."

"Are you still with your pilot? Who is he?"

"Darling, I'm with Reinhard Heydrich."

Heydrich was discussed constantly on the radio: The second-most feared man in Germany, and one of the most powerful—head of the SD, Sicherheitsdienst, the intelligence agency. Newly appointed Director of the Reich Security Main Office. Strategic mastermind. Hitler's favorite. He was also known throughout the Reich for being heartless and cruel, not just executing the more brutal Nazi policies, but enjoying it. She stifled a shudder.

"Reinhard isn't so bad in private," Hannelore muttered low enough to not be overheard.

"Yes, he's Hitler's 'man with an iron heart,' but mostly he's ambitious."

Ilse forced a gracious smile. "I'm sure he treats you well."

Hannelore brought them to a window seat ensconced in

velvet cushions, pillows, and drapes. It was colder by the window, which, under orders from the Reich, had been blacked out to prevent the light of the party from escaping. It was also quieter. Ilse began to feel at ease.

"I had no idea you were in Munich," Ilse said. "Have you been here since you left Heim Harz?"

"Yes, this is where Reinhard got me the apartment. He travels here on business frequently, which allows us to see each other. Munich isn't the place I would have chosen—the people are so dry, so conservative, with their work ethic and their dirndls. Berlin was what I used to dream of, but now Munich is my city of freedom. I take it gladly."

"You look better than ever. This life suits you."

Hannelore nudged her.

"How are you? How is Otto? How did you come to be in Munich?"

Ilse wanted to throw herself in Hannelore's arms and let loose her grief. Instead, she looked out the window as if there was anything to see besides black paint.

"Otto had birth palsy. They killed him. And I'm still in Lebensborn, proving my ability to breed. I can't leave."

Hannelore's mouth gaped open. She looked stricken.

"We shouldn't talk here," Ilse said. Too many emotions swirled within her. She wouldn't be able to contain them all. And she wouldn't be able to say what she had to say with so many SS ears nearby.

"Come to my apartment. Next week."

The valet announced dinner. Von Thiel reappeared at her side as everyone shuffled toward the dining room. She took his arm, mostly to keep him from wandering away and leaving her alone with a Fräulein Behrens or a Fräulein Löhr. Her head was still buzzing—Hannelore was here. They'd found each other, somehow. For once Ilse was grateful to the SS, if only for being such a tight-knit organization that paths might cross and recross.

They gathered around the large table, already covered with fine porcelain dishes and crystal glasses, the likes of which she had set many times for the Anschützes in Bremen. If she knew how to set these fancy tables, surely now she could eat off one. Ilse sank into the chair in front of her.

Stillness tightened the air in the room.

She looked up and realized that everyone else had remained standing. It was clear that she should have waited to be seated. Several footmen appeared, held out the chairs for the diners, and pushed the chairs in while the guests sat, all in unison.

Ilse looked down, as if she could will the people around her to disappear from her consciousness, and fixated on the light glinting off the crystal glass in front of her. She didn't understand why von Thiel had brought her when she so clearly didn't belong here.

When the first course came, she took care that her bites were small and delicate, while making trivial conversation with the older man next to her and trying to laugh airily at his jokes. Then she noticed she was the last person eating, which further embarrassed her, and for the first time in her life, she abandoned the rest of the food on her plate.

As with everything else that evening, the meal was entirely French: An herbed canapé, which tasted like a garden on a warm day. Then a touch of French onion soup, so savory it was almost sweet. Then herring, roasted lamb, Salade Lyonnaise. The glasses were filled with endless bottles of wine.

Ilse listened to von Thiel's conversation with the man on the other side of him. She leaned forward a bit to see: it was Reinhard Heydrich. Adrenaline burned and squeezed through her veins. Though he was considered handsome, Ilse hadn't thought so from pictures. But seeing him in person, she understood what others saw. It wasn't so much his long, straight nose, his tall, athletic build, or even his piercing gaze. She remembered Hannelore saying she'd never seen someone so intimidating. Every lie she'd ever told the Reich rose to the surface, and she felt sure he could see them in her eyes.

On Heydrich's other side was Hannelore, bright and bold among the painted porcelain and sparkling crystal, looking like a jewel herself and having a lively conversation with a slovenly looking man who must be Hitler's private secretary. Hannelore —alive and well and close. Ilse felt giddy.

"With Otto Rahn gone, the search is over." Heydrich's voice was high, cool, utterly controlled.

"Not if I can help it," von Thiel said. He almost seemed to be daydreaming, right in the midst of the dinner party. "I liked Rahn well enough as a person, but he didn't have what is required to find the Holy Grail."

Heydrich sipped from his wine glass. "Rahn was a degenerate. A homosexual has no place finding objects of mystical importance for the SS."

"I believe I am best suited to continue the search, for the Holy Grail *and* for the lost Aryan civilization," said von Thiel. He swirled the sherry in his glass, contemplating the middle distance.

"But I thought you were out of the Reichsführer's favor? Does he not have you in the barracks—"

"A temporary setback. We are all in and out of favor occasionally." Something flashed in von Thiel's eyes—a darkness, a danger perhaps. How casually he'd interrupted Heydrich, how Heydrich now looked like a bird of prey, eyes sharpened on his next meal. But von Thiel was not deterred from his original line of thought, and continued on. "After Rahn's death, I took possession of his notes. His search had gone on for years and he did not have many good ideas left—he'd already scoured France,

Italy, and Iceland for the object, but there is promising evidence in India as well as an island off Norway."

"My friend, our priority must be to rid our German blood of its impurities and reclaim our land," Heydrich said. "The treasure hunts can wait for the Final Victory."

"But why? The search has gone on for hundreds, thousands of years already. Perhaps items such as the Holy Grail will fuel us with the wisdom and power to achieve victory."

Ilse looked away. She kept her face straight, took a larger sip of wine, and stared at the Meissen figurines carefully arranged in the cabinet across the room for the rest of the meal.

As they drove home that night, Ilse asked, "Why is the Holy Grail important to the SS? Isn't it a Christian object?"

"Indeed, it was the last cup from which Jesus drank, and later it caught his blood as he perished on the cross. Artifacts like that carry immense power in them, regardless of the ideology from which they came. Think of Jesus's influence on modern civilization. I would like to harness that influence."

"I see. And what happened to that man you were talking about? Otto something?"

He glanced at her. "Otto Rahn. He was a researcher for the SS. He was also a homosexual. The Reichsführer overlooked this crime because of the importance of his work for the SS. As the years went by, it became clear that Rahn was getting no closer to finding the Holy Grail. That, combined with Rahn being caught in a . . . blatant act of indiscretion with another man, got him sent to be a guard at Dachau. That's how the SS are often punished."

Von Thiel's jaw clenched, briefly. The muscles fluttered, then disappeared.

"He couldn't stomach the duties, so he resigned and left.

But no one leaves the SS. He was tracked down and given the option to either take his own life or become a prisoner at Dachau. He chose the former; he froze to death on a mountain in Austria this past March."

She looked at him. His delivery was dry and his face was a mask. She wondered if he ever wished for a way out.

This was the moment to get it over with. She asked him to walk her to her door, voice soft and full of promises. He parked in the lot between the villa and the SS convalescent home and she led him up the stairs. He followed behind her, fingertips at her elbow, grazing down to her wrist, playing with the seam of the low back of her dress. She felt floaty and was glad she'd drunk more wine than she'd planned.

"No, Ilse." He caught her hand as she turned down the hallway to her room. "There's a better place for us."

She didn't understand. Was he simply important enough to be able to use whatever room he pleased? Or did he come here so often for this purpose that he had his own room? Ilse opted to believe it was the former. As he led her down the opposite hallway, she shot sideways glances at him. He was at the ideal age for a man: late thirties, fully grown into himself without the infantile look of youth and the uncertainty, or, conversely, the arrogance that came with it. He moved with confidence, and his uniform, once she looked past its frightening nature, showed off his square shoulders, slim waist, and confident gait. She wondered what his body was like under that suit. What kind of lover he was. She would find out soon enough.

Von Thiel took a key from his pocket and opened the door to what turned out to be a suite. There was a small sitting room with engraved mahogany furniture clustered around a fireplace, furniture her father would admire for its craftsmanship while being disgusted by the extravagance.

"I hope this will be comfortable for you." He leaned against a doorway. Beyond, she could see a bedroom almost entirely consumed by a large bed draped in black and blood-red damask curtains. Ilse trailed a hand along the back of the couch, trying to look like she belonged.

Von Thiel crossed his arms and the glint of his wedding ring caught her eye. So, she would be the other woman. His wife would raise the children, tied to the hearth, and Ilse would be the mistress, object of his desire.

She went to him.

All the while, she was somewhere deep within herself, watching his body and hers do things that seemed apart from her. She observed with the curiosity of an animal of prey. He was gentle, tender, worshipful. He took his time and seemed interested in how Ilse's body responded. She considered leaving her place of safety, truly feeling the sensations he was causing in her, and which she expressed enthusiastically for his benefit, but hesitated. Better to wait and see.

She couldn't help but think of his reaction if he knew the truth about her. That her Aryan blood had mixed with a Jew's and a child had been born out of it. That von Thiel was now also defiled as a result. She could picture him drawing away in disgust, banishing her from the room still naked, sending her to a KZ or straight to the scaffold. She couldn't breathe. She closed her eyes and forced herself to exhale.

After, she lay on her side and von Thiel curled his body around her. Then he shifted away, and the pads of his fingers ran across her back. She shivered.

"What are these?" he asked.

"Hm?"

"Scars. All over your back."

It was an exaggeration to say "all over." There were only a few. Ilse forgot about them most of the time; it wasn't as if she could see them.

"They're from when my father disciplined me as a girl."

"He hurt you?" Von Thiel's voice took on a new quality—commanding, almost harsh.

"That's how fathers command a daughter's respect. And it only left scars from one time. You must do the same with your children?"

"Never." He removed his hand from her back, sounding offended. He stroked the scar on her temple. "This is from him, too?"

"Not directly. Shortly after my mother died, I ran to him as he was leaving for work—I thought he would disappear, too. But I fell and glanced off the corner of a table. If my mother had been alive, she would have applied the right herbs so it wouldn't scar. But it was only him."

Von Thiel scoffed. "Do you still speak to this man?"

"No." Her voice almost cracked. Almost.

"Good." She felt his body relax. "He doesn't deserve your attention."

She tried never to think about her father. He'd hurt her so many times. He'd trained her like a dog to do as he said, believe as he believed. And he'd been so horribly wrong. If she'd been allowed to keep her own mind, if she'd been strong enough, perhaps her life would have turned out differently and she wouldn't be here. Her stomach twisted. It felt as if a vigorous laundress was wringing her out like a towel.

Von Thiel gathered her in his arms and held her all through the night, something she'd never experienced before.

Every night at this time, as she was falling asleep, she cried a few silent tears for Otto. It was a habit her body had developed. It happened even if she wasn't thinking about him. Her one daily release. She couldn't cry in front of von Thiel, not again. And, she found, she didn't need to. Von Thiel's arms, swaddled around her, were almost comforting.

Everything she'd ever known was unraveling. Here she was in bed with an SS officer, resisting the urge to feel safe.

Chapter Twenty-Three

Hannelore flounced out of the car, wearing an emerald-green dress and a jaunty halo hat. Ilse could hardly believe she was real, had almost convinced herself that Hannelore hadn't been at the dinner party, but here she was.

Ilse had told Hannelore before leaving the dinner party that it would be best if Hannelore came to her; she wasn't sure she was permitted to leave the villa without von Thiel, but she didn't mention that. So she'd requested permission to have a visitor, making it known that Hannelore was mistress to Heydrich. Frau Herta had not been pleased, but the SS hierarchy was a powerful force. She'd grimly given her permission, limiting the visit to two hours and certain rooms of the house.

Ilse brought Hannelore straight up to her room, where she had tea waiting. The less she and Frau Herta saw of each other, the better.

Hannelore made herself comfortable on the extra chair Ilse had brought in from the parlor. Ilse sat self-consciously at the edge of the velvet chair of her vanity and poured the tea.

She noticed that Hannelore wore just as much makeup as

she had at the dinner party. Her burgundy lips and black-rimmed eyes made her look like a cabaret dancer who'd never learned to create a day look, yet it suited her.

Then she remembered this was Hannelore she was talking to, so she said the thought out loud. Hannelore burst out laughing. The force of it threw her head back, sending her carefully styled waves cascading down her back. The sound bounced off the walls. Ilse was pleased with herself.

"You're lucky you can wear makeup. I'm tired of having to be 'naturally beautiful.'"

Hannelore stared at her. "How can anyone be that? Beauty takes effort. Not that I'm saying anything about you—you have as much natural beauty as it's possible to have. But we women must always do more."

Ilse shrugged. "I'm used to it. Being in an isolated environment all the time, only seeing the same people, other girls who aren't allowed to wear makeup either, makes it feel unnecessary after a while."

"That's not true. The others are wearing makeup, I promise you. I always did at Heim Harz."

"Well, some of them cheat, but most don't."

"Listen. Do you want to keep this von Thiel?"

She could see no practical alternative, so she said, "Yes."

"Then I will show you the tricks I can't believe you haven't figured out for yourself yet. Did you really think I was a natural blond?"

Ilse gaped. Hannelore's brassy waves had suited her so well Ilse hadn't looked twice.

"I needed to be blond to get the job at Heim Harz, so I became a blond. No one the wiser."

"What is your natural hair color?"

"Some shade of brown. I haven't seen it in years." Hannelore shrugged. "Now. You're the cook, yes? So you have access to everything you need. Take me to the kitchen. And bring your tea." She jumped up, looking ready to fly or to dance. Ilse smiled and stood, too, leading her downstairs to the kitchen.

"Excellent." Hannelore surveyed the gleaming, white-tiled surfaces. "I need beet juice. And cinnamon."

While Ilse fetched the ingredients, Hannelore retrieved a makeup brush from her purse. Then she sat Ilse down at the table in the alcove.

"In summer you can use blackberries and cherries instead of beets, but these are the best fall and winter options."

Perched on the table, Hannelore dipped the brush in the tea, then into the cinnamon.

"Close your eyes," she said, and lined Ilse's eyes with it. Ilse could feel Hannelore's breath on her cheek. It was oddly intimate, though she supposed this was how girlfriends passed their time with each other.

"Is Heydrich in love with you?" Ilse asked.

Hannelore's left eye twitched, just a little.

"I have no idea. Does your Gruppenführer love you?"

"He doesn't really know me."

"A man doesn't need to know you to love you."

"I'm not sure you know what love is."

"You're probably right. But do you know?"

Ilse had only ever loved one small person. "No, not that kind of love."

"That's my girl! Stay away from it if you can. It gets in the way of all the things that are good for you."

Ilse realized that neither of them had asked the other if they were in love with the men they were seeing—only if the men were in love with them. As if falling for Heydrich and von Thiel were not a possibility, not a consideration.

Their situations were not so different. And yet, Hannelore was living glamorously while Ilse worked six days a week in a kitchen. She wondered if she ought to set her sights higher, to something beyond subsistence.

After Hannelore filled in Ilse's eyebrows with cinnamon, she dunked a towel into the beet juice, staining it pink. She dabbed Ilse's lips and cheeks with the juice and gently rubbed the color in with her forefinger.

"There." Hannelore surveyed her work with satisfaction, then led her back up to the bedroom and sat her down in front of the vanity. "Take a look."

Ilse looked like herself, only brighter. As if something exciting had just happened to her, a run through an orchard on a summer evening, a kiss from a boy she liked. She looked the same, only better.

"No one will ever guess you're wearing makeup, because you're not. You're still a natural beauty. I've been a wonderful influence on you already."

"How did you learn to do this?"

"First, my situation in life was comfortable, and then it was not, but I'd grown used to looking a certain way and the advantages that came from it, and I wasn't going to give that up. Instead, I was going to make a career out of it—my first career, anyway. So I needed to find ways to look my best that didn't cost a pfennig."

"What was your first career?"

"I was a coquette."

Ilse almost laughed. It was a joke. But it wasn't a joke. Hannelore looked at her as if she'd said "secretary" or "teacher."

"Really?"

"Sure. After my parents died, it was just me and my six siblings left. Somehow it became my duty to stay home with the four little ones, to keep everyone fed, everyone clean. I love the adorable pests, but I couldn't stand the grime of their fingers, their constant tears and needs. And there was the tension of a violin string about to snap from my older brother and sister. We sold almost all the furniture in the apartment and kept the windows closed to keep the warmth in, and the stink of so many humans close together was wretched. Finally, I couldn't stand it. I needed to get out, be free, and fly. The means by which I got there were of little importance."

"And being a coquette gave you freedom."

"Yes. And no. It wasn't a bad profession, actually. The money was excellent—I earned five hundred marks a month, more or less."

It was as if someone had knocked the wind out of her. Five hundred marks. Ilse earned sixty-five.

"I sent a portion of my earnings to my siblings every month —still do, in fact. They're too much for me to take care of myself, so I do this instead." She leaned back on the chair. "Are you scandalized?"

"No," Ilse said. "I'm sure I would do it myself if a situation arose where it was necessary." Similar to her current situation, in fact. "How on earth did you go from the brothel to a Lebensborn home?"

"I was there for about a year before my two older siblings found me. They were horrified by the shame I'd brought to the family." She waved her hand to indicate the length and tediousness of their lecture. "They were quite bothersome. They told me about the opportunity at Lebensborn. My brother's friend knew someone who recommended me for the position. I knew I could do secretarial work in my sleep, and it would get my siblings out of my hair. I neglected to mention my previous experience in my application to Lebensborn, though considering how things work, it should have been an advantage. I figured working at Lebensborn could only lead to other opportunities, in one way or another. Before I met Reinhard, I was planning to disappear again after my siblings were satisfied that I was settled in. Find a new brothel."

"What was it like, being a coquette?"

"There's a level of skill in being a lady of the night that most don't understand. I went to the best brothel in Berlin. I wanted the most sophisticated clients, with whom I could discuss Goethe and Rilke late into the night. So I learned to move like water around rocks in a stream, like a snake seeking its next meal. I learned to pour drinks in a way that displayed my wrists without a drop spilled, and to speak with any man in such a way that he was stimulated without being made to feel that I was more intelligent than him. I soon found that what the men wanted was companionship, a kind ear to receive their secrets, a lap on which to rest their weary heads. The deed itself makes them feel like men; the rest makes them feel human."

Hannelore offered Ilse a cigarette from a silver card case. Lebensborn forbade smoking, and she'd barely smoked before that, only a cigarette here and there on particularly long days. She leaned over and opened the window, then slid one out of the case. Hannelore struck the match with a flare and a sizzle and lit both their cigarettes.

Eyes glazed, Hannelore let out a chuckle. "My first client was a round, balding man with weeping eczema across the left side of his face. My madame was testing me. Could I charm a most uncharming man? Of course I could. It was excellent practice for Reinhard. Though he's different, an equal. Every interaction is a battle of the wits. It's invigorating. We converse in French and English; we discuss politics and literature."

"And have you been able to fly again?"

Her face lit up. "It took some doing. After the war started, all the planes were claimed for the effort. But with Heydrich's influence and connections, I now get to fly a glider every Saturday."

Ilse studied Hannelore's blissful face. She seemed to possess the confidence of a man, certain that the world would grant her every wish, but maintained the warmth and grace of a woman. The ache that had lived inside her ever since Otto's death eased, just a little, for the first time. She could breathe.

A couple of hours later, Ilse walked Hannelore out. Waiting for her on the steps was a man. In the dying autumn light, she couldn't see who it was right away. But he turned his face to the light and she saw: Reinhard Heydrich. His close-set eyes fixed on her.

Ilse's mind scattered. Terror threatened to paralyze her. How could Hannelore be with a man this dangerous? But she gathered her wits in time to salute, and he accepted it with the casual wave of a high-ranking officer. At what rank, what level of power, could a man accept the salute instead of returning it? Was there an exact science to it?

Hannelore bestowed a kiss on his cheek, which he accepted with the same attitude with which he'd received Ilse's salute.

"And who are you?" he asked Ilse, though he sounded as if he didn't care.

"Ilse Rademann, Obergruppenführer. I was at the dinner party last Saturday."

"I see."

He penetrated her with his stare. It was meant to intimidate. Summoning up all her willpower, Ilse returned the gaze mildly. She looked danger in the eye every day. His was just another face of it.

As she went back inside, she saw Heydrich turn to Hannelore, who had become a golden sun, shining only on Heydrich. She wondered if she could ever be as good a mistress as that.

Chapter Twenty-Four

Ilse peeled potatoes in front of the window, eyes resting on the linden tree. It was bursting with green still, but soon it would turn red and yellow and its leaves would fall.

The war had gone on for over a month now. She was thinking about it in terms of food. What were people eating, and how much? On the rare occasion that she went to the parlor and listened to the radio, announcers recommended dehydrated foods over canned to save metal. Meat was discouraged—instead, flour dishes consisting of soups or noodles. They added, somewhat snippily, "It is wrong to say that such dishes based on flour don't 'fill us up.' We do not eat to fill our stomachs until the next meal, but rather to provide our bodies with the necessary nutrients." From this Ilse understood that the rest of Germany was hungry, while Lebensborn received as much food as it ever had.

Turn off the radio, and it was as if the war did not exist.

Thomas and his fellow blue-clad inmates came into view. She tossed the peeler onto the counter with a clang and ran to the door to meet Thomas and his rickety cart, stocked now with a dwindling supply of herbs.

She greeted him with a bushel of dusty purple plums. His eyes widened above his freckles.

"It's not as many as you had at your grandparents' farm, but I hope it's enough," she said as he fell upon them. He ate, not just the juices but the whole fruit this time, spitting the stones into a bowl Ilse provided for him. Soon he pushed the basket away, groaning in pain.

"What a kind gift," he said, gazing with longing at the remaining plums. "I can't eat anymore, or I won't be able to keep them down."

As they unburdened the cart, Thomas said, "I have good news for you. I was assigned to the research room at the Plantation, and while I was there, I found herbs for what you need."

Ilse's heart contracted with equal parts fear and hope. "You shouldn't have. Why take that risk?"

Thomas's jaw was set. "We must keep each other human. That is the one thing I know."

As he slid off his wooden shoe, the newspaper he wore in place of a sock came away, too. Underneath, his feet were gnarled, with open sores from constant rubbing and no protection. His toenails were jagged and dark. Thomas withdrew a folded piece of paper from the toe of his shoe and held it out to Ilse.

She hesitated. It was filthy with dirt and whatever else was on his feet, which looked infected. But she had to take it. He had done her a great kindness, and she couldn't repay him with disgust. She took the paper between two fingers, touching as little of it as possible, and unfolded it while he described his findings in low, rapid words.

"Couldn't find anything that does what we talked about—decreasing men's . . . abilities. Male scientists apparently haven't taken an interest in decreasing their own desire. Surprising, I know. I found chasteberry, which is said to decrease lust, but it only grows in climates much warmer than Germany's. But I found something else: contraceptive herbs." He gestured to the paper. "Wild carrot—also called Queen Anne's lace—is best: effective with almost no side effects. Needs to be harvested in the fall, so go soon. We don't have it at the Plantation, but look in the woods nearby and you should find it. Make sure the root smells of carrot—otherwise it's easy to confuse it with hemlock.

"Tansy is also effective, according to the book, but it's dangerous. You could develop stomach pain, nausea, kidney or liver damage. Hallucinations, convulsions, coma . . . death." He swallowed and looked at her. "Be careful."

"Thank you," she croaked. She would still have to sleep with von Thiel, but it was far, far better than nothing. She would happily choke down an herbal tea or tincture if that was what it took.

"One more thing," Thomas said, his eyes scanning the doorway and window. "I found this information in old texts kept for research. The Plantation hasn't succeeded with any of its experiments involving herbs. I can't promise you these will work."

"It's something to try," Ilse said. She examined the filthy note. It was hope. She yearned to express her gratitude for Thomas, and cast about the kitchen for an answer. "I'll hide you in the storeroom, then you can flee at nightfall."

For a moment his face reflected a longing that was all too familiar, though with more desperation than Ilse had ever felt. But he shook his head.

"Roll call before we leave the camp, roll call as soon as we get back. They'd know I was gone right away."

"Someday, we'll escape."

He nodded. "Isn't it pretty to think so?"

"What?" She cocked her head at him.

"It's from a book. You won't be able to find it. Ernest Hemingway."

With nothing left to offer, she reached out with a hesitant hand and touched his wrist. She knew he rarely got to wash his body, and his clothes were beyond cleaning. The smell of acetone and decay emanated from him. His wrist was so sharp and frail, Ilse was afraid she might snap it in two.

She looked him in the eye and thanked him. From the doorway, she watched as he walked into the autumn air to the far end of the grounds, where he blended in with the half-dozen anonymous bodies at work. Her skin itched; she longed to pull it off like clothing and take away all the parts of herself that were too cowardly, too self-preserving, to do something that would matter. Something that could save Thomas.

Her eyes fixed on the SS guard, Walter. He was pretending to ram his rifle up the emaciated bottoms of the prisoners, while they desperately tried to keep working.

An idea seized Ilse, so obvious she couldn't believe she hadn't thought of it before. It arrived with such force, such certainty, as if it hadn't come from her but from some external source, that she had no doubt that it was what was right, what was needed.

She'd been so dedicated to thinking about herself, her own self-preservation, that she hadn't given a thought to how she could affect the world around her.

She could administer doses of wild carrot to every Little Blond Sister in the villa via their food. No one would know. It would be impossible to trace a decreased birth rate back to her, and there would be fewer Lebensborn babies, babies who would grow up brainwashed, for she knew how easily one could lose one's own mind to the Reich and become the most brutal of

Nazis. Or, like Otto, be killed if they weren't considered worthy of life.

It wouldn't be revenge. That was a small reason, a selfish one. This plan was a way to take action. She had allowed Otto to die, and she was unable to protect Thomas. Not again. This act was ultimately a service to the world; it would allow her to make things, if not right, then a bit less wrong. It would help her live with the pain and self-loathing.

Each pregnancy prevented was one less girl becoming a breeder, a mother who would give her own child away before she learned how to think for herself. There would be fewer Walters and Maxes who lived to create terror and inflict pain.

There would be some burden to her conscience, but it would be manageable. A small voice in the back of her mind protested, but she turned it off. She gripped the paper in her hand until it crinkled into a ball.

❖

It was a sunny morning, the dew just beginning to evaporate, when Ilse ambled over to the two SS guards at the front gate.

"I wish to go gather herbs for the kitchen," she said as casually as she could. She passed them a note she'd secured from Frau Herta, permitting her a morning in the woods, accompanied by a guard.

She tried to meet their eyes but ended up studying the bindweed creeping up the brick wall just behind them. The two guards looked at each other. The older guard gave a sharp nod and a gesture with his hand.

"Lead the way then," the younger one said, passing the slip back to her. She set off for the small patch of forest beyond the lane, swinging her wicker basket, the image of a carefree girl. The air was rich with ephemeral crispness; leaves on the trees were tinged with red and a slight breeze made them rustle. She hopped over a swampy ditch and headed for the tree line.

Yesterday, she'd looked up Thomas's herbs in *Physica*. Wild carrot wasn't mentioned, but tansy was. Hildegard von Bingen prescribed it for use against "obstructed menses." Ilse had glossed right over it when she'd read it before. She felt foolish now; it was such an obvious euphemism for pregnancy. For a woman who is "in pain from obstructed menses," Hildegard prescribed an elaborate bath with several herbs, including tansy. But even if Ilse could obtain all those herbs and unlimited access to a bathtub, she wanted to take action *before* her menses were obstructed.

She would have to try this newer method and hope Thomas's mysterious herbalist had developed Hildegard's method into something simpler, but still effective.

Since wild carrot needed to be harvested in the fall, she had only a few weeks to find all she could. She wandered along, gathering various herbs and plants for cooking and medicinal teas and tinctures, to disguise the true purpose of her outing. She even sang old BDM songs to throw the SS guard, her shadow, off the scent.

All the while, she was on the lookout for the delicate fringe of green leaves, the white umbel of blooms. Thomas had seemed confident that the plant would be growing nearby.

She hadn't been walking long when she spotted plants matching the description, growing tall in the space between the road and the trees. She recognized them now: she'd never known the name, but this plant grew everywhere in Bremen. The answer to her problems, to the problems of so many women and girls, was growing along the sides of roads across Germany. If she'd known its effects, she could have saved herself all the suffering of the last year. But then she would never have had Otto. She wouldn't take back the short time she'd had with him for anything. Something like anguish threatened to erupt in her chest.

She shook off those thoughts and veered into the tall grass, her boots and hem getting wet with dew, and bent over to inspect the plants. Capping off each stem, tiny white flowers of the first-year plants clustered to form a dome, smelling sweet and delicate. Then there were the brown bird's nests, the seed pods of the second-year plants. With gloved fingers, she pushed aside the leaves as Thomas's note instructed and saw the hairy stalk differentiating the wild carrot from poison hemlock.

She tried to hum patriotically for the benefit of the guard looming over her, but her voice shook too much. Silence was safer. As casually as she could, she took out the small shovel she'd taken from the villa's gardening shed. Settling into a comfortable position on her knees, she began to free a plant from the surrounding dirt. Once she'd extracted the first root, she raised it to her nose and smelled. The faintly sweet, earthy smell of carrot. This was the second differentiation from hemlock.

She surveyed the waves of white flowers stretching across the tree line as far as she could see. So many of them. Plenty for the whole villa.

With a finger, she felt around for the fuzzy seeds from the debris-filled bird's nests. They looked like furry, gray-green bugs, something she'd prefer not to eat. She took out a knife and began cutting the stems below the blooms and bird's nests, surprisingly sturdy for how thin they were. She had to work her knife back and forth a few times before each stem came free.

On her way back with a full basket, as she reached the edge of the woods, her new eyes caught something that made her stop short. There, between the woods and the road, clusters of tansy grew, about two feet tall, each plant a small yellow sun. She went over to them, stooped, inhaled. Her nose tingled with the smell of camphor. She'd passed them that morning without look-ing, without noticing, so set she'd been on wild carrot.

Thomas had advised against using tansy, but it wouldn't hurt to harvest and store some, just in case. She put on her gloves and took as many cuttings as she could carry, depositing them into her basket, and when it was full, her pockets. Thomas had told her that tansy was "pleasant in taste." If it came down to it, at least tansy would be sweet rather than whatever foul taste she could expect from the wild carrot.

Back in the kitchen, having ditched the guard at the gate, she bundled up the first-year wild carrot and the tansy cuttings with twine and hung them from the wooden timbers in the ceiling of the storeroom. They looked like odd decorations. Soon, she would soak the wild carrot flowers in a bottle of the potato vodka and store them in glass vials for a month. The flowers from the tansy she would dry and keep in storage, just in case.

Then she moved on to the wild carrot seeds hiding in the bird's nests. She picked up the first one, and as soon as she peeled back the dried flowers, the seeds practically jumped out like bugs, and something powdery and tan scattered across the counter. It made quite a mess for such a small plant. She turned the bird's nest upside down and used a finger to scrape the seeds out. They fell neatly into a small pile. Then followed the tedious task of separating the tiny seeds from the twigs and powder, because she didn't fancy eating anything she didn't have to. The seeds were for her; she would chew them, that being the most effective method of all. Though Thomas's scrib-bled notes warned her the taste would be unpleasant, she would only have to eat them in the days following intercourse, and she hoped those events would be infrequent.

Her neck and shoulders were aching by the time she finished sorting the seeds and laying them out to dry. For the first time in her life, as far as she could recall, Ilse felt a sense of purpose, something beyond survival for herself or for Otto. A fire was lit inside her, and all her focus and energy were now directed toward the tiny collection of seeds and the drying flower heads.

CHAPTER TWENTY-FIVE

Frau Herta appeared at the kitchen door and surveyed the room disapprovingly. Ilse scanned the area for anything incriminating she might have left out, but she'd been thorough. The kitchen gleamed innocuously. Not so much as a speck of flour was out of place. She spoke out of sheer awkwardness.

"Were you hoping for something to eat? The meal isn't quite ready, but I can cut you a slice of last night's Obsttorte."

Frau Herta acted as if Ilse hadn't spoken. A disarming, clearly artificial smile crept across her face.

"Are you with child?" Her voice was reedy and grating.

Ilse lowered her gaze to the bowl. The brown eyes of the skinned potatoes stared back at her.

"Well?" said Frau Herta. "Your stomach remains flat. Have you menstruated this month?"

Ilse tried to think. What would get her out of this situation?

"Not yet, although my cycle has never been regular. I don't know, either way."

It had been weeks since her night with von Thiel. Perhaps

his work had taken him away from Munich. Perhaps he had gotten what he wanted and forgotten her.

"Until you know for sure, I advise you to keep trying. You're a healthy woman of good genetic stock; I can't imagine why you wouldn't devote yourself to creating another child for the Fatherland, especially now that we must replenish the German blood lost on the battlefield."

"Of course. You're right. I've been too focused on my work here"—she gestured around the kitchen—"and I have wanted to do well in this role. Good food is the foundation of a healthy life and I'm proud to serve the program." Now she was overdoing it. She clamped her mouth shut.

"Don't forget the other way to serve." The false smile wilted from Frau Herta's face. "A particular man who visits the grounds on Fridays has been asking for you. He will begin attending the mixers."

Frau Herta glared at the kitchen one last time before she left the room, leaving behind her the sickly sweet odor of her perfume.

Ilse sagged against the counter. That sneering, violent man, Thomas's SS guard Walter Streckenbach, wanted her. Of course, she'd wanted him to be attracted to her when she'd flirted with him, to keep Thomas safe. But the fact that it worked filled her with nausea. There must be something wrong with her if that kind of man wanted her. Against her will, she imagined his hard, violent body against hers. His smell, of rotting flesh, seeping into her skin, her sheets.

But there was another way.

She pushed herself off the counter and wound silently through a group of puff-chested administrators gathered around the fire in the foyer and up the stairs to the ladies' parlor, where among the knitting and embroidery supplies, there was also a cylinder desk with stationery. The room was dark and small and populated with a gaggle of Little Blond Sisters at their knitting.

Ilse sat at the desk and pulled out a page of stationery and a fountain pen. Her hand hovered over the blank page. The girls' voices rose as they twittered about the relative merits of various "conception assistants," as they called them. Ilse did her best to ignore their words as they bounced against the close walls of the room. She took a deep breath to steady her hand and block the girls out, and began to write.

Her first draft was cold and formal. It betrayed an emotional indifference. She took out a new piece of paper and tried again. This time the words were pleading and desperate. On the third try, she wrote:

Lieber Gruppenführer von Thiel,

> *I must confess I have missed your company these last few weeks. I enjoyed the short time we spent together. Though I am sure you're busy fulfilling some of the most important duties in the Reich, I hope I am not too small to escape your notice. I would very much like to see you at the villa again soon.*
>
> *Mit freundlichen Grüssen,*

Ilse

Having read the letter and decided it was the best she was capable of, she folded it in thirds, placed it in an envelope, and fled the room, glad to get away from the gossiping girls.

Frau Herta's office door was slightly ajar when Ilse arrived; she knocked on it, pushing it open. The administrator looked up from her desk by the window. The way the autumn light fell on her face, she looked much older, almost ghoulish.

"Frau Ilse, I wasn't expecting you."

"I have a request. It'll be quick." She held up the letter. "I've written to Gruppenführer von Thiel and am hoping you might have his address so I can mail it?"

Frau Herta's eyes narrowed, studying Ilse, and she did her best to appear rosy-cheeked and bright-eyed with hope so the administrator could read the purpose of the letter on Ilse's face.

"I'll take care of it," she said at last, stretching out her bony hand to receive the letter.

Ilse hesitated. Why did Frau Herta not simply give Ilse the address so she could mail it herself? But her hand was outstretched and her face grew impatient, so Ilse placed the letter in the outstretched palm, thanked the administrator, and left.

❧

Between lunch and dinner services, after making sure no one was near the kitchen, Ilse fetched the large bottles filled with her tinctures from their hiding place in the storeroom. She did this weekly, and as quickly as possible. She shook them, then sniffed the pungent, bitter liquid inside.

"Frau Ilse."

She flinched, her back tightening painfully under the eyes she hadn't known were there. She turned and saw Frau Herta. Ilse hadn't smelled her coming because her nose had been buried in the scent of the tinctures.

The tinctures. Ilse picked up a nearby rag and began fidgeting with it, holding it so that it blocked the view of the bottles.

"Can I help you?" Ilse asked. Her voice cracked.

"You have a visitor." Frau Herta stepped aside, and Hannelore appeared. Frau Herta grimaced at the sight of

Hannelore's radiant, unapologetic face. "Perhaps your visitors can schedule ahead next time."

She swept out of the room. Hannelore grinned. Ilse couldn't help herself; she grinned back. Hannelore made her feel as if the two of them were in on some great joke.

"She's not what you would expect in a madame, is she?" Hannelore said.

"She's no madame; this isn't a brothel."

"Don't be silly. I know what goes on here. Anyway." Hannelore shook back her hair. "I've come to snatch you away."

"I'd love to be snatched, but I have to cook."

"Well, when are you done?"

"In a few hours."

"Alright." Hannelore plopped down on the chair. She settled in and stretched out her legs, making herself look far more comfortable than Ilse thought it possible to be on that chair. "I'll sample the food and make sure it's acceptable. I'm famished after my flying lesson. It went long today."

"And how was it?"

"Wonderful. I stayed in the air for hours. I'm only supposed to fly for twenty minutes, but who can tell time up there? I flew as high as the wind would take me—it's not my fault it was a perfect day. I got to 13,000 feet."

"That sounds high."

"It is."

"Can you breathe up there?"

"Not really." Hannelore shrugged, as if such things were unimportant.

As casually as she could, Ilse picked up the tinctures and returned them to the storeroom. Back in the kitchen, she returned to the marinade she was preparing. Hannelore sniffed the sourness that wafted her way as Ilse poured red wine vinegar into the pot.

"Are you making Sauerbraten?" There was a note of hopefulness in her voice. Everyone loved Sauerbraten. Heavy and comforting, it was the perfect cold-weather dish.

"Yes, but it still needs to marinate for two weeks."

"Two weeks? One is fine."

"Look, I'm the one cooking, and I like the beef to be tender."

"Very well. Just don't tell me you're going to leave out the cookies because you're a northerner."

"Of course I am. Cookies as a thickener is ridiculous when cornstarch will do."

"Maybe your madame's been sucking on your Sauerbraten; that would explain her face. You need something sweet to balance out the sour."

Ilse stifled a smile.

"Careful. She could come back any moment and ask me if I'm procreating."

"And? Are you?"

Hannelore, sorting through a bowl of nuts on the table and picking out the almonds, didn't notice at first the stiffness that came over Ilse. But then she did.

"Oh, no, you're a rod of steel again. What is it?"

Ilse sighed, and with it came the full story of Otto's death. The postcard. The body that was discarded like trash, never to be returned to her. How she would never know the truth of what had happened in Brandenburg. The bargain struck between her and Lebensborn: that she must bear more Aryan children or risk death. And how she couldn't imagine having another child, much less one for the SS.

All the while, she worked on the marinade, adding juniper berries and cloves and thyme and rosemary. A smell like Christmas filled the kitchen.

She couldn't see what Hannelore was doing as she told the story—if she was uncomfortable, or if she was even listening.

Maybe she'd sneaked out the back door. But then arms wrapped around her from behind and squeezed her so tight she could barely breathe.

"When we first met, I could see all the hurt and fear in you. I wanted to raise you up out of it and show you how big and good life can be. It's the older sister in me, I suppose. I'm sorry there's been so much more pain since then."

Ilse set the ladle in the pot and rested her hand on top of Hannelore's joined ones, right on her solar plexus. She felt like she was standing in front of a warm fireplace after spending years in an ice storm of her own making.

CHAPTER TWENTY-SIX

The royal-blue satin dress hugged Ilse's curves in unfamiliar ways. She kept smoothing the skirt down, as if that would somehow keep it from clinging to her body. Her hair she pinned into her version of an Olympia roll. She hoped she looked attractive enough to be able to go with the "conception assistant" of her choosing.

The day before, Frau Herta had informed Ilse that she was excused from cooking for the next mixer; the local inn would provide the refreshments. Ilse understood this to mean she could have no further excuses; now that the war was on, and men were dying at the front, the Frau Hertas of the Reich would be even more obsessed with repopulation than before.

Another week had passed with no response from von Thiel. Ilse resigned herself to it; she would have to sleep with someone else. A strange man, who would be too rough in bed or too dull outside of it, who had no identity beyond being a machine for the Führer. Her only hope was to avoid the guard who tormented Thomas.

As she descended the stairs to the parlor, she contemplated ways to make it look as if she were going off with a man—how she might leave the room with him but then slip away once they were away from Frau Herta's watchful eyes.

She arrived at the double doors of the parlor. Tonight, a pianist was playing, a talented one, as far as Ilse could tell from her own untrained ear. Even she could recognize the triumphant Wagner he played. She was sick of Wagner. Everyone was.

Halfway to the bar, Ilse halted when she saw who was there, refilling his stein. Walter Streckenbach. She turned away before he could notice her, prepared to run straight to her room, no matter what Frau Herta would say to her later.

But someone in the center of the room was staring at her. She met his penetrating gaze with a glare, then nearly tripped over her foot when she saw that it was von Thiel.

A smile broke across her face. She was genuinely glad to see him. He walked toward her; she changed course to meet him. When he took both her hands in his, she felt the smooth metal of his rings. He kissed her cheek and said her name warmly.

"I'm so sorry I haven't seen you. I was called to consult with Herr Himmler, and I couldn't get back sooner," he said. "Come, I have a bottle of burgundy—a gift from the Reichsführer himself, which I've been saving for a special occasion. Not your usual burgundy that has given the wine from that region a bad name, mind you—this is the good stuff."

Ilse gave him a side-smile. "Is Burgundy a good place for wine then?"

"Herr Himmler believes Burgundy is the most overlooked region in Europe, for both wine and culture."

"You know him well."

"I used to," he said vaguely. Then, leaning over to the pianist, "For the love of God, play us some Chopin or something." He winked at Ilse as he sat and poured the wine.

The pianist—Ilse thought he looked as relieved as she felt—moved on to playing a much more tolerable tune.

She picked up her glass. The aroma, floral and sweet and light, danced below her nose. "Tell me, what has your work brought you to this time?"

For a hint of a moment, his expression shadowed, but just as quickly he blinked and it was gone.

"Herr Himmler has enlisted me to study Armanen runes. I spoke to you before of our desire to uncover ancient secrets that are the key to our future. Herr Himmler and I believe these runes, when deeply studied, can unlock great meaning that will bring the Aryan race to its full power."

Ilse fought the urge to recoil, reminding herself to glide around the unpleasant things he said, to forget them as soon as she heard them. She cleared her throat and took a sip of wine. "How do you deeply study the runes?"

"With meditation, contemplation, an analysis of each symbol's roots in Nordic mythology. And, if I'm fortunate, visions."

He took a delicate sip of wine and refilled Ilse's glass, which was nearly empty.

"How impressive," she said in a voice she made both breathy and admiring. For the first time, she was glad for the months of witnessing the coquettish behaviors of the other Lebensborn girls. All she had to do was pretend to be one of them. "Have you had these visions?"

"It takes years to cultivate a state of mind that allows for them. The man who revived the runes was only able to access visions when he experienced a period of blindness."

"Well, I hope it doesn't come to that for you."

"I wouldn't mind, except for not being able to see you."

Ilse wanted to gag, but forced what she hoped looked like a sheepish smile.

In the morning, von Thiel announced that he was taking her on a date.

"But I have to work," she said, slipping on last night's dress.

"I've secured you the day off already. I hope that's alright." He bounced on his toes, looking boyish in his excitement.

Ilse was flummoxed. She'd never been on a date.

"I would be delighted," she said.

Back in her room, she changed into her good day dress and a hat and her Ulster coat, still missing a piece from her futile offering to the juniper tree, and von Thiel escorted her downstairs.

"I'll need to stop by the kitchen to get something," Ilse said.

Von Thiel looked surprised, but didn't ask. She told him to wait outside the kitchen and slipped through the door. Inside, two Little Blond Sisters were up to their elbows in ingredients, running around each other.

One of them saw her and sagged with relief. The other whirled around, her braids swinging, and looked thrilled to see Ilse.

"I'm just here to pick something up. Carry on." Ilse only felt a little bad for them. They were doing for one day what she did every day. If she could manage on her own, the two of them would, at the very least, survive the day. She walked past them into the storeroom and closed the door. The sachet of seeds was where she'd left it, behind the potatoes. She retrieved them and poured into her open hand approximately one teaspoon of seeds. They looked like fleas, but she closed her eyes and tossed them into her mouth.

She gagged—they squeaked and popped against her teeth, turning into a viscous mush—but she forced herself to chew several times and choke them down.

Desperate, on the verge of vomiting, she searched the room for a chaser. Her choices were between cooking wine, pickling brine, and linseed oil. She chose the cooking wine, which she normally didn't even see fit to cook with. It burned her tongue and throat on the way down. Still, it was better than the taste it had replaced. With that flavor, the seeds had better work.

Ilse composed herself and picked up her wicker basket with the gloves, knife, and shovel in it, and left the storeroom, nodding goodbye to the girls as she went. She found von Thiel waiting obediently on the other side of the door. As she closed the door behind her, she saw the two girls one last time, with the expression written clearly across their faces: Why should the cook get a Gruppenführer while they were stuck doing the dirty work? Ilse gave them a shrug and a half-smile before the door clicked shut.

Von Thiel was looking at the basket in Ilse's hand.

"I thought we might go for a walk in the woods later. I enjoy gathering herbs and I so rarely get the opportunity. Would you mind?"

"I'd be happy to see you at your work. Your interest in *Physica* drew me to you from the first."

She stepped closer and took his arm. "Thank you."

Von Thiel's brows furrowed. He even seemed to lean back ever so slightly.

Then she realized. She'd downed wine straight from the jug before nine in the morning. He must have smelled it on her breath. There was no explanation she could provide, so she decided to pretend it hadn't happened. She followed von Thiel outside the villa to the small lot containing a handful of black, waxed-to-a-shine Mercedes. The SS flags on the hoods of the cars waved, sinister, in the breeze.

Von Thiel noticed she was looking.

"That Sig rune," he said, motioning to the jagged twin light-ning bolts that were the SS symbol. "It signifies victory—though before the twentieth century, it was a symbol of the sun."

The restaurant had the dim, cozy feeling of most inns. There was real butter, almost impossible to acquire since the war, though it was rancid. Ilse knew the flavor well, despite how it had been cleverly sauteed in onions to mask the taste—per the Reich's recommendation. Sometimes rancid butter was the only butter available, and in these times, it was not to be wasted.

She took a bite of bread and contemplated von Thiel's body. It was muscular and thick and sturdy; he was athletic, on the verge of going to seed. His body was nothing like Felix's, thin and lanky and soft. And there was another notable difference between the two: Felix's member had been shaped like a mushroom, while von Thiel's looked like a large one-eyed worm. She didn't understand how the same body part could look so dissimilar.

He caught her staring at him. She smiled and looked away, surveying the room instead. It was hard to keep from staring at the diverse sampling of people. Children too young to become parents, Opas and Omas far too old. She basked in the relative variety of people.

But everyone looked to be of German stock. It was because of the sign they'd passed on the way in: Juden sind hier unerwünscht. *Jews are not wanted here.* It was not a new sign—they had been everywhere since the beginning of the Third Reich—but she'd never seemed to notice them before. She didn't understand how it was possible for Jews to live at all in this country, when they weren't allowed to work or buy food. And now they were prohibited from leaving Germany, so they had no choice but to go on surviving here, or trying to. The sausage she'd just taken a bite of became a hard lump.

She forced herself to chew and swallow it, then put her fork down.

"Finished?" von Thiel asked as he dolloped strawberry jam onto his roll and deposited it into his mouth.

"I'm watching my figure." She'd meant it to be a joke, but the words came out dry and flat. Her fingers found the jagged edge of her coat where she'd cut into it. She traced the frayed edge.

"You have nothing at all you need to watch. It's important that you eat and keep up your health."

"All the same, I'm quite satisfied, thank you." Ilse took one last sip of ersatz coffee, the punctuation mark to complete the meal.

"Very well," said von Thiel, and called the waiter over to exchange the bill for a stack of ration cards. Ilse strained to look at them; she must be the only person in the country who had never used one. But the rectangles of stiff brown paper passed between hands and were gone. "To the woods, then?"

Ilse forced a smile.

Von Thiel drove them far out into the country. She rested her head against the window, taking in the views, the space, with no people in sight except for the guards at occasional SS checkpoints. Every time they stopped, von Thiel handed over his papers, which the men hurried to glimpse and return to him. They didn't even look at Ilse before waving them on.

Leaves had fallen and color had drained out of the earth. A gentle fog crept in, creating the essential eeriness of autumn. When von Thiel pulled over at the edge of the forest, Ilse led the way, walking along the tree line, where sun-loving wild carrot might grow. She breathed in the air and saw her exhalation as a puff of fog. Von Thiel walked beside her with his arms clasped behind his back. It was surprisingly comfortable being together.

She spotted some tansy and went for her gloves and knife to harvest the plant.

Von Thiel's head appeared next to hers. He sniffed.

"Tansy," he said.

Ilse's heart burst in her ears.

"Yes," she said as casually as she could.

"Centuries ago, Germanic people hung this plant outside their homes to protect against monsters." He reached out to touch it.

"Don't," she said. "You'll get a rash."

She curled and uncurled her gloved fingers before his face.

"It was also burned as incense," von Thiel said, his eyes drifting off. "I don't care for the smell myself."

Every muscle in Ilse's body tensed. She steadied her voice before she spoke.

"It's also a cure for migraines, worms, and, according to some, flatulence. I don't mind the smell. Of the tansy, I mean." She sounded mostly normal to herself.

She'd been a fool to gather herbs in front of him. She wouldn't make that mistake again, no matter how convenient it was.

As they walked on together, he said, "You look like a wood-land nymph."

Instead of answering, she smiled, hopefully in a mysterious way, and kept her eyes trained on the ground. It was difficult to identify wild carrot this time of year; the white blossoms were gone and only the deadened brown umbels would give them away.

"Did you know my name is based on a myth?" Ilse asked.

Von Thiel's eyes lit up, as she'd suspected they would. "I did not. Will you tell me the story?"

"It's a legend from the Harz Mountains, where my mother was born. Ilse was a princess, and one day, she was hunting in the mountains with her father and her lover when she got lost."

She bent and harvested some dandelion, the roots for tea, the greens for salad.

"The Fairy Queen met the princess and took her to her crystal palace underneath the mountains. Ilse stayed there for one year, alongside gnomes and kobolds, and witnessed the strange world of the fairies. But the princess missed her lover, and she demanded that the Fairy Queen return her to the world of light and humans. The queen made Ilse promise to never reveal to mortals what she'd seen in the fairy underworld. The princess agreed and returned to her lover, but he demanded that Ilse tell him where she'd been for that year. So she took him for a walk in the mountains and told him the whole story. Her lover's faith in her was restored. They fell asleep together. When he woke, he found that the princess had been turned into a river of clear, sparkling water—the River Ilse. That was the Fairy Queen's curse."

Von Thiel had been feasting his eyes on her, drinking in her words. At last she found the bird's nest belonging to the two-year-old wild carrot. She began cutting off the flower heads and placing them in her basket.

"What an enchanting tale," he said. "I wonder what it signifies for your life." Von Thiel leaned against a tree and squinted into the horizon. He didn't seem to notice what she was doing at all.

"I think my mother had some whimsy to her."

"Maybe she passed it on to you."

If she did, it was dormant. Ilse said nothing.

"Has she passed?" von Thiel asked.

"Yes, when she gave birth to my sister."

"I'm so sorry, Ilse." He looked down at her with softened eyes.

"Maybe someday I'll turn into a babbling brook. That doesn't sound too terrible."

"I can hardly picture you babbling in any form. And who is your faithful lover?"

Ilse tucked the last of the plants into the basket and stood.

"You tell me, Gruppenführer."

"Surely by now you can call me Erich."

"Yes, Erich."

He smiled, took her hand, and led her into the forest. Soon, he'd found a clearing—a suitable enough place to lay his black coat out and then lay her on the makeshift blanket.

That night, Ilse returned to her spot on the windowsill with her knees tucked in close to her chest. The cold pressed in through the glass, chilling the right side of her body. She swigged from the latest bottle of stolen whiskey.

Setting the whiskey next to her bare feet on the sill, she removed the pins from her hair and slowly unspooled it until it poured over her shoulders—the best feeling after a long day. Over time, each pin became its own pain point, one she did not notice until the discomfort was relieved.

She was waiting to see what would happen to her body after the wild carrot. Her breasts had begun to ache a few hours after taking the herb. She could be with child again already—though she felt as if her body would refuse such a thing, herbs or no herbs. All she could do was wait for her bleeding to start, the sign that the herb had worked.

A woman was supposed to know her body. She had heard of women knowing they were expecting even before a doctor could confirm it. Ilse had felt that, in a way, with Otto, though she'd ignored it for some time. Now, though, her body was a separate entity, one that she felt belonged to her less and less. She supposed it was a matter of having given birth. Her body had changed forever, in small ways. And she had never returned to the rigorous exercise of the BDM. Though she retained the musculature developed during her formative years, her body was no longer the agile, well-oiled machine it had been before.

Besides, what was the point of feeling a connection to something that didn't truly belong to her, anyway? The less she was aware of it, the easier it was to do what she had to. What the Reich demanded of her.

She longed, more than anything, to be a man. To have control over her own body. For bleeding and illness not to be part of its normal functioning. For it not to be a constant vulnerability, a liability, an asset to be used as those in power saw fit. To not, quite literally, carry the burdens bestowed on her by men.

These things filled her with a shaking rage that scared her. It felt uncontrollable. And in the face of it, all she had was whiskey.

A trickling feeling announced the arrival of the red wave. She fetched her supplies and headed to the bathroom down the hall. Her footsteps meandered, her body heavy and unwieldy, and she leaned every so often on the wall to steady herself.

A door opened and closed, and Frau Herta walked toward her with her swift, smooth, efficient steps. Ilse focused on walking steadily, mimicking the administrator's gait. How seriously the woman took herself. Ilse nodded at the administrator and wished her a good evening. Once she was past, she mimed gagging at Frau Herta's cloying perfume and silently giggled.

She felt wild with her new power—she'd found an invisible

rebellion. It was a narrow line she walked, between succumbing to the Reich and being destroyed by it.

"What are you doing?" Frau Herta's voice was sharp and demanding. Ilse whirled around. Frau Herta had turned back and was glaring at Ilse. Her eyes focused. Her mind cleared.

"I'm not feeling well. Perhaps it's morning sickness."

Frau Herta looked her up and down. She didn't believe Ilse, that much was written on her face.

Ilse said good night again and walked carefully to the bathroom. She could feel Frau Herta's eyes boring into the back of her head.

PART FOUR
SPROUT

At times I think I could survive anything on earth as long as it came from without and not from some devious trick of my own heart.

— ANONYMOUS AUTHOR OF *A WOMAN IN BERLIN*

Chapter Twenty-Seven

The tincture dripping through the cheesecloth into the amber bottle was painfully slow. Ilse twisted and squeezed the cloth, fingers aching as she extracted every drop.

As the tincture neared readiness, she'd started attending garden parties with Little Blond Sisters and Waffen-SS men, in gray uniforms instead of black since the war started. Instead of participating, she would find a secluded bench removed from the action and sketch plants, pretending that was her purpose for being out on the grounds, while keeping track of which girls were in need of dosing.

When she held no more than a pulpy mush of herbs, she set the cloth down and surveyed her work: four large bottles of tincture, ready for their tiny rebellion against the regime.

As at Heim Harz, every Little Blond Sister had to eat a salad every day, on special orders from Himmler. This meant that each girl received an individual plate of salad. Every girl who went off with an SS man would, for the following three days, receive a special salad dressing containing a tincture of wild carrot flowers. Ilse would have to calculate each girl's size and make each of their dressings individually to get the dosage right.

Now the tincture was ready, and she prepared doses for the first round of four girls. The meal served, Ilse lurked just inside the doorway between the kitchen and dining room. The first girl to take a bite of lettuce scrunched her manicured eyebrows and plump, red lips into a grimace.

"What is that dressing? Cow-dung vinaigrette?" Her voice was a loud drawl; she was used to others listening to her.

The others, taking reluctant nibbles of lettuce, grumbled agreement.

But they had no choice but to choke it down—Reichs-führer's orders if they wished to stay in the program. Ilse couldn't help but smile as they gagged; she had to duck back into the kitchen to hide it. A bubbling sensation, wild and reckless, rose within her. She felt powerful. Now she was the one pulling the strings of Lebensborn.

The next time, she added extra honey, lemon, and mustard, sweet and sour and pungent to mask the earthy bitterness. As entertaining as it was to see a one-hundred-percent Nazi have a bit of unpleasantness in her day, Ilse couldn't risk someone looking into the matter. Besides, she wasn't a sadist, though she sometimes had to actively try not to become one. It would make her no better than them.

Every day Ilse dosed at least a few girls, the ones who had copulated in the last three days, with wild carrot. She took responsibility for their bodies when they could not. With satisfaction, she noted that girls stayed longer, leaving less frequently for Lebensborn homes with a patriotic glow and a hand on their flat stomachs. She watched their growing dismay and Frau Herta's darkening glower with a smile. And then it began: girls started leaving with their wombs just as empty as the day they'd arrived.

As fall colors gave way to barren winter, Thomas's deliveries had dwindled almost into nonexistence. She sometimes watched him through the window, working alongside the other prisoners, chopping firewood, mulching, pruning. His ears and fingers swelled and turned bright pink with chilblains. It seemed impossible that the situation could get any worse for him, and yet with winter coming, it clearly was. She was helpless to do anything other than hide bits of food wrapped in brown paper around the garden and hope he would find them.

During the first snow of the season—big, wet flakes turning to rain just before hitting the ground—Thomas came to her door, damp and shivering.

"Come in, come in," she said. He stumbled inside. "I didn't think you were coming today, it's so cold."

"This is our last trip to the villa until spring." He sounded resigned. She brought over a Buchtel and joined him at the table in the alcove. He peeled off a soft strip of roll, revealing the bright-red jam within.

Over the last few weeks, a creeping shame had snuck up on her. She'd felt revulsion when she'd learned about Thomas's homosexuality. Just as the Reich would want her to. But she'd had time to get used to the idea, to not care that Thomas was different. It didn't matter that she didn't understand; she shouldn't have stepped away from him. He must have experienced so much of that.

"Can I ask you something?" she asked.

He flicked his eyelids, a silent assent.

"How did the Nazis find out you're homosexual? And why would they care enough to arrest you?"

For a moment he was silent, his eyes dark. Then he began to speak.

"I moved to Berlin in '29. It was the freest place in Europe. I could be myself there. Underground bars were packed with men like me. Everyone playing cards, gossiping, unbuttoning their shirts and rolling up their sleeves for relief from the heat of the iron stoves that were cranked up on purpose. The men I met didn't mind how timid I am. They seemed almost drawn to me for it. We all called each other the informal 'du' right away.

"When Hitler took power, it changed overnight. I didn't dare go to those bars anymore. I was already at risk. People passing in the street called me 'dirty Jew' and 'pig' and 'half-breed.'"

He took a breath and looked her in the eye.

"By then I had met Hans. We became lovers. I must have been infatuated, because after a couple of months I moved into his apartment. We pretended to be nothing more than room-mates and hid there in plain sight.

"Things could have gone on like that, but then Hans wanted to join the Party, to deflect suspicion. I said that if he did, I would end things." He set his jaw and his eyes blazed. "Hans followed me around the apartment, demanding that I come to terms with him becoming a Nazi, maybe even a Brownshirt. I said no, and no, and no again. Finally, I gave up on Hans and moved into a new place with a new roommate, who happened to be young and handsome. There was no intimacy between us, but one day I caught Hans following me home. He saw my roommate and must have drawn his own conclusions and gotten jealous, because the next day the Gestapo showed up at my door."

"Your own lover turned you in?"

"Neighbors denounce neighbors, children denounce parents. And scorned lovers denounce those who hurt them."

Thomas looked so tired. She reached across the table and took his hand.

"What a wretched creature Hans must be."

"I try not to think about him anymore." He sighed. "Then I was brought to Dachau. I haven't told you much about what happens there, but perhaps you should know. In case I don't make it."

She started to protest, but he stopped her.

"It will help me to know that someone on the outside knows. The SS are sadists, as you know. But the Kapos—prisoner guards—are sometimes worse. They especially enjoy tormenting Jews who happen to be imprisoned on other charges, like me. My Kapo makes me empty the buckets we use as latrines in the barracks. It's foul—with our diets, everyone uses it several times in the night, so I make many trips, regardless of weather. Last year there were so many sleet storms." He shuddered. "My Kapo forces me to remake my bed—what they call a bed, anyway—two, three times, and he beats me if I'm too slow."

She couldn't fathom how humans could treat other humans with such cruelty. Thomas was just as worthy of life as she was —more so. He was kind and gentle in the face of persecution, while she became hardened and angry.

"Something wonderful has happened, though." Thomas's gaze unfocused and a hint of a smile crept across his face. "I've met someone."

Ilse perked up. "Who?"

"His name is Peter. He has dark eyes with long, curling lashes. The most beautiful eyelashes I've ever seen. I met him on the Plantation when I was pushing a heavy wheelbarrow and I fell. People who fall are shot. I was moments from death, but Peter stopped his own work to help me up. He risked his life to save mine."

Though imagining two men in a romantic relationship was still strange to her, she was glad Thomas had found a respite in the camp. For some reason, she wanted to cry. It was as if walls were breaking down inside her. In their place, something was rising up. Guilt, grief, remorse, and bittersweet joy threatened to overwhelm her. She smiled at Thomas. "He sounds wonderful."

"He saves my life again and again. We share food, clothing, everything we have. If one of us is sick, the other props us up at roll call so we aren't punished. We keep each other alive, but we also keep each other human. No one survives the KZ alone, especially not through winter. This will be my second one in the camp."

He looked through the window at the wet, gray world outside.

"I have to go now," he said. "Splitting tulip bulbs and chopping firewood today."

She made him stand by the stove for a minute before he left, then wondered if the contrast would only make him feel colder. Then Thomas grasped the handles of the cart and squinted at the sodden grounds.

"I've seen you looking at the linden tree sometimes, through the window," he said. "That one is called a weeping linden, for the way its branches sag downwards. They can live for over a thousand years."

"How old is that one?"

"Three hundred, I'd say."

It had been here long before National Socialism came to exist. With any luck, it would be here long after it was gone, weeping and silent and untouched by the actions of humans.

Thomas looked away from the tree, back to the cart. With a simple "tschüss," he pushed the cart over the lumpy, soggy path that had been carved out by previous deliveries.

Ilse thought of how Felix's life must have been before he left Germany. Once, when the two of them had been picnicking in the park, a drunk had stumbled upon them. He'd sized up Felix and said, "*You.*" The word was drawn out to be multi-syllabic, his tone disgusted. Then he spat at Felix's feet before stumbling away. Ilse had been shocked, confused—but Felix had brushed it off with his casual elegance. He moved on to a rousing story about his little sisters' latest antics, and it had left her mind. Now she realized why the man had treated Felix that way, and she also knew that he must have endured that treatment daily. Beyond expulsion from university and public spaces and ridiculous laws like the one forbidding Jews to buy bread after 5:30 in the afternoon, he must have faced cruelty from his own neighbors, every day, with no respite. Except for those few hours he'd spent in the park with Ilse, she hoped—though that had only been possible because of her ignorance.

She wished she could find Felix somehow and talk with him, actually know him. Tell him about Otto. He was the only person who might long for their baby as much as she did. But it was impossible.

That night, in bed, she paged through *Physica* until she found Hildegard's passage on linden. It signified frailty, and then there was something about carving its wood into a ring and adding a green stone bound with spiderwebs to prevent all diseases.

Her mother had added a note in the margin: "Its flowers can be made into a tea, as a sedative."

Chapter Twenty-Eight

Whenever von Thiel visited Ilse, she loved him while he was there and stopped as soon as he was gone, and ate the harsh seeds in the storeroom. She even grew accustomed to the taste.

He sometimes visited two or three times a week; other times he would be called away to Berlin or some other far-off land Ilse could only guess at, perhaps even to his family in Pomerania. He never told her the details. They went into the city for meals and plays and films, but most of their time together was spent in the suite, where a few things, women's things, had appeared since her first visit—a rose-colored robe, a small bottle of perfume. They drank fine wines in the sitting room and discussed mysticism and identity. For those brief hours, it was as if they could both forget the world around them, absorbed only in receiving the attentions of the other. Von Thiel seemed happiest when having a deep conversation about his desires and origins, or hers, or Norse mythology, or the destiny of Germany. This was easy enough for her to oblige. She pretended her attraction to him—but in some ways she didn't. She'd always been drawn to him, his sincerity and kindness and optimism. All she had to do was forget what he represented and ignore his references to Aryan superiority. She'd spent her whole life doing what was necessary to survive; now seemed a poor time to stop.

Overall, she was pleased with her choice in a lover, such as it was. Another man's preferred pastime could have been far worse than mythology. She didn't want to know how the arrogant younger SS officers spent their time, but she imagined it involved harming small creatures—or worse—and bragging about it.

Once, she asked him about the suite they spent so much of their time in. He absently scanned the sitting room, as if her mention of it had brought it into being.

"I have it kept ready for me. I stay here sometimes."

"So it's yours and only yours?"

"Yes, it's at my disposal."

"Do you stay here often?"

"Sometimes."

The question was on her lips. She swallowed it. It was not for her to ask if he brought other women here, now or in the past, and it was better if she didn't know anyway.

With the regularity of von Thiel's visits, Frau Herta had stopped glaring at her and asking if she was expecting. If Ilse wasn't mistaken, the administrator was even looking at her with some respect. No longer the lowly cook who'd escaped sterilization, she was now the special friend of a high-ranking SS officer, who could do away with Frau Herta without a thought, an insect squashed beneath the heel of his boot.

Ilse sometimes wondered why von Thiel never brought her to his home. He must live alone, in a grand place, and he could surely override any rules about her staying a night away from Lebensborn. It would make sense for the two of them to be alone in his apartment rather than holed up in a room in a villa crawling with people. But there must be a reason he never suggested it. Maybe his wife was there.

Sometimes she woke to find that von Thiel had wrapped her up tight with both his arms and his legs. The leg and the arm and part of his torso were a comfortable weight on her body. His chest expanded and contracted against hers. She pondered how the simple presence of another being could be a comfort. Knowing that something warm and breathing was nearby, someone who could be touched and touch her back, made some part of her unwind in a way that nothing else could. How odd that von Thiel was providing this service.

Much of winter passed this way, and 1939 gave way to 1940. The radio continued to announce certain victory. Germany's allies, the Soviets, had invaded Finland. Propaganda Minister Goebbels's New Year's speech spoke of Germany and its values being attacked on all fronts, and how they must defend themselves—by invading other countries, clearly.

Ilse wondered how her father fared. He would not be doing well, alone in a war-torn country. She hated having the time to think. She especially didn't want to think about him, but the thoughts crept in. He was surely better off without her, as she was without him.

Hannelore was her source of sanity. She came to the villa whenever she pleased, sometimes succeeding in pulling Ilse away from her work, for a walk on the grounds or a game of draughts. But more often than not, she sat on the chair and kept Ilse company while she worked. In turn, Ilse kept her fed, sneaking her the best treats. She longed to tell Hannelore about Felix and Otto and Thomas and the wild carrot, but something held her back. She couldn't say her secrets out loud, because then they would be alive in the world. She imagined the words riding the wind and reaching the ears of the Reich, which would rain down on her the consequences she was only postponing.

Once, in Bremen, when Ilse was twelve years old, she had gone into the cathedral. She'd never been inside any church before. Struck by a moment of curiosity, and having finished the shopping early, she climbed the stone steps. Her heels clicked on the floor as she entered. It was a Friday, and she was the only person in the church. The air was full—of what, she didn't know—but she felt compelled to take only slow, shallow breaths and small, quiet steps. The feeling was ancient. Enormous. Impossibly tall ceilings arched toward the heavens, making the air still and pregnant with unknown meaning. She sat for a moment in a creaking wooden pew and took in the altar and the engravings along the walls, letting the feeling seep inside her.

Too much had happened to her since that day. The ability to appreciate art was a luxury reserved for those who had nothing more on their mind. It could only come when the mind was relaxed, at ease. Safe enough to leave the body and sink into an experience outside of it. She could no longer rest in an unnecessary feeling.

She knew, though, that this was what she was supposed to be doing, as she stood in front of a painting at the Alte Pinakothek in Munich. It was one of the oldest and largest art galleries in the world, von Thiel had told her as they drove up to the estate.

She recognized a few names from school, like Albrecht Dürer, but there were many she did not recognize—other European artists, from France, Holland, Norway. These should be the most stunning sights she'd ever seen in her small life. She could see von Thiel thinking it as he watched her expectantly.

Yet she felt blank. An empty awareness that said, So?

What had happened to her, that she could no longer feel beauty?

But it didn't matter how she felt; she'd had plenty of practice at pretending. As they'd wandered from room to room, viewing the Old Masters, her face glowed with awe. Of the art, the place. Of him, for bringing her here.

The painting she studied now was particularly ugly. The subject was a woman with a bulbous forehead, a receding hairline, no eyebrows. Her eyes rolled back in her head. She looked like an inbred dog. But it was clear from the way she stood with her ample hips tilted, almost completely naked, covered only by a slip of fabric draped over the loins, that this woman was meant to be attractive.

Ilse leaned forward to read the plaque.

THE SUICIDE OF LUCRETIA
ALBRECHT DÜRER

WHEN LUCRETIA OF ANCIENT ROME, WIFE OF LUCIUS TARQUINIUS COLLATINUS, WAS RAPED BY HER COUSIN, SHE WENT TO HER FATHER AND HUSBAND AND EXACTED AN OATH OF VENGEANCE FROM THEM. THAT DONE, SHE PULLED A DAGGER SHE HAD CONCEALED IN HER ROBES AND STABBED HERSELF IN THE HEART.

A huff escaped Ilse.

"I prefer the *Lucretia* by Lucas Cranach the Elder, myself," von Thiel said. "A more formal version, yet far more original."

"Have you heard this story before? About Lucretia?"

"Oh yes. A very important story from the *Library of History*. I've read the whole of Diodorus Siculus's works."

That meant nothing to Ilse, though it was probably impressive. She crossed her arms over her chest. Unable to contain herself any longer, she said, "Such a waste of a life, to die from shame, when it was someone else who did the shameful thing."

"It was a different time. Purity for a woman was everything."

It's not so different now, Ilse stopped herself from saying.

"I'd much rather see a woman who finds a way to go on living. I don't understand why anyone would paint this story."

"I suppose," von Thiel said mildly. "Perhaps it was what her story represented: her death gave birth to the uprising that took Rome from a monarchy to a republic."

In other words, they used her death to pursue their own means and called it honor. Vengeance.

Von Thiel clasped his hands behind his back, making his SS dagger glint in the harsh museum light. With the handle's inlay of the silver eagle of National Socialism and the Sig runes of the SS that spoke of violence, it was out of place in this house of art.

Ilse was forgetting herself, why she was here, with him. She smiled and said, "I'm sure you're right."

She uncrossed her arms and led the way to the next room, trying to leave behind her irrational anger at a woman who'd been dead for over two thousand years. No—anger at the men who'd idealized her for centuries after.

The next room contained religious art, and Ilse returned to her stupor, pretending to be enthralled by brushstrokes and light and depth. She would be extra good to make up for her outburst. If she proved to be more difficult than she was worth, von Thiel could easily move on. That could not happen. She laced her fingers around his arm and he squeezed them close.

Chapter Twenty-Nine

Ilse stared at the deflated bag of seeds tucked in the back of the shelf. The tincture had run out yesterday; this was all she had left, and it contained less than two doses. She hadn't planned on so many girls participating in their duties so vigorously. She hadn't planned that for herself either.

Her head pounded from too much whiskey the night before, but sometimes it was the only way she could sleep. She rubbed her fingers against her forehead.

It was too late in the year to gather more wild carrot. Tansy wasn't as safe, nor as effective, but she had to try it. Her mouth went dry at the thought of having another little Otto. They said his disabilities were incidental, related to the birth itself, but Ilse couldn't be sure that her next baby wouldn't have the same affliction and meet the same fate. Even if the baby was healthy, she might be forced to give it up to the SS; she didn't actually know what was expected of her once she'd achieved this ultimate goal of bearing a child, but every girl passing through the villa seemed intent on adoption. If she would be allowed to keep the baby, she'd live in fear as a single mother in wartime. She would have nowhere to raise the child. Perhaps von Thiel would take her on as his official mistress, as Heydrich had with Hannelore—set her and the baby up in a nice apartment near him, and look after them.

She shook herself. No, she did not want to join her life with a Nazi officer's any more than she already had. She would use the tansy. It would have to work.

Thomas's note warned that even the slightest overdose could result in hallucinations, convulsions, kidney damage, liver damage, coma, death. It was a new level of risk—not just of being caught, but of harming the girls. But she couldn't bear the idea of brainwashed girls giving up their own bodies and cranking out babies who would be child soldiers.

She gathered the ingredients for a tansy-based salad dressing and brought them into the kitchen. Tansy was more difficult than wild carrot to slip into the food; it had to be made as a tea, which she would then add to the salad dressing.

Out of habit, she looked out the window, where she used to catch her weekly glimpse of Thomas. Feeling flat and hopeless, she reached for the tin of tansy to count out the dosage.

"Frau Ilse."

She jumped. The bowl filled with ingredients spun a few times and tansy scattered across the floor. She whirled around to meet Frau Herta's narrowed eyes. Ilse's reaction hadn't escaped her notice.

"Is everything alright?" the administrator asked.

"Yes. I'm sorry." Ilse collected herself and shifted so her foot hid most of the faded yellow tansy flowers. Her heart pounding in her chest must have been visible to Frau Herta, even from across the room.

"I see." Her eyes flicked over the scene, taking it all in. The administrator rarely came to the kitchen. Had she somehow traced the decreased birth rate back to Ilse? Everything went still as she focused her energies on looking unfazed and innocuous. Evidently, the administrator found nothing amiss, for she carried on. "I've brought you someone to help with the cooking."

Frau Herta gestured to the door. Half-hidden behind it was a young girl Ilse hadn't seen at the villa before. She looked no more than twelve years old, with almost translucently pale skin, straight white-blond hair, and turquoise eyes. She was every inch an Aryan specimen, except for her frame: though taller than the average girl, she was very slight. And she was far too young to be here.

"I'll leave you to it," Frau Herta said, taking her usual non-nurturing approach to leadership, and swept out the door. The girl barely got out of the way in time.

Ilse exhaled, willing her nerves to gather themselves, then approached the newest Little Blond Sister and held out an arm in invitation.

"Come in then. I could use the extra hands. What's your name?"

"Anneliese Stahlecker."

"No last names here," Ilse said. Even she was surprised at the briskness in her voice. "I'm Ilse."

She fetched the girl an apron and directed her to wash her hands.

"Do you know your way around a kitchen?" Ilse asked.

The girl nodded unconvincingly. Ilse sighed as she brought the girl to the counter by the stove where the dough for marrow dumpling soup was rising under a towel. She demonstrated how to roll the dough in the palm of her hand until it was perfectly round. Anneliese rolled a satisfactorily round ball, and Ilse told her to do that a hundred more times.

The girl got to work, and Ilse gathered the precious tansy back into its tin. She waited for Anneliese to grow bored, to complain of her wrists and neck and feet aching. If this girl was from the upper class as she seemed to be, she wouldn't last long in Ilse's kitchen. That was fine—she didn't need anyone asking questions about the unmarked bags of dried flowers in the storeroom. But Anneliese rolled a dumpling and another and another, chattering excitedly. Ilse learned that Anneliese was from Berlin and she was fifteen years old and she loved playing piano.

"Why in the world are you *here*?"

"What do you mean?"

"Surely they've told you what happens at this villa, yes?"

Anneliese nodded vigorously. "Oh yes. It's the most important thing we can do for the Führer. That's what my BDM leader says, and I've been to lots of talks about it. I simply couldn't wait any longer to get started."

"But your body hasn't even finished growing yet. You think it's ready to create another one?"

"The doctors examined me and they said I was ready." She sounded so confident, her words pat, as if the matter were settled.

This fifteen-year-old girl, sweet and innocent, was about to go to bed with monstrous men. Her body would be used and torn apart by childbirth and used again, cementing the girl's belief that she was nothing but a vessel to be filled.

Ilse was too depressed to discuss the matter further. Anneliese carried the conversation.

"What was your favorite activity in the BDM?" she asked.

Ilse pondered. "Foraging. We've forgotten that our forests contain everything we need for life."

Anneliese nodded seriously.

"Mine's knitting." A simple, brilliant smile spread across her face. "I can make sweaters, shawls, mittens, and socks. I'm working on becoming so fast my needles are a blur. Would you like me to make you something?"

Ilse normally didn't accept anything from strangers, but

Anneliese was so eagerly awaiting her response that she said, "That would be nice."

Anneliese studied Ilse. "A hat for you, I think. It will go well with your face shape."

She began talking all about her piano lessons back in Berlin and how much she missed her teacher. Ilse studied her as she put the water on the stove to boil. Her artlessness made Ilse trust that Anneliese was who she said she was, something Ilse was not used to seeing inside Lebensborn—she couldn't even see it in herself.

When Anneliese finished with the dumplings, Ilse sent her to fetch the mountain of walnuts she'd stored in the cellar during the fall. When Ilse was alone, she added the tansy flowers and leaves to the pot of water, now at a rolling boil. Shriveled and yellow, they floated on the water, riding the bubbles.

Von Thiel had visited the night before, so after it steeped for twenty minutes, she poured the tea into a mug for herself. Though she knew the taste would be nothing compared to wild carrot, she braced herself anyway and gulped the tea down. The flavor was mildly bitter, with an herbal quality. Though she wouldn't describe it as "pleasant in taste" as the herbalist had, with a touch of honey, it would be easy enough to avoid complaints about her salad dressing. As long as it didn't make her, or anyone else, sick.

She'd already lined her underpants in preparation for the bleeding that should come, and only a few hours later, it did.

Chapter Thirty

Today would be Anneliese's first day on her own, and Ilse was fairly certain the girl wouldn't be up for it. Nevertheless, Anneliese was bright-eyed, tracking Ilse's instructions and ignoring her rather obvious lack of belief in her when von Thiel discovered her.

"Ilse, you're not working today, remember?" he said, stepping into the kitchen.

"Oh, don't come in," Ilse said, reaching behind her to untie the apron she'd thrown on over her day dress. "I'm coming out."

She really was coming out anyway, but some irrational part of her was afraid that he would see Anneliese, this walking angel, and his affections would transfer to her. Her grasp on him felt tenuous, based only on his illusions of her, which at any moment could be shattered. Just the other day he'd said, "There is so much darkness in me, but I look at you and see such light. You brighten my life." Ilse didn't think any description of her could be less accurate. He didn't know her at all. And he mustn't.

Von Thiel chuckled and stepped out to wait in the hall. Ilse followed him out a moment later.

"That's the new cook," she said with a sigh. "I'm training her, but I think I'd be better off on my own."

"It will be good for her to learn from you," he said as they headed for the front door. "And if you have help, then I get more of you to myself."

She gave him her best crooked smile.

"Shall we go for a drive?"

As they roamed along the countryside, early spring rain pounding against the windshield, Ilse found herself pressing her feet against the floor of the car, trying to go faster, yearning to have control. She glanced at von Thiel's hands on the steering wheel, on the gear.

"Once, you said you'd teach me how to drive. Do you remember?"

"Are you saying you want to learn now?"

"If you're still willing."

"You know I want nothing more than to acquiesce to your every wish. Nothing makes me happier than to see you happy." Ilse doubted this—what about his children, his studies, Himmler's approval? "But you would need to be discreet. I can teach you while we're out here in the country, and when we go back to the villa, it will be as if you never touched a steering wheel. I would be in considerable trouble if it were known that I let you drive a government vehicle."

"I understand."

"Alright." He pulled over, then got out of the car and looped around to the passenger seat while Ilse slid over to the driver's side. Once he'd settled in, he eyed Ilse, who felt giddy behind the wheel.

"You're too happy there," he said.

"I'm exactly the right amount of happy. You know the value

of independence, even if it's in the form of a skill I'll probably never use."

"I do, I do. I just have to get used to this." He shook his head, smiling. "Here we go. Put your foot on the left pedal and make sure your gear is in neutral—give it a wiggle, that's how you know—good. The key is in the ignition; go ahead and turn it forward and you'll feel the engine turn over."

Ilse followed his instructions and felt the engine rumbling through the car. When it settled into its purr, it was quite satisfying. Von Thiel showed her the various gears, how to ease pressure on the pedal and coordinate the timing of the two. It seemed easy enough, though he told her it was not.

She set off, and immediately stalled. She restarted and then stalled again, and again, and again. Frustration bristled inside her; she swallowed it. He remained patient. He assured her that stalling was normal, and it would take her several sessions to learn. She began to hate the silky leather seats, the feel of the steering wheel beneath her hands, the taunting sound of the engine as it failed over and over.

"I think I've had enough for today," she said after the car stalled for the thirtieth or the hundredth time. She hopped out of the car and stomped over to the passenger side, trying to work her frustrations out on the dirt road so she wouldn't take them out on him.

Von Thiel, looking rather relieved himself, resumed his place at the wheel and drove them to lunch.

In the red room, von Thiel's attentions were especially ardent. Ilse fell asleep within moments of completing the act, though it was only mid-afternoon. As she drifted away, she thought she heard von Thiel mumble, "I can't wait for you to have our child." She was too close to sleep for the tiny bubble of panic inside her to rise.

Some time later, she woke from a thick and unpleasant sleep to a pain stabbing away in her gut. Cramps. Or gas. It was mild, already beginning to recede. She draped an arm over her stomach and blinked open her eyes, feeling disoriented and groggy—she never fell asleep during the day. Now it was dusk.

Von Thiel's face loomed over hers; he was gazing at her with an intense ferocity. And then she realized.

He loved her.

Maybe he had this whole time, or maybe the feeling had snuck up on him today. It was an overwhelming thought. What did it mean? Did she love him too? She did think of him constantly. She enjoyed their conversations, the feeling of safety he gave her.

"What's the matter?" he said, eyes full of concern. His eyebrows knitted and rose to the center of his forehead. It was painfully endearing. *Did* she love him? His ideals were wrong, but his focus was on improving the lives of Germans, not on destroying everyone else. He was thoughtful and gentle and would never hurt anyone.

Still half-asleep, she blurted out, "How can you be in the SS?"

And then she was not half-asleep at all. She was wide awake, heart thundering in her chest. This had been the danger all along, of getting close to a Nazi and letting her guard down. One moment of ease was all it took. This was why she should have stuck to quick encounters with the foot soldiers passing through. She lowered her eyelids, trying to look as sleepy, or innocent, or seductive as possible.

But, she saw through her eyelashes, he wasn't looking at her like a traitor. Instead, he was contemplating her. He drew in a deep breath.

"I was young when I became very passionate about Germany and our people's right to take up space, our own space, our own land. I believe there is something special about us, that we have a destiny to fulfill. When I attended my first National Socialist meeting, back in the twenties when Hitler was nobody, there was something in the air; I was swept up in it."

Ilse propped herself up on an elbow. She remembered that feeling. She'd felt it at the Nuremberg rally.

"Are you still swept up?"

"I've been challenged. But those challenges only remind me that the sacrifices I make now are for something more important."

"What kinds of sacrifices?"

His deep-set eyes hid in shadow. It was as if a wall came down behind them.

"Nothing for a lady like you to think on."

She began drawing feather-light circles on his arm.

"What about your family?" she asked. "I know you have a wife and children."

Von Thiel lay on his back, so they were both staring at the red canopy of the bed.

"What would you like to know?" His voice was low and even. It was clear that he didn't want to talk about it, but he felt he must.

"What is her name? How long have you been married?" She strove to keep her voice like his.

"Emmi. Almost twelve years."

"That is quite some time."

"I suppose. It was more or less an arrangement between our families. I liked her, enjoyed her company. It seemed a strong partnership. And it is: we have a balance between the two of us, and have always agreed on how to build our family."

"Does she know about me?"

"Not specifically. But we have an understanding. Emmi didn't do well after our youngest was born, and we don't know if she would survive another birth. She knows it's my duty as a member of the SS to have at least four children."

"I see." That was where Ilse came in.

He looked at her. She could feel his breath on her cheek. "And she knows that I must have affection for any woman I am with."

Her breath was shaky in her chest. She exhaled. It was important to understand what she was doing, not just the reality for her, but what it meant for others. She had von Thiel on loan from another woman who probably was less understanding about it than he believed. At the end of all this, he would go home to his wife, kiss her in that habitual way that comes after a thousand kisses, when there will be at least a thousand more. And Ilse would be nothing.

"And your children?"

"I have three. Two boys and a girl: Mani, Alvis, and Sigrun." She could hear the smile in his voice. "The boys are little men already, wanting to help around the farm, push plows like field-hands. The youngest, the girl, is only four, and full of questions. I don't spend as much time with them as I would like. My work keeps me away from them."

"They sound wonderful." Ilse's stomach panged.

There was a pause. She wanted to know more, but if she asked the wrong thing, they could find themselves in a place from which they couldn't come back. What he might reveal, how it might make her feel . . . It was better not to know.

"So many questions tonight," he said.

"I want to know you," she said, and found that she meant it.

"It's only fair now for you to tell me something about your-self that I don't know."

She didn't want to hide anymore. Von Thiel had been honest. She would be, too.

"Wait here," she said. She got up and threw her dress on and darted to her room down the hall. She retrieved *Jane Eyre* and wrapped it in a silk scarf von Thiel had given her but she felt was too nice to ever wear. Back in the suite, she returned to the bed where von Thiel lay waiting. His eyes flicked to her hands, and he grinned.

"Your scarf? I've already seen it. In fact, I gave it to you."

Hands trembling slightly, she unwrapped the scarf to reveal the book, which she handed to von Thiel. She sat on the bed next to him as he took it.

"I found it underneath the floorboard in my room." Ilse didn't add that it was her room in Heim Harz, and she'd brought it halfway across the country to the villa. "I assume it's banned, if it was hidden."

Von Thiel ran his hands over the cover and cracked open the spine. It fell open and lay flat.

"It's not banned explicitly, but only because no one bothered to ban it," he said. "This book isn't popular in Germany anymore; it must have been difficult to find a translation. Your predecessor may have had an English parent or a tutor who gave it to her."

He flipped through the pages, fluttering her with a cool breeze.

"Because it's written by a non-German author, especially because she was English, it would probably have gone into a fire had there been one nearby," he said. "Its focus on women's independence and Christian values wouldn't have helped it."

"You've read it?"

He stopped at a page.

"Yes. It was a long time ago. But I remember enjoying Jane's strength of character and her philosophical fireside conversations with Mr. Rochester."

"I enjoyed those things, too."

"So you have read it. What do you think?"

Ilse studied his face. He seemed curious, perhaps even excited.

"I haven't read many books," she began hesitantly, "but I think Jane is an admirable character, and the author's wisdom makes far more sense to me than the wisdom of our age. Only I don't like the ending."

"Oh?"

"I wish Jane had continued on her own, found her own way, instead of going back to the man who tried to trick her into bigamy."

She clamped her mouth shut. Von Thiel himself was a bigamist, and she was taking part in it. No trick was needed.

"In literature, as in life, a woman must end up married," von Thiel said, appearing not to have noticed Ilse's misstep. "What else would there have been for her?"

She bit back irritation. "She could have gone on teaching and helped many children who would have remained illiterate without her."

"You don't think Jane deserves happiness?"

"Marriage does not have to equal happiness. Quite often it's the opposite."

Von Thiel looked a little put out at that. It was a clue. His marriage was not a happy one after all, and he was not glad that she'd pointed it out.

"Of course," she said, trying to save the situation, "I believe that respect and honesty are essential aspects of marriage, and Mr. Rochester is lacking in both. He's a lovable man, but not a good one. Jane could have done better."

"I only hope that you keep such high standards for yourself, my treasure."

"I do." She leaned forward and pecked him on the lips. He looked up from the book, pleasantly bemused, then he took her face in the palms of his hands.

"The ability to think for yourself is a powerful one. I'm going to take you to Wewelsburg Castle soon. It's a special place; I want to see what you make of it."

He slid a hand to cup her head, stroking her hair with his thumb. It drove all thoughts out of her head. It felt so good not to think. She closed her eyes and curled her body into his.

CHAPTER THIRTY-ONE

Anneliese appeared in the kitchen wearing a new smile, sly and coy. Ilse assigned her to the tedious task of mincing herbs, but the girl immediately bubbled over with her news, brandishing the knife as she spoke.

"I wish you'd been at the mixer last night. You could have seen the dashing soldier who chose me. Well, we chose each other."

A stone dropped in Ilse's stomach. So, it had happened. She should have been there, gone to the mixer to stop it. What kind of a man would take a girl like this, her breasts barely formed, hair just out of pigtails? Had he at least been gentle with her? Had it been her first time? What if it was Walter?

"And . . . how are you today?" Ilse asked.

"Never better!" Her face was bright and knowing.

Now she had to dose Anneliese. The stone in her stomach grew to a boulder.

She began mentally calculating Anneliese's weight, trying to figure out the proper dosage for someone so small. Perhaps it was too dangerous. But she imagined an infant passing through those narrow hips, getting stuck, and that seemed even more dangerous. Anneliese wasn't ready to have a child—they could both die in labor, and Ilse wasn't going to let that happen. She would have to be the one to get her hands dirty, bear the burden of responsibility for Anneliese.

Ilse sent her on an errand to the wine cellar to hunt for a wine she was certain they didn't have. She knew because she'd made it up: *Chateau Thomas*. Anneliese would be down there for a while. Ilse felt bad about the frustration this fruitless hunt would cause Anneliese, but she had to dose her now.

She opened a drawer and lifted out a box of recipes. Hidden underneath the felt bottom of that box were Thomas's instructions from all those months ago. She looked at his neat, careful handwriting. Soon that handwriting might be extinct. Thomas was dying, slowly. And she sat in her villa, well fed and warm, drugging girls as if that would make any difference at all. Her blood roiled and, out of a need to do something besides stand there, she threw the recipe box across the room. The clattering echoed off the hard surfaces. One of the recipes landed in the pot of boiling water. Others floated to the ground dreamily.

Ilse breathed heavily for a few moments, taking in the chaos she'd created and the temporary relief it had brought, then gathered herself and picked up the box. The recipe for tansy was under the false bottom where she'd hidden it. Even though she had them memorized, she reread the instructions and calculated the dosage for Anneliese, then checked it twice. The girl was so delicate; there was no margin for error. Ilse retrieved the needed amount of dried flowers and leaves from her hiding spot in the storeroom and poured them into the pot of water boiling on the stove. Hands resting on the counter, her elbows locked so she could rest her weight in her shoulder sockets, she watched the water darken.

Without warning, pain stabbed her stomach. She'd felt it several times now. It was sharp, insistent, demanding her attention. She doubled over, leaning her head toward the counter. It could be cramps again—she took tansy, and before that, wild carrot, so often that she sometimes bled several times a month. The world shifted around her as if she were on a ship and bile rose to her throat. She bit the inside of her cheek, straightened herself up, and poured the tea into a mug.

Anneliese returned empty-handed, as Ilse had known she would.

"Oops!" Anneliese said when she saw the scattered recipes on the floor. She began to gather them up.

"Don't do that, Anneliese. I'll clean it up in a moment." Ilse's voice felt weak. Anneliese continued gathering the recipes.

"I couldn't find the wine," the girl said from the ground. "I'm so sorry."

The world reeled again.

"Are you ill?" Anneliese's voice came from far away.

"I'm fine. Fine."

Ilse looked at the steam rising from the cup of tea. Could the pain be caused by tansy? It seemed likely. It had come on only a few weeks after she'd started using it, and she already knew it was dangerous. This pain, as much as she tried to tell herself otherwise, was not like any cramps or gas she'd had before. And for all she knew, it would get worse.

She'd been exerting her will over other people's lives and bodies, much the way the Nazis did. A sudden feeling of disgust with herself overwhelmed her.

She wasn't Jane Eyre; she was Mr. Rochester—meaning well, or perhaps not, but in any event, totally misguided. It was not up to her to trick people into doing what she wanted, to drug teenage girls who had no choice in becoming what they were.

Had she hurt anyone? She probably would have found out if a girl had more severe side effects, but any one of those girls could be having cramps, nausea, pain– pain that Ilse had caused.

"Would you like your tea now?" Anneliese, looking concerned, held the cup of tansy out to Ilse.

She snatched it away from Anneliese, splashing hot water onto her own hands. Red welts appeared on her skin, but she barely felt it. Anneliese gasped, her hands fluttering to her face.

"No," Ilse said, pouring the tea out into the sink. "I made that by mistake."

She dismissed Anneliese early. As soon as she'd left, Ilse burned Thomas's note.

That night, as she got into bed, she picked up *Physica* and opened it at random. The page naturally fell open where Hildegard's writings ended and her mother's began.

Her thoughts went to the girls she'd drugged. Had she really thought she'd been doing good in some way? Helping Thomas, indirectly? She'd been naive and caused harm. Revulsion twisted and surged up from her gut, merging with the pain that still throbbed faintly.

Out of habit, she almost reached for the bottle of whiskey she hid between her bed and the wall.

But she stopped herself. She didn't want to numb herself anymore. Instead, she pressed her fingers against a purple Siberian iris that her mother had found and pressed herself, over twenty years ago. She read page after page, about every kind of plant—edible, medicinal, beautiful.

CHAPTER THIRTY-TWO

Ilse waited on the villa's front steps for von Thiel to pick her up, basking in the beginnings of warmth in the spring air. She looked forward to seeing him. Since the night she'd shared *Jane Eyre* with him, she felt closer to him, an intimacy that felt at once safe and dangerous—if she was right and they could trust each other, he could be her strongest ally; but if she had it wrong, she could reveal the wrong thought to an SS officer who held her fate in his hands.

The gates opened and the black Mercedes with its flapping flags glided up the driveway. Ilse approached as the car pulled up. As always, von Thiel got out and opened the door for her.

But today, his eyes were bloodshot with shadows underneath, and his shoulders were hunched.

"Are you alright?" she asked.

"What? Yes, yes. Get in, treasure." His smile looked forced.

Whatever it was, he would come out with it eventually, she thought as she slid onto the leather seat. They drove toward their usual restaurant in pensive silence. His preoccupation filled the air. She eyed his clenched jaw and stiff back, wishing he would open up to her as he had before. For the feeling of closeness to return and for him to seek solace in her.

They were out in the countryside now, no buildings or people for miles. He pulled over. "You wanted to continue your driving lessons?"

"If you're up for it."

"Of course."

They switched sides and he instructed her in a quiet voice that seethed underneath, bristling with an unsettling energy. She tried to be a good pupil, as if that would cheer him up. She held back her frustrations, even when she stalled the vehicle, twice.

First, he grabbed her arm so hard it hurt. Ilse lay beneath him, pushing against his chest as if to make him stop, too afraid to ask him to. He didn't seem to notice. He bit her lip and she tasted iron. Worst of all, as he drove himself into her, he seemed far away, gone even. Some other man had taken up residence in his body, a stranger who cared nothing for her, only used her.

What had happened to him that would make him do this? How far would he go? He was still von Thiel, wasn't he? He wouldn't truly hurt her.

And yet.

Her eyes shut, she bit her lip against the discomfort and retreated into herself, to the perch where she was safe.

Afterwards, he rose and produced a bottle of cognac from his briefcase. He poured two, three fingers into a crystal glass and downed it, then poured another. When he ran his hands through his hair, it stood up, pointing every which way.

He'd gone from kind to aloof to aggressive so quickly. What had changed since his kindness toward her? Ilse put on her robe and sat on the bench at the foot of the bed, ignoring the blossoming soreness.

With her legs crossed and her hands folded together in her lap, she asked what was wrong in her most soothing voice.

He flopped back down on the bed and took a swig from the bottle. His mood seemed to morph almost at once from anger to a desire for comfort. He rested his head on her lap. She ran her fingers through his hair, grotesquely slick with pomade. Care and fear warred inside her, but it didn't matter which emotion won; she had her part to play.

"I thought I could remain above it all, keep my mind on the abstract, be with a good woman," he squeezed her thigh, "and the taint wouldn't reach me. But I'm like everyone else. The man doing monstrous things becomes the monster. I've signed orders, not thinking, because I had to. It was on paper, not real. But now I've looked into their eyes. They're dead and their killers are rewarded."

Ilse stopped stroking his hair. Who was dead?

"What are you talking about?"

He rolled over to bury his face in her lap. "What matters is the purpose. We must remember that. We'll become a pure civilization and live as gods on earth. I will find the secret in the runes and show them all."

His words were incoherent, but disturbing. What did he mean that someone was dead and the killers rewarded? That he was a monster? Was this how he would be from now on?

Something told her yes. He was SS. This was the man the Reich had shaped, only he'd hidden it better than others. He would hurt her as all men had, because he could. She'd learned that lesson already.

She forced herself to resume stroking his hair, slow and steady, so he wouldn't feel her hands shaking. She murmured soothing words into his ear.

It wasn't as if she could leave him. As advantageous as being in his favor was, being out of it was that much more dangerous. If he didn't care so much for her, he'd already suspect her of her crimes. With his resources, he could find out everything if he started looking. She trembled. She was going to crumble into pieces, and no one would be there to put her back together.

A memory rose clearly in her mind of Max, the SS man at Heim Harz who had so much beer he couldn't fulfill his duties in the bedroom.

Beer was made from hops, which even without alcohol were a sedative, but she didn't have hops. She would have to order them, claiming she wanted to brew her own beer, and then she would need to actually make the beer.

What she did have were linden flowers, now in bloom. Her mother's annotation in *Physica* indicated linden flower as a sedative. Instead of the tea her mother suggested, she would make a tincture, a potent one, that could be added to a beverage. With any luck, and the help of von Thiel's drinking, it could lead to sleep instead of intercourse.

She couldn't believe she hadn't thought of a sedative tincture before. Perhaps it was because, until now, she hadn't been able to imagine interfering with the violent bodies of men.

He rolled to look up at her in the dark, sloshing the contents of the bottle onto the bedspread.

"Why have you never gotten pregnant?" he demanded. "I know I'm virile. I have three children at home."

Her mouth fell open, and her heart stopped. Her palms instantly became slick with sweat. She focused on poise, aloofness. She could not think of the truth.

"I don't know," she began slowly. "It depends on my cycle— we have to make love at the right time, and since my cycle has always been irregular, it's harder to know when that time is . . ."

She squirmed with discomfort at having to talk about her bodily functions.

He scoffed. His eyes bulged at her.

"We can try harder," she said. "If you want a child this much."

"It's not just that I want one. It's that something doesn't add up here. Frau Herta has spoken to me about your odd behavior."

Adrenaline rushed to Ilse's extremities. All over she burned.

"What did she say?"

"That birth rates for the whole villa have declined. That you've been here the longest—almost a year—and have yet to conceive. That you jump a mile when Frau Herta enters the room. I've always thought your oddness is part of your charm, but perhaps I was wrong."

She'd been so brash, drugging everyone. It was bound to come to someone's notice. Well, she'd stopped that now, but there was no way around dosing herself. No matter what, she would not have von Thiel's child, or any other Nazi's. She took a breath, held it, and let it go.

"I'm used to being alone in the kitchen; she startles me," she said. "And maybe it's a little harder for me to conceive after . . ." she trailed off, not wanting to say Otto's name in this conversation. "My body could be taking some time to recover after the difficult birth. I'm sure we can figure it out together."

"We must," he huffed and took another swig. "Whatever is going on with you, Frau Herta has made it clear: If you're not expecting by the time you've been here a year, your place will be reconsidered."

That was only a few weeks away. She felt as if she were floating away, watching the two of them from above.

"My place? What does that mean?"

"In Lebensborn. In the Reich. Remember, you were on trial

before you came here. The investigation will be reopened." He clutched her hand. "Ilse, we must have a child, for both our sakes."

Ilse's hand hesitated over the dried tansy. She must stop taking it. She must become pregnant.

But she was overwhelmed with the need to void herself of any remnants of von Thiel. He'd hurt her. He'd called himself a monster but wouldn't tell her what he'd done. Her imagination filled in the gaps. She felt the revulsion for him that she'd once thought she should feel for Felix. He'd finally shown her what was hiding behind his warmth and kindness and sophistication. She'd wanted the two of them to be honest with each other, and she'd gotten her wish. Though a part of her mourned, any tenderness she'd felt for him had now vanished, replaced by steely resolve.

She spooned out a full dose of tansy. The dried leaves crackled and crumbled as she dumped them into the boiling water. Once she'd gulped it down, she went out to the gardens. This she often did; no one would suspect anything as long as she didn't behave suspiciously. She meandered over to the linden tree, as anyone would. In full bloom, its scent was intoxicating, enticing. She could see the individual blooms now, clusters of yellow-white, small and feathery. She withdrew a knife from her apron pocket and began to cut. A few minutes later, she returned to the kitchen with full pockets and set about preparing her tinctures. She'd never made a tincture with fresh flowers, but how different could it be? In small brown glass vials, she added the flower heads and potato vodka, sealed them each with wax, and hid them away in the storeroom.

She needed a plan, an escape before the end of June, when her time ran out. After all this time, her lies would be discovered, and everything she'd gone through this last year would be for nothing.

A dull ache grew in her stomach, which she ignored as she kneaded dough and looked out the window at the linden tree.

Then there was the familiar sight of Thomas with his cart.

He was alive. Her chest contracted. With the earliest harvests coming in, she'd been looking forward to finding out how he was doing, talking with him in Low German, feeding him. And most of all, confirming that he was, somehow, still alive.

With floury hands, she ran to the door and opened it, bursting with a smile. But her face fell instantly. It wasn't Thomas pushing the cart. It was another man, older, with a sturdier build and dark eyes framed by long, thick eyelashes.

"Delivery," the man said brusquely. "I'll leave it outside."

"Sorry," she said. "Where's Thomas? The man who usually brings the produce?"

The man examined her face—looking for what, Ilse didn't know—then lowered his gaze as he began to unload the cart.

"Thomas went in for castration." His voice was flat. "They give that option to homosexuals in exchange for freedom. He took it, of course—better to be castrated than dead. I got the news from someone I know who works in the infirmary and saw it. They castrated him, alright, and then they let him bleed out. They cracked jokes while they did it. He knew better than to beg at least, and he kept some dignity."

The world tilted; Ilse leaned against the counter to keep from falling. "He was awake?"

"They wouldn't waste drugs on a Jew." His voice was filled with bitterness so strong she almost took a step back. "They would never let a Jew walk out of a KZ alive, either. This is a place where guards kill when they're bored. They make a man run for his life while they riddle his back with bullet holes, or drown him in the carp pond, or stomp on his rib cage."

She felt sick. She knew Thomas dying was a possibility, a likelihood. But at the thought that he'd been killed, and in such a way, she wanted to vomit. The man was watching her.

"I tell you because you should know this," he said. "Someone should."

She nodded, forced herself to remain calm and help the man unload the cart. Her arms felt like levers in a machine. The triangle on the man's arm was red; Thomas had once told her that was the symbol for political prisoners. Perhaps he was a communist or a social democrat.

"Did you know him?" she asked.

He stopped and looked at her again.

"Very well." His voice was rough.

She noticed the man's eyelashes again, dark and thick and curling. She wondered if he was Peter, Thomas's lover. Ilse opened her mouth, to apologize perhaps.

"Do you have any food?" the man asked. She nodded and fetched some roasted pork and slathered a roll with a thick layer of butter. The man wolfed it down and left with his cart. It was a relief that he didn't thank her as Thomas had. She didn't deserve it.

Ilse closed the door and sank to the ground. She tried and failed not to picture Thomas's final moments, the pain and then the realization. The SS men laughing at him, the butt of their joke. Thomas, his body, being hauled away. She ran to the sink and vomited.

Ilse and von Thiel lay sprawled across the sheets. Von Thiel was drinking. Not savoring a French red, as he had in the early days, but taking large gulps of Schnaps. How could it be that her only hope was to bear his child?

She felt hollow. When she touched her lip, it came away spotted with bright-red blood. He thought he could hurt her, that it was his right to do as he pleased with her, so she would spite him by remaining unaffected. She extricated the bottle from his inebriated hands, drank out of it, coughed at the sharpness.

She was seized by an impulse. Deflection from his suspicions and his punishments, she told herself, but really, she was angry. That he was acting like a stranger, that he thought he could hurt her. She sat up in bed.

"Why don't you ever get me out of this life?" she said. She was the demanding lover now. He would focus on calming her. It was unlikely to work, but she could hardly tell anymore what was right and when to do it.

Von Thiel rolled his bleary face toward her.

"What?"

"I'm trapped here, cooking three meals a day, six days a week. It's not easy work. You take me to romantic places and buy me gifts, when what I really want is to be able to walk out of these gates of my own accord. You're powerful. You could free me."

"Ils-sah, Ils-sah," he slurred. "I'm the reason you're here at all."

She froze. Something told her she would find out what she didn't want to know, what she maybe already knew, but kept hidden from herself.

"This was the trade I made for you," von Thiel continued. "If not for my interference after Otto died, you would have been sterilized and then been a subject of study for the doctors perfecting and scaling the procedure. A human test subject. Would that have been better?"

She gaped at him. It seemed so obvious now.

"What did you do?"

"I knew—I *know*—that our fates are intertwined, that we're meant to be in each other's lives. I had to protect you. So I had documents made that proved Otto's death was a defect caused by a lack of oxygen during the birth—not a genetic condition, but a traumatic one, highly unlikely to occur again. Which, by the way, I believe is true. I said we needed more Aryan mothers and that you deserved the opportunity to fulfill your duty of motherhood, to serve in a position of honor as a reward for your dedication and your resilience. It was another chance for you to prove yourself. I promised to personally ensure that you lived up to the potential that I knew lay within you." His eyes flicked to her stomach. "Now I'm not so sure."

Ilse wrapped herself in a sheet. So he was the reason she'd become a breeder, trapped in the SS. "Why didn't you pull me out of the program and take me as your mistress instead?"

"Ah. That. My power is not what it once was. I do not have enough of Himmler's favor anymore to remove you from the program. Everything must appear to be in service to Lebensborn."

She continued to stare, heart pounding.

"You look at me like I'm a monster, Ilse, but you have no idea who I am. What I've had to do. See this?" He raised his fist and the silver skull-engraved ring glinted at her. "This is the SS honor ring, the Death's Head Ring. You must have noticed it's not standard issue for the SS. It is a personal gift, given to me by Himmler himself, as one of his inner circle. That was before I fell out of his favor and was stationed at Dachau."

Ilse stiffened. Against her better judgment, she leaned away from him. He worked at the camp, at the place that tormented Thomas and Peter and so many others? Where people were drowned and stomped on and used for target practice? She fought back bile.

"Yes, I thought you wouldn't like that. It was a punishment. I told you that all this time I was working with Himmler on my occult pursuits. But the truth is I fell out of his favor months ago. We'd been friends, good friends for ten years at least. We bonded over our love of mysticism. But I pushed. I wanted to be involved in the development of Wewelsburg Castle, the search for the Holy Grail. Himmler reminded me that my role as a RuSHA officer is to ensure that German people are living on German land, that our most pressing duty is to purify our race, free it from Jews and Slavs, Poles and Gypsies. Wewelsburg was not in my purview.

"When I painted runes on my office floor in Berlin, that was when Himmler decided he'd had enough of me. He didn't pull me from my role in RuSHA—yet—but he did send me to Dachau for 'hands-on experience.' That's what he does with members of the SS who displease him. We do his dirty work and he teaches us a lesson. That's where I've been for the last several months, as punishment for my obsession with the historical, the mythological, above all other National Socialist values."

He looked her in the eye. She forced herself to meet his gaze. She felt dirty down to her core.

"I understood the purpose of the camp, to reeducate and provide much-needed labor for the Reich, but I wasn't prepared to see the conditions. The men were dirty and downtrodden, emaciated. The sight of what could be done to human beings filled me with revulsion. But even if I weren't disgraced, I would be powerless to change what happened there. When I arrived, I vomited into the dirt. There wasn't even a bush nearby, so desolate was this land. I was told it's like that for everyone at first. Then they get used to it."

It was all Ilse could do to stop herself from running away from him. The thin sheet wasn't enough; she gathered the blankets around herself, a barrier between her flesh and his.

"I managed to distance myself from the daily operations. I buried myself in administration. I signed orders without looking at them, because it was easier for me not to see. But I know I have arranged for men to be killed. Assigned them to work orders a healthy man could not survive, much less a starving one. Then, a few weeks ago, Himmler caught wind of my tactics. He wanted me to see for myself what I was doing. He put me in charge of the castration of homosexuals. I did my duty. I looked the prisoners in the eye when I told them their options. They all made the same choice. And then, of course, the guards got carried away with my orders. They decided to let the Jewish one bleed out, for their own entertainment. I found out after, when they were joking about pulling the balls off the Mischling. They're rewarded for their sickest acts."

A sudden cold filled her body. Von Thiel had made the order that led to Thomas's death. She felt filthy. She'd touched this man. She wished for her clothes so intensely that it felt as if a part of her had picked them up, gotten dressed, and left the red room for good. He'd been leaning against the headboard, but now leaned toward her, his face wretched.

"You see," he continued, "I'm not the kind, sensitive man you think I am. I have orchestrated several events in your life to bring you closer to me. I arranged for the second doctor to examine Otto. I brought you here as a Little Blond Sister. You've been the one bright light in my ever-darkening life. My burdens grow heavier and there's no way out. You know that as well as anyone. Even if I could get you out of Lebensborn, of the SS—which I can't—I need you with me."

Ilse forced herself to remain composed. "Did you know what the doctor would determine when he saw Otto?"

"I knew you wanted the examination. I suspected what may happen, but it was inevitable. The only thought in my mind was to ease your suffering in that moment. I care for you, Ilse."

He reached a hand across the bed and laid it on hers. It was hot and clammy and repulsive. She forced herself not to pull away.

"You have to find a way out," she said, beginning to feel frantic. She thought she'd been playing him this whole time. She should have known better. Everyone knew that all SS were frightening men who did terrible things. Better to do anything else than become entangled with one. She should have run away, gone underground and sold her body on the streets instead. It would have been better.

But she forced out the words she knew he needed to hear, made them sound genuine.

"You *are* a good man, deep down. You've had to do bad things, but you haven't changed yet. I'll help you find a way out, so you can be who you really are: a scholar, a mystic. Not a killer."

"Yes, Ilse." He reached out and patted her hand. "That's what I love about you. You see that side of me. I need you to keep believing in me, treasure. Promise?"

She took another swig from the bottle and passed it to von Thiel, who gulped it down. It would be better if they both didn't remember this night.

"It's time we finally make this baby," he said. "It's been far too long."

Then he pushed his mouth against hers until their teeth crashed together. The spot on her lip where he'd made her bleed screamed in protest. She went silently along, for what choice did she have?

A piece of her was being taken away, something vital, that would change her forever.

Images haunted her: von Thiel standing by as Otto, helpless and tiny, passed from one indifferent set of hands to another while he wailed for his mother, until he was silenced. Thomas running through plum orchards with stained feet. Thomas tending to the rose gardens of Berlin. Thomas's shy, averted gaze, until he was sure about something—then, his face blazed with determination. Thomas at Dachau, standing for hours at roll call, inhaling his food so it wouldn't be stolen, being beaten. Then taking von Thiel's offer, and his final moments on a table in some wretched surgery.

When von Thiel began snoring loud enough for the whole villa to hear, she sat up in bed, trembling in the sharp night air.

On the floor by the bed, she could see the collar of von Thiel's tunic bearing the insignia of three oak leaves, illuminated by the moon. According to Hildegard, oak signified worthlessness.

How could she bring him to justice? Was such a thing possible?

She could kill him right now, with his own gun, with poison. But she would never get out alive after murdering an SS officer. Even if she somehow managed to escape—which seemed more impossible the more she thought about it—she'd never be able to live with herself if she became a murderer like him.

But was she so different from him? She'd gone along, played her own role within the same system, her feeble rebellion aside. Perhaps in his situation she would do the same, if she felt she had no option. She'd already done so much she knew was wrong.

Disgust and despair mingled, rising to her throat. She ran to the toilet. Her wretched fingers clung to the seat as she shuddered and heaved, her nose burning, her coughs echoing in the porcelain bowl. When her stomach was empty, she slumped against the golden walls.

She lived with the SS, slept with the SS, was the SS. It was in her blood. There was no way out.

CHAPTER THIRTY-THREE

Hannelore and Ilse sat in the back seat of a Mercedes, watching houses turn into fields and then meadows, as they headed for the hangar.

It was her first time leaving the villa without von Thiel. She was allowed to leave only with a permission slip and an SS guard as escort. He was too young, but his silence and sharp movements revealed what his training had made him capable of. He was there for her protection, Frau Herta had said, from those who "do not properly appreciate the work Lebensborn is doing." Ilse didn't believe this; she was being watched and tracked.

She was going to fly for the first time today. Well, she would ride while Hannelore flew. She tried to look forward to it, to overflow with excitement as Hannelore did, but Ilse's world had gone gray and flat, except for the moments when she was overwhelmed with horror and disgust.

Hannelore must have noticed, for she reached across the back seat and squeezed Ilse's forearm. They wouldn't talk here, with the SS guard in the car.

"What would you do, if you could do anything?" Hannelore

asked. She wore her fur-lined flying suit and the yellow scarf Ilse had knitted.

Ilse shrugged.

"I've never had a reason to think about it."

"You don't need a reason," Hannelore said. She stuck her hand out the window to catch the breeze. "Think about whatever you want, all the time. That's what I do."

A faint pain stabbed at Ilse's stomach, again. She wondered wildly if she was pregnant.

"You would fly planes," Ilse said.

"Of course. Maybe even machine planes if I can get my hands on one. I'm going to be Hanna Reitsch, remember."

"She's in the Luftwaffe, isn't she? Would you enlist? Would you be able to?"

Hannelore shook her head, bouncing with irritation at the irrelevant questions. Her eye twitched. "Go. Your turn."

Cook, housekeeper, secretary, pilot, carpenter. She didn't know how to dream. She stretched her mind but, like cold dough, it wouldn't budge.

Ilse leaned against the headrest.

"Maybe I wouldn't do anything. I'd be outside all day, running through forests, swimming in rivers, living off the land." She couldn't think of anything else she'd want to do. Her mind was too full of her only options: have von Thiel's baby or continue to resist, futilely, and meet the fate that had been chasing her for two years.

Hannelore appraised Ilse with squinted eyes.

"You could be a botanist, or an herbalist. The woman in the woods everyone goes to see for their cures, perhaps with a bit of magic slipped in."

"I'm not sure 'curing' is what I do."

"Well, soon we'll be in the air. You'll see how much none of it matters."

Ilse studied Hannelore's face, her lips upturned. She wondered if anything ever troubled her. Perhaps flying was the secret to her carefree spirit.

They arrived at the hangar and spilled out of the car. Hannelore's flight instructor, a Hauptmann in the Luftwaffe, waited for her, tall and spare and still as a statue. He had the personality of one, too. He didn't seem to be thrilled about giving weekly private lessons to Hannelore, and she wasn't the least bit fazed. Hannelore had told Ilse it was a favor to Heydrich. No one said no to him.

The Hauptmann gave Hannelore her instructions for the day in a monotone voice Ilse was sure the man himself wasn't listening to. Hannelore certainly wasn't paying attention, tugging at a curl and eyeing the plane as men set up the ropes to prepare it for takeoff.

Hannelore and Ilse greased their faces for protection from the elements, climbed into the cramped glider, single file with Ilse in the back, and put on their helmets, gloves, and goggles. Four strapping men held the bungees attached to the nose of the plane. A few more men held the tail steady.

The Hauptmann gave the order, "Heave!" and the men ran forward, pulling the plane after them. The cable stretched, the men at the back let go of the tail, and the bungee slipped off the nose as the plane broke free.

The wind thrust them upwards, higher and higher, until the air was thin and cold. Below, the world became smaller, fading away until only the sky was real.

She closed her eyes against the sun as it appeared from behind a cloud. Hannelore let out a whoop.

Ilse's heart was racing. She placed her hand on her chest. Her hand didn't feel like hers. Her body didn't feel like hers.

She was being sucked up into the sky. She would burst into a million particles. The feeling rose and rose; her body would explode any minute, and then, what relief. An odd sensation—one she was sure had nothing to do with flying.

"Should we head back?" Ilse called over the roar of the wind.

Hannelore's voice sounded tinny and far away.

"Why ever would we do that? Ilse?"

But everything was black, and then there was nothing at all.

⁂

The blanket was heavy, pinning her to the bed. Hair, not hers, feathered across her cheek. She seemed to have sunk through her body to somewhere deep inside the bed and was unable to get out.

Her eyelids must have twitched, because a voice said, "You're awake."

Hannelore.

The best Ilse could do was emit a garbled sound, so unlike words. She had to get up. Time was running out.

A cold rim was pressed to her lips. Water trickled into her mouth, down her throat, down her chin. She swallowed.

"You're in my apartment," Hannelore said. "The doctor says you had convulsions. Have you ever had those before? He says just about anything could have caused it."

A towel dabbed at Ilse's chin. Hannelore's presence was comforting. Ilse felt so warm.

"Don't worry about the villa. I told them you had scarlet fever and I was bringing you back here so you wouldn't get the rest of them sick. They didn't seem to mind that."

With effort, Ilse opened her mouth and garbled something else.

"You're on bed rest for a while, darling. Don't try to talk.

Don't think about cleaning, or cooking, or seducing von Thiel, or anything else that involves getting up."

Ilse shook her head. But it didn't matter what she wanted. Her eyelids were crusted shut. Outside, car horns tooted and trams clanged. The sounds of life, so exhausting. She sank again.

She slept, she didn't know for how long, sometimes coming to the surface at the sound of people coming in and out—Hannelore, maybe her maid, maybe the doctor. But she couldn't bring herself to open her eyes.

Ilse did not know how he found her, but there he was when she blinked open her eyes, standing at the foot of the bed. Through clouded vision, she saw that his face was contorted in what looked like anguish.

"Erich." Her voice came out scratched and broken, surprising her as much as him. He swept around the bed to sit beside her. She tried not to recoil as he took her hand.

"How are you feeling?"

"I'm fine. It's nothing, really."

"Convulsions are not nothing." He rested a hand on her forehead. "Was it . . . did you lose a baby?"

His voice shook, just a little, and she realized how devastated he was at the thought of it. She shook her head. His face melted; he buried it in her stomach. Before, she would have rested a hand on his thick, wavy head of hair. Now she couldn't bring herself to touch him if she didn't have to.

She wondered if he was more upset that there hadn't been a child at all than he would have been if there had been one who'd been lost. After a moment, he sat back up, looking gray.

"Then what was it?"

A thought punched her in the chest, woke her up. If Lebensborn found out about the convulsions and decided she was epileptic, perhaps she would be killed as Otto had been. They had taken everything else from her. She wouldn't give them her life. Von Thiel had to be on her side, fighting for her, not angry and estranged. She sat up.

"I think it was a reaction to some herbs I've been taking." Her voice sounded thin, but steady. "Motherwort."

Von Thiel stared at her blankly.

"To increase fertility."

"Please be careful. Without you . . . you're my last hope for myself." He leaned in, vibrating with something like desperation. He looked haunted. "You will redeem me. Promise me you'll be more careful."

"Yes, Erich."

He sagged in relief, the stiff collar of his uniform brushing his ears.

"I brought you something to read while you recover." He handed her a small object wrapped in brown paper and string. "It's the *Library of History*, the book I told you about, which tells Lucretia's story. I thought you might be interested in studying it further."

The contradictory feelings in Ilse created a storm that swirled inside her. Before her was everything she hated, encased in the form of a flesh-and-blood man, but one who cared for her and gave her thoughtful gifts. She didn't know what to make of it. So she looked at the book and cracked it open. It was stiff and smelled of leather and glue—the first new book she'd ever owned.

"Thank you," she said, and turned to Lucretia's story.

The apartment Heydrich had arranged for Hannelore was spacious and bordered on opulent. The wood-paneled walls were painted pale blue with gilt reaching up to the curved ceiling.

On every wall was a vibrant painting, upgraded from the prints pinned to Hannelore's wall at Heim Harz. One was abstract, another was a dreamy watercolor, and yet another a meticulously wrought oil painting. There was a painting of a woman, distorted and almost ghoulish, but the expression in her eyes was tragic.

Hannelore once saw her looking and said, "That's Anna Göldi. She was the last woman in Europe to be tried and killed for witchcraft. In Switzerland, of all places."

"Interesting choice for decoration."

"I have diverse tastes."

Ilse gradually regained control of her mind and body, wiggling her toes and fingers. Hannelore began sleeping in the bed with her, forsaking what she claimed was the most uncomfortable settee in the world. At night, they stared at the ceiling and talked until they fell asleep. Hannelore told her stories from the literature and history she'd studied. Ilse told her Bremen folk tales and the more entertaining uses for herbs she'd found in *Physica*.

Lucretia's story continued to haunt her. Reading *Library of History* hadn't helped. One night, after they'd been lying in bed for a few minutes, Ilse sat up, switched on the light, which Hannelore met with groans and scrunching of the face, and read aloud the passage. It told of the man's lust, Lucretia's defilement, the promise she'd extracted from her father and husband, then the suicide—a dagger to the heart.

"She thought she wasn't worthy of life. She thought that because she'd been violated she had to die."

Ilse looked at Hannelore, fuming.

Hannelore, awake now but still lying down, looked up at Ilse in the dim light and said, "Tell me what's bothering you."

Ilse tossed the book toward the end of the bed. It landed on the quilt with a thud.

"Ow!" Hannelore retracted her foot from where the book had nicked it.

"Sorry." Ilse patted Hannelore's foot over the covers. "It's terrible what happened to Lucretia, but it's not rare. If every misused woman took her own life, there wouldn't be any of us left. She shouldn't have let them do that to her."

"There was the revenge-killing," Hannelore supplied helpfully, still rubbing her foot.

"What kind of a trade is that?"

A wicked grin spread across Hannelore's face. "Maybe Lucretia faked her death. That would show them."

"They paraded her bloody corpse through the streets."

"Ah. Well. That's what she *should* have done then. If everyone believed she was dead, she could escape from society and be free."

Ilse didn't think a lady like Lucretia could survive on her own, but decided not to mention it. With Hannelore, she was learning to imagine possibilities, no matter how unlikely.

"She believed she wasn't worthy to look at the sun."

"The sun in most mythologies is masculine. Maybe that's why." Hannelore spread her arms, pretending to bask in the nonexistent rays.

"I think the sun is a woman, in Germany, anyway: die Sonne. She makes life possible." Something was shifting in Ilse. Certainty took root deep inside her. Certainty of what, she wasn't sure yet, but it made her feel taller, stronger.

They lapsed into silence. Hannelore became still and quiet, drifting closer to unconsciousness. It was after midnight, but Ilse couldn't sleep with the city lights shining through the curtains.

"Do you ever feel bad about . . . who you're with? Knowing what he does?" Ilse asked.

Hannelore groaned herself awake. Then registering what Ilse had said, she shook her head.

"The question is irrelevant. We're all in *this*, anyway." In the dark, her pale hands flapped to indicate the general predicament of the entire country. "There's no point resisting the inevitable. Whether Heydrich sleeps with me or someone else, the outcome of this war will not be changed. No one suffers, yet my life is improved."

Ilse saw her point. But it didn't change the fact that she couldn't stomach any more of von Thiel.

There was a pause. Then Hannelore said, "I see what you're doing, and it's stupid, and dangerous."

Ilse stared at the arched ceiling, blue in the dark, and felt blank.

"What am I doing?"

"You know what I mean."

And she did. But how could Hannelore possibly know that Ilse had gathered a weed, dried it, and regularly made a tea out of it to prevent pregnancy?

"You're doing something foolish to keep from having another child."

Ilse felt hollow. She knew it must be the tansy that had caused the convulsions, and she knew it was foolish. Her stomach pains and nausea, creeping up, had warned her, and she'd ignored them. She'd been taking tansy for months now, and von Thiel had been visiting often—sometimes several times a week. If she wasn't already bleeding, she took a dose. Her monthly was more like a weekly, her spotty bleeding almost constant.

She longed to tell Hannelore about everything: the wild carrot and the tansy. What von Thiel had revealed to her and the narrow line she walked. How her time was running out, and to save herself she would have to do the last thing she wanted, the thing she'd been avoiding all this time: have a baby with a monster. She was sure Hannelore would keep her secrets, but Nazis loved listening devices. It was more likely than not that Heydrich had bugged Hannelore's apartment.

"Say you do know what I'm doing. Do you have an alternative to offer?"

"There's been an alternative for ages. Prophylactics." She tapped Ilse once on the wrist with each word. "The rubber, the jimmy, the nightcap."

Ilse sighed.

"Remember Lebensborn? I'm supposed to be trying to have babies, and so is von Thiel. I could never even ask him."

"Oh." The sound of an off-put Hannelore was foreign to Ilse's ears. It was an unsteady, delicate sound. But she soon recovered. "Right. There has to be another way. You're going to kill yourself, Lucretia."

Ilse's chest hurt. "Maybe I'll have a baby instead."

Hannelore stiffened and looked at Ilse. "Why would you do that?"

"Perhaps there's no other way."

"You could stop sleeping with von Thiel. Then you wouldn't have to take anything." Hannelore's voice was strained.

"And cease to be useful? It's the only thing that makes me useful to the regime."

"What happens if you don't have another baby?"

Nothing good. But she couldn't bring herself to say it. She only shrugged, and tension filled the air. The silence said everything Ilse could not.

"We're in the same boat, I think," Hannelore said softly. "Heydrich's sick of me."

Ilse jerked up. "What? How could he possibly get sick of *you?*"

"Beats me. I've used every trick I have, in bed and out of it." Ilse felt suddenly uncomfortable, realizing this was the bed she referred to. "But men like him want variety. A new mistress or two every year." Her face looked ashen. "He told me about a place called Salon Kitty. It's a pet project of his. A brothel. When government officials from other countries come to Berlin, they enjoy the city's nightlife. And when you get a man a little drunk, a little homesick, and possibly a little scared, he will find himself confiding in the nearest warm, soft bosom. To the right bosom, prompted by the right questions, he'll reveal anything. The girls at Salon Kitty are spies. He thinks I'd be perfect for it."

Her voice sounded clear and strong again, but for the first time, there was a hint of fear.

"No. He can't force you to do that."

"Men like him get whatever they want. Most of the girls are there because they've been blackmailed. They all have something to hide: abortions, theft, illegal prostitution, other crimes. It's Salon Kitty or prison. If there's no crime, he makes one up and it's as good as real. He could say my Berlin brothel was unlicensed, and the madame and everyone working there would go to prison, too."

"That won't happen to you. You'll find a way out."

Hannelore's voice lowered to a whisper. "Sometimes I think about escaping to Switzerland. Maybe move to Anna Göldi's town and rewrite its history. You could come with me."

Ilse turned to look at Hannelore's profile outlined in the window, all straight nose and pointed chin, her curls splayed against the pillow. It was nearly impossible to get across the Swiss border, legally or illegally. Everyone had heard of the Swiss guards and their dogs, turning refugees back, sending them into the hands of the SS and the Gestapo, and then to a

KZ. Sometimes refugees even made it across the Swiss border, only to be sent back days later.

"Leaving Germany is impossible," Ilse whispered back.

"Not for someone with access to a glider plane, plus a few feminine wiles up her sleeve."

Ilse shushed her. "We can't talk about this. And you have more than a few wiles."

"Maybe you'll come with me?"

Ilse hesitated. Two girls against two powerful SS officers? Against the Reich? Escape was futile, they both knew it.

But then, what did she have to lose? The illness had eaten up the last of her time. It was June now, and still she was not pregnant.

So she said, "Yes."

The air around her buzzed. Hannelore rolled over and hugged her. Ilse could feel Hannelore's heart beating rapidly in her chest. Soon, they would leave here. Soon, they could be free.

A while later, when Hannelore had rolled onto her side and disappeared into sleep, Ilse leaned over and kissed her on the shoulder.

PART FIVE
SEEDLING

Glance at the sun. See the moon and the stars. Gaze at the beauty of earth's greenings.
Now, think.

— HILDEGARD VON BINGEN

CHAPTER THIRTY-FOUR

Ilse removed her apron and tossed it down the chute. It was the end of her second day back at the pristine prison of the villa. Hannelore would have just gotten back from the hangar, where she was finalizing her plan. Their plan. To steal a plane and fly across the German border.

She swallowed the familiar nausea that pulsed through her —the gift of the tansy—as she returned to her room to change out of her uniform.

When she put her key into the door, it swung open.

Her heart skipped. It must be Hannelore inside, having used one of her tricks to break into Ilse's room and wait for her.

But Hannelore was not seated on the velvet chair or sprawled across the bed, bright-eyed, copper curls shining. Standing at attention was a man in a gray Waffen-SS uniform, holding himself with the rigid posture of an officer on duty. He shifted to allow Ilse to enter and on his arm she saw the white piping of the insignia of the SD, the intelligence agency. Her body went cold.

"Ilse Rademann," the man said. "The Obergruppenführer would like to speak with you."

Heydrich. In her room? Ilse stalled. She did not want to go in, but she had no choice. Stepping inside, she was entering a chess board; every maneuver must be played strategically. And everything was a maneuver. She began to tremble.

Heydrich was seated at the vanity, which he'd taken over as his desk. This was the last place she wanted him to be—past all her defenses, already inside her private space. He looked at her with an amused arrogance that told her he knew something she did not. Where was Hannelore?

"Ilse Rademann. You're right on schedule," he said, picking up Hannelore's date book. "I knew you would be. You seem to be someone who keeps her engagements. Have a seat."

The SD man produced a straight-backed chair. As Ilse sat, she noticed that he resumed his post in front of the door. Keeping others out, or her in.

Heydrich contemplated her. She refused to speak first. This was a tactic, she knew. Make the other person uncomfortable until they start babbling—then the power lies with the other. Well, she was used to discomfort. She stared back at Heydrich. Seconds ticked past. At last Heydrich spoke.

"Hannelore fled via plane last night."

"Fled?" Pain stabbed her stomach. It wasn't caused by tansy this time.

"Fled. It seems she was reluctant to fulfill her duty, so she stole a glider plane and crashed. She was killed. We found the burned wreckage at the Inn River this morning. Perhaps it was suicide, or perhaps it was a failed escape attempt. It doesn't matter now."

A tingling sensation spread across her skin, across her face and over her hands.

"What did she tell you of her plan? What was your involvement?" Heydrich asked.

She curled over her stomach, trying to compose herself. She

would not lose control in front of him. Through a strange new ringing in her ears, she heard Heydrich telling the SD man to bring her a glass of Schnaps.

A crystal glass filled with brown liquid was held before her until she took it between her fingers. A voice in the back of her head sounded an alarm: Hannelore had told her that Heydrich, in the business of extracting information, was known for drugging people he wanted information from. What did her glass hold?

She took the smallest sip she could manage. Pear brandy. If there was anything else in it, she couldn't tell.

Heydrich did not seem to be at all upset over Hannelore's death. He seemed focused, full of an energy that could either be agitation or excitement. Perhaps he truly didn't care for her— but then why the apartment, the allowance, the attention, for all these months?

"Tell me what you know," Heydrich said.

"I'm sorry I can't help you, but she told me nothing of this."

"Forgive me, but I find that highly unlikely. She must have talked, perhaps hypothetically. You two were confidants. Perhaps collaborators is a better word. How could she have failed to mention a plan for escape to you?"

Why had she left without Ilse? If Heydrich decided to send her away with no warning, she would have had no time and possibly no way to reach her. There could have been any number of reasons. Hannelore wouldn't have left without Ilse unless she had no choice. She pictured it: the two of them flying off into the clouds and mountains, wild and free. Though if she had, Ilse would probably be dead now, too. But what a perfect way to die . . .

Yet another person she cared for was on the other side of life. Ilse must be cursed; everyone she cared about died. Prematurely and horribly.

"I suppose we weren't as close as you thought," Ilse choked out.

"The two of you had plans to meet today. What were you going to do?"

"Have tea, talk, play cards. The same as always." Her voice wavered.

Heydrich eyed her. He picked something up, a scarf. Hannelore's yellow scarf. He played with it, letting it fall through his hands. She saw that it was stained with dark smudges of ash and something rust-colored. Hannelore's blood. Ilse's eyes burned.

"Have a cigarette," Heydrich said.

"I'm alright."

"I insist."

The snap and sizzle of a cigarette being lit. The SD man handed it to her. She took a drag.

"And make sure you actually inhale. If you find that you can't do that on your own, my friend here will help you." He nodded at the SD man, now hovering behind Heydrich.

So she inhaled. Instantly her head felt light, her problems farther away. Her mouth was dry. She lifted the glass to take another sip, then stopped herself.

"Go on, have some more," Heydrich said.

She wondered if drugged people ever volunteered information. They probably did.

The moisture had been sucked out of her mouth. Her thirst was all she could think about.

Heydrich asked her again what she knew about Hannelore's escape. Nothing, Ilse said again. The yellow scarf rippled before her eyes.

All she wanted to do was lie down and rest. Why did Heydrich insist on talking to her?

She fought the urge to let her head loll to one side. He asked her if she, too, had a plan to escape. She almost laughed. Not anymore, she didn't. Hannelore was all she had, and she was gone.

Had she said that out loud? Heydrich was smiling, so probably.

He was asking now if Ilse had spoken to Hannelore today.

Today?

"No," she said. "I cannot yet commune with the dead."

The questioning continued in this circular vein for hours, while Ilse longed for a sip of water and sleep.

CHAPTER THIRTY-FIVE

The sun was bright in Ilse's eyes when she woke in her bed, fully clothed on top of the covers. It was early evening, judging by its angle.

Her body and her mind felt sticky and unclean, as if she'd had far too much to drink. Why was that?

Hannelore.

Ilse started. Something had happened to Hannelore. Why couldn't she remember? She leaned forward and buried her head in her knees, her arms wrapped around her legs. Remember, remember.

Slowly, small details trickled back.

The puckering dryness of her mouth, so fierce her mouth now watered at the memory.

Heydrich's smug face floating before her.

Hannelore's bloody yellow scarf.

Hannelore escaped last night.

Hannelore was dead.

A hollow horror struck Ilse's chest. She gripped her knees and stared unseeing across the room.

Heydrich wanted something from her. He wanted to know

what she knew about Hannelore's plan. He wanted to know if she had spoken to Hannelore today. It was an odd question to ask. He would only ask that if Hannelore were still alive, which she was not.

Her eye caught on a crumpled bit of white paper under the door. She dragged herself to it and picked it up. A clear boot print was etched in mud across the page. It was a phone message the secretary had taken.

Her heart skipped. The message was from Hannelore. She must have called shortly before she escaped, before she died. Ilse had spent the previous night in the red room with von Thiel, where she was not to be disturbed.

The cat tried to take me today, but I'm a bird. I'm so sorry we couldn't fly together. It is now or never. Don't be Lucretia.

Ilse shook her head. Her fogged brain couldn't make sense of it. She stumbled to the water pitcher, poured herself a glass, and drank it all at once, willing her head to clear.

She sat back on her bed and studied the words.

The cat tried to take me. That must refer to Salon Kitty. Heydrich had sent her there.

Don't be Lucretia.

Hannelore had said something that night: "Maybe Lucretia faked her death. That would show them."

Heydrich said they found the wreckage. He did not say they found a body.

No body meant no death, everyone knew that. No one ever gave up on a loved one until they beheld the beloved's remains with their own eyes. Wasn't there a part of her that would always wait for Otto?

Hannelore was not dead.

Ilse jumped up. Her vision went black. She collapsed again. Her body would surely explode from this happiness.

Now that she thought about it, the way Hannelore faked

her death wasn't particularly clever. No one would believe she was dead just because her plane had crashed and a bloody scarf was found.

She rubbed her eyes. *Don't be Lucretia.* Hannelore was telling her that if Ilse let these men keep her life, if she remained, kept poisoning herself, allowed them to do whatever they wanted with her, she would be the same as Lucretia.

Hannelore had no fear. She had no practicality. She probably barely had a plan: Crash the plane, and then what? Walk to Switzerland? If only they could have gone together. Ilse would have taken care of the practicalities.

There was so little she could recall from the interrogation after the cigarette. The drugged cigarette. What had Heydrich told her? What had she said? At least she knew nothing of Hannelore's escape plan. But she could have revealed anything at all about herself. Not everything, because she would have woken up in a KZ. But she could have said enough to guide an investigation, about the herbs, about Thomas, about Felix and Otto. Any of those things could send her straight to the noose.

She jumped up, paced the room a few times. She couldn't stay around to find out. Hannelore had chosen not to let happen to her what may; Ilse would do the same, and they would both be free. Perhaps they would even find each other as they trekked through the mountains and forests of Germany. They'd found each other twice; they could find each other again.

She was throwing her few belongings into her canvas knapsack, mind racing as she ran through idea after idea to get herself out, when she heard the knock at her door. A confident knock, made by someone who knew he was going to get what he wanted. She cast a wild look around the room. A map of central Europe, ripped from the villa's atlas, lay on the bed and clothes were strewn about, clear evidence of her plans.

"Just a moment!" There was a tremor in her voice she couldn't control.

The knock rang again as she swept up the map, the clothing, and the luggage into the wardrobe and closed it, then unlocked the bedroom door. Von Thiel practically fell into the room.

Had he spoken with Heydrich? Was he here to save her or condemn her?

"I wanted to see you." His eyes darted and his hands twitched with nervous energy; he was clearly agitated. "What were you doing in here?"

"Private things. Surely you don't want to know everything a woman does in her own bedroom?" She hoped she sounded more confident than she felt.

"I've decided," he carried on as if she hadn't spoken, "that we must go to Wewelsburg tonight. I must show you the castle. I thought our child would be the key to the new Aryan civilization, but now I see there's much we must do to be worthy of the baby. We will perform a ritual to the fertility goddess Ostara. Then, at last, our union will bear fruit. We leave tonight."

"Tonight? Isn't it far away? I would need to pack."

"It has to be tonight; the solstice approaches. Throw a few things in a bag, sleep on the drive. We'll be there in a few hours."

She stood, staring at him. He seemed to know nothing of what had happened with Heydrich. But he was out of favor. Just because Heydrich hadn't confided in him didn't mean she was safe.

"Jetzt," he said, clapping his hands twice.

She went to the wardrobe, careful to not open the door all the way and reveal that her knapsack was already packed and that she was, in fact, removing items from it. Her mind raced as she searched for a way out. The linden tincture wasn't ready yet, but surely it would have some effect. She could drug him with it and he would fall asleep.

"I'd like to stop by the kitchen, if I may," she said casually. "We'll need refreshments for the journey."

"No. We must go now," he said, and marched her down the stairs, past the kitchen, and out of the villa.

CHAPTER THIRTY-SIX

The only visibility came from the headlights. Darkness pressed in on her eyes. They stopped at several SS checkpoints, von Thiel handing over his papers and travel permit. The guards scrambled to salute von Thiel with the proper deference.

Von Thiel stopped in a small town, in front of an apothecary. "Get what you need," he said.

"For what?"

"Fertility, of course."

"But you told me to be careful, for my health."

His wild eyes bored into hers. "It is essential that you bear my child. I spoke with Heydrich today."

Ilse stopped breathing. "About what?"

"Apparently you said some very interesting things."

"Such as?"

He raised his eyebrows and leaned in, wafting whiskey and sweat. "Enough for Heydrich to take an interest in you and your file."

Did von Thiel not know what she'd said, or was he withholding in the hopes that she'd reveal more than he already knew? She clamped her mouth shut.

He sighed. "You have not been honest with me. I thought I could count on that from you. But I still believe we have a shared destiny. You have a way with herbs, treasure. Use them to give us a child. It may save you."

She swallowed. "Save me how?"

"To bear an SS officer a child of good blood, in wartime, may help the Party overlook certain . . . indiscretions. I'm trying to help you. I'm always trying to help you."

She took a breath, looked away from his shadowed eyes. She couldn't bear the sight of him. With a shaking hand, she opened the car door and walked with von Thiel into the apothecary.

The scent hit her: old wood and dried herbs, tangy and bitter and sharp, alerting and calming at the same time. The apothecary, a shriveled old woman, emerged from a curtain behind the counter. Von Thiel swept a hand, inviting Ilse to join him at the counter.

"Tell the good Apothekerin what you want."

Ilse stepped up and looked into the woman's rheumy eyes. She didn't dare try to order the wrong herbs, not with von Thiel watching and the woman who might give her away.

"Motherwort, please. And sage. I'll make a tea."

Perhaps she could order licorice for decreasing fertility in men, add linden, and convince von Thiel to drink it?

No, she couldn't try anything tonight. Not here, when she didn't even know where *here* was. And no plan to get away.

She watched as the woman placed the herbs into small sachets. If only she could signal what was happening to her. But it wasn't all that different from any other woman's situation—the requirement to become a mother or die trying.

. . .

Sometime after midnight, the car came to a halt before a triangular stone castle perched on the edge of a steep hill. Where each of the three exterior walls met, there was a solid-looking tower. Von Thiel, months ago, had called this place *the spiritual home of our sacred brotherhood.* She imagined human sacrifices. Satanic rituals. Fear chilled her bones.

They were greeted by an SS guard as they emerged from the vehicle, stretching cramped muscles.

"You received my orders?" von Thiel said.

"Jawohl," he said. "Everything is waiting for you in the Crypt."

"Good. And bring some hot water for the lady."

She fought the instinct to panic—she could only think of one reason to bring someone to a crypt. But she couldn't bear his child if she was dead. She swallowed. Von Thiel took her by the waist and led her across the grounds to one of the three towers. They entered and went down and down the spiral staircase until they entered a large, circular room made entirely of stone.

The only source of light came from torches affixed to the round walls. The high ceiling arched, much like a church, and at the center of it a stylized swastika was engraved, its four legs elongated, spider-like. The air felt cold and dank and cursed.

"Impressive." She choked the word out; it was better to play along.

"And it's only the beginning," he said. He seemed pleased. Once again, Ilse could not discern whether he was proud or ashamed of the organization he belonged to.

In the center of the room, which was sunken, were several items: a dozen or so lilies, a small sack bulging with invisible contents, a red velvet cloth, and a live hare in a small cage. Dread coiled in her stomach. Von Thiel stepped down into the sunken space, bringing Ilse with him, and brought her to the center, on the red blanket. He collected the lilies and scattered them in a circle around her.

"Last night, I was in the depths of despair. I couldn't sleep, so I went into my office. The air was stale. I wanted to open the window, but it must remain closed to keep out the constantly falling gray snow generated by the crematorium. I wished for your warm body to cling to. Sometimes I feel I could absorb your purity and honesty if I hold you close enough. But I don't deserve it.

"Have you ever asked yourself who you are and come up empty? Have you ever lost your one true purpose? My collection of ancient manuscripts was scattered across my desk. On my wall was a map that tracked the journey of the Aryan race through its diaspora, as well as a table of Armanen runes, which I had commissioned years ago. These runes contain the quarterly per square—the swastika—and the three-pronged fork which has become the Lebensborn symbol signifying to mother, to increase. These objects once held the answer for me. I was a man who got lost in the study of ancient utopias and mystic runes, who found beauty and hope in those things."

The soldier arrived with a silver teapot of hot water and a matching cup. Ilse added the herbs, waited a few moments, then poured the tea. It needed to steep for much longer, but she wasn't about to tell von Thiel that.

"There was a heaviness in me—my hands, my arms, my chest." Von Thiel opened the bag, which contained soil. He walked in a slow circle, sprinkling it inside the circle of the lilies. "There has been so much death, and my part in it has weighed me down. So to ease my pain, I threw the drawing of the runes across the room and swore to give it all up. But discarding my old ways created an emptiness that was even more terrifying than the pain.

"A few minutes were all I could bear. I replaced the drawing on the wall. Then I meditated on the symbols, contemplating their meanings and possible applications, until this idea came to me. It is now clear to me that my role is to make up for lost life by creating life. Purer life."

He spread the red velvet blanket and faced her, holding her hands in his.

"Now, we begin the ceremony to appeal to the German goddess Ostara." Von Thiel closed his eyes and rattled off a poem, or perhaps a prayer, in Old German. Though she couldn't understand a word, if she didn't listen too closely, it sounded almost as if she could discern the meaning. She thought she heard something about *Blut und Boden*. Blood and soil. Next, he pulled out the dagger he always wore at his hip, and reached for the hare.

"What are you doing? Stop." Ilse's shrill words escaped from her mouth before she knew she was saying them, before she could stop herself. It didn't matter; von Thiel ignored her—he gripped the hare in his hand as it squirmed, red eyes darting. He raised his knife to the creature's throat and drew it across. Blood ran over the floor. It reached Ilse's shoes and she jumped away, horrified.

"Come back, Ilse." Von Thiel's voice was eerily calm. The hare was still. Von Thiel used its blood to mark the stone floor with a circle of runes. Then he laid the hare's body and the blood-drenched dagger on the ground outside the circle. He carefully wiped his hands on a handkerchief. He sat on the red cloth and patted the ground next to him. "Now that we have offered a sacrifice to the goddess, we may proceed with consummation."

"What is this ritual?" Ilse asked, still unwilling to return to the inside of the circle.

"It's my own invention. You see, the hare is a symbol of Ostara. Easter would be better, as it is her holiday, but the solstice is also auspicious. Lilies signify fertility, and the German soil is inextricably linked with our blood. The child we create tonight will be destined for greatness. He will be the future of Germany."

Whatever that meant. She wished she could have brought her tansy. She eyed the cloth, the color of blood. Von Thiel seemed to intuit her thoughts.

"Don't worry, treasure," he said. "The hare's life force will not touch you."

Regardless of how she felt about anything, she saw she had no choice in the matter, and she stepped back into the circle and sat next to von Thiel. He leaned over her; she lay down, shivering, feeling sick, trying to hide it.

The back of her head, her spine, her ankles ground into the stone with every movement. She stared at the swastika above her for an eternity.

Dawn was obscured by a grumbling, damp thunderstorm as she collapsed onto the stiff four-poster bed. Apparently this was the Nordic decor he'd promised her.

As she lay in bed, as far away from the sleeping von Thiel as she could get, a feeling of disgust overwhelmed her. She'd slept with a murderer, Thomas's murderer, and the only way to escape doom was to bear his child. And then she would be trapped again—forever, this time.

Unless Heydrich had already found enough from his investigation and called for her arrest. It was possible that as soon as they returned to Munich, she would be taken away. Even carrying von Thiel's baby wouldn't save her then. They would simply wait until she'd given birth to do whatever they would do to her.

In fact, if von Thiel truly was out of favor, they might not care if she bore his child at all. He was delusional to think the Reich would value the offspring of two out-of-favor Germans, no matter how "pure" their blood.

She wondered how long an investigation would take, what it would entail. However long, she would have to act faster.

Adrenaline pounded in her thighs and made her want to run, but she had nowhere to go. Von Thiel had brought her to the very center of Germany. She was hundreds of miles away from any border.

Von Thiel snorted and rolled over, draping an arm over Ilse's stomach. His breath stank and his arm on her was heavy, stifling. She forced herself to take a deep breath. It shuddered on its way out. Another breath, and another. Von Thiel did as he pleased with her, with his rough hands, rough movements. He used her body like it belonged to him, but he could never have *her*.

For no reason at all, she became aware of her ankle bone—its protrusion, the smooth skin over it. When she was growing up, in the bath or as she was falling asleep, she would sometimes examine her body with curiosity, almost a sense of marvel that all this was hers. It *was* her. But when her body stopped changing, she stopped noticing its details, unless something hurt. Now, this small bone was a marvel to her; she could feel it from the inside. It seemed that an awareness grew there, as if that small protruding bit of bone was its own life.

Her eye caught on von Thiel's ankle, hanging off the edge of the bed. It wasn't so different from hers, pale and prominent. She scanned the rest of his body and hers in the gray light of the moon.

With perfect clarity, a stillness, the last element of her plan clicked into place. There was only one way out.

After a few hours of sleep so light it was little more than a doze, Ilse woke without so much as a moment of grogginess. It was time to go.

She stood and went to the window. Vibrant green trees lined golden fields. A herd of sheep grazed by a narrow, lazy river. It made sense that the SS had chosen a location that fit the pastoral National Socialist ideal, but to Ilse the peace so close to the darkness was eerie.

Von Thiel was still sleeping. She shook him lightly, then harder. He groaned and rolled over.

"Erich," she said, punching him in the back. It felt good to do that. She wanted to do it again, but resisted. At last he woke, mumbling unintelligibly.

"We have to go," she said. "I have to get to work."

"It's just as well." Von Thiel's voice was thick with sleep. He rolled onto his back and stretched. "Himmler is coming later today."

"To the castle?" The thought of that little man occupying the same space and breathing the same air simultaneously repulsed her and filled her with fear.

Von Thiel grunted his confirmation.

"There is a ceremony for the solstice tonight. We should leave before he arrives. Technically, we're not supposed to be here."

"We're trespassing?"

"In a sense. The guards here believe I'm allowed. It's only Himmler who doesn't want me here without him."

"Let's leave then." Ilse didn't want to imagine what would happen if Himmler discovered what they had done. Had all the blood been washed away? She pulled on the clothes she'd worn the day before while von Thiel dragged himself out of bed.

. . .

The drive felt longer in the daytime. She watched von Thiel drive, how he maneuvered the gears, changed lanes, sped up and slowed down with perfect control. They drove most of the way in silence.

She bounced a leg. It seemed to her that von Thiel had never driven so slowly before. Maybe he was taunting her. Her fate was in his hands, or so he thought.

For a long time, Ilse had felt untethered. It was as if she'd been swimming and decided to stop and float, letting the current take her anywhere and everywhere, to drag her down to the silt or to wash her up onto shore. It had become impossible to tell right from wrong. She'd lost her own innate sense of such things long ago, if she'd ever had it.

Perhaps a part of her had been holding on, waiting for Otto. She would never see his body, so she'd never see for herself that he really was dead. But there could have been no other fate for him once he was taken to Brandenburg; she'd heard the confirmation herself when she eavesdropped in the dumbwaiter. To save him, she would have had to run away with him before they could take him. She should have done whatever it took to save him, and she hadn't. She had failed. She hadn't been smart enough, hadn't understood enough. Waiting for him all this time had done no good. All that was left of Otto, she carried inside her.

But she knew what to do now. She was done floating, done following. There was nothing she wouldn't do to be free.

CHAPTER THIRTY-SEVEN

It was well after lunchtime when von Thiel dropped Ilse off at the villa. She half-expected Heydrich's men to be there already, waiting to arrest her. But the foyer was empty—for now at least. Perhaps they would come tonight, or tomorrow. She wasn't going to wait to find out. She dashed straight to the kitchen, brewed herself a cup of tansy, and got to work.

A big pot of soup with everything thrown in it. Salad with wilting lettuce and a few, sad spears of asparagus. It counted as a meal, and that was all she cared about.

When she was done, she grabbed her knapsack, which she'd thrown in a corner of the kitchen, and stuffed it with enough food to last a few days. She also grabbed a vial of the linden tincture, which she slipped into her pocket, then ran out of the kitchen, still wearing her soiled apron.

Von Thiel had never given her a way to contact him, probably to hide his location at Dachau, but she needed to reach him now. She ran up the two flights of stairs to the administrative floors. This close to dinner, almost everyone would be downstairs, smacking their Aryan lips in anticipation. Tonight, they would be disappointed—though compared to what people were eating outside the villa, in war-torn Germany, it would still be a feast.

She arrived at Frau Herta's door and knocked tentatively. Waited, then knocked again. After a solid minute of silence, she opened the door and slipped inside. Even when she wasn't there, the smell of the administrator's perfume was overpowering. Ilse hoped this was the last time she would smell it. She began looking through the administrator's desk. In the second drawer, she found Frau Herta's book of contacts and flipped through the pages until she came upon "Gruppenführer Erich von Thiel." She wrote the phone number on a scrap of paper, rearranged everything the way it had been, and fled the room.

Downstairs, in a room off the foyer, a bank of phones was kept for calls. She'd never used them before, but she went there now. She picked up a black receiver and spun the dial for each number. It seemed to take a lifetime. She waited, not breathing, as the phone rang. Someone—his secretary—answered and put her through to von Thiel. His voice on the other end warbled a gruff hello.

"Erich," she said, forcing her voice to sound breathy, ecstatic. "I had a revelation today. I admit I was skeptical before, but now I believe the ceremony worked, only it has just taken effect. I feel . . . different. We must meet. This is the night, I can feel it."

"Really?" She could hear the eagerness in his voice. "This is wonderful news. I will be there in two hours. Is that too long?"

"No, no. Just come as soon as you can." She smiled so he could hear it in her voice.

Back in her room, she changed her clothes, putting on her one pair of trousers and a blouse with a thin but sturdy jacket. As she repacked her knapsack, she thought of *Jane Eyre* under the floorboard. She decided to leave it for the next lost girl to find.

She met von Thiel in the foyer as sunset turned to dusk. He looked like a child at Christmas. She grabbed him by the hand and led him up the stairs to the red room, the image of a good Lebensborn woman who simply could not wait to be impregnated.

She kissed him before the door was even shut. Something rose up in her, small and fierce. She went to the other place in her mind, her perch. As long as she had herself, that was all she needed. Von Thiel could have her body, one more time.

Tonight, she was someone else, the best actress she'd ever been. She pulled him into the bedroom, undressed him, climbed astride him. Though she was sore from the previous night, she pushed past it, hoping he took her grunts of discomfort and eagerness to get it over for enthusiasm. Von Thiel seemed to notice nothing amiss. In fact, he seemed to be enjoying it all, gripping her hips and rocking her into him.

It was over quickly, and they collapsed into a panting heap. When their breathing regulated, she said, "I'll get us some drinks."

She went into the sitting room and retrieved the vial of linden tincture from the pocket of her trousers. As she poured two glasses of whiskey, she shook the vial of linden over one of the glasses, once, twice. She added some bitters in hopes of masking the taste.

Back in the bedroom, she handed him the drugged glass and watched out of the corner of her eye as he took a sip. His nose wrinkled. The von Thiel of the past would have turned to the well-stocked wine cellar for something of higher caliber, but this was a new von Thiel—one who drank to forget. He knocked the glass back and downed the rest in one gulp.

"Another?" Ilse asked.

"Please."

He held the glass up for her to take. She prepared him another drugged glass and he downed it as well. His tongue loosened, and he began babbling about ancient stones he'd recently had shipped from his remote village in Pomerania. He'd meditated on them, asking for an epiphany from his ancestors, a message from the Aryan gods. As if she'd care about something like that, when at any moment she could be arrested for treason.

Within three drinks, he was slurring his words, sinking into the bed. He was still on top of the covers and looked ridiculous in his nudity. If only Germany could see its Gruppenführer now, the hairy legs, a newly rounded stomach from his increased drinking, his flaccid member resting against his thigh. She found things to prattle on about: how fertile she suddenly felt, how Wewelsburg had been every bit as amazing as he'd promised, how she understood now his fascination with the occult. He seemed pleased and kept kissing her face with wet, whiskey-scented lips. Outside, darkness fell, but a full moon hung bright in the sky. She watched it as she spoke, as if it would anchor her.

He drank a fourth glass, a fifth, a sixth.

As he drifted off, he said, "Are you with child now? I think you are."

Snoring took over the room, practically vibrating the framed artwork on the walls.

"Absolutely not," she said.

She waited a few minutes to be sure he remained soundly asleep, then sprang up and got to work. From among von Thiel's clothes, she retrieved his SS dagger and took it into the bathroom. Looking in the mirror, she grabbed a chunk of long blond hair, pride of the Aryan race. Then she lifted the knife and sawed it off. She worked her way around her head, shearing it all as the pale locks floated to the ground. She'd never cut more than a few inches off at a time, and it was almost as if a part of herself was falling away. But it was not a part she would miss. The resulting hairstyle was choppy and uneven, though she'd cut it as smoothly as she could. She gathered up the hair and shoved it in her knapsack to be disposed of when she was somewhere far away.

Back in the bedroom, she slid the knife into its sheath and put on her own clothes, then von Thiel's black breeches, which were too long for her, though it was hardly noticeable when they were tucked into his high black boots. She slipped into his stifling wool tunic, heavy with medals, and the cap, which thankfully covered her poorly shorn hair. For a finishing touch, she belted the knife and scabbard at her waist. She checked the tunic pockets—there were his papers, his universal travel permit, and the keys to his Mercedes. Ilse returned to the bathroom to inspect her new self.

Even with her own clothes underneath, the uniform was loose in the shoulders and the waist. As for her face, she shared the light eyes and strong jaw required of anyone involved in the SS. She didn't look like von Thiel's twin, but she didn't look dissimilar, in the dark, anyway. If only it was a new moon tonight.

With one last glimpse at von Thiel, naked and reeking of whiskey and sweat, Ilse left the suite. She did her best to walk with the unswiveled, commanding stride of a male officer, though there was no one in the halls. As she strode out of the building, she pulled on von Thiel's leather gloves.

The shiny black surface of von Thiel's car caught the light of the moon. She climbed into the driver's seat, forcing her mind to slow down, concentrate. Then she put the key in the ignition and turned the engine over, put the car into gear, and pulled out. She exhaled; she'd remembered all the steps. So far.

She didn't know if any of the SS guards at the villa knew von Thiel well, or at all, but she decided to leave through the back gate, where newer guards were usually stationed. She cleared her throat a few times, preparing to lower her voice several octaves.

With the darkness of night on her side and the imposing nature of the three oak leaves on her lapel, few people would dare to question her. She idled the car up to the waiting guard, hoping with everything she had that the car wouldn't stall.

"Heil Hitler." The guard thrust up an arm with the exuberant heel click reserved for those of high station.

"Heil Hitler," Ilse said, striving for von Thiel's ambiguous accent, Pomeranian with a hint of his early years in Austria. She handed him von Thiel's identification papers and travel permit exempting him from the nationwide curfew and watched him inspect them.

Her blood should have arrived, but it hadn't; she'd forgotten to take her dose of tansy, now sitting cold on the counter, and she hadn't brought any with her. She could turn back, run into the kitchen and find some—but she couldn't. The chances of her successfully backing the car up, going inside without them noticing her child-bearing hips, and making it all the way back here a second time were slim.

She had to compose herself. The guard was mere inches away from her. That will be a problem for another day, she thought. Or it won't be.

The guard handed the papers back to her and saluted again —she couldn't bring herself to reciprocate—and he opened the gates. The creaking of the iron was the best sound she'd ever heard.

She put the car into gear and it didn't stall, and she drove into the night. Huge breaths shuddered out of her, as if she were crying with no tears—the relief of leaving Lebensborn.

There was a road that would take her past Memmingen, through Austria, and into Switzerland by Lake Obersee. She unfolded the page of the atlas to track her journey. It wasn't even far. It would be a matter of hours instead of the days it would have taken to walk.

Not half an hour down the road, Ilse encountered another SS checkpoint. She avoided eye contact, hid her shaking hands, tried to look bored. The SS guard merely glanced at the papers while stifling a yawn and waved her on.

As she drove on, she came to a fork in the road. The faint lines of the map were barely visible in the moonlight and Ilse couldn't decipher which path to take. She paused between the two of them, squinting between the map and the two roads, both equally dark and tree-lined and empty. She decided the left one looked more promising and continued on.

A feeling came over Ilse, so sudden and intense that she pulled to the side of the dark, empty road. Her head felt as if it were spinning around and around, becoming so light it could float away, leaving her body in the car, to crash into a tree or drive off a cliff. She leaned her head against the steering wheel, willing her body to know that she would never take a dose of tansy again, that it could begin to heal now. But her head continued to whirl around the roof of the car and she felt the wrongness in her body, a dull ache always in her abdomen, telling her she had done perhaps irreparable harm.

At last the dizziness subsided, and she resumed driving, faster now to make up for the lost time.

She wished she would start bleeding. Still, she did not.

After a few more minutes of driving, Ilse came to a sign indicating a town. Her heart leapt as she pulled close to read it. Tegernsee.

There's a castle outside of town where young men and women of Aryan stock go to breed.

Himmler's family lives there.

Lucie and Metta had told her that, back at Heim Harz. Ilse had no desire to be anywhere near this place. As she squinted again at the map, it became clear she'd driven in the wrong direction. She should have taken the right fork toward St. Gallen.

With a nervous glance at the sky, which would soon turn gray with pre-dawn light, she began the three-point maneuver to turn the boxy car around.

Then the car stalled.

She tried and tried again to restart the engine. It sputtered and died. Twice. Three times. Hysteria began to rise in her throat. She swallowed it. She didn't know much about the inner workings of vehicles, but she worried that if she kept trying this way, the car might be destroyed and never start again. Pushing open the door, she put her feet on the ground and gasped in fresh air. It smelled of fresh grass and damp earth. Overhead, the moon was bright and so close she could almost touch it.

She wished Hannelore were next to her.

Hannelore had understood something all along—that women could use their own bodies to suit their needs, just as men used them, without being defined by what happened to them. That last part—that was what mattered.

Nothing belonged to her and she needed nothing, only herself.

She closed the door and took a breath. Held the clutch. Turned the key. A sputter and a purr as the engine started. A laugh escaped her lips, nervous and giddy. She sped back the way she had come, every muscle in her body tense.

CHAPTER THIRTY-EIGHT

It was not yet dawn on the shortest night of the year when Ilse pulled up to the Swiss border check. Her hands were sweating inside the leather gloves. She slid them low on the steering wheel to hide that extra space at the tip of each finger that her hands didn't fill. Putting on her best surly, powerful man expression, she rolled down the window. A German guard lounged in the back, reading a newspaper. When he glanced up and saw the black Mercedes and the black uniform, he stood at once and saluted. The Swiss guard, a pockmarked young fellow, took the papers from her hand.

"Where are you coming from?"

She tried to be as honest as possible. "Munich."

"Where are you going? What is the purpose of your journey?"

"A short holiday by Lake Obersee."

"Will you be meeting anyone there?"

She cleared her throat, trying to make it lower.

"No."

"Perhaps you will meet a nice girl."

"I'm not sure such a thing exists."

The Swiss guard smirked and held the papers out to Ilse. She thought she would pass out with relief. She took the papers and restarted the car.

Then it stalled. Silence pressed in. With it came a cold clarity—these were her last free moments.

"Having trouble?" The German officer approached. He was older than the Swiss guard, his face chiseled with cruelty. She frantically tried to get the car to restart, but he sidled up before she could. His eyes bored into Ilse's. She was certain he could see her heart thumping through two layers of clothing.

"No. Car's just a little finicky. I gave my chauffeur the weekend off."

"Why did you drive through the night? Why break curfew just for a vacation?"

He could tell. This was it, but she would fight to the last. Normally, she would look sweet and pretty and harmless, but now she had to be von Thiel, handle this situation as he would. She forced herself to meet his gaze, even though he could surely read her secrets in them. She remembered von Thiel ordering her: *Halt. Jetzt.* The way he kept her at bay with a single raised hand and drew her to him with his power and charm, the way he assumed those around him would follow his orders. She sucked in a breath.

"I am a leading officer in the RuSHA department. I have no curfew. I'm entitled to enjoy the quiet night roads if I wish. You'd do well to remember that." She looked him up and down and let disappointment flash in her eyes. "Who is your commanding officer?"

A pause.

"I don't think we need to involve him, Gruppenführer."

"We'll see," Ilse said, sizing him up.

Then she started the car and drove away, relief tingling across every cell of her body.

A howl threatened to escape from her, loud and primal and terrifyingly sad and unbearably happy. She had made it, though a part of her felt like she was still, and always would be, on the night roads of Germany, leaving behind everything she'd known.

She drove fast now. It felt good to put distance between herself and the border, and safer, too; she didn't know how far the SS would search for her. How much von Thiel would search on his own. Men didn't like things being taken from them.

With the inch-thick windows down, her shorn hair whipped in the wind. She was getting used to driving, even beginning to like it—the smooth approach of the road, bending the car to her will. Though she shouldn't get used to it; soon she would need to leave the uniform and the car behind. It was only a useful disguise as long as no one was looking for it. After today she would be on foot.

She'd fled Germany, just like Felix. She hadn't fully understood his need to leave before, focusing on the fact that he'd left her. But he'd done the right thing. The only way to be free and safe was to get as far away from the Reich as he could.

Perhaps she would never return. She couldn't imagine a world where it would be possible. But here everything seemed brighter, more beautiful. Crisp, clean, and free.

When the fuel gauge became dangerously low, she took a side road into the woods, stopping when she found a rippling body of water. She parked and hobbled out of the car, her body cramped and fatigued from the fear that had permeated every muscle in her body. Leaning against the warm hood of the car, she took big gulps of air.

The two SS flags waved obscenely. She snapped them off and hurled them into the lake. They landed with a splash. The mass of blond hair that had once been hers followed after; she used a stick to push the strands below the surface. She stuck her hands in her pockets and watched it all sink.

Her hand touched something hard and smooth in von Thiel's pocket. She pulled it out. It was his card case, with layers of folded banknotes on one side—she counted eighty marks. Enough to buy fake papers and have a bit left over. She would be on the run now, concealing her identity, for a long time. But she knew how to lie low. She took the money out and stowed it in her knapsack.

There was something tucked behind the notes. With pinched fingernails, she pulled it out. A neat-looking woman with tired eyes sat with a small boy standing on either side of her and a little girl on her lap. Von Thiel's family. Ilse tucked the photo back into the case. She was sorry, but she could not allow herself regrets.

As the sun began to set, she gathered enough wood to start a fire and set up a makeshift shelter out of leafy green branches, drawing from skills she'd learned in the BDM.

The air grew cooler, and her head was pounding with fatigue when she finally sat down to eat some of the food she'd stolen from the villa. Here she was, a town girl out in the wild woods, making her way. But she wasn't really of the town; her mother came from the mountains, and her mother's blood ran through her veins. The trees and earth were more a part of her than any town square or apartment building. She would trade the green spires of Bremen's gothic town hall for a copse of fir trees any day. As long as she was not being forced into a choice that was really no choice at all.

All her life, until recently, she had taken the path laid out for her. First by her father, then by Fräulein Glücks when she'd given her the flier. Ever since then, it had been what Lebensborn wanted. Take her child, sterilize her, send her to the villa, breed her—she'd gone along with what they decided. It was a strategy that had failed her, dismally. It had included her little rebellions, first her relationship with Felix, which got her into trouble in the first place, then the herbs, which had left her with a mountain of guilt and damage to her body. Now, her life was uncertain and the vast abyss of her future was terrifying, but it was no less frightening than her past.

That night, inside the small shelter, she was nearly asleep when another pain struck. There were no words to describe this pain—not aching or searing or burning. It simply felt as if her insides had turned into a monster that was trying to claw its way out. But this pain was a part of her body now, perhaps forever. This pain was the cost. She would take no more tansy, but the tansy remained with her. There was no point in crying out; there was nothing to do but lie on the earth, with the pain.

Then she was rising out of her body. She would bump into the thatched roof soon. Her vision blurred and darkened. It was that feeling again, the one she'd had that day in the plane with Hannelore. Part of her mind, the very back of it, began to panic. After everything, she could die out here. The rest of her gave over to the darkness.

She woke to aches throughout her body, a dried crusting of saliva around her lips. It was still dark; unfamiliar shapes surrounded her. The trees beyond the entrance to her shelter leaned over her, whispering softly. Beyond them, rocks and ferns and the lake glinted in the moonlight.

She had escaped. She remembered now. Nothing else mattered but that. A smile crept across her face, cracking the saliva. She raised a heavy hand to wipe her mouth. As she faded into sleep, she decided to look for raspberry leaf or willow bark in the morning to help with the pain.

Dawn broke. Faint beams of light streamed in through the branches and moss that made up the thatched ceiling, waking her gently. The pain was gone for now. She crawled out of the relative warmth of the shelter. Though she'd slept fully clothed, the dewy air cut through to her flesh. She crossed her arms for protection.

Her mouth was dry, but most of all it tasted foul. She went to the lake and kneeled at the edge to scoop water over her face and cup it in her hands to drink. The coldness sloshed in her stomach and made her shiver.

She prepared a breakfast of cheese and bread and gathered nearby clover-shaped wood sorrel. She contemplated what to do with the car. Drive it into the lake? Leave it where it was? Perhaps it didn't matter.

There was no sound, but she felt a presence near her. Slowly, carefully, she looked up. A doe stood only a few feet away, nosing through the foliage. She looked at Ilse with warm, brown eyes, then returned to her meal. So did Ilse. They ate together for a while until the deer wandered away. Ilse watched her brown and white coat disappear into the trees.

She was about to leave, too, when she saw the sparkling water in the morning light. It would wash away von Thiel's touch, the horrible ritual, everything that had happened. She peeled off her clothes and jumped in. The water was cold enough to make her want to shriek. Instead, she dunked her whole head under and made quick, long strokes until her body warmed up. She floated to the surface and rolled her body over and over, then began to scrub herself clean. When she raised a hand to wipe the water from her eyes, she saw a shocking red smear across the side of her thumb.

The hare's blood. She fought the urge to vomit and plunged her hand in the water, scrubbing at it. More blood floated to the surface of the water, and she began to panic. The hare was haunting her.

Then she realized the blood was coming from her.

She turned her face to the sky and exhaled so sharply it sounded almost like a laugh. Her courses had arrived. Von Thiel would leave no mark on her body.

When even her bones were warm, she gathered moss and leaves to replace the usual rags, then dressed in her own clothes. She put von Thiel's uniform, papers, card case, and SS dagger in the car. Then she drove it to the end of the lake, rolled down the windows, put it in neutral, and pushed it into the water. It bobbed and sucked, the air inside competing with the rush of water, until the lake claimed it.

She picked up her knapsack.

Today she would travel south, toward the sun.

EPILOGUE

May 1946
Somewhere in Switzerland

Crouching under a linden tree, the girl baring her bottom didn't notice the woman of the woods approaching until she was almost upon her. To be fair, Ilse hadn't noticed the girl either until a moment before; her eyes had been scanning for umbels and florets and hints of hidden tubers.

When the girl finally did see her, she jumped and pulled down her dress, covering the angry welts on her backside while her tearstained face mooned up at Ilse.

Any time she spotted a girl in the woods, Ilse foolishly hoped it would be Hannelore, coppery hair bouncing, her smile unconquerable. But this girl's dark curls sprang out of a long braid down her back. She reminded Ilse more of Mitzi.

"Come with me," Ilse said, holding out her hand to help the girl up. She took it and stood with a grimace. The scars on Ilse's back pulsed in memory. She led the girl toward the abandoned hunter's cottage she'd claimed as hers for the last few months.

With the war finally over, she'd stopped running and found a forgotten corner of Switzerland, dotted with small villages and teeming with trees.

"I've heard of you," the girl said. Her eyes were as round as her face, so innocent. She looked about twelve.

"Good things, I bet."

"It depends who's talking. But many swear by your cures."

Ilse smiled. She'd taken care when she settled here to be a friendly, helpful presence to the nearby villagers, but a woman living alone in the woods caused talk anyway.

"Don't be scared. I've learned to work with plants, that's all."

They arrived at the cottage and Ilse held the door open for the girl. The two-room house had fallen into a state of disrepair, but she'd added touches to make it cheerful. Yellow curtains were a particular point of pride. And plants, plants everywhere—in vases, in pots, hanging from the rafters, dried, and canned. Ilse gestured to the girl to sit down at the table, which she'd whittled all over with crude renditions of flora and fauna.

From her stores, she gathered ointments and clean cloth, and set water to boil. As she brought them over to the girl, her stomach pains came back, and she hunched over a little. She was used to them by now, but the girl looked alarmed.

"Are you alright?"

"Of course. The choices you make, they follow you forever. This one probably won't kill me; it hasn't yet. Now pull up your dress and turn around. Don't blush. I've seen you with your buttocks out already, so there's no point in being shy about anything."

The girl turned and pulled her dress up to her waist. Whoever had done this had at least not whipped in the same place twice, which was the worst. Skin had broken in a few spots, but mostly it was crisscrossed with bright-red, raised welts.

Ilse cleaned the wounds with warm water and applied a pot marigold poultice.

"This isn't how it's supposed to be, you know," she said.

The girl said nothing, but bowed her head. Tears trickled to the tip of her nose and dropped off. Ilse gave her an extra bandage to dry her nose and eyes.

"Do this, today and every other day you remember: Find a tree and place your hand on it. Feel that it is alive. That's what you are; there's no difference. Always remember: you are as worthy as the tree."

The girl's bottom quivered as Ilse applied the last bandage. "There. You're all fixed up now."

After the girl had drunk up a tea from yarrow and willow bark while staring at Ilse like she was a member of some new species, she set her mug down.

"I have to go back now. I haven't finished my chores," she said.

"You won't want to do much sitting for the next few days, but you'll be alright. Come back in two days so I can check on you. Come anytime you want." Ilse squeezed her shoulder.

The girl smiled and ducked her head in a nod. From the doorway, Ilse watched her scamper off until she was out of sight. Not far away from her little porch, Ilse spotted a patch of sunlight. She stripped off all her clothes and lay in the glow of the sun.

She put one hand on her stomach and felt the muscles expand and contract as she breathed, and another hand on her chest and felt the bones of her rib cage, strong and steady. She noticed her toes and feet, her calves and knees and thighs, the widening of her hips and the narrowing of her waist. Her breasts, her shoulders, her neck. The pain in her gut. The blood coursing through her, the connection of her tendons and sinews. Her nerves sending and receiving messages. Every element inside of her and every element outside of her, thrumming and vibrating and pulsing.

Hildegard said that herbs dried in the sun were the most potent. Ilse basked until the light and warmth soaked into her bones.

Author's Note

At the beginning of the pandemic, I was going through old notes, looking for inspiration, when I saw the words "Nazi breeding program."

I think I first learned about this Nazi maternity home when I was a teenager. I think my mother told me, but I don't remember for sure. In our long car rides when I was growing up, she told me many stories about fascinating moments in history, embellished with her dramatic flair.

Well, I thought, on this day in 2020 while I was scrolling through my notes, let's see what really happened before I decide if I want to write about it. I opened my laptop and immediately found Lebensborn.

There wasn't much reliable information available on the internet, but that only made me dig harder. I found a whole documentary on Lebensborn and pressed play. About halfway through this documentary, the historian Dorothee Schmitz-Köster takes a trip to the Lebensborn archives. Schmitz-Köster thumbs through records with gloved hands. She pulls out a yellowed postcard. It is a confirmation of the euthanasia of a six-month-old infant who did not meet the genetic criteria for Lebensborn. For life in the Third Reich.

When I looked up from my screen, ten hours had passed. It was summer and only just beginning to grow dark. I had barely eaten. I decided to write this book.

I spent the first six months researching and planning as my full-time job. As soon as Germany opened its borders, I traveled from Munich to Bremen and many places in between. I criss-crossed the country by train and met dozens of people who generously helped me in my research. I found myself constantly buying bouquets of flowers as the only small thanks I could think of for these kind strangers.

I learned plenty about the bizarre microcosm of Lebens-born. And I learned about the Third Reich, and what it meant to be an everyday German at the time. I found chilling similari-ties between Germany in the 1930s and the United States today.

To many people, Nazi Germany is synonymous with World War II, with Holocaust. But it's not as if Hitler came to power one day and started invading countries and setting up extermination camps the next. For many years, Nazi Germany was a relatively peaceful dictatorship. There were people who loved Hitler. There were people who hated him, and there are many stories of heroism and sacrifice from those in the Resistance. And—this is even harder to believe today, with all our hindsight—there were people who did not want to be involved in politics and went about their daily lives, saluting as needed, avoiding Jewish shops, and donating to the Winter Relief Fund when the Stormtroopers came knocking. Some people found small rebellions, like avoiding situations where they'd have to salute, but anyone who survived the regime made compromises. I learned that last part from an interview I read with Freya von Moltke, whose husband was executed for his participation in the July 1944 plot to assassinate Hitler.

I wanted to write about these people and the early years of the regime because they are so often glossed over on the way to the war that followed and the many heroes, victims, and villains it produced. Of interest to me now are the times before the war and the Holocaust. What did people think then? What were the warning signs, and how could people have looked past them? What was it like for them when they realized what was really going on, but it was too late to stop it?

The sterilization program Ilse faced began in the first year of the regime. Anyone deemed to be of less-than-desirable genetic stock was at risk; even people who had conditions that couldn't be passed on were sometimes sterilized. Extensive experiments involving X-rays and injections were conducted, mostly at concentration camps, to find the most efficient way to sterilize people. There were approximately 400,000 forced sterilizations during the Nazi regime.

Also of note is the Aktion T4 program, which was instituted to kill people with mental and physical disabilities, like Otto. There is almost no surviving documentation for this program. We do know that a version of it began with Lebensborn, and by September 1939, using the distraction of the war, full-scale euthanasia began. The public did find out about this program because their institutionalized family members began dying at alarming rates. The program ran until 1941, killing hundreds of thousands of people, until Catholic bishops stepped in and put a stop to it. However, these people continued to face sterilization, or worse, in the concentration camps.

My obsession with isolated microcosms led me to focus on life inside the homes, but many more books could be written about the children of Lebensborn.

During the war years, thousands of children from invaded

countries who met the "racial criteria" were kidnapped and brutally "Germanized" to be adopted by German families. Those who survived the process never saw their true families again, and often had no idea they were from other countries.

After the war, German-born and kidnapped Lebensborn children faced terrible treatment from their families and the public. One can imagine the shame cast upon children of an SS institution by a post-war society that wanted nothing more than to leave their country's Nazi legacy in the past. They were called "SS bastards," mistreated and often unloved by their own families, and kept in the dark about their true origins. Some of these children have unraveled these mysteries and told their stories in powerful and devastating detail. For further reading on this subject, I recommend starting with *Hitler's Forgotten Children* by Ingrid von Oelhafen.

A few small notes on timing: Two Lebensborn mothers were beaten by townspeople in 1942, rather than in 1938 as happened to Ilse. Also, the villa that inspired the fictional one in the novel was not purchased by Lebensborn until 1942.

Acknowledgments

It is stunning to me how many people helped bring this book to fruition. I would like to offer my deepest thanks to them all.

Ms. Lena Fellman, for her extraordinary generosity in volunteering to show me her hometown of Bremen, introducing me to women who remembered the Nazi years, serving as a de facto translator, and providing her notes to ensure the authenticity of the novel.

Ms. Gabriele Ros and Mr. Sebastian Gruber for graciously allowing me to visit the original Lebensborn home in Steinhoring and for their passion for helping others.

A volunteer with the Gröpelingen Historical Society who wishes to remain nameless but who walked me through the entire neighborhood, and surprised me with a bonus tour of a 1940s home.

Ms. Angela Piplak for her passion and knowledge of Bremen's history.

The Bremen State Archive for allowing me to camp out and peruse their documents for many hours.

The International Center on Nazi Persecution, where the Lebensborn archives are located.

Richard Koret, for consulting with me to ensure thoughtful representation of the Jewish experience.

Nan Cole for her insights as a master forager.

Rebecca Allen, for her enthusiastic copyedits.

Jessica Bell, for her cover design.

Susan Leon, Ellen Baker, and Maryka Biaggio for their feedback and mentorship.

And of course my critique partners, including Justine, Lily, Julie, Jenny, and Sheila, and all the other beta readers along the way, most especially Constance Remillard.

So many books helped me along the way that it is only possible to name a fraction of them: *Of Pure Blood* by Clarissa Henry and Marc Hillel, *Master Race* by Catrine Clay and Michael Leapman, *Frauen* by Alison Owings, *German Mother, Are You Ready?* By Dorothee Schmitz-Köster, *Account Rendered* by Melita Maschman, *Hitler's Girls* by Tim Heath, *On Hitler's Mountain* by Irmgard A. Hunt, *School for Barbarians* by Erika Mann, and *A Woman in Berlin* are a few. In this last work, the brutal honesty of the anonymous author provided invaluable and unexpected insights into what it was like to be a German woman during this era.

My sister Aly, for her humor and love. And for getting a wild carrot tattoo.

My parents, for their support, and for fostering in me a love of history and literature, and never doubting that I could write a book.

Patrick, for being my crew, for his unrelenting support and belief in me, for motivating me, for his endless ideas. For too many things to name.

About the Author

Shannon St. Hilaire is fascinated by forgotten microcosms and the complex women who lived through them. She spends just about all her time reading and writing stories about them—also, traveling, being roommates with her cat, and finding cottages in forests.

Thank you so much for reading *To Look Upon the Sun*. As an independent author, reviews mean everything and it would mean so much to me if you'd take a moment to leave a review on Amazon and/or Goodreads!

Want more Hannelore?

Scan the QR code to read chapter one of her story!

Follow her on Substack for sneak peeks, book recommendations, and updates on her writing.

facebook.com/missivesfromthemargins

instagram.com/shannon_sthilaire

amazon.com/stores/Shannon-St.Hilaire/author/B0CSWXFRHX

bookbub.com/profile/4177095120

linkedin.com/in/shannonsthilaire

pinterest.com/saintshannon

Also by SHANNON ST. HILAIRE

The Ones Who Stayed

In the heart of war-torn El Salvador, an iron-willed American nun crosses paths with a visionary priest. Driven by a desire to transcend her duties, she joins him on a perilous journey to aid war victims, challenging her beliefs and confronting the harsh realities of war.

As they navigate this tumultuous landscape, their bond deepens, forcing her to face a world of moral complexities. In a land where each day teeters on the brink of tragedy, she must make a life-altering choice before all she holds dear is lost.

Printed by Amazon Italia Logistica S.r.l.
Torrazza Piemonte (TO), Italy

58998542R00208